Frankie 1 Stigma

A Novel by Olga Soler

Frankie 1 Stigma

A Novel by Olga Soler

©2020 Leap over the Edge Publications Olga Soler

Dedication

To my Brother Frank the gentile giant who first taught me about heavenly things even when I wasn't listening. Also to Frank Patterson who helps unasked and whose kindness is legendary.

Last but not least to Frankie, a baby born on October 11th 2020 to a remarkable woman named Krysten who has fought with the monster of addiction and is winning. May he be a champion for justice like the Frankie in this book.

Preface

This book has been in me for years as I have worked with the infirmed and the addicted. My brother Frank who is a wonderful person and the classic victim of poverty, drug addiction, naiveté and all the other illnesses and pain associated with it, was my inspiration for the character. Even though he lives with terrible physical discomfort (that I would love to ameliorate but can't), he hobbles on and helps the homeless. This in conjunction with my love for the character in Mary Shelly's book "Frankenstein" moved me to write.

I have long thought that "Frankenstein" was a woman's cry against pain both physical and emotional and that it has been hijacked by men for centuries and made a story of horror. I wanted to reclaim it replace in it the sensitivity of a woman's touch. No doubt horror comes into it though now in our post "Chuckie" and "Psycho" world a creature that kills out of longing and pain is almost benign. As one concerned for the wounded of this world, as well as an artist the question plagued me, "what if the creature had been nurtured?" What if it moved towards the light?

I always felt that the plodding thing featured in movies and books to date robbed the character of its spiritual aspects. Shelly, though inclined towards atheism, still gave the character a soul capable of pain and choice. Hollywood's bolt in the neck was never in Shelly's version and the plodding orthopedic footwear did her character a great injustice. A smidgen of the dejection of her character was part of the Hollywood version but not the intelligence. How differently the story might have unfolded if the monster had some respite from the stigma. Real monsters are more often made not born and all of us must question our part in the making or unmaking of them.

As a human services worker you will see my frustration with a system that has the means to end all physical human misery but does not, because of greed. This too is monstrous and something for us to think about. If we viewed it all as Frankie does (without bias) how would we see it? In this story the setting is modern not gothic and the character has more tech but I trust his essence is still there. It is my hope you will enjoy this fantasy and that it will help *you* in your pondering.

Frankie

1

The Servant King

Elaina was used to walking in neighborhoods no decent person would walk in. She just put her money in her bra, didn't carry a purse, and walked on. Warding off the bite of the New York winter just meant wrapping the coat she got at Good Will a little tighter around her.

She followed the GPS on her phone through grey, streets of cracked concrete full of cigarette butts, trash and dead rodents, to the place indicated; a ramshackle house that reeked of frozen mold, urine and plastic tape reading "condemned". Getting what she needed these days was safer than it used to be but as full of intrigue as ever. It was always a different time and a different place. Oh, and she could not be late. Her provider was nothing, if not punctual.

The circuitous path that led her to this dependency was never far from her memory. Urban poverty produced millions of assaults to the human psyche but these could all be arrested by sweet chemical escapes from reality. This however, led to the moment when her mother, Rosa, finally got tired of money, electronics and her cheap jewelry going missing. Mother's solution was to toss Elaina's rear end out of the house, at the green and impulsive age of fourteen.

That period of her life found her on the asphalt of their filthy, unforgiving hood. Of necessity, the small, once curvy but now wraith like, teen ager went to "couch surfing." Sheltered by the benevolence of friends she continued till she burnt those out as well; then she had to go to strangers. This she did, till they too, wearied of indulging her habit at the cost of their stuff. How she avoided arrest was a remarkable feet of ingenuity; though the frigid streets can be less kind than a warm cell. She kept moving, and move she did; from slum housing, to the corners and alleys where both windblown and human garbage come to stasis.

Summers witnessed her sleeping on stoops, roofs or fire escapes and winters had her tearing boards off of abandoned doors, or taking chances in hovels that were fire traps or abandoned buildings. This she did with other human shadows nodding to the inebriation of latest stuff. What used to be the wild intoxicated raves of her early years became membership in the club of the shuffling dead whose eyes sparked only when loading syringes.

Then she got pregnant. This was good and bad. Bad to feed two on what one wasn't eating; and good because she had a diminutive ticket to shelter with a wait list for a dingy vermin infested rooming house. But even that didn't stop her using, till the day she heard the most horrifying sound in all her inebriated nightmares--the scream of her new born baby, purple with pain and going through withdrawals.

Instead of pity she got venom from the nursing staff of the hospital and of course the Department of Child Protection got involved and the trouble didn't end there. The supposed sperm donor whose name was "Panic" had a short fuse and a financial plan for his habit. This included DTA (Department of Transitional Assistance) money for the support of the child and cash from pimping Elaina which would provide him dope and a place to use it. When the child was taken and put in Grandmother's custody "Panic" took it out of Elaina's hide and tossed her out. She was on her last leg. That was where Frankie came in and it was the reason she was still alive.

Wherever Frankie arranged a meeting she noticed others in the shadows waiting. Unknown to Elaina, she and her baby (Dee Dee) were not his only dependents. They too received the message on their phones with a beacon that led them to places like this, out of the way, run down, and more than a little scary.

She walked into a room half lit and half in shadows, on time, with the jitters as usual. The rendezvous points were always different but the set up was always the same. Today she was dressed in scrubs for work at the hospital where she had landed a job as a clerk. She stood, with her back to him, vulnerable, near the well lit wall. She could see the blue scan run down her body on the wall. Whatever the scan was for, she was certain it revealed all her secrets. From his point of view it was not really necessary. He knew everything that was going down in the street. Still the scan had a dramatic affect that served his purpose. She turned and sat at the table between them. Shrouded in darkness, and seated, his massive form was almost approachable.

He pushed a small box into the light containing two pills. Her eyes lit up despite her attempt at dissimulation. It was an addict's reflex she had not yet learned to arrest. He sighed with disappointment knowing she was still so bound to the formidable substance. She was, however, following the plan and for that he commended her.

"You're sticking with your program. I'm glad." he said, then queried, "The child?"

Elaina squirmed in the broken chair she had been provide. She was an addict in a time when few resources were left for the treatment of this disorder, but she was also a mother, with concerns that this bizarre but philanthropic creature had an interest in her child. He truly meant no harm by it. The child was precious to him. Never the less, she didn't really know that or anything else about Frankie. So she answered curtly,

"She's OK. Good. Doing good in school," then added tentatively. "My mom is sick though, and we had some high co-pays for her medication and the hospital. Had to take it out of the rent."

He was as poor as she but he could access resources. He knew what she was asking and reassured her.

"I'll take care of it."

He could hear her sigh with relief and he wished his own answers could come as readily.

"Thanks Frankie. Don't know what we would do without you."

Without him? Well, he supposed, like a magician he could produced the things that brought her peace, but if these could be obtained without him he was sure she would not bat an eye to affirm her need of him. The child, however, was different and that is why he loved her. Slipping a corps like hand out of the darkness that occulted him, he poured Elaina's dose out of the box onto the table. Then with a potent thread of light from his finger tips, (a gift from his re-animator), he cut the dose a few micro grams. She acted like he had cut off her arm.

"What are you doing to my dose?"

He had seen this behavior before and had to be firm. He forced a dramatic harshness in his voice.

"You know that's the deal. A little less each month till you don't need any."

She looked like she might weep, which of course, would have undone him. He had to remind himself this was for her good and for sweet little Dee Dee.

"But ..." she protested.   He interrupted her with a snarl, to good effect.

"Don't push me Elaina. You know the deal. You deviate from it one inch or go to another dealer for more and you can start getting your fix the old way-- by selling yourself on the street.   You lose your daughter, your job and everything else. Cut back till you are free and rejoin the human race. What's it gonna be?"   She was duly humbled.

"You're way Frankie."

She took the pills and walked out with a half smile and quiet gratitude. The play was over and he breathed deeply.   It was difficult for him to be caustic with Elaina. She was his first charge. There were, however, others he needed no patience for. As Elaina took the bend in the dark creaking stairway another came around in the direction of his temporary audience chamber.

It disturbed him that such a one had accessed their network to approach him, but working with the street's former "living dead" had its limitations. This was one reason why their meeting places had to keep moving. The intruder sat in the chair like he belonged there, a little jittery but entitled, spreading his legs and leaning back with a hard affect and a gangster's posture. Frankie scanned him but it really wasn't necessary, he already knew who this clown in dingy boxers and drooping jeans was and where he had gotten the gun under his jacket and the gold chains in his pocket.

"Why are you here?" the question was rhetorical.

"Thought you knew everything?"

"You've been misinformed." The visitor smiled like a poker player with a winning hand and moved the toothpick in his mouth from left to right.

"Well, I heard you helped people who like, were in need and shit."

"You in need?"

"Dude, I am so in need. I gots kids that need support and my woman is sick but I gots this Jones and..."

The face in the dark clenched at the jaw and his eyes narrowed. The Don of the Living Dead had heard enough.

"I don't know everything but I know you. Your woman is in the hospital, put there by you. You kicked her half to death in the alley where you deal, near 149th St and Hunts Point."

The man adjusted his hoodie and squirmed.

"Na that ain't me."

The answer to this blatant falsehood came with venom.

"I hates bull shitters."

The creature in the shadows had mastered the art of stealth but whenever he did revealed himself he understood his appearance was grand and ghastly. He rose slowly and stepped into the half light. His yellow cat like eyes gleamed with a relish as he saw terror radiate from the liar's face. In the dealers jaundice eyes the man could read thoughts of what was to follow. The fear sank into his soul. The shock ripped through the hoodlum riveting him to the spot, and he shouted as if to stop the on rushing "locomotive of flesh" that was heading his way,

"Woah, Woah, WOAH!!!!"

The following day police and fire department joined forces as they had 22 times before, in the last few months. This was to retrieve a cocoon made of rope, the contents of which, was human. It was dangling from a high profile designation as usual, by its feet. This time the rope was tied to a Spanish anti drug bill board in the Bronx that groaned in the breeze and threatened to let its petrified ornament plummet to the ground. Each time the wind blew him back and forth he relived his potential death. This of course added to his terror. When the hook and ladder brought him down, like the others, he was not in his right mind. He was babbling and screaming about ghouls and aliens. He was also covered in bruises and gashes produced by what looked like animal claws and he was not fit for questioning.

Detective Andre Poloche watched as the ambulance swallow the gurney with the babbling, disturbed wretch. Walking over to an officer that was directing traffic around the site, he stuck a stick of gum in his mouth to ward off the desire for nicotine. He wanted to quit as he needed every edge to stay vital at his age. The Hispanic widower was still in great shape for his forties but he had seen lots of officers go soft in the belly and did not want to be one of them. He needed his job. He had lost his wife to a terrible accident and then a brother to an unsolved crime. His devotion to his work eased the pain like a drug. It was his only vice outside of womanizing and his biggest distraction.

His partner Jasmine was young and black and was having too much fun busting heads to settle down. She was smart and sick of "dumbing" things down to accommodate her on line dates, besides, she loved her work. She lived alone with her son and liked it.

As protocol dictated she questioned people but didn't get far with her inquiries. Whoever or whatever was doing this strange business was stealthy and no one seemed to know much of anything as in all the other cases. Poloche commented to the traffic cop:

"Well, that makes 22. Did the guy in the cocoon say anything?"

"Nothin'. Just Big Ugly monster, laser beams and crazy stuff like that. Same as the others. You think we got some alien invasion thing going on behind this? It's kinda creepy."

"More likely vigilantes of some sort, with high tech. Whoever they are, they seem to be doing us a favor. Victims seem to be known wife beaters, dealers, slum lords and one dirty cop scared shitless. Of the ones we couldn't arrest, three of them moved out of town completely. Some pattern huh?"

"Well I don't wanna meet up with whatever it is. I didn't sign up for this."

Andre looked at the officer and made a note on his phone of the badge number.

"Got something to hide Pat?"

The officer smirked and got in his car. Meanwhile Jasmine stood there thinking then turned to Andy with a scowl.

"Whoever is doing this knows as much as we do about evidence. They cover their tracks well. Then whatever they do to their victims, messes with the mind. That guy was babbling like a monkey eating chili peppers, he couldn't even say his own name."

"Torture will do that, but you know this guy. It's Casaba from Hunts Point; the SOB who almost killed the prostitute last week."

"Yeah? Well, well what goes around comes around." Jasmine answered with satisfaction, but Andre was far away in his thoughts.

"Common, I hear the wheels turning." Jasmine quipped.

"It's nothing. Just remembered something Frank used to say."

"What's that?"

"We were both old spaghetti western fans and we used to get so pissed about all these fuckers who had good lawyer and would get off legally without a scratch. He used to say he wanted to round these guys up and "hang 'em high" – like in the movie."

"They never found his body, did they?"

"Na but he's gone. We were tight. Even if he was in witness protection he would let me know.   Anyway he would never do a thing like this. He was a good cop; the best. He disappeared with others who were mob targets.   I'm sure there was nothing left when they got done with him.   It was just something he used to say. We all say stuff like that. You said you wanted to hang that "bottle top" rapist by his...

"By his nuts, yeah, still do. If this vigilante had been around at that time I would have given him the guy's address with special instructions.

"OOO! Ok its lunch time. Meat ball sub?"

"Shut up."

All the while, from the roof top, eyes that seldom slept were watching. Watching and wondering why the detective with the graying temples who had been following his exploits, seemed so likeable to a blank slate of memory like his own. Though the data in Frankie's mind was vast and impressive he was yet a child and to himself he was a great mystery. Children were born but he was constructed. He knew that at least. Watching children from a distance was a great pass time of his. He watched and remembered being like them (emotionally at least) and looking at the world with unaffected wonder, but he was never small, never frail, never cherished. There on the roof as he mused, he knew his introspective focus must shift. He was now an administrator, he had to forget himself to deal with the business at hand.

"I am slave and I am king. I own my subjects and they own me. In this my kingdom, my darkness I rein and serve. Here now I hold audience with this one or that, of my subjects, once lost souls, oppressed on every side. These my people, lost by degrees of which I am the lowest. They are finding their way but I remain."

He placed a box in the crevasse of an air vent on the roof then disappeared over the side just as an old woman emerged from within the building. Claiming the few dollars she found in the cardboard receptacle she sighed, knowing this would keep her from eviction. She kissed what she found then looking skyward she closed her bathrobe against the chill. Scurrying back inside her anxiety was pacified, like that of a mouse finding precious grain in a winter's famine. She returned to her apartment and disabled child while the "king" retreated to the hovel that served as his present "palace".

Loneliness tugged at him like the sad and lingering chord of a cello, softened only by this tentative connection to the troubled souls who needed him, for his strange abilities. It was morning but He tossed himself on a pile of bedding commandeered from nature, dumpsters and trucks that pedal stolen goods. Then with yellow eyes opened part way, he slept, till the moon rose to evening and met the night.

2

Lost Things

He walked miles and miles each night, in dark places where his shadow would not even cast his form. Foot falls as silent as a cat; he wished to remain a myth and a rumor, as long as possible. Human kind once aware would fear or hunt him. Unafraid of their pitch forks or guns it was their screams and jeer that wounded him deeply. Rejection was a lacerating and inescapable component of his short eventful life.

Frankie was a people person but people where not Frankie people. His greatest heartache was that his form produced only terror in others. This exasperating detail of his existence made any attempt to relate, a mysterious process. He had become very good at making the acquaintance of others under strange and unusual circumstances. Because of this the dark was often to his purpose, but darkness covered only part of the day. A great deal of his time was therefore spent alone, though not by choice. It was during this part of his day that he reviewed millions of hours of human history and present news through his access to neurological artificial intelligence. A giant with the curiosity of a precocious 8-year-old he learned the beautiful and the uglier facts of life from his NAI or from unfriendly encounters.

NAI or Neuro-Artificial Intelligence had a data capacity surpassing that of the Pentagon and was a feature, installed in him by his re-animator. It provided an endless source of data. This internal tutor could teach him to speak many languages and produced an intellect that was rivaled only by his social angst and nerve-racking size. Dr. Stein, the scientist that parented him, did not wish to waste his time teaching the creature he brought into the world. He therefore, provided him with a sophisticated cyber baby sitter and mentor.

Frankie was beginning to get the idea that he knew more about stuff than most people, but people knew secret things he could not access on the cyber highway. Things that lovers, saints, poets and artists knew. Therefore, his great mind full of information did not prevent him feeling ignorant and naïve in the presence of actual humans. Because of this, in 8 years of life his closest community consisted of giant Brown Bears. These were the proud Kodiak that frequented the McNeil River in Alaska's vast and beatific southwest. Frankie's access to knowledge surpassed even his maker's but he would trade it all for one genuine face to face encounter with a real friend that wasn't covered in fur.

Then again the city made him nostalgic for the woods. He missed standing at his full height in the light of day under cloudless skies unencumbered by the shadows of building. He also missed the radiant blue of the skies. He missed the riotous yet inconspicuous life of forest glades all around him, and pristine snow-covered peaks and dells. It enriched his memories but it was also part of his misfortune, to call all that, his brief past.

The Alaskan wildlife sanctuary exposed him, to many scars as well. After all, some animal encounters and accidents he had would have been fatal to normal men. Never the less nature had shielded him for a time. Fangs and claws and primal beauty became a barrier between him and the far more painful rejection of human beings. He wished he had been satisfied with it. But He wasn't. He needed more, and to get it, he had to do what he was doing now; facing his fears, even as he caused no end of fear himself.

Watching the salmon spawn in Alaska's surging rivers he had for several seasons marked their yearly return home. After ranging freely across the wild places of northern America, like the salmon, he was prompted to return to the only home and the only father he knew; to Stein the scientist who pieced him together in the concrete and human wilderness of New York. He wasn't sure why he was returning but he had to retrieve something---something lost.

His present foray into the peopled lands was an experiment he had entered into tentatively. He took the risk and found he adapted and decided to extend his stay. That extension lengthened to two years. With the help of great agility and his cyber network he was able to stay hidden. This was due to the fact that NAI did not work like other internet access. It was highly specialized with impenetrable protections. His whereabouts were therefore undetectable by technology. Therefore, NAI could help him find just about anyone or anything and that was how he found Stein.

Asking after the Dr's location NAI navigated him to a mansion near a conservation reserve and lake, in Connecticut near the NY border. It also informed him through access to the house security that the doctor was alone. Skulking and hiding had become a fine art for Frankie. His size was a problem but his agility and quick faculties compensated nicely. He could avoid the detection of the most cunning or curious hunter and was certainly invisible to those who were not paying attention. If he stood in plain view he was formidably frightening; a half naked 7 foot giant with long black matted hair and grey green skin. Face and body were scared and his twisted mouth wore a permanent grimace. His eyes gleamed yellow and one would not wish to encounter them in the darkness of a city alley or anywhere else. Even Stein winced when the patchwork carcass he had pieced together was reanimated as a gruesome twitching mass of flesh and muscle. Monster was the only accurate moniker for him as he was in fact, a large living corps.

If Frankie was desperate for society, Stein was the contrary. He thought the whole human race irreparably flawed and didn't care if he ever saw another human being in his life. This was probably why he didn't have a problem with cutting up dead ones and putting them back together. The large house he lived in also accommodated an extensive lab funded by the mob. Stein was confined to it but much as he liked his work he hated compulsive confinement. This was never the less, the real price of his funding; forever dwelling in his own little corner of hell.

The only human being Stein had valued was his wife Elizabeth, but she was taken by cancer and he never got over it. A gifted researcher and surgeon he became devoted to the idea of reanimating dead tissue. Obsessed as he was to find the answer to "life eternal" in a test tube he was too late to salvage his beloved. Cloning was something he considered, but in the end, it would not serve his purpose. He would be an octogenarian by the time a clone was old enough to favor a spouse and at that ripe age even a test tube bride wouldn't pick him.

He therefore returned to his experiments surrounding reanimation. If he succeeded, the stakes were high. He might prolong his own life and fund centuries of experiments with the revenue. An initial endowment was what he needed. His obsession turned to finding it. To his bitterness and shame, he did find it, along with the initial "raw materials". Then-- after Frankie disappeared he repented of the project and drowned the reason for it, in gallons of booze.

Shockingly, here now was the monster returned like the proverbial bad penny. What kind of welcome would he receive? Frankie placed a hand on the iron fence and gingerly vaulted over it. He had already disarmed the security system with the use of NAI as anything computerized was within his power to affect. The element of surprise was his. The large house was empty except for the shuffling sound of a man's slippers and the pouring of liquid into a glass. These sounds took the Monster to what proved to be, the library.

As Stein poured his 6th drink of the evening he knew his senses did not perceive accurately. The creaking of the old house was familiar to him but there had been no wind that night. All was still. Some music would perhaps solve the problem of his jitters but he had not gotten to the stereo remote before he heard another sound; the door creaking. Could a burglar, wanderer or even a rat be in the house? He turned and what he saw dropped the drink right out of his hand.

Frankie ducked slowly under the arched door frame and walked in looking very much like a heavily scared Tarzan emerging from the jungle. When he was reanimated his head had been shaved bald but now his long black hair greasy and streaming down his back added to his creepiness. What was left of the scrub pants he had escaped with was tattered and he was without shoes.

Eight o'clock in the evening and Stein was already drunk. The monster kicked the glass out of the way while the scientist stared. He was shocked but not without repartee.

"So, where ya been?" he quipped. The answer from the giant was low and even, like a bowed base string.

"Going to and fro upon the earth."

"A biblical reference, Satan answering God in the book of Job, I believe. That's appropriate. And your speech, it's quite refined thanks to NAI I presume. Where have you been?"

"I believe the answer is Canada and all the places between here and Alaska."

Stein thought it remarkable that this enormous eccentricity could have ranged so far without hitting the pages of the Inquirer or being killed. He marveled at his resilience but was still disgusted by his appearance. Drunk and without social filter he commented and was surprise by the response.

"You look even more like shit than you did before."   Stein slurred.

"<u>Your</u> speech is <u>not</u> refined. It is vulgar."

Frankie said this in a matter of fact way, but was actually very pleased to be having a real conversation, with a person that wasn't running in the opposite direction. For a moment he indulged a longing for connection to the man who had formed him. That was short lived, as Stein had no desire of even the appearance of sentimentality.

"Well what a sissy I seem to have created."

Frankie stood to his full height and slowly took the scientist off his feet by most of the fabric on his shirt. He ripped it in the process.

"YOU did not create me--ex Nihilo--out of nothing. You stole raw materials and patched them together. You were not even a clever artist. You are what they call -- a hack."

"But a brilliant one, you will admit...and the boy speaks Latin. You should go to med school."

Frankie slammed him against the wall and held on. Stein strained to speak changing his approach.

"And now that you are thus gifted with knowledge you are surely more reasonable than when I last saw you. Please, please...let me down."

Frankie complied slowly and Stein, composing himself, answers soberly with a hint of respect.

"Thank you. Please, have a seat. Sherry? Scotch? Kalifa Cush? Name your poison."

"I do not want intoxicants."

That was unfortunate news to Stein since his life's blood was "intoxicants". He thought his "handiwork" quite a wuss but dared not comment again in that vein. Stein also lamented that being clear headed this enormous brute might have an advantage in a battle of words. He decided to temper his own fluid intake and smoke a little weed instead. Frankie brushed the smoke away from his face. He was used to air as clean as the modern world could provide and still had something of the lost child in his demeanor. He looked around and finally sat on a couch which deflated and collapsed under his weight. Compensating he crossed his legs in the manner of those who are used to sitting on the ground.

Thanks to the Kalifa Cush Stein was able to deescalate the conversation and be sociable. He was not expecting company else his "jailers" in New York might come down and deal with "the problem" for him. That is, if "the problem" could be dealt with using knives or guns. No NY phone call was forthcoming so he assumed the surveillance was not working. In fact he hoped it wasn't, as Frankie was a well kept secret even from them. The scientist regarded Frankie's arms and torso and noted healed gashes and what looked like large bite marks. The ability to heal, even massive physical trauma like this was apparently a side effect of his re-animation. What might this creature have endured in the six years since he walked off the table of his lab? But the motive for the visit was presently, more to the point for Stein. The scientist gritted his teeth and attempted polite conversation.

"Why are you here? Why have you waited so long to return?"

"Has it been long? I cannot say what long is I only know what happened this I will tell you. This was more information than Stein had bargained for but he sat and began to take mental notes.

"When I first was, I babbled but had no words. At least I had no words that were understandable. I looked at things like a cub that is new. You were there, I remember, and I was tingling all over. Something had run through me-- a heat with great force. I was awake but weak and there was pain in all my parts. I stumbled, and everything was flying everywhere. That is what happened isn't it?"

Frankie paused for some assurance, that he had not imagined this so long ago. Stein obliged him.

"That was in the lab. I'll show you if you like. You were disoriented. I anticipated you might feel pain and had prepared NAI with a neuro intercept to deal with it. You began to feel better, isn't that right? But go on what else do you remember?"

"The discomfort did go away. I felt good, strong. I was happy. But you were not happy. You were full of something--disgust, I think. I stumbled as I was just learning to move, and you became angry. You wanted to restrain me, but I would not be restrained. As I looked at things and reached for them NAI began to speak. "Cobweb, test tube, Dr. Victor Stein, wall, window, door..." I walked out of the door and I was hungry to know. That hunger drove me."

"You destroyed my lab with your clumsiness. Then you disappeared."

"Disappeared? No, I went out to understand. Shouldn't you have found me?"

"I suppose...I didn't want to. I just didn't." This answer wounded Frankie but he went on.

"By the river in Alaska I bent down and made a man of clay the size of my hand. I dried him in the sun and valued him because I had made him. If you could not value me for myself then why could you not value me because I was your work?"

"That is all a bit too existential for me. Not my field I'm afraid. I was never good at that sort of thing. I could not have anticipated my reaction. I still can't."

"You disappoint me. I don't know what I expected but it was not this. Now I have a question for you Doctor. Why am I thus? All other species have one kind of DNA. According to NAI I have many. "

"The raw material I acquired to build you came from five different corpses of men. But that is all I can tell you at the moment."

"Very well, that will be a question for another day."

Stein did not want any more days with this creature and his questions, but he had a few questions of his own.

"What happened after you left? You were gone for years."

"Yes, the revolution of the seasons, I suppose that was years, but there were so many things out there; endless things to know. NAI taught me anything I wanted about things. What is a tick? Tick is an insect, I don't like ticks. What is a quasar? Brightest of the heavens. I like quasars. The more I learned the more I wanted to know. I guess I was curious. Were you ever curious?"

Stein answered with sarcasm.

"Curiosity killed the cat."

"I can't die."

"Can't you?"

"I don't think so, but regardless, I am not a cat."

3

De Lacy

They spoke for a while longer and Stein, remembering something that happened on the day of the big man's genesis, started to call him, Frankie.

"Is that my name?"

"It can be."

"Thank you. I have never had a name." Frankie voiced this with an emotive tremor. He was moved.

"NAI has no reference for me outside of your work, it calls me monstrous."

This stung the scientist who despite his desire to totally obliterate his own feelings now realize, Frankie must have some access to his e-files and the tissue he had given life to was sentient and capable of emotional pain. His marijuana was wearing off and stuffing the tender moment down, he regained his irritability and his thirst. He had endured all the socializing he could manage especially when he started to note Frankie's desire to engage further. The creature was lonely, and this added to the scientist's revulsion. Next to stupidity he hated neediness above all things.

Still, he felt a certain responsibility towards the creature. Never-the-less, the big oaf couldn't stay with him and he made that clear. It was, in fact, a matter of life and death for the doctor to live alone. Though a temporary shutdown of the surveillance cams could be explained, a permanent one could not be. Besides, Frankie was not supposed to exist. Though the house's spy system had been installed after Frankie there was a little white lie the scientist had told his "Keeper". He reported the "experiment" had been successful, but he said, the subject was euthanized and disposed of. That was how he explained Frankie's disappearance. If any of Don Lupo's people found out he had lied there might be mortal consequences for Stein. The doctor well knew that once liquidated no one would be left to piece together and reanimate him.

He told Frankie he could not stay but invited him to come back from time to time when there was no one else around. Frankie could easily promise him he would never come when Stein had company. Stein also made him agree to continue disarming the security when he came. Frankie thought all this uncomfortably odd, but he did not question it at present. He wanted another conversation, even if it was with a man who didn't seem to like him. Stein told him to come back in a couple of weeks and he would give him some clothing. He would need clothing, he told him, if he were ever around other people. He would also need a bath as his smell might have been alright around bears but not people. In addition, he asked Frankie to restore the surveillance when he left or trouble might befall the scientist. Frankie would comply with all these things. Moments after he jumped off the veranda, he leaped over the 14 foot high fence and was gone.

Stein explained the pause in surveillance to his jailers with "I had to party a little with some girls." And the gangster that watched him half asleep from a penthouse in Manhattan understood and let it go. Meanwhile Stein was good for his promise and with the Cart Blanche card that Lupo had given him purchased a new couch and some items on line from the "Big and Tall" catalogue for men.

Trusting the word of his Re-animator Frankie appeared again a few weeks later. Because of the doctor's question about years, Frankie had made an NAI study of time and how people marked it. In fact he studied the theory of relativity and knew what the space time continuum was basically referring to. Now he understood what was meant by nano-seconds, minutes etc. all the way to centuries, millennia, eons and so forth. He also knew that a few people, such as the Hopi Indians, did not mark time. He thought he might be a good Hopi because time was not to his liking. He preferred not to keep track of the passing of moments. Now that he was doing so he felt encumbered, but he did it for the sake of renewing human dialogue with this enigmatic man who had brought him into the world.

Frankie also researched the concept of "bathing" and found out that body odors were offensive to people in western civilization and that personal hygiene was desirable for health and social interaction. He certainly did not want to pollute the environment so he concocted natural products to help him cleanse and treat his unruly hair. He looked and smelled a great deal better. He also saw he had an aptitude for preparing things from natural materials. Manufacturing natural cosmetics required a bit of chemistry which he was fascinated by. He was pleased that Stein had a slightly different reaction to him the following visit. His cleanliness slightly mitigated the unpleasantness of his visit and how the scientist reacted to him. This was good.

It went without saying, Stein was not glad to see him but true to his word he had some sweat pants and a very large hooded sweatshirt for the gentle giant. He even bought him some boxer shorts and some sneakers. Frankie was alright with everything but the socks and sneakers. Stein assured him he would grow accustomed to them.

Instructing him on how to put them on was a great inconvenience to the doctor and he recalled why he had never wanted children. Still he would get some benefit out of the visit by way of research. Thinking about the last visit his scientific interest had been peaked by certain things Frankie said. On the off chance that he might sober up and renew his work, he needed some clarification on these subjects. Was the reanimation process ongoing? Was the product invulnerable or even virtually immortal?

The answers to these questions might be a ticket out of this elegant, albeit musty, prison. Most of all, he needed to know, could Frankie's unique NAI be used to obtain funding as well as information? Stein did all his shopping on the phone. He was not allowed internet access by his patron because his patron did not want him sharing information with anyone else. Still, Frankie had that glorious NAI which Stein had obtained, back when he still had friends among the finest minds in Silicon Valley. The schismatic for it had been lost because of Frankie's clumsiness at his inception, but this model for NAI existed within him. Perhaps the oaf was naïve enough to be played?

Not so, for Frankie had also done some thinking. It did not sit well in his opinion, that Stein, who was the equivalent of a father to him, did not like him or offer him hospitality. The giant intuited this man was somehow, not as honest or good as the animals he had communed with. There was something shadowy about him that Frankie perceived with concern. If the bears had taught him anything it was how to sniff out danger. Despite this, Frankie was grateful to Stein for the new clothes. They would take some getting used to but he was glad for them just the same. He wondered if they would make a difference in how people perceived him. He didn't yet know, that hoodie, with the design that could hide his face, would soon become his best friend.

Stein, who was on the scent of making money, now put his plan into action. He told Frankie he had done him a favor by purchasing the clothes and that it was good protocol for him to repay. Frankie did not know what that meant. Stein explained that it had to do with money. Frankie told him he would study money and would pay him back the next time he came. Stein offered to show him how to do some banking and how to deposit money into his account in payment for the clothing. Frankie listened and logged how to use NAI as the doctor recommended but he did not follow through because he felt a bit strange about it all. Where was money coming from? He was sure he didn't have any. And why did people use it? Stein seemed a little obsessed with it in a way that bothered Frankie. He decided he would feel better learning more about money and working it out for himself.

Instead of making his first transaction in that moment, Frankie decided to answer more of Stein's original question. "Where have you been?"

As Frankie traveled there were times when he met people. He found them generally untrustworthy and not very friendly. He felt more at home with animals. In his travels, he was always attracted to beauty, and beauty was found more in wild places than in those made by man. The noises of urbanity were also not to his liking. He preferred the whispers and twittering of nature by day and the symphony of the crickets and the spheres in open space as his night sounds. Temperature was not problematic for him subsequently he could enjoy the natural world, at all times, without obstruction. When he was able to establish himself as "not food" for certain predatory types of creature, he was quite like primordial man in an Eden. Sadly, like Adam, he lamented, all other creatures had counter parts and there was no creature like himself.

He recalled traveling through sultry sun-scorched places where he watched prairie dogs romp and where he could run. And how he ran, like a tireless race horse. He chased prong horn and raced giant bison. Then walked through the desserts, examining snakes and lizards, and climbing majestic outcroppings and plateaus with stones of staggering size and varied hues. He traversed snowy divides with rock strewn elevations that allowed him to see across miles of tundra in a landscape free of the human environmental mutilation he had seen elsewhere. These, ensconced in blue mist and ice, were pure and pristine and he was pleased and at peace with all he beheld.

However, if he went far enough in most directions, people would be there. When he arrived in Alaska his welcome was a shack with a rickety sign in the middle of nowhere. Two toothless Inuit women were there to welcome him with flirtatious smiles, till they saw his features in the half light, and ran screaming to the back of the building. He followed them and found a white man drunk over a table and a few others belly's up to the bar. They smelled stale and babbled in fear when they saw him. Then they gave Frankie his first exposure to gunfire. He thought it most unwelcoming and even though he answered them with both English and Inuit words he considered their reactions disheartening and unbearable. There was no conversation to be found there. This experience drove him as far from people as he could get. He would go elsewhere to recover and lick his promptly healing wounds.

Stein paid attention to this and the tiny remnants of the bullet marks on his shoulder and arms. Noting this with interest he attributed it, to the reconstructing micro bots he had place in the monster's system. These repaired his wounds and left the multitude of scars that decorated Frankie's face and limbs. As Stein observed him he continued his story.

His travels finally took him the path of Alaskan savage beauty and he stood many days and nights knee deep in the shimmering river gazing enraptured at the northern lights. He listened to the gentle sound of the water and it soothed him. Then day began to dawn in that seemingly endless darkness and spring came with its vivacious color and emerging life. He marked the surging of the rivers with salmon and for the first-time tasted flesh. Mimicking a huge bear with a face the size of manhole cover he grabbed a wriggling three foot salmon and thought to try it. The bear tore into a fish and held it in his jowls just across the river and the huge man did the same.

The bear watched with intense curiosity, as Frankie tore and chewed the fish, savoring it and deliberating about the flavor. Then to his dismay he realized that the fish would not reanimate and he understood that his taste test had cost the life of the creature. He laid it in the river reverently and determined he would not eat such things again.

Turning his attention to the bear, Frankie noticed it did not run and this intrigued him. He therefore, began to cross the river to make its acquaintance. The bear satiated with perhaps his fifth large salmon, was not of a mind to be social and sauntered off looking behind him. Frankie sensed no fear in the beast and his curiosity got the best of him. He walked on after the bruin but this seemed to annoy the bear and a perturbed roar in Frankie's direction told him he had best be polite and wait for a more favorable time to make friends.

As he explained all this to Stein, he noticed the scientist was drifting from genuine interest to the impatience he had shown before. Stein looked like a bear that was full and wanted to take a nap. It was not long before he started saying Frankie had to leave while reminding him about the money. This time Frankie did not mind leaving. He had clothes now and he would try his luck going down to the place where the people were.

Walking north, in few hours, the big man began seeing houses and cars. It was night and the people were obviously in their homes. Many of them did not even have security systems on. However, peering through windows he started to get a sense that people did not like anyone looking into their houses. A few screams brought black and white cars screeching into the area and soon he was being chased. Apparently the clothes did not help him. He would keep them anyway as they were comfortable. Besides Stein had taken such trouble showing him how to put them on, the least he could do was wear them. In time, this large hooded sweatshirt would give him some anonymity as those who saw his face would go mad with terror. As a vigilante, however, the hood could easily be removed when he needed to apply some righteous anger.

He continued north where he started to see tall buildings and streets, that even at this late hour, had quite a few people in and around them. Many of them wore clothes like his. There were others with hoodies and baggy pants. He sort of felt, a camaraderie to them, but again, as soon as they saw his size and face they became alarmed and ran. While he was sitting on the edge of a fountain in a park, one hooded man, who was full of intoxicants approached him in a hostile manner. He pointed a gun at him and said something about money, but when Frankie stood up to talk, the man lost consciousness and there was no reviving him. Frustrated, Frankie just stuck his hands in his hoodie pockets and walked on.

The following day was just a series of bad encounters, with people screaming or running away or worst, attacking him with guns or objects hurled at him. He was hungry and ate half the cabbages at a fruit stand and for this he was pelted with rotting fruit and another black and white car arrived. By the end of the day he was ready to go back into the wild. The only thing that stopped him was the heaviness in his heart and a sound; an amazing sound. It was music coming through the window of an apartment on the ground floor of a two level house, in a quiet part, of the outskirts of the city.

Frankie had heard all sorts of music that day blasting from stores and cars. Some of it had a beat that moved him, other music seemed to whine in his ear and he didn't much like it. Some made him a bit jittery. He even saw someone dancing in the street and of course, when he tried to imitate him the man ran like a rabbit.

This music lilting through this window was different. It was like the river, soothing and sweet. The night had already come, and with discretion this time, he looked in the window and did not let the inhabitants of the house see him. There were three people there; a young man, an elderly lady and a young woman with white hair and pale blue eyes. She also had white eye lashes as fair and delicate as a flower petal. The music he was hearing had enigmatic but enchanting words,

> "High vibration go on
> to the sun, oh let my heart dreaming
> past a mortal as me.
> Where can I be?
>
> Wish the sun to stand still.
> Reaching out to touch our own being
> Past a mortal as we
> Here we can be
> We can be here,
> be here now.
> Here we can be."

These words and music floated on the still night air like the flow of a gurgling brook, or like scintillating moonlight streaming down from space. He was enchanted and slumped quietly against the wall of the house to listen. He peaked back in to see the older lady taking a loaf of bread out of the oven and placing it on the table. The smell of this was enchanting as well. Frankie could smell the homely waft of warm yeasty food and he thought he had never been so content in all his days. Then he heard the young man speaking loudly, and the music stopped.

"Mom, you missed the plate."

"Sorry Jean Luc I was caught up in the music. "Yes" will do that to me every time. "

"Ok you love the band, but maybe you should listen to something else when you're baking. Just don't drop it on the floor please. I want a hunk with lots of butter."

"Jean Luc De Lacy, when have I ever dropped a loaf on the floor? You're the one that dropped the chicken picatta into the sink last week and you are sighted."

"You distracted me. I thought you were going to fall. That's why we moved the table."

"Don't blame that on me. You just don't like picatta."

"Well it's not my favorite. But I got the pizza didn't I?" at this point the girl chimed in.

"You can't compare pizza to mom's picatta even if it's not your favorite. You are so spoiled."

"But you still love me don't you sis? Listen, I think you and mom should put your feet up and I will read some Neruda to you while we eat bread and butter and cheese and drink a little Beaujolais. What do you say?"

Frankie quickly asked NAI what Neruda and Beaujolais were and found out the former was a Hispanic poet and the latter was a mild intoxicant made from grapes. The light it took to make this inquiry alerted Jean Luc and Frankie had to hide as the two young people looked out the door to investigate. No one there, they returned to the inside were the girl whose name was Stacia and the woman whose name was "Mom" seemed excited by the suggestion of such a simple meal. The elder sat in a comfortable chair putting her feet up on a cushion; the girl brought out the cheeses while the young man, whose name was Jean Luc, furnished the bottle and glasses and poured.

"Brie and Provence OK?" Stacia said almost with a giggle and he answered,

"What about some Roquefort also?" Said Jean Luc, but mom quickly added,

"I want a little Morbier."

"OK we will have a cheese feast."

They chatted and munched and drank and all were placidly content. This, despite the fact, that the elder woman seemed impaired in some way. Something was wrong with her vision.

The music never came back but in a few moments the young man began to read from a book and what he read sounded like music. This kind of reading far surpassed anything that NAI had ever read to Frankie. Jean Luc recited melodically and what he read was as mysterious as the swirling green northern skies Frankie loved so well.

> "I gather this delicate day like a ribbon to girdle the world's sad encirclement.

I turn it into a belt or a cup, a boat to cross over, an ocean of dew.

Come and see it: over the bee a platinum zither, the honey,
the waist of my lucent beloved,

I took life as it came – lucky or unlucky—this life."

Moved with emotion, Frankie mimicked some of Neruda's poetry,

"The waist of my lucent beloved,

I took life as it came…lucky or unlucky…this life."

Then he sighed and listened again and at the end of the night as they all wandered off to nocturnal rest he determined that, even hidden by shadows -- he would return.

4

Demigods of Different Sizes

Romeo Lupo was a short man that might have made a good jockey if he were not a maniacal and egotistic example of the worst sort of humanity. He broke his knuckles in as a child, against a taunting bully who took exception to his thumb sucking. He did this with his mother egging him on. He learned to fight at his uncles boxing gym but torturing other children was a talent he developed all on his own. Soon stealing milk money turned into stealing six packs from the corner liquor store. He started selling his auntie's Johnnies to make pin money and buy muscular support. Revenge was sweet, when as a teen, he finally made the bullies pay, in the most exquisite and painful ways, for all their taunts in his diminutive youth. This was right around the time he replaced thumb sucking with a cigar.

Lupo was incurably short and he made his doctor suffer for giving him this news. Compensating for this with ambition he superseded his vertical challenge, by exceeding the violence of all local gang leaders and psychopathic criminals in the scope of his knowledge. It followed that in "short order," all the bullies would be breaking bones for him.

Meanwhile, his family cleared the stones in his way, as many families do, and this accelerated his climb to the top of his field. Thus through lies, fear and murder Romeo Lupo became leader of the criminal cabal controlling all underworld power in three of the five NY boroughs. Eliminating all pretenders, even among his own kin, he sucked his cigar all the way to the top of the scummy bottom. Now Lupo's very shadow struck fear through the intestines of all who saw it and caused grown gangsters to void their pants at the mention of his name.

There were those however, who actually liked him or at least liked his power and money. His oldest son Angelo, who was rumored to have no conscience at all, was one. He took after his mother in height, at a healthy 6 ft of pure pathological violence. There were rumors about Anglo's mother. Some said she was in Italy but others said she had not survived after burning Lupo's calamari in a jealous rage. Either way she was replaced by Lupo's only other true fan, his statuesque significant other, Wanda.

"Naturally" blonde hair gave Wanda the reputation of being a Viking but she was actually a Pollack from Jersey. When Angelo occasionally asked about his mother, Lupo would only hit his forehead and say, "I told you it just didn't work out." Left to his own conclusions Angelo suspected his mother had been liquidated, and in his heart he blamed Wanda. This caused him to frequently bite his hand and desire 'Venganza.' He also had two other brothers who appreciated the college money but seldom visited. Angelo didn't mind because he liked being treated like an only child.

Lupo also had a loyal staff and urban army that didn't always like him but uncompromisingly feared him. He owned them completely and they were usually quick to comply with his every command. Paying them well he also punished them without mercy. They understood how expendable they were to him because at his price new recruits among the poor and desperate were always easy to find.

Lupo was also a man of vision and he understood that blue collar crime was penny anti compared to white collar. He was not afraid to diversify. For the purpose of investments he had a guy who loved money and talked "Wall Street". Alexi Breughel was his name, and in addition to hot tips on the stock market, he would provide exotic entertainments for the affluent famous and for the infamous.

This stock broker from Austria had clients that included media moguls, industrial royalty, and political officials, but his specialty was for the wealthy and unscrupulous. He was an artist of sorts with his own taste for the bizarre and twisted. Lupo always said he like him because he was smart enough to do business with, but sadistic enough to be fun. To Wanda's slight dismay, Lupo said if Breughel was a woman he'd marry him.

In the cosmic war against good and evil it was just a matter of time, for two people as malevolent as Mephisto and one as innocent as St Francis, living in the same vicinity, to intersect. The ironic fact was that the two were actually the cause of the one.

Frankie visited the outside of the De Lacy home many times. Stein warned him that this was called "stalking" and that he would be thought a pervert to visit secretly and frequently but Frankie felt it could not be helped. He would probably not be welcomed as a real visitor, and his solitude rankled in him all the more, since he noted the love and conviviality of this exceptional family. He learned so much from them and about them. The mother's name was not "Mom" or "ma Mere" but those were short versions of mother. Her name was Ann De Lacy and she had been a school teacher. She was blind (which meant she could not see) and she was also in a great deal of pain because of a back injury.

Jean Luc was her oldest son and he was a social worker and activist. He was dark and handsome with very black eyes and thick eyebrows. When he was curious he would raise one eye brow and everyone would know he wanted them to listen to his questions. From what Frankie understood, he helped people who were poor and who no one else wanted to help. Jean Luc was serious but he could also joke around, especially to cheer his mother up. Jean Luc was a good man and Frankie liked him very much.

The girl Stacia was the most fascinating of all. Her hair was white and her face was almost white as well. She had large pale blue eyes and wore dark colors that contrasted so nicely with her skin. She was delicate as the petals of a rose and he tried hard not to look at her all the time because he didn't feel he had the right to. She was also a school teacher like her mother but she taught small children. She was compassionate and bright and always had a soft, kind word to say to her students. In addition she was a dancer. She took classes a few times a week. Frankie knew these things because he spent some days watching her from the roof of the building next to the school or from the skylight at the studio where she danced. This would definitely be considered stalking but he had no intention of approaching her.   At least he knew he should not. This did not dispel his desire to speak to all of them; in fact it increased it. His dreams were filled with this obsession.

Frankie had been looking into the subject of money as he promised Stein he would do and he now realized that in the world of money there were many things that did not seem good or fair. Some people had it and others did not. With it people could buy things and power. Without it people would get sick and even starve and die. He came across an ancient text that even asserted that "the love of money was the root of all evil." Yet the world seemed to revolve around it. This was very enigmatic for him but he accepted that it could be a tool to make things better or worse for many people, not just a few. Through NAI he discovered that he could move money here and there. In fact he could access all he wanted using money, through NAI, but he determined that he did not want to be overly influenced by it.

With this knowledge he decided not to give Stein any more of it than necessary. He found out the cost of the clothing he was given, and much to Stein's dismay, only transferred that much into his account. Frankie now understood that people got money by different means. He had no means of getting money other than NAI so that is how he did it. He also understood that the De Lacy family did not have much of it. That was probably the reason they were happy but it was also the reason why they didn't have a lot of things they needed; like medicine.

Ann was in a great deal of pain and her doctor did not want to give her medication that would help her. Her insurance (the means of using money for sickness) was not good and would not pay enough for her to get better. There was also some kind of rule about opioid medications that also prevented the doctor from helping her. That was another study Frankie had to make. In the end he decided that Mrs. De Lacy had three options: Live in pain, get enough of the pain medication to help her or find another solution for her pain. The doctor seemed afraid that she would want the medication too much but the alternative was terrible. Frankie remembered the pain of his reanimation and he could not see this lovely lady afflicted this way every single day. He decided to ask Stein to help her with neuronal pain blocking stimulation (NPBS) like his own. For this he went to see the doctor. Stein did not like his visits but he would have to get over it.

The next night Frankie knew Stein would have no company. He ran the many miles to the dilapidated mansion on the conservation land near the Connecticut, NY boarder and disarmed the web cam surveillance with NAI. He leaped over the fence then realized a new layer of protection had been added, as five vicious dogs came from all directions. Their hackles up and their teeth barred the K-9 pack surrounded the giant but they soon wished they had not. He sent three whimpering into the bushes with one blow. The other two were tossed like rags against a brick wall. It was not Frankie's intention to hurt them but they would never attack him again.

Dispensing with the door he climbed up the wall and headed straight for the light of the library window, where he found Stein in his usually inebriated condition. Stein might have had a heart attack if he had not been drunk. Sitting down unbidden Frankie broke the couch again while Stein sighed with deep perturbation. They did not speak for a while but simply observed each other. Stein hoping the giant would go away and Frankie, wondering how to request what he wanted. He was beginning to understand that how you asked for something was as important as what you ask for. So he quoted Neruda:

"I took life as it came...lucky or unlucky...this life." The scientist looked at him like an impatient parent looks at a wise cracking teenager.

"What is that supposed to mean?" said Stein, and Frankie smiled glad to know something the knowledgeable man did not.

"It is poetry. Poetry moves my emotions."

"Now that's a concept. I never had any use for it myself. Did NAI teach you about it?"

"No, NAI reads poetry very blandly. It has no soul. My friend Jean Luc reads it like music."

Stein had warned Frankie about his secret observation of this family.

"Well I can't help you there. NAI is what it is. Like everything else it has limitations. As for your, so called friends...If they discover you, they will hate you. Don't do this to yourself Frank."

"I know... but while I can I want to. I help them you know. I protect Stacia. The other day a man took her purse as she was walking home at night. I stopped him without her seeing me and left her purse for her to find on the street. I brought some school supplies for her children; two boxes full. I also help Jean Luc. I brought him some bathing products for the people he works with...a whole box of them. He said the ones with no home like me did not take baths. I bath in the river but it is too cold for them I guess. But mostly I help Ann. I found a cane for her."

This was all unequivocally boring Stein to death so he cut to the chase.

"That is all very nice. Now to what do I owe this visit?" Frankie fidgeted like a child.

"Can you help me with a friend that is in pain?" Stein drew back and knew what he was asking.

"I can't and you know it. I'm as much a prisoner of this technology as you are. I can't share it, can't take it out of here. Even if the people who...who own my life, learn about *you* I would be a dead man. "

This angered the giant more than he thought possible. He grabbed Stein by the lapels and squeezed in frustration till the scientist began to sputter and cough.

"You could help so many people. Stimulate nerves to do their work again, interrupt pain like NAI does for me, "the man answered, winded and in a hoarse whisper.

"No I can't Frank. Ironic isn't it. If I help I die, but I'm no Christ." Frankie just dropped him and climbed out the way he came.

Plan "A" had failed but now he would implement plan "B". He would get the medicine, carefully dispense it in proper doses and deliver it to Ann. More than this and most exciting of all, he would deliver it personally.

For weeks now Frankie had been thinking how wonderful it would be to have a conversation with Ann. In fact he had been hungering for it. She could not see and perhaps his appearance would not be a problem for her. Of course he would not be able to speak to her when Jean Luc and Stacia were there but Ann was often alone.   He would bath in the river and he would even purchase new clothes for the visit, but that created a new problem.

Ordering through NAI needed an address for deliveries. The things he bought for the De Lacy's were sent to their home without trouble but he had no address. So he put a mail box out in front of an old abandoned house a few miles from Stein's and reconciled it with the local post office on line. When one could navigate the cyber universe like NAI did, it was easy to create just about anything or anyone virtually. He had things sent in the name of Mr. F. Smith, because it was a popular name according to NAI. After a few deliveries Frankie noted the post man and the UPS seemed rather skittish about dropping things off and they drove away in a hurry but that didn't matter.   Frankie had an address. Now what he needed was a plan.

In observing the De Lacy home Frankie had noticed nurses came to visit Ann on a regular basis. He decided that with a little research he could come as a nurse. In fact he would be the best kind of nurse--a practitioner. He would wait till Jean Luc and Stacia had gone out for the evening and using NAI he would make a phone call to their home. He would tell Ann her insurance had approved the medicine and an NP would be by to deliver it every month. He also would tell her it was through another agency so her regular nurse would know nothing about it. The plan would work wonderfully.

A few nights prior to his visit, the large but agile cat burglar, approached a country drug store in upstate NY with surprising stealth. He had actually learned stealth from "big cats" in the wilds of Dakota but who knew that such a large person could be so intriguingly silent.   Disarming their locks and surveillance with NAI he went in and directed his steps to their computer. With NAI he logged in. Soon he had printed out several labels with Ann De Lacy's info and secured six months worth of medication. As NAI analyzed the medication for accuracy Frankie noted that there were elements in the pills that might be better arranged for pain relief and far less dependency. He made a mental note of this. He had been doing an awful lot of research on pain medications and their contents. He was not sure why but all this chemistry came very naturally to him and for Ann's sake he was glad. He filled the bottles and affixed the labels.   Where the name of the prescribing physician should be, he used a pencil for the keyboard and typed in DR. Frank. Reversing and restoring the security process he took what he needed and left.

Three evenings later, Frankie was at the De Lacy home listening in his usual spot. Jean Luc was reading to Ann from Dickens and mimicking the British accent to amuse his mother. Frankie, as always, was enjoying himself quietly, by mimicked Jean Luc, but his joy turned to concern when he noticed Ann was having a particularly difficult night. She was squirming in her seat and dealing with so much pain she could not enjoy the reading. Jean Luc closed the book and also looked at her with concern.

"Mammah, you OK?"

"Relatively." Her usually positive demeanor was turned upside down. This answer provoked a powerless feeling inside Jean Luc. They had tried so many things and now with this opioid issue, that had everyone so up in arms, there seemed no hope at all. He was afraid she was giving up.

"What does that mean?" said Jean Luc, because Ann was almost in tears. Frankie could hear it in her voice and so could her son.

"Maybe I don't want to die this minute but if it doesn't stop…"

"Mammah please, don't talk like that."

"How shall I to talk then? The same doctor that gave me my pain medication for ten years since the accident stopped giving them to me. No one else will give them to me. We got an advocate and still no one will help. You know I never even used to take an aspirin before the accident. Now I can't think and I can't work for the pain. I feel like I'm losing my mind. I can't live this way. Besides I feel so useless."

"Oh mamma, what was it Dickens said, "No one is useless in this world that lightens the burden of it to anyone else." Your baking does that for me. It lightens my burden even as it expands my waistline. Besides the doctor says pain is in the mind. If you will try the mindfulness exercise he gave you..."

"That doctor's a quack; I did child birth without anesthesia. I know how to deal with pain but this is beyond all I can do, even at my most mindful. I've got metal grating against the nerves of my spine. What do you expect?"

"He just doesn't want you to be addicted to those meds."

"Then why won't he give me something else?"

"We tried everything else."

"Then shoot me and put me out of my misery." Her body heaved with weeping and she winced and turned away as he tried to hold her and comfort her. She knew she was taking it out on him and that was not fair. She finally composed herself.

"Never mind. I'm alright now. The spasm has passed. You go. Go ahead to your meeting. They need you there. You have to stand up for all those poor kids who need bus passes. All these government cuts are crippling the people who need them most and somebody has to say something about it."

She tried to suppress another visible spasm. She then looked at him as if it were the last time. She touched his face and kissed him on the cheek and sent him off with a tremulous hand. This made him more nervous than he had previously been. What could he do? He tightened his lips and said,

"Breathe, try to relax, listen to music... Stacia should be coming soon. She's tutoring till 8." Her answer was almost convincing,

"Yes I'll be fine. I'll be fine."

The big man in the shadows smiled with satisfaction and justification. This dialogue convinced Frankie that what he had done and would do for Ann was right. He recalled what Jean Luc had quoted and repeated it in a whisper with a perfect English accent.

"No one is useless in this world that lightens the burden of it to anyone else."

He walked to the other side of the house till he was sure Jean Luc had gone. Then he peaked in the window and watched Ann. She was listening for something; for Jean Luc to be gone and his footsteps to fade away. Then in a peculiar, uncharacteristic move she slid down the side of the oven, turned it on, opened its door and then blew out the pilot.

When he was in Alaska and survived a bear attach he wondered about end of life or what NAI called "death." He made a study of it and saw how fragile people were. They could die for many reasons and they even killed others of their kind. Most curious of all, in great emotional distress, they could even kill themselves. He read about all the ways people did this and wondered deeply what would make a person so despondent they would do such a thing. One way people "offed" themselves had to do with gas in an oven. When he saw Ann enacting this terrible ritual he could not imagine a life without this lovely person.

He had to act and now. Forgetting to call first he just knocked at the door. Ann jumped at the sound

. She waited in silence hoping whoever it was would leave. Then she heard a deep sonorous voice with a British inflection.

"Mrs. De Lacy...Mamm, I've come from the VNA office with your medication."

Ann could hardly believe her ears. "Mon Dieu" she thought, "Could this be?" She turned the dial of the oven off, closed the appliance, and with great effort rose and went to the door. She wanted to be sure she was hearing clearly so she asked,

"Who is it?"

"I hope the North End VNA office called. My name is Frank and I'm a Nurse Practitioner. I've been reviewing your..."

She opened the door and he proceeded with his rehearsed speech.

"Begging your pardon Ms. De Lacy but the office was supposed to call, did they?"

"You know sometimes my children are so busy they forget things. The office might have called and my children did not tell me, but welcome. I didn't know that prescribers did house calls."

"Well house calls seem natural to me, I'm from Britain. National health you know. It's hard for people like you to make their appointments. I'm only sorry it took so long for me to get here. My agency is apart from yours and specializes in chronic pain.”

“Young man you have no idea what music this is to my ears.”

“Well yes I do. I suffer with chronic pain myself.   I do understand. “

“Oh Bless you. Until it happens to you it’s hard to sympathize isn’t it? And what a pity, you sound so young.”

“Well, I’m much better now. But I’m here about you not me.”

He pulled out the medication and told her she could take one three times a day. It was not as high a dose as she had before and it was a little different formula (he had tampered with it) but hopefully the pain would be manageable soon. She was just thrilled to have anything at all. Assuming there was some protocol that involved documents she asked him something he was not ready for.

“Do I have to sign anything?”

“Dear me this was the last stop of my day and I seem to have run out of forms. I will mail one to you. You can sign it and keep a copy for me when I return in a month to renew your script.”

“Well I suppose that will be fine. You poor man, working so late. It must be close to 7 o’clock.”

“I don’t mind. I’m alone in this country and I try to keep busy.”

“We are from France. I understand how it is. My children were young when we came over but for me there was so much cultural shock. You must come and join us for dinner sometime. You would enjoy a conversation with my son Jean Luc. He is a social worker. And my daughter Stacia is a teacher. I’m sure she would love to meet you.”

He almost cried to hear this invitation. Everything in him wanted to jump at the chance to sit and eat fresh bread and enjoy the company of the whole family. But he did not know if that would ever be. He answered and she could hear the sincere regret in his voice.

“That is splendid of you to offer but I’m adjusting to this job at present and things are so busy. It is all I can do some nights to get home and get a good night’s rest. Perhaps when I am better adjusted.”

He noted the time and knew that Stacia would return at 8. He had to go.

"If there is any problem with the medicine please call me. Would you like to take my number down in brail?"

She took a note book out and a stylus and he gave her a number that would reach him on NAI. He gave her a last warning about the medication and she promised to follow his instructions.

"I will count these pills when I come if there are any left. Please take them as prescribed."

"Oh I will, be good as gold. I never abused them before I won't now. Just glad to have them. You were like an angel coming to me now. I've been very low."

"I quite understand. Here sit down. You can take a dose now if it helps." He got her some water and she took the medicine.

"We hope this will make things better. And by the way, its smells like gas in here. Oh look the pilot has gone out." He took a match and lit the pilot then continued.

"There also might be a leak. That would be very dangerous. You might have someone check that. We don't want anything to happen to you. Good night Mrs. Delacy."

"Oh please call me Ann."

"Good night Ann."

Ann was ashamed about what she had attempted. Frankie hoped this would ensure she would not try self-harm again. On the other hand, his heart was beating out of his chest. His emotions were running away with him. He was never so excited, not even when facing Kodiak attacks in the wild. He had turned a corner in his life...he had a reciprocal friend.

The "paperwork" had to be researched and the best way to get it was to break into the VNA office at night and pick up some documents which he "doctored" with NAI to indicate they were from North End VNA. That was easy but getting the stamp on the envelope to mail it was not. Big fingers with difficulty in tiny motor tasks made him wonder why Stein made him so big. He got the answer in later conversations, when the scientist explained that even as a child learning to write needed to scribble in large letters, so Stein, learning to build an organism as complex as Frankie, needed to make it big. Besides Frankie had already perceived, he was built from several bodies and this meant some creative construction. All things considered he was not badly built, but his corps like coloring didn't help his aesthetics and the pupils of his eyes had so little pigment they were a frightening cat like, yellow.

Stacia and Jean Luc were curious at first, about the meds, but when the documents came they were more at ease. They assumed that this prescriber with a more "enlightened European" point of view had seen her need and her ability to be responsible with the medication and had rearranged things for her comfort. They were in fact happy to see their mother in good spirits and more satisfied with her functionality.

Ann asked them not to report this to the agency as "house calls" might not be standard procedure. She did not want to get this delightful young man in trouble for being kind. They were alright with it since one does not questions good fortune too much. After all, when *they* received certain recent "donations" they were just grateful; curious but grateful. They did wonder about the gifts and asked people they thought might have been responsible but when the mystery persisted they just assumed the benefactor wanted to be anonymous and they respected that.

True to his word Frankie watched for Ann to be alone and came each month to bring her medicine. He sat at her table and ate her bread and chatted about music, literature, theater and poetry, which he researched, and which she was very knowledgeable about. She kept thinking what a wonderful friend he would make for Stacia but she could never persuade him to stay and meet her. He looked forward to these visits as much as she looked forward to them and to the medicine that gave her good quality of life.

At the end of three months Frankie was culturally educated and had observed plays and movies and dances through NAI and by hiding in the rafters of theaters and cinemas. He observed art in museums and galleries at night by disarming their security systems. He became expert at evading security guards when they were doing their rounds but he still longed to saunter through such places with warm bodies walking all around him. Instead he had to be satisfied with viewing the products of human emotive genius all alone.

It was a day in the spring when windows are opened and flowers bloom that Frankie was preparing to see Ann with her last refill. He had been wondering if breaking into pharmacies was the most effective way of getting her medicine and he had also been thinking long and hard about the medicine itself. Frankie had determined that there were certain herbs and chemical combinations with properties that were much better for humans and were not addictive. In fact there were other things much more compatible with human neurology for the purpose of interrupting pain. He wondered to himself if this kind of knowledge came easily to others and why others had not discovered such helpful remedies. He also questioned if perhaps, one of his "parts" was a man of medicine, and logged that in his subjects for future investigation.

Becoming a self made pharmacist, he was certain that with the proper equipment, a formula for more effective and non-addictive pills could be designed. Ann would need to wean off of the meds she was on but alternatives could be introduced once she was at a low enough dosage of the opioids. For this purpose he had created a make shift "lab" and pill factory in his ramshackle home. Short on chemicals he discovered through NAI that clandestine shipments of bad and good chemicals from China and herbs in great quantities from other countries had been confiscated by the police. A little sleuthing and listening in on criminal conversations with NAI and he was able to determine the arrival of two such shipments along with parts for pill making apparatus. Much to the upset of local mobsters, those shipments mysteriously disappeared, and Frankie was in business manufacturing safe pain meds. His next visit to Ann was to introduce the plan. He would properly cloak it all in medical terminology and she would never know.

That evening was going splendidly. Jean Luc was at the theater with his lady friend Luna and Stacia was at a dance class. He and Ann were chatting and sharing as usual then Frankie got technical. He told her he had marked out a plan to wean her from the opioid and put her on another much more efficient medication that was not harmful or addictive. She was concerned about the transition but he assured her she would not be without relief if she followed his instructions to the letter. The medicine might in fact help her body start manufacturing its own endorphins more effectively. She reiterated that he had come as an angel of help to her and that she would trust him. Then a terrible thing happened.

Jean Luc had forgotten his wallet with the tickets he had purchase for the concert. He and Luna, his girl, drove all the way back to the house to get them. Frankie heard them coming in the front door and chatting. So did Ann.

She was happy because Jean Luc and Frankie would finally meet. But Frankie was terrified. He put the bottle of pills in her hand and made his excuses quickly escaping through the kitchen door. He was quick but not quick enough to avoid Jean Luc seeing a huge man dashing out of his mother's kitchen with less than professional clothing which included a hooded sweatshirt.

Frankie was terrified of discovery. He leaped over the fence in the back yard and was gone before Jean Luc got out the door but Jean Luc was filled with fear over what he saw and his queries also terrified Luna who was a nurse. Only Ann defended NP Frank as someone who could do no wrong. Jean Luc called the VNA office and they knew nothing of an NP Frank or of North End VNA. This terrified him even more. Who was this frightening stranger that had been visiting with his mother for months? He would be hyper-vigilant in future and Ann would never be left alone again.

Ann wondered what Jean Luc would do about her medicine. She feared to lose her assistance in this matter. She had also enjoyed the company of this gentle and knowledgeable young man who visited her monthly. Since her illness all her visitors had dwindled till there were none. She was isolated and quite lonesome. What if NP Frank did wear a hoodie and sweat pants instead of scrubs? What did clothes matter? She was an old hippie and she recalled the revolution that made it possible for people to go to work in business casual or even casual, casual. Besides, her son was being condescending. He was treating her like a child.

She didn't need eyes to know a genuine person when she met one. She remembered Frankie's authentic, kindness and concern. It was unpretentious and refreshing. He had never hurt her. As for their belongings, nothing had ever been missing in the house because Frankie was not a thief. He had never required money from her. His only interest was her comfort. She could see nothing wrong or harm in the arrangement but rather a great deal of good. Ann's suicidal despair began to return, when suddenly, she remembered the brail phone number in her purse. She found it and clutched it to her breast like a life line.

Questions remained and the police were called but no evidence of a person could be found. Apparently the medication was of an unusual kind. It had no identifying label or mark. Analysis provided a list of ingredients in combination that were heretofore unidentified as a street drug. The dosage was not getting her high it was just doing what it was supposed to—easing pain. It was a strange analgesic that for these days, had minimal side effects, and did the job well. In fact, unknown to them, it had some added benefits for human neurology.

As far as the crime scene was concerned there were no fingerprints anywhere. Everything the stranger had handled was free of tell tale marks. He knew how to cover his tracks. When the investigating cop mentioned this at the precinct, that fact tickled the ears of a certain lady detective and her Hispanic partner. "Space Alien" might be working another side of the street and he might have a "Robin Hood" angle as well.

No harm had been done which left all investigators concerned and befuddled but not angry. Even Ann was left with some hope. She had no pain killers but she had his number and was sure he would not leave her stranded. The only ones who seemed "put out" by this were the ones who were expecting the illegal shipments of chemicals and herbs. These people and in particular, this person (Romeo Lupo) were enraged by the whole audacious scenario. He of all people had been "robbed".

Lupo of course blamed the Don of Brooklyn and Staten Island and this, in weeks to come, resulted in unprecedented bloodshed. Suspicion did not need justification and the war was on. The police were picking up the pieces for weeks as one family blamed the other and exacted revenge at gun point. For law enforcement it was like a purge. Minor gangs also got blamed and their ranks thinned in the crossfire. The morgue was busy but the arrests were surprisingly few. However, Romeo felt no better for all the corpses that could be laid to his credit. He had been wronged and he didn't know how. This disturbed him and gave him awful dyspepsia. What could be done but to make everyone else pay? If he only knew that as Stein's keeper, the cause was of his own making, but he didn't know, and not knowing made him vicious and crazier than usual.

All he did know was that business was bad. Still a man had to make a living. So, while the drug trade seemed to be in flux as large shipments continued to go missing, and his customers were screaming for product he turned to another line of business to boost his numbers.   For this he consulted his associate Alexi Breughel.

The short diamond encrusted demigod in the Bottega Veneta cashmere jacket was in the mood for a visit. Securing the keys to the private elevator of the Park Avenue Penthouse, he left his boys in the lobby with a duly intimidated doorman. He ascended in brass and velvet silence and knocked on the door of the luxury suite as if he were there to borrow a cup of sugar.

Alexi knew only one man, who had the audacity to come calling unannounced, and at this hour. He also knew the rap of his Safire pinkie ring on the door. He had been apprised by the evening news, that his client was not in a mood to be spurned. Letting his valet retire for the night, he adjusted the cords to his Dior Homme dressing gown. Then like a fellow demigod in the halls of Olympus the pale, lanky financier and sex trade monger unlatched the door himself and opened his arms to receive the Don of three boroughs.

5

Masks and Dolls

Frankie was inconsolable after Jean Luc uncovered his ruse to help Ann. His whole pill manufacturing operation stopped and he felt purposeless. What was he to do now with the sacks and sacks of chemicals he had brought from the docks and stored in several caverns in the area? Worst of all he was alone again and his solitude threatened to consume him. He was even afraid to lurk around the De Lacy home for fear of discovery. What might they have told Ann? Nothing good, he was sure.

"Your so called NP is a gruesome gargoyle," "You befriended a monster and a liar." The scenarios of travesty replayed themselves over and over in his head as did the words of Stein, "If they discover you they will hate you." Now the worst had happened. They did hate him and the most heart wrenching part of it all was that Ann was in pain again and subsequently in danger of her life. He felt so incredibly lost and helpless till, for the very first time ever, NAI declared he had received a voice message.

When he gave Ann the phone number he knew any call would be processed by NAI and the source of the number would be heavily protected like any other communication he might receive. Stein had asked him to refrain from using it to call him because of his dubious benefactor but he knew that giving it to Ann was not a threat to him. It now might be for her. Was anyone monitoring her calls? Would she be accused of colluding with a drug dealer? Was it safe to answer? He decided to throw caution to the wind. She might be calling to reprimand him. He must take the punishment of her anger if this was the case. He had no ill intention and he wanted to have an opportunity to tell her so. He took the call but did not know how to answer. Ann broke the ice.

"NP Frank?"

"Yes... is this Ann?"

"Yes it is?"

"I'm so sorry, I..."

"I don't know who you are but you have done me nothing but good. You have nothing to be sorry for."

He had never wept but now the tears ran freely down his corps like cheeks.

"Is it alright for me to talk to you?"

"Well I ordered a cell phone on the television that my son knows nothing about. So yes, I can talk freely. He is not here at the moment and Stacia is out in the garden."

He breathed more easily and thought with regret, of Stacia. She had been lacking his protection on her excursions to dance class and he had been missing her grace. He was glad to know she was safe and he determined to study gardening, to at least become acquainted with what she was currently doing. Frankie paused in his thinking now. Since he last saw Ann, he had been holding his next question night and day.

"How are you feeling?"

"Terrible, of course. The pain has come back with a vengeance and I can't even get out of bed."

"I am so sorry."

"Again mon ami this is not your fault, you have tried to help me more than I can repay and have done me no harm. My pain consumes me but more than this I wish to know about you."

"Oh, Madam, calling me a friend is more to me than all that is precious. I do not know what your son saw of me but it is my monstrous size and aspect that has made me a pariah to humanity. I became aware of your plight and being gifted with certain abilities I knew I could help you. But my sin was to desire your -- vision impaired company--in return; for never have I had a friend. Now that you know my secret you may not want to have further to do with me, but it has been my greatest pleasure to converse with you and I will help you if you wish, even if I never speak with you again."

Now it was Ann's turn to weep. She imagined some poor deformed sod, lonely and rejected, because of circumstances, (not of his own making) rendering him freakish. A student of literature she envisioned him, a Quasimodo of legend with a pure heart, in modern sweats. She was also a teacher of years and she evaluated him now as a pedagogue might examine a student. Her evaluation found him erudite and intelligent. His voice, now free of the British accent, was charming, genuine and passionate. She herself was an incredibly compassionate person who had taught her children it was the responsibility of the strong to help the weak. As an elder and someone with a handicap, she had endured human isolation and modern callousness with regret. She had felt its painful sting. But this young man was enduring sadness beyond words. She needed him but he also needed her and she would not abandon him.

"You are all the more my friend now that I know something of you. In the future if you will be honest with me I will return the favor."

Frankie could not believe what he was hearing. She was proposing a future for him, in her kind association. He would do anything for such a gift.

"I will be as honest as I can. I seek to do no one harm, but people do not always perceive what I am as harmless. You have seen this already, haven't you?"

"Every great person I know has been misunderstood."

He paused and felt warmed by the compliment. He did not know how to take it. She had to break the silence.

"Frank? Is that your real name?"

"As far as I know."

"Then Frank, can you help me again?"

"With the greatest pleasure."

They decided on a course of action whereby he would leave her medicine on the window sill at night, on the 1st of the month and she would pick it up. He told her he would give her the first bottle that night due to the unforeseen circumstances. She in turn would give him a loaf of fresh bread. They would converse on the phone when she was able. She would call him the day before just in case there was a problem. He explained to her that he was working on a formula that would not include opioids at all. This would be experimental but he assured her it would not be harmful in any way. It would include a period of weaning from the present medication but he would keep her supplied during every change. Never would she be without relief.

She was surprisingly gratified by this news and thought he could be a wealthy man if he developed such a helpful and innocuous medication. But she also thought him so ingenuous that he might be corrupted by money. Oh, the people he could help... but that was a conversation for another day. As something of a revolutionary in her own time, she was not afraid of bending unjust rules for progress. She was in fact thrilled to be his "guinea pig". They said their goodbyes and he felt like he was floating on rainbow colored clouds. In this mindset he went straight to work on her medicine. She rose, slowly and painfully, to prepare her dough for the bread she would bake and leave for him that night.

Evil minds grind like machinery oiled by greed and profit. What they produce is the worst of what humanity is capable. While Lupo's boys were seeking and destroying their opponents, on the suspicion of them stealing their imports, the boss was in consultation about a new scheme that would keep the flow of cash coming. Breughel had been indulging a new perversion that he guessed would be terribly popular among certain high profile individuals with certain proclivities and money to burn. People of this kind needed access points for the indulgence of their secret pleasures. But the occasional sex object with loose lips was one of their greatest fears. It was Breughel's challenge to secure objects that would be, alluring, silent and that were still breathing. If these human commodities, were also flexible enough for kinky utility, that was a plus.

With the help of Lupo's funding such an enterprise was made possible. The prototype of this project would be located in a quaint two story building with the front of a high end bistro in the East Village. The location had to be accessible to "john's" doing business on Wall Street or elsewhere in the city. "Quick and available" needed to be an implicit feature of the business. The rooms were furnished with the finest décor and the restaurant had food to make the mouth, and even imagination, water. Astutely, it was offered at prices that would assure only the wealthiest patrons. The music was live and sensual; a foreshadowing the "entertainment" to come. The wait staff was tastefully clad, impeccably professional and handsome enough to model for Esquire or Vogue. The culinary critics gave it five out of five stars with the proviso that some ambiguity hung on the fringe of its entertainment but this only added to its mystique and desirability. Anyone who was anyone wanted to eat there or imbibe of its legendary wine cellars, at least once. It was simply called, Ealú. Now all that was needed was the distinctive product.

Frankie was encouraged to continue his usual rounds with slight modification. He felt accepted by Ann. This gave him tacit leave to continue providing in small ways for the family and also to keep clandestine guard over Stacia when she was out at night. He love Ann's bread but watching Stacia and her peers dance fed his soul in a way he could not describe. They glided and flew across the boards in ways that defined elegance. The music was also the stuff of dreams and he felt its ethereal ministration in the depth of his being.

It happened that on a cool night in spring Frankie took to the alleys and silently followed the girl to her destination. He then, as always, climbed the wall holding on to drain pipes and window ledges, coming finally to the sky light of the two story building. There he had an over head view of the dance studio. He could also easily see the alley where many of the dancers went at break time to quench their thirst for water, electrolytes and or nicotine. Frankie was please to know that, Stacia neither smoked nor vaped, as he had studied this smoking practice and found it most pernicious and unhealthy.

They were rehearsing for a ballet called, "Swan Lake" and he thought that of all the swans in the chorus Stacia was the most swanlike and beautiful. He had seen the great white birds on his journeys across the continent and felt they were more splendid and powerful than anything else in the sky. When they beat their wings, the sound was thunderous, and he wished he could leap and take hold of them somehow accompanying them on their way. Stacia was similarly glorious and she certainly had a power over him that no creature had ever exerted...and that, without a single touch. He did not dare even mention this to Ann. It was his secret, and well he should keep it, for what did a monster have in common with a swan.

He watched and mused, till the dancers started exiting the building. Some stood in groups that congregated for one last smoke and some wandered off on their own. Stacia had a question about a certain kind of lift and a male dancer showed her how it was done. Frankie felt a twinge of something he had not felt before. He later learned it was jealousy, but he calmed inside to see that the dancer was more interested in another male dancer than in Stacia. Still, he knew eventually this would happen. She would find a mate like the rest of creation and he would still be alone. He would have to prepare his heart for that, but not today.

As the dancers socialized a very large vehicle drove up. Frankie would learn it was called a limousine and it seemed to catch the attention of all those on the side walk. A man emerged with a long tan leather vest and a petulant, attitude of impatience. Frankie did not like him. His animal instinct, honed to a fine skill in the wild, raised his hackles and alerted him to danger. The man looked around, like a hunting hyena. Then he started to speak,

"Well whose coming?"

None of the dancers knew what he was talking about but there were many conjectures.

"Common now I don't have all night. I was supposed to pick up ten dancers for the audition and if there is no one here I will move on to the Martha Graham's studio."

Martha Graham's was a rival studio and this started quite a buzz. Obviously this man had made a mistake because no one was apprised of an audition. This "error" could be fortuitous for them. They all wanted more work, except Stacia who was not really interested in being a professional dancer. She did it for the love not for the work. One girl ventured a comment,

"I've forgotten which audition this is for."

"*Wicked* of course…on Broadway."

These were apparently the magic words that were needed to clear the street, as at least 11 dancers poured themselves into the limo. Stacia stood alone in her lace up sneakers and jeans pulling her lilac sweater around her in the evening chill. The man looked her up and down, which provoked a bear like grunt from the vigilante on the roof.

"There's room for you next to the driver doll. If you're interested?"

The other dancers all started to call out to her encouraging her to come along. She refused at first, but soon peer pressure overcame her reluctance and she shrugged. Then causing Frankie great concern, she got in.

The limo took off and Frankie felt fear like he had never felt. Something was wrong and Stacia was not safe. He was not sure what, but he only knew he must follow that car. This would challenge both his stealth and his speed. He ran along the edge of the roof and when it ended he leaped onto the roof of the next building. After this he lunged from one object to another like an orangutan. A series of fire escapes drain pipes and light posts became means of transit, and when those failed him, he streaked across streets and alley ways following the limo as fast as stealth and city transit would permit. He kept his hood down and after a few miles he was spotted and briefly chased by a black and white that remarked on his running speed and yelled at him to stop. He ducked instead, into a tight space between two buildings, just as the limo parked in front of the elegant Bistro called Ealú.

When the police car had passed, Frankie slipped out to hear all the dancers commenting excitedly about being at this place. Frankie did not understand. They were speaking as if this was a good thing, the best in fact, and they were happy, but something was not right. He gingerly mounted the side wall of the building and was on the roof in moments. From there he could see the man from the limo escorting the dancers around the building to the back. Their excited voices mingled as a woman came out holding a load of strange clothes. These outfits were offered to the dancers who took them with gratitude. Later Frankie would learn these were called, costumes. They were told showers and dressing rooms awaited them within. The excitement and giddy laughter mounted. The dancers were absolutely drunk with it. One by one they entered, Stacia was the last. She held up her costume and it was a black, white and red flimsy thing, with a big red flower.

As soon as the last dancer entered Frankie descended. Alone in the back alley he groped for a plan. Somehow he had to get into this place. He found a diagonally slanted double door that seemed to lead to the under part of the building. He yanked at the handle and ripped the door off. He went in then placed the door gently back on so that nothing looked out of place.

It was soon discovered that he was indeed in the building. There were many voices and noises above. He heard the sound of music in one area and the smells of food wafted down to him from another. It was a fairly large place. Exploring a bit he finally began to hear the unmistakable sound of the giggling dancers. They appeared to be coming and going with much excitement.

He went up a stairway to a place with a small window that looked out onto a long hotel hallway with modern art and carpeting of geometric design. There he saw some of the dancers running in and out of two rooms vaping or giggling about what they had been told. They would apparently need to do some sort of improvisation related to their clothing, whatever that meant. Most of them felt confident they could execute anything they were given to do. That supposedly meant that most of them might be in the show. Stacia also came out but unlike the others, she was quite uneasy about staying. Frankie thought her very perceptive for this, and wished more than anything that he could walk her right out of there. Disappointed he saw, it was her choice to stay. She looked lovely in her strange new clothing and like some of the others she also wore a mask.

Finally they were asked to wait in the hall and one by one they were called to come in. This took a few minutes. Frankie thought it was taking forever, but the dancers were saying it was too short a time; too short for an audition. It must be that they were getting reviewed and shown into another waiting area. This was the first time during the evening that they were finally showing some quiet concern. A little fear, was filtering down into their midst. They too were sensing something.

When it was finally Stacia's turn she went in, leaving absolute quiet in the hall. Frankie could hear the music in the restaurant and the street noise but not one peep from the frivolous band of performers. Frankie went to the door where he had seen them enter and listened. He heard nothing.

In the restaurant there were murmurs among certain exclusive customers that their "desert" had arrived. They would soon be called into their rooms to enjoy it. Upstairs, however, Frankie waited helplessly by the door where Stacia had entered wondering what to do. He heard footsteps and found only a window at the end of the hall to exit from and keep watch. What he saw was this.

Big men with clothes like kitchen staff and others with suits went into the room he had been standing near and came out with limp, lifeless dancers in their strange costumes. Frankie was terrified thinking they were dead but one was close enough in the quay for him to see she was breathing. This temporarily relieved his angst but again, he wondered what to do. To come out into the hall would allow him to be seen, but he would never let anything happen to Stacia whatever the cost to himself.

The men hefted the performers like organic baggage distributing them into different rooms. He decided to scoot around the dark periphery of the building, peering in the windows with open blinds. He saw the men placing the dancers in strange positions on the bed or furniture like exotic manikins in a grotesque pantomime, then they pulled blinds. One room had two girls placed in it and another had a boy and a girl. Stacia was also placed on a bed with candles all around it, like a macabre offering to a perverse god; the flower from her costume in her hand like a bridal bouquet. She resembled the peaceful dead.

In that room, as soon as the man took hold of the blind to close it Frankie lifted the window and grabbed the man's hand in an iron grip. He yanked him out and threw him unconscious, like a rag doll into a trash filled dumpster below. Frankie slipped into the room like smoke, silent and unseen.

Now he was alone in a room with Stacia. How could this be? Embarrassment engulfed and befuddled him for a moment, and he wondered how he could even touch her to save her. He pulled the blanket around her and then peered out of the door into the hallway. There he saw well dressed men and a couple of women entering the rooms. At once he understood that Stacia would never be content with being the only one saved. He had to save them all or he would not be able to live with himself. In his naiveté he questioned if what was about to happen in the rooms was bad. After all, the people who went in seemed well dressed and harmless enough. Then he heard what sounded like a vicious snap and a low moan and he had his answer. Following the noise, he entered that room to find a man, half dressed in a tuxedo, with a whip in his hand. He was lashing an unconscious young man whose face and chest were bleeding from the first blow.

The man with the barbed whip saw him and started to scream. Frankie did not hesitate. He grabbed the man and smacked him rendering him mute with shock. Then he did something he had never done before. He shoved a pillow case into the man's mouth for silence and in less than a minute he neatly wrapped the whip around the terrified torturer. Following this, electrical cords were yanked from appliances and used to bind the man head to foot. Looking at the man full in the face he then raked that face with his sharp black fingernails, all the while growling like a hungry animal. The man was petrified enough to void himself. Frankie anchored the cord to the bed and tossed the man out the back window to hang by his feet. The giant paused for a moment to note that he looked quite like a caterpillar in a cocoon, yet he understood this worm would never turn. No time for philosophizing he moved on.

Other rooms were similarly filled with luxurious implements of torture. He went from room to room cornering and binding the tormentors as quickly as he could. He hung five of them out the windows and left them there to moan. But things were moving too slowly. There were too many. Then he noted the door to Stacia's room was closed. He had left it wide open. Someone must be in there. He ripped the ceiling light out of the hall way and ran in the darkness.

When he got to the room all was dark except for a few candles. The blanket had been removed and she lay disheveled on the bed. A man stood over her in a black silk suit sliding a long knife to surgical sharpness on a jewel studded stone. He was tall and slim and sure of himself. Frankie almost envied his confidence with her but he had something else that was not to be envied. Something even fanged serpents in the dessert didn't have; pure sentient evil.

A crooked smile on his face, the man stood then moved as if in an ecstatic trance. He turned slowly to the sound of the door creaking open and there he saw a shadow that filled the doorway. A wave of a large sepulchral hand knocked over the candles and slapped the knife away like a fly. Fire erupted and livid, the man took to the hallway escaping into the dark. Frankie' would not follow him. His only thought was to save Stacia.

The giant lifted the girl onto his shoulder like a feather and raced down the hall punching the doors open as he ran. In his former search for "causes of death" he had noted that fire was a big one. Subsequently, he researched "fire safety" and knew to call out "fire" as a warning to others. Now by experience he noted how effective this was. In moments it seemed people were screaming and fire engines were arriving while a herculean figure lowered three dancers at a time out of a window in blankets and tossed 4 more would be tormentors into the dumpster.

Frankie hated to leave Stacia on the street in a blanket but he saw that rescue was coming and he could not stay to be seen. He also noted the man who had almost hurt Stacia. He was speaking to some people with cameras and microphones as the fire fighters battled the flames in the background. He later found out from NAI, and the news that his name was Alexi Breughel the owner of the establishment. He claimed to have called out "fire" and saved the people within. Breughel had no explanation for the drugged dancers or the five men dangling from the back windows. He said he was not responsible for any eccentricities his guests might have. The people in the dumpster had obviously gotten away. Among the human "cocoons" were found a visiting Midwestern senator, two local business men, a foreign diplomat and a famous comedian. They were all babbling and crying like babies when they were found. Even weeks later, they were incapable and unwilling to make comment.

Breughel was the only one that seemed to have his wits about him but even he had to take a break to recover. The best of lawyers and a trip to the French Riviera settled his bad PR and his nerves. Still, Lupo would want his money back and the Austrian had an image in his mind of a certain large shadowy figure from which he wanted revenge.

After two weeks he felt more like himself and returned to the states ready for business. Insurance settled things with the gangster but pride could not so easily be appeased. That monstrous Shadow in the doorway had cost him a good time and a bundle of money. He would somehow find him and get a return for his "hardship".

Frankie later recalled his own feelings after that night. He stood on the hill he always retreated to, overlooking Manhattan, and wondered about the city below. He had seen too much of the world to deem "the Big Apple" a universe but it was so illusive and absorbing. Like F. Scott Fitzgerald in his lamentation, "My Lost City" one could consider it a universe indeed, all its own. Frankie knew the green beyond this obscenity of concrete and smog but at the moment he was absorbed with the ephemeral sensation in his arms where the warmth of an angel had been. He then understood how a universe could be in a city as large as Manhattan and in something as small as a feathery white eyelash.

6

Memories and Phobias

Things had a tendency to cave in and fall in Frankie's new house so he started improving on the structure. Finding materials in the woods or occasionally in catalogues with money he "borrowed" through NAI he made the house (on the inside at least) look quite decent if not a bit eccentric. MC Escher might have enjoyed the unusual staircases that went nowhere.

Though his choice of décor was a combination of interesting trash, natural objects and a few things he made, it was all his. Loving trees and branches he made much of his furniture out of trees without refinement. This gave his home the look of a curious forest. The chairs were large and the bed gave the appearance of an enormous nest among golden birch trees in a grove. It was marvelous.

Obtaining money was not a problem for him. He noted through NAI there were some people who had lots of it and some who had little. He therefore, without being too extravagant, took what he needed for himself from these large coffers in Switzerland, New York, the Isle of Mann and many other wealthy places. They didn't seem to miss it and he didn't over do it. It seemed a good arrangement.

His gardening was coming along nicely too. Realizing that gardening out in the open would expose him he learned about indoor gardening and hydroponics. A local cavern with a narrow entrance, that was rumored to have bears but didn't, served as his cellar. LED lights were purchased for the purpose and soon he was growing things underground, with earth enriched by bat guano. This garden gave him a far more balanced diet, and as he had studied about diet, he thought this a good thing.

Meanwhile, Stacia was now among the suffering at the De Lacy home and Frankie was desolate to hear this. Terror filled her at the very thought of leaving the house. A victim of post traumatic stress, she not only quit her dance classes but took a leave from her job. She was even afraid to venture past her porch. Even the gardening she loved did not tempt her. Like her mother before Frankie's intervention, Stacia lost much of the joy of life. Jean Luc tried to get her to counseling but she would not leave the house to go. Ann watched this with great concern and spoke to Frankie who already sensed something terrible had happened. The dance studio was shut down for a while and when it reopened all the students were new and the beautiful "swan" Stacia was conspicuously absent.

Satisfaction filled Frankie knowing Stacia was safe but he lamented the fact that she was housebound with terror. What could he do to coax her back into life? The answer came to him and the next morning, when she awoke, she looked out the porch window to see two, 6' X 4' elevated gardening boxes complete with dirt and packets of seed. Ann knew by now that Frankie was the one leaving presents and she covered for him. She said that some friends from the Garden project had furnished her with these. This produced Stacia's first smile since her trauma.

It was a wonderful turn of events as Stacia began venturing out to water her seedlings and care for her plants. Ann had long been considering a way that Frankie could expand his talent to others. In fact she had been doing a lot of thinking. She called the school and asked if, under the circumstances, Stacia's class might be allowed to come and visit so she could teach them about gardening. If they did this, she said she could speak to her "friend" about a raised garden at the school. The principle thought this would be a great field trip and loved the idea of the raised garden. Missing their teacher quite a lot the children were thrilled by the prospect of seeing her. Frankie was in, but secretly of course.

Stacia was told to expect her "company" on a Monday and there was much baking of cookies and muffins for all. When the children arrived she immediately took on the teacher's persona and even went into the yard with the children crowded around her. She taught the class, explaining which plants were which and giving them a plan of organization to "help" each grow with maximum sun. Then they had lunch and laughed and simply enjoyed each other's company. Soon they were gone for the day and Stacia realized she had been away too long. By Wednesday four full garden boxes had appeared on the sunny side of the school yard along with boxes of seed. By Friday Stacia was in class teaching them all about seed germination and photosynthesis.

Ann was, of course, delighted and she was also convinced that Frankie had more to offer the world. His talents must not be lavished on her family alone. At times she wondered if he were independently wealthy since she could not get a clear answer about where he got his money, but she felt that even good friends had to have some secrets. She did encourage him to patent his analgesic formula because many others were in pain like she was and needed his help. He told her he would consider what she said but in his heart he feared exposure more than anything and so did not act upon her suggestions. Still he began to watch for others to help and found Elaina and Dee Dee.

Dee Dee was one of Stacia's students. When Frankie observed her class at play he noted that one little girl was not like the others. Her clothes were shabby and her expression, though sweet, was different. She had a flat, round face with large slanted eyes. Her light brown hair was wispy and straight. Sometimes she held her tongue out between her lips. He was told by Ann, that when she first came to the class the other children shunned her but Stacia would not permit this. She made Dee Dee feel welcome and expected the other children to do the same.

When the children came to the house to visit on gardening day Frankie observed through the tall fence. He usually did not venture out by day but this was an exception. Well hidden by foliage he watched Dee Dee who had become a point of fascination for him. Now able to hear her he noted she spoke with impairment and her speech was not like that of the other children. That night when he spoke to Ann he asked her about it.

"She is what they call Down's syndrome." Ann explained. "Many children like her are not able to go to regular school but Dee Dee is high functioning for her condition. Dee Dee's mother is addicted to drugs so she was forbidden to see her by Child Protective Services. Her grandmother Rosa was given charge of her. When Rosa got her she didn't know much about this condition so she was at a loss. Stacia had me call to explain some things since I can speak Spanish as well as French."

"So she does have a mother?" Frankie asked.

"Yes but her mother can't take care of her, she is chemically addicted."

Frankie felt he should not ask more. Ann might think him awkwardly ignorant. Still he had many questions and when he had a moment he inquired of NAI about Downs and addiction and the habits of such people. This made him wonder what would make a mother prefer something else over her own child. What he found was heart breaking. As far as he could see bad medicine turned a mother into a monster; this was terrible and sad. Could this somehow be changed with good medicine? He noted the methods of dealing with addiction in the United States were not as efficient as they were in other countries. Places like Portugal for instance were dispensing the drug itself legally and helping the person wean off if they were willing. He consulted with

NAI for days over this. Then one day, moving roof to roof, he decided to follow Dee Dee's bus home.

He watched as the grandmother came out of her building to get the child and noted the little one waved as the bus drove off. Rosa stopped to speak to a neighbor and after a short while a woman approached them. This woman was rather dirty and did not look well. Dee Dee ran to her and hugged her but grandmother pulled her back and addressed the woman gruffly. The woman asked for money but the grandmother gave the woman nothing. Instead Rosa turned away and took Dee Dee inside.

The woman held her stomach and ran around behind the building to the clothes lines and fire escapes of the back alley. Subsequently the ragged woman started yelling towards one of the upper windows. Rosa looked out and told her she would call "La Policia". The woman yelled demeaning things at Rosa's window and soon a black and white car drove up and policemen started to walk towards the woman. She ran and the police waved her off. Apparently she was not worth chasing. They stood around for a little while, spoke on the radio then drove away.

All of this disturbed Frankie more than he could imagine. He had to do something about it. He needed to know more. That night he went to the building where he had seen Rosa and Dee Dee enter. There was a fire escape next to the window that Rosa had looked out of and he easily accessed it. Peering in he noticed several things. The fire escape was at the window of a child's bed room. The other window accessed the living room where grandmother and child sat watching a Spanish soap opera in their pajama's and slippers, eating rice and beans.

During the commercial Rosa told Dee Dee to brush her teeth. The grandmother took the dishes into the kitchen and helped the little girl brush. Then the child was told to get in bed. Dee Dee was very compliant. Grandmother kissed her goodnight and she was off to her room.

As she entered Frankie witnessed a little ritual that he would learn she performed every night. She turned on her night light, got in her bed and looked at a book. She held is upside down but she looked at it for a moment then closed it and put it on her night stand. She folded her hands and bowed her head. Then she turned off the light and she nestled under her covers. On the many subsequent nights he secretly visited it was always the same. This was her routine and he came to enjoy watching it. In fact he look forward to it. It gave him ease. After a week of observing the comforting segue he was not prepare for what happened.

One night he was climbing down the fire escape after her little ritual and he inadvertently made a noise. He froze hoping he had not alerted anyone. Satisfied that all was well he continued his exit when he saw a little round face pressed against the window. He fully expected she would be terrified and scream but she did not. She examined him only with curiosity and then waved like she did with the bus every day. He was not sure what to do so he waved back then hurriedly completed his decent.

This surprised and amazed him. The child was not blind but she had no fear of him. He had never experienced such an extraordinary thing. It was the first time he ever had anyone look at him straight in the face and not flinch. Though he feared she might alert her grandmother to his presence he could not get that little face in the window out of his mind. He was drawn--compelled, by a great depth of emotion. Regardless of the consequences he would have to return but it would not be today.

It was a few weeks later and the chill in spring air was turning balmy. He had been working on making his kitchen functional by hooking it up to a local solar farm. He was happy to have some success and he had been thinking this would be the night he would go to see the child. He had chosen a gift to show his intentions were good. Something the child could enjoy. He put great thought into it and finally settled on a little flower pot with a cherry tomato plant. In school Stacia had been teaching them about plants. She could have one of her own. She would know what to do with it and might enjoy the fruit when it came in a few weeks. He was thrilled about his choice and worked very hard on selecting just the right pot to put it in. He settled on a pink one with a teddy bear motif and ordered it through NAI.

When the pot arrived he picked a perfect little plant from his indoor garden, fertilized and potted it. He put on his best hoodie and went to deliver his gift. The days were getting longer and he had to wait till dark. He hoped Dee Dee would still be awake but when he got to the window he saw she was already nestled in her bed.

He accepted that. It was enough to see she was well. He would leave the plant and remain satisfied with its delivery. But again, just as he was leaving, he made a noise in the constricted area of the fire escape and Dee Dee turned towards the window, as if she had been waiting. She sat up and she waved. He waved back and she ran to the window. He picked up the plant and showed her. Her eyes lit up and she opened the window. He placed the gift in her little hands. She then put it down on the sill and rapped her small arm around his neck giving him the first human hug he had ever experienced. After that she quickly shut the window and got back in bed.

You could have moved him with a puff of air and he would have gladly fallen, the three stories down in a cloud of bliss. After a few moments he came too, and made his way down the fire escape. All the while he was thinking he wanted to help this child any way he could. She would need good clothing and school things and food. But he knew this was not enough. The best gift he could give Dee Dee was to somehow restore her mother to her. He would apply his mind to all these thing, but especially to that.

Elena was 15 when she had Dee Dee. She was living in the street and she did not really know who the father was. Her pimp whose moniker was "Panic" did not wish to assume the responsibility of a child but he liked the benefits. Welfare and food stamps could be use to supplement his income. Elaina also thought to use the child this way—that is, until she held it in her arms. Then a motherly tenderness took over which threatened to eclipse even her addiction. She wanted to be a mom but that tenderness mixed with terror, after the baby's first heart wrenching episode of withdrawal from heroin. Elaina heard her screams and ran. She simply could not deal with the guilt.

Rosa took the baby home and when Elaina finally got the nerve to visit she was told it had Down's. Though. this was genetic and not due to the drugs, Elaina blamed herself and took off again. Rosa got custody and Elaina was alone and without shelter. Her resources had dwindled to almost nothing. She went to see 'Panic' who had already moved on in his "affection," to another girl he could hustle. When he opened the door and saw Elaina he slapped her down the stairs and told her never to show herself at his door again.

What could she do? She became a thief till she recovered from the pregnancy and could sell herself again. B & E along with shoplifting and any other rip offs became her daily routine. Once pretty, now she looked the worst of the worst and so had to proposition the lowest of the low. This meant sleeping with and stealing from SSI recipients in the bowery who were also addicts and eating out of garbage cans. In this way she managed to eek out 6 years of existence. She seldom went to see Rosa who occasionally gave her some food or money if she agreed to go to detox and treatment for a couple of weeks. Then the whole syndrome would start over again. The department of child protection banned her from seeing Dee Dee and that was fine with her, though occasionally she would steal a stuffed animal and give it to Rosa for the child which was promptly thrown in the trash for fear of lice.

One day the ambulating addiction who used to be Elaina was making her way down the alley for her first rendezvous of the day with her dealer. She was short a couple of dollars but she hoped being a regular customer Casaba might be in a good mood and might cut her a break. She didn't like this dark alley as it had no back exit and no fire escapes, but it had the locked back door to Casaba's place and he wanted things as convenient as possible. The shock came when a gi-normous shadow in a hoodie showed up in the ally instead of her supplier. She was spooked witless and when she tried to slide past him out of the ally he blocked her way. If she had believed in God she would have been making her peace in the face of looming death. Then the shadow spoke.

"Casaba is not coming."

Her heart was racing, though at the sound of the familiar name, the edge was taken off her angst. But she was in need and was afraid her source had dried up.

"Why? Was he busted?"

"No, he's busy."

"BUSY? But I got to see 'em."

"You can see me instead. I have a deal for you."

She wondered at his speech. It didn't exactly go with the hoodie. The desperation was mounting and she remembered her funds were low.

"Look, help me man. I really need to get straight. I'm a little short on cash now but I can get you the rest by tonight."

"No money."

She thought that if he wanted a trick he might break her in two but she was desperate.

"Ok how do you want it?"

"No payment."

Her nerves were already jangling and she couldn't think.

"Whateva, what's the deal?"

"You get these for free."

She looked at his hand and it was even more frightening than the shadow he cast. In the darkness of the alley the hand looked scared and a slightly greenish color. Like the hand of a ghost. It held two pills. She had never seen Fentanyl or Ecstasy or any other pills that looked like these.

"You screwing with me? What's this?"

"You take these for free. They will put you right. Then you take this phone and I will call you with instructions tonight. One for now and one for later. You won't need a syringe. Take it or leave it."

She took it of course. This guy was an idiot. She would take the pills, keep the cash and maybe even sell one pill if she didn't like the other. Or this might kill her, then it would all be over. Who knows, it might be the best high she ever had, but he wanted something. Still, if he was stupid enough to wait till tonight for it she could get something from somebody else. He was going to call her. She needed a phone too but she might sell it. Then again in the darkness of her mind there lurked some curiosity. If this stuff could get her "right" this might be an opportunity. What did she have to lose? She took the pills and the phone.

"If you lose the phone I will know. If you get any dope from anyone else I will know. I will know and you will be out of luck. If you try to trick me you will be tricking yourself."

That sounded like a threat in a weird, Polly Anna sort of way. What was she getting into? Still, she needed something. She swallowed the pill, expecting she did not know what. In a few moments her stomach settled and she felt...well...pleasant, clear, at ease. It wasn't a high exactly but it was--nice. Nicer than she had felt in a long time. She even felt a little hungry. She heard his voice at the end of the alley with no exit.

"Use your money for food. I will call later," and he was gone.

Elaina had probably disarmed every endorphin in her body through drug abuse. That meant her body had lost its ability to feel good and negotiate pain. Without her "fix" life was a kind of torture that only opioids would put a temporary end to. *This* new "medication" seemed to wake all those little "feel good" suckers up again and make them do their work. She felt alright, not euphoric but nice and she wasn't nodding and slumping in a corner either. She felt like, well, like spring. Wandering the streets she found a Spanish cuchifrito and bought herself two empanadas and a flan. She ate every bit, enjoying it, as if she was eating for the first time in years. She wasn't done either and got a side of rice and beans and ate that too. The other pill she had for later was zipped and safe in her ragged jacket and that was all she cared about. The big dude said he would call her after a while and whatever she had to do to feel this good might be worth it. She put the phone in her hoodie pocket and decided to take a walk.

That evening found her smiling in front of the Museum of Natural History in Manhattan. She had walked all day. By this time she had taken the second pill. As before, her returning pain was relieved and she felt alright; more than alright. When she was a kid in school she went to the museum on a field trip. She had never seen anything like it. Now she sat on the steps and watched the people passing by in endless parade. She was thinking how great it had been to see the dinosaurs and gems and other cool stuff inside. She thought it would be nice to take Dee Dee there someday. Dee Dee...her thoughts had not run in that direction...in forever. The phone rang.

"How are you feeling?"

"Good, really good."

"Did you go to the Museum?"

"Well I'm there but I didn't go in. You know where I am? Who are you? What do you want?"

"I want to help Dee Dee's mom get back on her feet. Your little girl needs you."

"WHO ARE YOU?"

"You can call me Frankie." Ann had started calling him that and he liked the sound of it.

"So Frankie, what do you want me to do? In another few hours I'm going to need to dose. What do I have to do to get my dose?"

"You have to agree to my terms."

His "terms" were the strangest she had ever heard. She would go to a stone in the park under which she would find $20 dollars. She would buy food and eat it. Then she would go to the Art House Hotel on W 77th St and ask for the room which had been reserved for her. She would find two more pills on the dresser in the room and she would find clothes. She was to take a bath and get a good night's sleep and she would get a call in the morning after she had breakfast. It was all paid for. Again he repeated that if she bought anything by way of drugs from anyone else this would end the deal. As long as she did what she was told she would get free medicine. This was too good to be true.

"Is anyone going to be waiting for me at that hotel?"

"No, you need *rest*. Take it. Call no one but Rosa and Dee Dee. You can tell them you are alright. I will call you tomorrow to tell you where to find your next dose."

Elaina was thunderstruck. She did not know what was going on. Was she dreaming all this? Was she hallucinating? Had she lost her mind?   She had been forced to do many devious things to get her fix in the past, things that had been wicked and shameful. She accepted all that because she thought she was a dirty druggy that deserved nothing but pain. But this was crazy absolutely crazy.

She bought a hot dog at a stand, a pretzel and a Pepsi. She didn't remember the last time a hot dog tasted so good. Then she started walking. At the hotel the concierge looked her up and down restraining his disgust, then with a raised eyebrow and a cordial manner he confirmed that she was in room 502 and gave her the key card. She raised her head and tossed her hair, almost proudly, then walked towards the elevator.

The room was simple and elegant. She could not believe how clean it was. She had not seen a place that clean since she lived with Rosa as a kid. She ran to the dresser and saw that Frankie was good for his word on the dose. Relieved she looked around and found some flannel PJ's on the bed and some clothes hanging in the closet. They were a little big but OK. She then went into the bathroom. She had one cigarette in her pocket but there was a sign on the door that read "no smoking" so she refrained thinking she might go out and smoke it before she did anything else. Then she saw the porch. She stepped outside to a warm breeze and the view of the city below. She had her cigarette or what was left of it then went inside for the first shower she had in 6 months.

The pain in her stomach woke her the next morning. She had slept like a baby and was a bit shocked in the morning when she found herself alone in this spacious place under clean sheets.   Her dose was now on the bed stand by Frankie's phone. She took it then went to the bathroom where she found some coffee. She sat out on the porch and drank it smoking the last of the cigarette from the night before. The phone rang.

"Those things are bad for you. You should quit."

"You are really creeping me out you know."

"You have no idea how creepy I can get." Frankie thought a little fear was good for her at this point.

"Did you sleep well?"

"Why do you ask, weren't you watching me?"

"No I wasn't but you never know when I am. I will respect your privacy to a degree."

"Yes I slept well. Thank you. Thanks for all of this. Now what do I have to do to deserve it."

"You have to become a responsible, loving mother."

"Wow is that all? Why don't you ask me to grow six legs and crawl around like a cock roach? I could do that better than be a mother."

"You will have my help."

"You can't put me up here forever. Not unless you are as rich as Eminem."

"You will be here a few more days. It isn't easy to find apartments in this city."

"You're finding me an apartment? Who are you? What do you want?"

"I already told you. Now call for breakfast. I paid for it. And I will take care of everything else. I will call you later. Remember our agreement."

In the days that followed Elaina ate, slept and let the dirt of thousands of days of wandering flow down the drain of the bathtub. Frankie called her and she received doses in the mail. Though she was still very suspicious of everything that surrounded him she started to believe that this strange man had her best interest at heart. The plan he unfolded included her continuing to dose for nothing and then move forward in her life. He asked her what she wanted to do for honest work and she mocked him by saying "brain surgery". He then asked her if she would like to go to school. She said she had never graduated high school.

He began to feel a little out of his depths so he decided to tell her that on a certain day she was to make an appointment to see a social worker in Queens named Jean Luc De Lacy.   Ann recommended this when Frankie asked her who his new friend could talk to regarding things like education. Frankie warned Elaina not to say who she was getting her help from only that she was getting help. He wanted her to ask Mr. De Lacy's advice with vocation, school and parenting. She did as he said and so her journey began. She was soon "forced" to get her GED, which without having to forage for scraps in dumpsters and steal for her drugs was not as hard as she thought.

The day Elaina came into see Jean Luc, he commented at home, how his family would never guess who came in for help, looking like a regular human being. Because of confidentiality he could not tell who the person was, but his comment started a "20 questions" game that ended up revealing it was Elaina. Jean Luc wanted Stacia to know because of her special little student and she thought it was good news indeed. Ann was also impressed, and putting two and two together, decided she now knew who Frankie's new friend was. She asked him about it in their next telephone conversation.

"I think it's a wonderful thing you are doing. You have a gift with medicine. I'm glad you are sharing it."

Frankie thought about that for a moment. He had been wondering why medicine came so easily to him, as if he had done it all before. He had also thought about what she said concerning selling his product to pharmaceutical companies.

"I simply cannot do what you ask and give what I have discovered to companies that may abuse it. It strikes me as strange that their researchers have not come up with similar formulas. If they have they are not sharing and it all has something to do with the corrupting influence of money. Besides I have looked into this. I have no credentials and who would take the word of a monster for medical issues."

"Don't talk like that. You are not a monster. If your exterior matched your soul you would be an Adonis."

She always knew what to say to make him feel twenty feet tall. If he had a mother he would want her to be just like Ann.

"As for Elaina, she has led me to others who are similarly in need. In fact there seem to be thousands of them. I want to work out a way to help them but I haven't figured it out yet."

"I'm sure you will and I want to hear all about it when you do."

With such certainty from Ann, Frankie was emboldened to accomplish anything. That night after sending Elaina her instructions to meet him at an abandoned warehouse on the East side, he started out to find help for another person—himself.

The tall, agile, hooded character, walked quickly up a winding road to a creepy house, isolated on a hill, overlooking the lake of a nature reserve. He was angry and he did not know why. He arrived at the iron gates of the house and disarmed the security system with NAI then tried clicking the code into the number pad but he just couldn't. He tried another code and that didn't work either. Losing patience he took hold of the Gates and vault over them. His footsteps were loud and his pace was snappy. He used none of his stealth skills as he wanted his coming announced. In minutes he was surrounded by the guard dogs that approached viciously but paused in short order as soon as he was in sniff range. Their teeth hidden and tails tucked they backed up slowly and let him pass. He marched up to the house and banged on the door loud enough to wake the drunk or the dead.

Inside a man was drinking in a room shaking his head at the blank surveillance screens of the houses perimeter. He understood what that meant. He cliqued a switch and said,

"Come up Fran..." But his invitation was preempted by a crash through the window that broke the pain and unhinged the library door. The scientist rolled his eyes and again had cause to lament his experiment. His inebriated peace was not often disturbed but when it was, especially by Frankie, it was very off putting for his reclusive spirit. How would he explain this to his patron?

"Why can't you just use the key pad?"

"My fingers are too thick, you ought to know."

"Use a pencil for God's sake."

"Don't…"

The Doctor poured a bit more scotch into a glass and downed it in one gulp.

"Oh dear, I've insulted your ecclesiastic sensibilities—where ever did you get that nonsense?"

"That is a story for another time. If it even is a real question."

"It's rhetorical actually. You know me so well. Did you hurt the dogs?"

"No, they are just dumb animals not brilliant vermin like yourself, FATHER."

"Do you have to call me that? Well I suppose anger as an emotion is long overdue in you. It was bound to happen. What do you want from me?"

"Some adjustments. Why else would I want to visit my father?"

"For the NAI or the body? I'm drunk you know. Not up to delicate work right now."

"Drunk or sober you're the only one who can do this. It's not body or NAI. It's my head." Frankie paused and groped for words."

"I see things when I rest. I suppose you call them dreams."

"Fascinating, but not my field."

The giant straightened to his full height and grabbed Stein's clothes in such a grip that his sports coat ripped in the back. Then lifting him up he met his gaze.

"Make it your field."

Stein trembled and sobered rather quickly. In a course voice he tried to pacify the monster of his own making.

"Alright, alright. Tell me. I will try to help."

"I was obviously stitched together somehow. You told me about the tech. Nano-bots repair me, and self generating neurological energy keeps me reanimating. Artificial intelligence answers all my questions and keeps my pain at bay.   Further, you also spoke to me about the "raw materials" that compose the train wreck of body parts you have given me. I know your connections with evil men in what they call "the mob" and I have begun to suspect my parts were people they wanted to get out of the way;   perhaps other criminals. But I've been having these, these visions. Visions about things I have not experienced in my short life. Families, children, a loving touch from a spouse, a large stately office, a transcendent experience of something I can only call--worship. I have dreams of ending human pain. I think these are not dreams but..."

Stein turned pail and knew he had to deviate him immediately.

"Memories? NOT possible. I would say the process of your origin wiped away all of that. You are alone in the world and your dreams are wishful thinking. I have them myself at times. I swim in oceans of vermouth."

"Why do I feel so strongly, in my fabric of my kishkies that you are lying through your stained dentures FATHER! And "kishkies" where did I get that word DAD? I have never read it."

Frankie pressed the side of his head and pointed towards the wall. Illuminated images came up and NAI showed him the meaning of the word as his eye movements had requested.

"kishkes - Yiddish Slang - the innermost parts; guts. I also speak fluent street Spanish and now it seems I speak Yiddish as well. I never studied these languages. Who the hell was I?"

"I don't know. I DON'T KNOW I TELL YOU! I made a point of not knowing. I just knew I could reanimate them, but they were mangled."

Frankie had done a great deal of thinking about this and he remembered the dancers and the vicious people who wanted to hurt them.

"Tortured?"

Stein had thought about that too. He knew the mob was not kind to its enemies and the bodies had been...to put it nicely...distorted. They were also used to frighten him into submission. His answer was tight and low.

"Possibly,   Look, I didn't torture them I only salvaged what was left."

Frankie answered with mixed despair and rage.

"You call this SALVAGED!!!"

Stein stood there with an odd expression on his face. These disclosures were bringing up his own, long buried emotions. All at once he could not contain the angst he was feeling. He began to sputter and weep like a child.

"I didn't mean any harm."

Now it was Frankie's turn to be therapeutic. He had pressed some emotional buttons in his re-animator that he had not expected to. Contrary to all he had seen up to now, the brilliant but pathetic man, going to pieces in front of him, did have feelings, but his Creature still wanted answers.

"Tell me how you did it."

Stein had enough presence of mind to know what telling (even Frankie) might mean. For another to know his secrets would send this technology into "the wild" and that was capable of producing things that might never allow him blameless sleep again. He had given the monster an abridged version of his "construction" with unsophisticated language a few times before, but Frankie wanted more, and he had become informed enough, to understand such an explanation. Stein had to give him more without giving him anything.

"Haven't you heard that bedtime horror story enough times by now? I can't keep reliving it."

Stein went for the bottle but Frankie flung it out the broken window.

"You owe me." Stein started crying and laughing with hysteria. The Giant was powerful enough to carry an elephant but compassion was his weakness. He gave in and handed him another bottle. Stein gratefully acknowledged it with a nod and a lift of the glass. Frankie continued.

"Alright-- tell me what happened before—about the people. Where did you get them?"

Stein sat back in his chair. Frankie sat at his feet crossed legged, hunched shouldered and attentive. The man took a swig and began.

"How would you feel if you were on the verge of discoveries that were going to revolutionize modern science? You can't judge me Frank, not till you've been there. My wife had died. She was the only human being I had ever been able to tolerate. I had to have her back and this drove me on. Cloning was within my field of study but it was out of the question because of the time factor. I would be ancient before a clone was old enough to be a companion. I got to the place where through amplified magnetic stimulation and nano-tech I was able to reanimated dead tissue, but to do this with an organism I would have to have incredible electronic power and funding for specialized equipment.

Reanimation was fraught with prejudice. The scientific community was being influenced by powerful lobbies, tree hugging naturalists, animal rights people and religionists of every sect, all of these had something to say about it. It was dangerous, immoral, and unnatural according to them! Still, even though the time was well past to save my Elizabeth I felt that all I had was my research and all I knew was that it was possible. How would you feel if you were close to causing a resurrection and the world was tying your hands? I felt like a god with my wings clipped."

Frankie grunted like a bear then commented.

"Hardly a deity, more like an plagerist." Stein looked at him incredulously.

"Insult and satire Frank? I never thought you would stoop so low."

Frankie knew he was being made light of. He rolled his eyes and waved Stein on impatiently.

"Then one night, I was at my favorite bar and I had a few too many. I spilled my frustrated guts to a bar tender. He predictably thought I was mad, but other ears were listening too; ears that took me seriously. People you don't want to know Frank but they had money. They took me in and sobered me up just enough to confirm I was not a nut case and the man in charge believed what I was saying was true. This wealthy and visionary man lived with nightmares of being killed and wanted to know if I could bring him back in such an eventuality. I told him almost certainly I could but I needed money."

Frankie was not stupid. He had his hand on the pulse of all the news-- globally.

"You have to be speaking of Romeo Ernesto Lupo."

Stein turned away in fear.

"How did you know?"

"It makes sense. Money, power, blatant cruelty. The biggest name in all those specialties is Romeo Lupo, the wolf."

"For both our sakes, forget that you even think that." This was evidence that what Frankie suspected was true.

"As proof I showed my patrons what I could do on a small scale and they decided to fund me. It was wrong to take their dirty money but in the name of science I was prepared to do anything. You know how I have paid for this. I'm like a prisoner here. They said they would fund my research materials and when the day came to test it, they would provide the, the... organic materials."

"Bodies you mean."

"Yes, the bodies." He chased that one with a full glass.

"Why bodies? Why not just one person?"

"I... I needed them all to make one person. Parts were damaged. I couldn't..."

"Did you damage them?"

"Some by accident but mostly they came that way.

My "Employer's" men set up my lab with the state of the art equipment but it was not yet operational when they brought in my raw materials. They were newly deceased and this was optimal but I had to work fast against decomposition. This was not a problem for me. I had waited for this moment so long and now I worked like a man on fire. Feverishly I took what I had been given and formed, a man, a real man out of the parts I could salvage from the trauma they had been through. The cosmetics were not important to me. You have to understand it was the function that mattered. It was also my first attempt and as a neophyte to all this I was somewhat clumsy.

I worked tirelessly--truly a man obsessed or perhaps inspired, I will always wonder which. Then the first big hitch happened. The power for reanimation was not yet fully in place. I had to do something and quickly. My first attempt at powering up shut down the grid for miles. I decided I would harness the power of nature. It would perhaps be overload and far less controlled than what I had planned, but I had to take the chance. A few days passed. I kept my work in cold storage till finally news of a storm brewing came and I positioned the subject. The lightning cooperated with my set up and did its work."

"Just remember you are a hack not a God! Now, WHO WERE THEY?"

Frankie was revolted by the things he called him. "The subject," "his work," he did not call him a man. The giant seethed and showed no sign of relenting without an answer. Stein tried to dispel his efforts again.

"Why don't you let the dead rest in peace? You don't want to know these things."

"You didn't let them rest in peace? What you really mean is you don't want me to know or to put your benefactors on a gibbet and watch them pay for their crimes."

"You don't know who you are dealing with. I made you strong and fast practically indestructible but your powers have not been tested. You can be hurt. You can be killed."

"I hope so. I really do. And someday you are going to fix it for me, but you are not worried about me. It's your own hide that worries you. Who would be left to reanimate you? Now tell me what they were like? How many bodies?"

Stein squeaked out the answer.

"There were five bodies."

"Bullet wounds?"

"One had an old bullet wound just below his right rib. I saw the repair work."

"OK one old bullet wound. Knife wounds?"

"One was young and had several lesions and two fingers had been freshly cut off."

"Anything else?"

"One was quite elderly and had a tattoo on his arm."

"What kind of tattoo?" Stein hesitated. He did not want to give too much information. But Frankie insisted.

"WHAT KIND OF TATTOO?"

"Just a number."

"Do you remember the number?"

"No."

"Why do I think you're lying?"

"Please Frank…" Now the monster asked the question with the most weight for him.

"Why Frank?"

"You could not speak at first as you know, but when you awoke you seemed to have an artifact of speech. You actually said, Frank…and mumbled something then you said some numbers. After that you lost language and just groaned or made meaningless noises.

"I was in great pain." Frankie said this recalling, then added, "So, more numbers you don't remember I'm sure."

"There was a 571 in it but I can't remember the others."

"What was the cause of death for these people?"

"My guess, mind you, I didn't really explore that. But the old one died of heart failure. One looked like he had been electrocuted. He had burn mark across his chest. The rest were smashed up in different ways. Some had spinal injuries, one had leg disjointed at the knees. Some sort of impact like a bad landing from a sky dive or something."

"Racial profiles? Any of them look to be of some unusual ethnicity?"

"One might have been Hispanic or Middle Eastern; he looked tanned and was a great strong man. The old man might also have been Middle Eastern or perhaps Jewish but was lighter skinned. The boy had long dark hair maybe Native American. Or he might have been a musician or something? Which could be complicated by the two missing fingers. He was the biggest mystery to me. Why would they kill a man so young? Please can we stop now?"

Frankie stroked his own long hair for a moment. He had come off the lab table with a bald head but recalled that he had no trouble growing a mass of hair in short order. It was the thing he liked best about his body. But he quickly came back to the matter at hand.

"Why kill anyone? Are you kidding? You work for butchers." As Stein started to whimper again Frankie thought to relent.

"We will stop there… for now."

Frankie stood up and Stein looked away for a moment. When he looked back and the Big Man was gone. He peered out the window after him and he was already vaulting over the gate. The night promised to be a stormy one and the scientist uncharacteristically and superstitiously took it as a bad omen. He collapsed in a chair as the dogs began to bark at a marauding owl flying overhead. Then the surveillance screens came to life again. He sighed deeply and whipped the dribble that was escaping his nose; remnants of the tears he had shed for the first time in years.

Out of his desk drawer he pulls a small box. It contains an unusual combination of objects. He pulled out in turn, a watch, a set of dog tags, four guitar picks, a cuff link and a patch of human skin encased in plastic with a series of numbers. Much as he tried to convince himself these things had belonged to "raw materials", he knew they belonged to human beings. The objects spoke to him often, like the spirits of dead men and told him what Frankie most wanted to hear. Stein closed the box and replaced it, drank deeply and lowered his head in drunken oblivion.

7

The Tolling Bells

Andre Poloche's mind never seemed to shut off. Sleep was then a problem when hard to solve cases occupied his cerebral space. He had been trying to find a link between the targets of "Alien guy", as Jasmine liked to call him. It seemed the only commonality was that they were criminals. High profile or lowlife they were illicit, illegal and immoral. There was no pattern otherwise, only the unusual habit of binding people, like sausages and hanging them by their ankles from places where they could be seen as they swung in the breeze. It was obvious they were to be exposed as well as apprehended. Or shall we say "shamed" as it were.

The detective thought if it were not so creepy it would be humorous. The only problem was that finding the perpetrator, would mean trying to stop him. He almost didn't want to do that, but he had to do his job. People couldn't take the law into their own hands. Still many on the force including Jasmine and Andre thought this Alien guy wasn't all bad. He was more like a fairy godfather granting them justice filled wishes.

The guy had to be really strong. The targets were never drugged. Subduing them fully awake and quickly had to be a challenge. They were sort of "hog tied" like ranchers do live stock. Neatly bound and gagged they were then tossed like fish on a line to dangle in space which added to their trauma. The guy was kind of geeky too. He was smart enough to perfectly cover his tracks and he sported a space alien mask of some sort. There was evidence that he was able to disarm surveillance so he must be tech savvy and perhaps had sophisticated equipment. Could "he" be a team?

If he was, it had to be the "A" team. They worked as one, with the precision of a watch and the speed of a hummingbird. A fast weight lifting geek was kind of inconceivable but so was this case. The only guy he had ever known who was smart and buff too was his brother Frank. But he was dead...or was he? He walked the streets at night thinking about it all when he couldn't sleep, and yellow eyes watched him with more than curiosity.

Frankie's nightly strolls often had regulars he observed and Andre was one of them. By this time in his life the big man made it his business to know everything that was going on in the street. His dependants needed protection and provision so he had to know who might hurt them and who had the components of what they needed. He had to be aware of "shipments of supplies" for their medicine and he had to know what mischief in general was going down. The people he helped were a good source of intel, but he also listened in on phone conversations and security systems in numerous places thru NAI (police channels being one of them). So he maintained a bead on all the dirt in town. The rest he figured out and by these means he would have given Sherlock a good run, if Sherlock were not a fictitious character. The FBI had nothing on the giant. He had no history, no record, no credible witnesses and no evidence against him. He did not even have a president. There was no one like Frankie.

Long after Andre retired for the night Frankie would walk on. The dark streets would always finally wind his way around to higher ground on a hill overlooking the city. There he would sit to think his tormented thoughts. The only thing he could really label memories were the recollections of his short life since re-animation. He reviewed what he could remember of the house in Upstate New York near the lake. He recalled the sound of water fowl mingled with humming equipment. Unlike most infants, his "birth" was vivid in his thoughts. Frankie could see himself in his memory in the place where a frantic man was completing the process of awakening him and all that transpired after. His clumsiness and how he broke the fateful laptop that Stein could never forgive him for.

He recalled the bots healing and scaring his skin and putting clothing on for the first time like a child. Then he could see himself running out into a world of wonders like the first man on all the earth.

He remembered NAI teaching him speech and the birds by the lake and one great swan in particular that resisted his curios grasp with its mighty wings. He ate mud, fought off insect pests with a lazer-like potential he could generate that covered his skin. He also saw that things died and could not reanimate like he did and he sorrowed for them.

NAI had an explanation for everything and he, like a precocious child, learned voraciously. He ran with delight into his surroundings madly pointing, batting his eyes to inquire of NAI and speaking the names of all creation. He had no sense of time and so continued this way over many changes of light and darkness. Moments of discovery both good and bad, coupled with forward movement, soon become years.

Returning to people was far more complex than living with bears but progress was painfully slow for his socializing. He despaired of ever achieving society. This was painful. Frankie often spoke to himself as NAI was good for data but not for conversation and all these memories produced many unsatisfying nightly monologues.

"Words, how I hate them, but they bring back the things I have to unravel yet in all this data there is no answer for the question of why regarding myself. WHY?"

Stein mumbled replies on their visits but his mouth was full of falsehoods. There were few answers with him. As far as Frank could see Stein had made him because he could, like a man with no love for a woman that impregnates her without a thought for her or the child that is born after. Stein did not think he just had his way.

He also recalled his friends the stars, the moon and the bears. In the end it was always the same. He would weary of the monolog with great longing for conversation.

Hiding by day and wandering by night became his routine while in the city he watched the people. He observed couples strolling romantically entwined, some eating at café's others shopping in toy stores with their children. He listened to people arguing, fighting and watched them hurt and steal from each other. He noticed the difference between some who had much and others who had little. He noticed people running in exercise, moving to music and worshiping in churches. He saw it all but could not put it all together; love, hatred, need and greed and the angst for something greater.

He heard the exhilarating beat of street drumming and the magnificence of organ music. Street violins or guitars and singing enchanted him. Music was to him, a heartbreak and a joy. He could not resist it and often stopped to listen from hidden places for symphonies being practiced at the back door of theaters. He also watched dancers practice from the skylight of studios and back stage doors. He experienced the passion of Rock concerts and the enigma of plays from theater rafters. Just as he had loved the beauty of the natural world he loved the creativity of the human one. Museums and galleries he frequented by disarming their surveillance and protections. He did all this from the periphery while suffering the impossibility of joining the human race.

Then one day he turned his steps towards an impressive old place with high walls. There was a mystery about it and it was surrounded by graves of what he now knew were the remains of the dead. NAI told him it was a holy place full of those who had sought solitude to find peace. He thought perhaps they would understand his condition but fearing censure he kept to the shadows. In an occulted crevasse here and a hallway there, he watched and noted that those who lived there also hid their faces. What were they hiding under cowls and robes? Perhaps a kindred spirit, in a place where he might find, such anonymity.

They rang stately bells which apparently called them in for their rituals. Daring a venture he entered in his own hooded garment and he was absorbed by their chanting. He allowed their voices to swell in his ears and work their peace. However, even as he surrendered to the mood and felt he could do this forever, the inevitable happened. He was noticed. Men ran screaming and stumbling in all directions. His presence, as always was offensive to them. He ran in frustration, then climbing up into their loft he disappeared and some wondered if he had been an evil apparition. This could not be refuge for him, but like everything else he longed for, he could hide within it, he could enjoy it in the shadows. He would return for thirst of their sacred music. He would just have to have greater discretion.

Shortly after this, things started to change for him. He became acquainted with the De Lacy family and Ann and Dee Dee became his dear friends. Elaina happily occupied much of his time from behind the scenes and was progressing. She and Rosa were living together again and Dee Dee had her mother back. But all this was still done from a distance. He was still suffering with isolation but beginning to see there were so many others who in the multitudes of people walked alone. Was there an answer for them? This question brought him again to the high wall as he listened to the bells toll.

As he stood in this place, pondering the loneliness of millions, he discovered it was complicated by grief and death. He was fascinated by the dead and well he should be as they were the raw materials used to form him. The dead, he understood, were called corpses and the living had to painfully detach themselves from these. When bodies ceased living some thought their consciousness went into a great unknown and there were other theories. Much study was ahead of him regarding all this. He wanted to discover if anyone else had gone to corps state and returned to say for certain what happened after. He had done this but he knew nothing.

Standing near the wall where there were many memorial stones for graves he continued to ponder. In the half light he walked among them feeling their cold wet finality, contemplating what remained of them besides these carved monuments. He paused at one and his large hand reached down into the earth with the power of a steam shovel. Then he recoiled feeling somehow that he had no right.

Consulting NAI he was informed that all peoples objected the desecration of their dead. He replaced the earth and patted it down apologetically. Then looking at the grave stone he said,

"Begging your pardon, Mr. Johnson, I meant no harm." His curiosity would have to be satisfied in other ways.

The services or rituals for the dead had also been his study of late. People perish and their loved ones mourn. The corpses were buried or they were burned. Information about the dead was often published in a newspaper and NAI made record of it. He discovered that if a loved one was missing they would often be remembered with a service even though the body was not present. He was wondering, about his "parts" and if their loved ones had done such things. Could there be someone out there mourning for them--for him? He had been asking NAI about this. It then commented that such services often happen in holy places like this one called a chapel. It was not something Ann could help him with. She did not know the details of his history. He wanted to ask a person about it and he was wondering how.

While he considered all this he climbed the wall. He sat on top of it watching as people who were *not* wearing robes went in to pray. Apparently there was no objection to them being there. They kneeled in the pews and bowed their heads then they entered these boxes for a time and came out. NAI explained they were making confession of their wrongs. This was a ritual for cleansing the soul. They did it for forgiveness. Frankie wondered what else was in the box and NAI gave him a schematic. He learned a priest (robed man) was in the middle and there was a partition, on either side, separating him from the people who went in. He would listen to them without seeing them. Frankie thought this was perfect.

Having been there before Frankie had explored the belfry and steeple of the building. He looked at the large bells and thought about how he had enjoyed hearing them in all their solemnity. NAI had mentioned that bells tolled to announce sacred services and for the dead. It had also quoted (very badly) a poem by John Dunn that Frankie liked very much. He tried repeating it the way Jean Luc might recite it. "Do not ask for whom the bell tolls, it tolls for thee." And now, as he spoke this in his own hearing, it whispered something to him about himself. All the memorials for these people inside him had been said for him. He was moved, somehow felt honored, and then, he he thought to cautiously descend.

He was familiar with the choir loft where he had hidden before from the brothers who lived in the adjoining monastery. Sitting on the floor of the darkest corner he waited and when the last person exited the last box he silently climbed down and went in. The priest in the confessional was a young man but he had been very busy that evening and thinking he was done for the day, was disappointed to hear one more "parishioner" enter the box. He sighed and slid the dark screened door open waiting for the ritual response from the sinner on the other side. Strangely he heard breathing but no words were forthcoming.

"Go on." He said.

"Hello, I am here to ask a question."

"Are you interested in confessing my son? Because if you are not I would be happy to make an appointment to see you in the rectory tomorrow."

"I would like that very much but I don't think you would want to see me."

"And why might that be?"

"I seem to frighten people."

"Come now, is this a joke? Because if it is, it's not very funny."

"I don't know how to joke sir."

"Are you a Catholic?"

"I don't think so."

"Is your question about God?"

"Well, I do have questions about God but if I can only ask one question it would be about remembering someone who is dead."

"My son, it sounds like this is a question that cannot be answered in a hurry. Will you come and see me tomorrow?"

"I will if you promise not to be frightened. My appearance is surprising but I will not hurt anyone."

The priest thought this very strange but the voice of the subject was deep and ingenuous. He guessed that the man might be very ugly or a homeless person or something of that kind. The priest had committed to serving even the poor and the outcast so he crossed himself and responded.

"All right, fair enough I promise not to be scared. This time tomorrow?"

"Yes."

"Next door is the rectory; my secretary will have gone home by then so just come in."

"Thank you, I will be there."

Frankie spent that night and the whole next day fretting about seeing the priest. The man had promised he would not be frightened and he sounded honest and kind, so the gentle giant comforted himself with that promise and hoped he would get the information he needed at least. If he was very lucky and the priest kept his word, he might perhaps even make a friend.

On the other hand the priest had been quite impressed with this conversation and prayed about the meeting all day. His ministry at the large church building had here to fore, consisted of weddings for people who never came to church, hearing the confessions of elderly people in a small congregation that seldom did more than gossip or lie, an occasional wife who was being beaten and parents with wayward teen agers or adult children who needed prayer. He had never ministered to a non-believer. If the man was ugly, oh well, a soul is a soul. In his part of the woods converts were rare, scarce indeed, and he wondered if this person with the deep and plaintive voice might be a seeker, whom God was calling. If so he, as a priest, would have a great opportunity. If this were the case, he didn't want to flub it. He promised the Lord that whatever came through that door he would welcome him like a long lost brother.

The next evening Frankie had to bow his head to get in the door of the rectory. He felt somewhat awkward, actually walking into a building through the door. Never the less he walked into the empty place with his hood on and hearing the door the priest came out of his office and froze on the spot. Frankie pulled his hood back shyly and held his breath for a moment anticipating a scream. The priest slowly crossed himself as he swallowed hard. He held his ground as the blood drained from his head and he almost swooned, but Frankie spoke first.

"I told you I was frightening. I'm sorry to have troubled you. I will go."

In the aftershock of the initial meeting, the priest had, what he later called, "an unction of grace". Though he had never seen anything like the creature before him, in that moment, he heard the plaintiff voice and he knew he had to make good his promise.

"If you come in peace my brother, please, stay and... and sit down."

Frankie looked at him with eyes that were moist with emotion. He sat down right there in the anti-room on the floor and his head was level with the young priest who pulled up a chair. The conversation that followed was prefaced by the priest with an assurance of strictest confidentiality. Frankie told him his story would be unbelievable. The priest said he imagined it might be but encouraged him to go on. So Frankie unburdened himself, though he omitted real names, so as not to put the priest in danger, but he told him everything.

As he told his chilling tale the priest saw before him not a monster but a tormented soul and he felt that this was a divine appointment. There was nothing in his experience or in his catechism that he could compare this too. He did wonder what God thought about it all, but he had to go with his gut feeling. This creature before him was innocent of what evil men had done to him and anything he could do to bring him peace must be done. It would be like saying masses for the dead to help him.

Frankie bowed his head and cried at the compassion of the young man. His name was Father Fergus and young as he was he had a very fatherly way about him. He was also no slouch. Intelligent and top of his class he knew something about law as well. There was little he could do about the murders of the "body parts" or of the reanimation but there was something he could do about helping Frankie uncover their identities and perhaps bring their loved ones some comfort.

The father told him that finding his people might be done through records of memorial services. All these men had died at the same time and, in New York of course, because that was the territory of the killer hoodlums. Frankie told him the year this happened and Father Fergus told him he would go to work on digging up some information that very night.

Just then the bell of the church struck 10 and Frankie like a Shakespearian actor quoted John Dunne.

"Send not to know for whom the bell tolls, it tolls for thee."

The priest was impressed at his poetic knowledge.

"John Donne said in the same poem that "no man is an island. I often think of that when the bells ring."

This was not the reason though, that Frankie was quoting the poet from Tudor England. He was burdened.

"I am a desecration of the dead. I am an island."

The priest took on that therapeutic look that the sensitive and compassionate often take.

"You are that if you dishonor them with evil deeds. But if you are just in the administration of your vast gifts you will honor them instead."

"I might even avenge them."

"Vengeance belongs to God my son."

Frankie Har-rumfed and turned his back on his new mentor thinking,

"But does he not use even earthly tools to direct it?"

He did not want to cross Fergus since they were just getting started in their acquaintance. After all, only two people had looked passed his grim exterior to what might be his composite soul. One was blind and the other, was a child, tiny and unusual herself. Now he had this young man with a sage's wisdom who told him the truth about himself. Were not three true friends a greater gift than he had ever dared to expect?

As Frankie rose to his full height the priest craned his neck to look at him. He made the sign of the cross over his visitor, and Frankie said he would like to know more about such things. This brought thoughts to the priest of the demoniac in the cemetery, when Jesus walked the earth. He remembered Christ's tenderness towards him and how grateful the poor wretch had been. In that moment it occurred to the priest that Frankie might be more than just a scientific travesty. In the end if Frankie continued his work and his inquiries he might be more of a radical and divergent agent of justice. God worked in mysterious ways. Surely the big man, before him, was one of the most mysterious of all.

8

Wanted Dead or Alive

Alexi Breughel had an invigorating day at the stock market and made a bundle of money but that did not make him happy. He went home to beat a call girl he hired but that didn't make him happy either. He tried the same with a boy toy but nothing changed. He was miserable and he knew he needed to take care of the cause of his misery; the giant shadow.

In the past when he wanted someone out of his way he just hired some of Lupo's men and they got the job done but this was different. First of all he was somewhat out of favor with Lupo and secondly this was much more personal. He decided to call in an expert he had used before. She was a bounty hunter with a flawless record of bringing in her targets and she had curves like the Allegany Mountains. Her name was Babe.

Babe was tall and had auburn hair that cascaded down her back like a river of rubies. Part of her success at hunting men had to do with her disarming gender and looks. She was stunning, but "deadly" was a euphemism for what she was capable of. Alexi could not pay her enough to subdue her but he could pay her handsomely to dispose of targets for him. It was not sexual, but a satisfying relationship none the less.

Still it tickled his manhood to walk into a place with her on his arm. Therefore, while she was in town for the operation he decided to throw a party and show her off. To regain Lupo's good will, Alexi invited both he and Wanda along with a few others. It would be a small intimate soiree with his pent house as the venue. Lupo of course thought his "blonde bombshell" would trump any female on the premises, but Wanda almost hissed when they walked in and she saw how Lupo looked at Babe. He looked her up and down then kissed her hand. For the Blonde that was a call to arms.

Babe had been told to play nice but really, she was totally unimpressed and walked away. Lupo played it cool but this lit his fire like a Jersey torch. Wanda bit her bejeweled knuckle and told Lupo to take her home. Lupo told her to relax and get him a drink. She wouldn't budge and finally he obliged her wish but said she would go home with Johnny, his right hand man. This nearly caused a cat fight but Alexi whispered to Wanda to be careful as Babe could cut her in two. He really didn't care about Wanda. His real concerned was his white carpets.

So Wanda gathered up her full length ermine and Lupo patted her on the behind. She walked out with Johnny but was silently swearing vendetta.

Shortly after that and to Lupo's dismay, Babe declared she was a working girl and was retiring early. Lupo blew her a kiss and not to seem overly anxious told her to dream expensive dreams and see if they wouldn't come true. When she was gone Alexi informed Lupo of his frustration with Babe and warned that she might not even like men. He also informed him of her expertise. That was all fuel for the fire. The next day there were ten dozen roses delivered to Alexi's apartment, all for Babe, but she never saw them. She was up and out at the crack of dawn on the scent of the Giant Shadow.

Andre Poloche could not help but notice the gorgeous red head in uniform that walked into the station with transfer papers from Jersey. These were all fake but no one was questioning them except maybe the lady officers who all thought she looked more like a hooker than a cop. Those around the station soon learned she was great on the firing range and everyone wanted a crack at sparing with her in the gym. That is, till they discovered how hard she could slam a man on the mat. Half the precinct went home maimed but in love. In addition she was good at detective work and the chief was not going to waste her on traffic duty or other mundane tasks, especially when she asked so nicely. She was on the beat in no time and shortly thereafter she was in plain clothes. The highlight of their day at the precinct became finding out what she was wearing especially during the progressively warmer weather.

Jasmine noticed right away that officer Lonagan, as she called herself, had a lot of questions about "Alien Guy". His biggest performance had resulted in the bust of the S&M sex ring in the East Village and she was fascinated with the details. She asked Andre out for a drink, much to the envy of all the other officers, and what was her subject of choice? Alien Guy. She also asked about all the other cases that seemed to have the same MO.

Jasmine started the evening out with them but had to go home to her boy. Before she left however, she took Andre aside and warned him. Andre took note that Jasmine had her hackles up about this red head and she was seldom wrong. The detective knew this about her but, Hispanic to the end, he thought he could handle himself with any woman. He had no idea.

The next call Jasmine and Andre got on this case came from the docks. A ship had been pillaged that had remnants of heroin and chemical constituents of fentanyl. Three Chinese hoods and two Italians where wrapped up snuggly and dangling from the aft of the ship babbling in Mandarin and Sicilian-ized English, their heads a foot above the oily water. The thick metal access to the hold of the ship was actually bent and the lock broken off. What kind of machinery could do that coupled with such stealth?

By the time the two detectives got there they were met with Officer Lonagan coming out of the hold. Jasmine pursed her lips and looked at Andre with that expression that reeked of "I told you so". Babe just walked up to them as if she belonged there.

"No finger prints, or prints of any kind. No trace of hair, cloth or anything that might have DNA. Don't know what they used to pull that open. If it weren't totally ludicrous I would swear those where giant paw shaped marks. Like a bear's. The two detectives looked at the indentations on the hold and had to agree. Was Alien Guy humanoid with the paws of a bear or was it some sort of weird symbol. This was the first break they had in a long time but what did it mean? Babe seemed to have ideas of her own and wasn't sharing. The imprints were analyzed and found not to be alien or human. It was good old cow hide and therefore had to be some sort of device. They did not suspect Frankie with hands gloved in thick leather using only his palms (no fingers) and pressing the access open with his weight from above.

When officer Lonagan was satisfied she knew more than the police she simply disappeared. It was time to take to the streets. For a few years now the addict population had been undergoing a strange metamorphosis. Experts were at a loss for ideas of how but the number of active addicts was somehow diminishing. This was alarming news to Lupo and his ilk but somehow addicts were finding sobriety appealing and growing out of their habit. When cornered by their previous dealers they simply said they had been to rehab. Somehow that just didn't seem right. Many of them had gone to rehab continuously for years and never managed more than a few months sober. What was making the difference? Whatever it was if it continued Lupo would be a poor man.

When Babe probed on the street she found many people who had taken the "cure" but they were silent on the matter. They also seemed confident that her scare tactics would come to nothing. They were not afraid. She followed several of them and she found them quite normal. They had apparently truly beaten the habit. She thought to find one in process of normalizing but it was hard to spot them. Sometimes addicts would just disappear and show up elsewhere as regular citizens. Jasmines brother was one of these people. He was attending school for HVAC and Air conditioning repair and his 8 year addiction to heroin had abruptly stopped and turned into the life of a good and responsible man. Jasmine could not get him to say how it happened. But when the gorgeous red head started asking questions and then intimidating former addicts he had to say something. Jasmine went straight to Andre with the news.

"I found your girl friend."

"Jazz you know she hasn't talked to me since I stood her up for that dance last month. But I'm working on..."

"Spare me the sorted details of your love life. I mean that cherry top hooker in the fake uniform that you were divulging all our process to."

"Lady Lonagan, I thought she was transferred to..."

"Men are so royally stupid. She booked it out of the precinct. She went AWOL. Everybody knew that."

"Yeah well...you know how rumors get started..."

"No rumors...facts! She's on the street pushing former addicts around-- like James."

"WHAT? Shut up girl. She playing bad cop?"

"She ain't no cop no how. She probably a shill for Romeo."

"I always fall for the bad ones."

"Get over yourself." Andre stopped cold and changed gears.

"Ok Jazz this is pertinent to that. Well just FYI I been digging around the street myself and what I found is giving me the chills, but you gotta keep this off the record. I mean like that time when I didn't report James and we got him in rehab instead. You with me?" Jasmine nodded yes then answered.

"Common man, you know I owe you and you're scaring me."

Andre sighed and deliberated for a moment then began as if he was busting to tell somebody.

"You know my cousin Elaina. She's a recent recovered addict. I mean she is really clean now and working at a hospital. Well, I was at a birthday party for her kid; you know the one with Down's syndrome. I was sitting on the couch having a beer and the little girl comes over to me with this flower pot. It had cherry tomatoes on the plant; she is seven now but really little and cute. Anyway, I asked her where she got the plant and she said, "My big friend." Then I noticed Elaina turn white as a sheet and walked over. She scooted Dee Dee to her room and said to everyone,

"That's her imaginary friend. I told her not to talk about it but she's a little slow. Sorry."

"No problem," I said. "We all do stuff like that when we're kids. I use to tie a towel around my neck and say I was Superman." Everybody in the room laughed but something was not right about the whole thing. Elaina went into the room and started talking to Dee Dee and Dee Dee put the plant up and would not come out again. I couldn't get it out of my head, the thing about her "big friend." He continued,

"I waited till everyone else had gone and Rosa was watching the Novela. I was helping Elaina wash the dishes and told her I would take the party trash out for her. I wanted an opportunity to talk to her. I said,"

"You know the wave of recovery that has hit the city."

"Yeah, I'm part of it. It's time. We all been f—d up for too long. There's a lot of deadly crap out there."

"True dat, but you also know about this guy they call the "Alien". The one that's been tying up people and hanging 'em.' He's got something to do with this wave I'm sure. I've been looking into this for years and..."

"I don't know nothin' about it. Besides this Alien guy is getting rid of a lot of scum. You should give him a medal, not hunt him down."

"The only reason I've been draggin' my feet about this investigation is just what you said. Respect Elaina. This Guy has my respect but the law is the law. No one has a right to take it into their own hands."

"If the law moved a little faster maybe people wouldn't have to do that. I know you gotta do what you gotta do but don't count on me to help you. Alien guy is the best thing that ever happened to this city."

"After that I had to leave it alone. She was really bent out of shape over it and even the kid was on Alien guy's side."

Jasmine was thinking and finally said,

"I agree with James and Elaina I don't know that I wanna collar this guy. But I can tell you who I do wanna drag into a cell and that's that bitch who was impersonating an officer. If she knows something it might help us do our job so that Alien guy doesn't have to. I say we go after her."

What Andre did not tell Jasmine was what happened next that night. Frankie climbed down the fire escape to Dee Dee's level and peeked in. The child had fallen asleep on the floor waiting for him but he had not been able to come down for all the people that were coming and going from her party. The big man noted that the last visitor was the detective that had been tracking him for a long time. He watched the man get into his car but he didn't drive away and this concerned him. Frankie opened the window entered quietly and put the little girl in her bed. He then kneeled by her covered her up and placed a pink teddy bear next to her. With eyes still closed and almost as an impulse she lifted her little arm and wrapped it round his neck then tucked it back under the covers and slept on.

Charmed by what he had just experienced he climbed up the fire escape and onto the roof. He looked down and with dismay noticed that the detective's car was still below. Then a noise behind him made him freeze. He slowly rose to his full height, silhouetted by the street lamp, and turned to see Andre standing there holding a gun. The detective's eyes were wide but he held his ground at the site of the huge shadow and as they stood starring at each other. The intensity of this caused Andre to step back with eviscerating fear and he land on his back side still starring. Frankie also was incredulous and in his shock he spoke words, the source of which he did not know,

"No me hables con balas," to which the detective answered impulsively and with awe.

"Frank, is that you?"

Overcome with emotion the agile giant jumped over the side of the building and was down the fire escape in moments. Then he was gone.

The next day Babe phoned in as promised, for a report. Alexi was pleased with all she had done so far but not so pleased with the results. "Large and strong" was no great news. He had seen that with his own eyes but who was, he? Where was he? and What could be done to bring him to his knees? Those were the things Alexi wanted to know. Babe did not like being reprimanded and she told him she would get what he wanted in due time. She told him, if he continued being so "naughty", she would not give him the additional news she had. He promised a few more dollars for her expense account and she relented. She told him the Shadow was also involved in the missing shipments that were driving Lupo's gang war. This was news but soon would be public since dangling prisoners had been photographed by reporters at the docs. Babe basically had nothing. "Alien" and "Big Shadow" might be one and the same but he or it would have to leave the planet when both mob families discovered he was taking their shipments, that is, unless Alexi got to him first.

Meanwhile, now Andre had to step up his investigation. Not for his job's sake but to save the life of the giant that knew something only his brother Frank could know. When they were kids they played quick draw cowboys like most other kids. Their dad kept a licensed fire arm in their home for protection which their mother hated and always fretted about. The boys were told never to touch it and it was always kept in a safe place away from their curious hands. One day, Dad was cleaning it and he put it down to go to the bathroom. In the few minutes he was gone the boys ran in to speak to him and in typical kid fashion, simply could not keep their hands off of the pistol.

Andre the oldest picked it up first but Frankie the biggest snatched it away. In retaliation Andre took the bullets that were on the cleaning cloth and started waving them around victoriously. Frankie was pissed at the taunting and said, "No me hables con balas." Which means, "don't talk to me with bullets." Then he tossed the gun carelessly onto the table and it went off. Frankie ended up in the hospital with a wound to the right rib. In all the time he spent in the army and on the police force he never got wounded but both boys, respected guns a great deal more, after that day.

Andre's mind started racing and his emotions crisscrossed his psyche with dozens of mixed signals. No one else could know the story about his father's gun, but if this was Frank what happened to him? He had not attend his mother's bedside through her illness or attended her funeral when she died grieving his disappearance. And what the hell was so important that he could not tell his brother he was alive? Then again what if he was in witness protection or something even more intense like national security? But if this were true what was he doing sneaking around tying up and hanging criminals, and stealing shipments of dope? And what had happened to his face?

Well, one part of that sounded so like him. He always had a zany sense of humor. Hanging them could be a manifestation of that but what had happened to his body? He was always big but this was…was monstrous. Whatever the case, if this big hulking thing had anything to do with his brother he had to know? And if it *was* his brother he had to protect him. This last incident would no doubt tip off the mob that Alien Guy had ripped them off. After two years of stealth he had finally gotten careless enough to let someone make a connection. Alien Guy's goose was cooked. He had to find him and he had to find Lonagan, if that was her name, because she might know more.

Jasmine was way ahead of him. After she talked to Andre she had spent the whole evening looking through criminal records. There was nothing on anyone like Alien Guy (this she already knew) but she did find "Red". Babe Lonagan had a long record of bounty hunting and general violence. She worked for heavy hitters with the bucks to hire lawyers that never lost a case. She had been booked but never convicted and she lived large on what she made at finding her client's targets, dead or alive. She had never sustained the charge of murder but she certainly had the capacity to kill both targets and collaterals. Jasmine had pinned her as a cold killer from day one.

Meanwhile Babe was struggling with her own issues. She had performance standards and she knew she was not meeting them. She wanted to adjust things for greater client satisfaction and maximum remuneration. Knowing Alexi's primary objective for the manhunt was revenge with a secondary motivation for reconciliation with Lupo, Babe formulated a plan.

The lady had copious international connections. Some quick calls and she could shift things to make a deal that would compensate Lupo for all the losses he had sustained recently. She dressed in her best business suit and went to see Alexi. He was intrigued (and stimulated) but still reserved towards her. He knew she would never submit to him and he didn't like pain which he knew she was capable of inflicting. The match would be a power play. They would never get anywhere sexually. Then she whispered her suggestion and he experienced a whole different kind of elation. He called Lupo immediately.

"Romeo, Alexi here. Listen I know our last deal fell flat but I have something for you that will change everything."

"I'm listening."

"Babe knows some people, who know some people; Russians to be exact."

"Really, she certainly gets around."

"Not really. She is very selective as a matter of fact, but what she wants to whisper in your ear will make you smile, like a Krockodile."

"Tell her to get those ruby lips ready to whisper. I'll be right over."

9

Artifacts a Plenty

While Lupo, Babe and Alexi were having their "business meeting" Frankie was fretting about his encounter with Andre on the roof. He was so disturbed by what had transpired that he had made his way to the rectory of St Andrews and perched in the cool night on the side of the steeple like a gargoyle. He needed more than data. It was assurance he needed and not a little wisdom. His yellow eyes peered through the evening haze and waited to catch a glimpse of Father Fergus through one of the open windows. NAI was finally engaged to dial the priest. Fergus answered excitedly but told Frankie to wait till the admin assistant had gone. He settled himself down to wait, feeling a little less anxious knowing the father actually *wanted* to see him.

Frankie cast a massive shadow in the lengthy hall outside the vestry; one that despite their acquaintance still sent a shiver up the spine of the cleric. Frankie had very little room to turn in the compact space but when he finally took his place on the floor he looked much like a gorilla seated, cross legged, in all his primal splendor.

"How have you been my son?"

"I have many concerns but I will not trouble you with these. It is my internal people I seek you about. There is a man...a detective..." and Frankie went on to explain what had happened.

The priest crossed himself and sat quietly with his eyes closed. Frankie had noticed him doing this before.

"Are you praying?"

"Yes my son."

"How?"

"I talk to God about all I experience and all that perplexes me?"

"And does He talk back?"

"Yes, in a manner of speaking. He gives me clarity and peace about things."

"And why do you do this?" He did the sign of the cross.

"I do that to remind myself that the death and resurrection of Christ gives me access to the ear of God."

"He is your Creator. Does he care about you?"

"He loves me."

"He does not love me. I was created by Stein who hates me."

"I have thought about that Frank. Stein only reanimated you. What you are made of was created by God. There is much good in you. This is evidence."

"Of what?"

"That you are also loved."

Frankie began to moan and weep. The priest closed all the windows and tried to hush him.

"Quietly, my friend quietly; the whole city will hear."

Frankie doubled over his long hair cascading to the ground. He whimpered then finally looked up. The priest tried to divert him.

"My son stay your course, talk to me."

"Explain then, what happened with this detective."

"I think you said something that reminded him of someone. Why did you say that?"

"I don't know. It was Spanish and I have never studied that language. It comes to me. Like other languages. The words had to do with what was happening in the moment but also reminded me of another time--one not experienced by who I am now. I saw two boys in a room and had a piercing pain in my side."

He lifted his hoodie and there by his well defined abs was a healed puncture scare near his right rib. Stein had told him about it belonging to one of his "parts." The priest stood and paced.

"The body remembers things. I have gone to see amputees in the hospital and they claim to still feel their amputated parts. I have heard of others who have received organ donations and begin to take on certain traits that are typically not their own. I knew of a man who hated the taste of beets and grew to love them after his kidney donation. His wife who donated the kidney loved beets. We can't begin to know what part of our spirit infuses our corporeal self. These are mysteries we must ask the Father in heaven about all this someday."

"So this was a memory?"

"More like an artifact, something that remained of one of the persons you have as part of you."

"But this detective...he knew my name."

"Now that is something. What you said obviously "triggered" a response if you pardon the pun."

"No problem, I like puns."

Frankie blinked a few times and pointed his finger at the empty air. Pictures were projected into it with the names and photos of several Hispanic detectives in the immediate area. Andre was one of them and was selected. Frankie blinked again and it brought up his profile. He continued blinking and news events that were associated with him emerged. Frankie moved his finger and scrolled down the list. He saw Andre was decorated as a police officer for exposing a drug ring in 2005 and that he currently helps with the local Boys Club.

Continuing to scroll Frankie experienced a kind of emotional vertigo. His feelings enlarged and he had to swallow hard not to break down again. There in the darkened office NAI was, as it were, pouring this man's soul into his psyche and it was moving him deeply. Frankie saw many other things about Andre, places he had lived and things he had done. Then he saw something that chilled his blood. There in the bluish light was a photo of Andre along with his mother and many fellow police officers. They were at the memorial service of a policeman. That officer was Andre's brother--Frank Poloche.

The article said the body of the fallen officer was not present because he was missing, along with four others, after doing security for a conference against mob violence. Next to the article was a picture of the officer who, after long search and investigation, was thought to be deceased. Finally, the date registered in his mind as he read it in print. It was ten years ago; the year of his reanimation. In that moment the monster who caused strong men to quake and weep, trembled. He felt what some old wives believe, that someone had just walked across his grave.

Fergus was very empathetic and perceived what the big man was thinking sitting there shaking, with his fists next to his jaw. Breaking the silence he gave words to what was on the giant's mind,

"You must speak to him."

"How can I? He will shun me. I am not the brother I was. I am a freak."

"If my brother had passed I would take any remnant of him I could find. I could help you with this."

"I can't, I simply can't. You don't know what I have endured, so many turning their faces in fear when I offered only kindness."

"People are quick to stigmatize anyone that is different from themselves, with many it's a terrible, judgmental reflex."

"What is stigmatize?"

"To label or denounce someone even when you really don't know or understand them. Christ was stigmatized. In fact the word comes from the crucifixion."

Frankie thought deeply about this and Fergus noticed.

"How like the Lord Jesus you are in some ways, he was rejected and marred more than all the sons of men."

"Truly? Then He is more my brother than the detective."

Frankie began to stand and Fergus touched him for the first time easing him back down to the ground.

"My son you have asked my advice and this I will tell you. Go and spend some time near the works of God and far from the world of man, as you have before. In that retreat ask for guidance from the Creator of all things. Ask and it is His promised that you will receive. Then you will know what to do."

Frankie's heart said, "yes" in every way to this suggestion. He knew this was what he must do. He had faced the Kodiak without a weapon and lived but now this fear of rejection was crippling him like the pain he had before NAI was activated. He knew Fergus was right. Only in the wilderness had he been able to think clearly. Also, all this emotional upheaval was making him careless. People like Dee Dee, Elaina and Ann depended on him and if he were not doing what he must for them their troubles would return. There was a problem however, how could he leave even for a short while and not take care of them and all the others? He had to think but his mind was a deep well of chaotic thoughts. He made a clumsy and deliberated sign of the cross over himself and looking up he said,

"If You are for me then send me help...Thank you."

Fergus sat back in his chair with awe then whispered,

"Amen."

The house where Frankie received his mail looked dilapidated and abandoned. That is, it looked this way on the surface. Packages were delivered and they disappeared so they kept delivering, but to the mail carrier and the little staff of the country Post office, it was a mystery as to who Mr. Smith was. Why would anyone want their stuff sent to this site? Surely no one lived in the house itself; at least no one alive or human. Rumor was, it was haunted and some said a ghoulish creature had been seen a time or two skulking through the woods and disappearing into the night. The postman was sworn to deliver so he did, but quickly and only by the light of day.

Such fairy tales did not disturb Gunta Doree. His father was a Parisian intellectual and his mother a German nurse. He was a realist, whatever that meant, but he was now learning that "there were more things in heaven and earth than were in his philosophy". Gunta was interested in medicine like mother but drank like his father. This unfortunately got him kicked out of medical school and cut off financially from home. Mother was so disappointed she tossed him his hat like she did his old man. Propelled by this action, he kept moving, cycled across Europe then made his way over the Atlantic bartending on ships. He ended up in America sticking out his thumb to get from the city to who knows where. Perhaps he would make it to Canada.

The journey from one place to another was as easy to him as the journey from one high to the other. All these flowed together and mattered little. When one had lost as much as he had life was a mute point. He would live it and die. So his existentialist father had taught him, in the short time he had been around. Gunta therefore had tried it all. For the moment he settled on crack cocaine, and he needed a hit but he was save it till he found a place to crash. Right now, it was getting cold and he needed a place soon. Night was encroaching and it looked like it might storm. The old house looked like hell but had a sturdy roof. He was far too smart to believe in ghosts and this seemed ideal. It might even be good enough for a few days or to squat for a season. He had about 48 hours worth of stuff and some ramen noodles in his satchel; he would get by very nicely.

The door was bolted shut and so was the back door but he finally found a window that was not warped by settling and got in. What he found inside was, to his amazement, both enchanting and unnerving. Stairways that went nowhere carpeted by moss and corners decorated with drift wood. Boulders arranged in elegant designs, furniture made of trunks and branches of golden, silver and white birch saplings uprooted and placed for best effect. There were occasionally regular furnishings like a sturdy wooden table, a pot or pan hung with deliberation in high places or a fine couch with no legs. The roof had obviously been repaired and overgrown by moss and other plants. The house had settled a good deal and the roof and upper story were held in place by large rocks or telephone poles. There was no electricity that Gunta could find. What he surmised was that this was not an abandon domicile. But he very much wanted to meet the person who lived in such a place. Wandering through the house he finally did.

Gunta should have noticed that the furniture of stone or wood was large. This should have given him a clue. But nothing could have prepared him for the creature he found asleep on what looked like the largest bed or nest of trees moss and other soft things that he had ever seen. In fact only special effects in epic fantasy movies could have rivaled it. The door creaked as it swung, closing slowly behind him. This sound paralyzed him but turning quietly to leave he hoped the gigantic figure had not been awakened by it. The lightning flashed outside and there he was.

The fact was the Titan slept lightly. By the time Gunta had turned around Frankie was sitting up in the bed and the height of his head cleared the top of Gunta's blond crown. The young man had seen medical anomalies, large people, and phenomenon of all sorts at med school but nothing to compare with what he saw now. Gunta thought he was going to die but the expression on the things face was not hostile, only surprised. The visitor thought to exit through the door but remembered it had closed behind him. As the giant rose and moved to hold his hand over the door, the young man fell to his knees in sheer terror. Frankie lowered his head like a bull ready to charge and his eyes surveyed the intruder. Then he said.

"You will have to be my guest for a while." And Gunta fainted.

In the days to come Gunta discovered much about Frank and Frank about him. The interaction became more and more mutually appreciative. Gunta had nowhere to go and no one to go to. He was educated enough to accept what he was told of Frankie's origins and Frankie was able to help him with his own alienation from himself. Frankie's gentle soothing way and his unconditional acceptance made Gunta finally feel like he belonged. Frankie was also able to help the young man detox and move away from intoxicants and Gunta was fascinated by the process.

The young man saw the genius of this benevolent creature and thought for a moment, to exploit it but, coming to himself, he knew why this must never happen. Life on the road had taught him the folly of materialism and material simplicity was now his default. Now that he was drug free, what would they do with money? Buy stuff? What they already had as friends was better than stuff. Besides Frankie had the money thing all figured out. If they needed something he could get it. What more could they want? The only thing that bothered Gunta a little was that Frankie thought he had come to him as an answer from God.

"Yes Gunta, God sent you."

"If you say so but don't expect me to believe in that religious mumbo jumbo."

"This is not about rituals it is about a spiritual connection. You don't have to accept it. I will live it none the less. I'm leaving you know."

"Leaving? When will you come back?"

"I'm not sure. When God speaks to me."

"That could be a long time. What about my dose and the doses of all the others?"

"I must consider how trust worthy you are, or are not."

In many conversations over the past few weeks Gunta had been told he would be released and established somewhere. He would also have to go back to medical school at some point in order to continue getting his medicine. Frankie would take care of it. But he was strictly warned that Frankie would know if Gunta betrayed him by revealing his existence, whereabouts or activities. He would know and Gunta would pay for his betrayal. Now he was being tested for a different level of trust. Gunta was abashed by the idea that Frankie would suspect him.

"Do you think me so low as to betray the only person who has ever believed in me? I have told you I want to stay and help with your work."

Frankie was taken aback. None of the other addicts had said such words to him. Then again none of the other addicts had even seen his face. They did express their loyalty in obedience to his demands for their good, but in his view they did it for fear of losing their dose or the resources he provided.

"Can it be that you would keep my secret for friendship? So many depend on my help. If I am harsh it is for them."

"You are selfless. This is a strange and rare thing. If you were a regular human you would know that such qualities are almost unheard of among us. I would sooner crush a child as betray you. In fact I want to be you. When I was an addict I might have sold you for gain but now that I am clean it would be inconceivable. You are better than a father to me."

Frankie was now acquainted with falsehood and knew it could be very convincing. On the other hand he did "consider" and the answer came quickly to his understanding. Gunta had been sent to him by God. This meant that whatever happened, even betrayal, Gunta's presence in his life would be God's will for some higher purpose. He had thought many times that if he did succumb to death someday all his work would end. This was the way things would be. He would work all the good he could as long as he could and then God would have to use someone else to do his work. Perhaps it was this boy who could look him full in the face, with an intact intellect and still call him friend. Perhaps his replacement would be Gunta.

Frankie had been busy in his cavernous lab making a large stock of tablets for his clients. He had helped thousands but the current 500 addicts that depended on his medicine could be dosed for at least a month on the present stock. If he took longer than a month more would be needed. He would have to turn Gunta into a pharmacist/manufacturer/distributer in a few days. Gunta was a quick study but even so he was in awe of the whole system and he also came up with ideas on how to do what he would need to do.

Frankie knew that with Gunta's limitations as a regular human he would need a phone and a vehicle. He provided him with a modified smart phone, complete with instructions, times and places of drop offs, doctored with certain protections and loaded with all the national and international features. It also had a scan feature that would detect weapons or even remnants of other intoxicants. If any addicts were scanned and found with these on their person their dose was to be cancelled.

A great many of the addicts in need now had addresses thanks to Frankie. They could receive the drop by mail. Only about 85 needed personal attention and these would need scanning and meetings in hidden places. Frankie had a black Mercedes Van delivered in short order fully insured, registered and paid for by F. Smith courtesy of NAI. In addition Frank gave Gunta a credit card with quite a bit of money on it for gas and anything else he might need while Frankie was away. The Mercedes-Benz Corporation never even noticed they were the ones who actually paid for it all. Amazing what the movements of a few ones and zeros could do on the cyber exchange.

This would be Gunta's test. If the young man absconded with everything and tried to disappear, Frankie would find him and he would make him the next cocooned offering to the police while he himself would retreat to the wild. Frankie also asked Gunta to water his plants which were many. If the plants died then he would really be mad.

Frank had one stop to make before he took off. Seeing Dee Dee was out of the question since her apartment was probably under surveillance by the Police at the moment. However, he had not visited Ann this week and he wanted to drop her medicine off and get some of her lovely bread. He waited till dark and made his way to the neighborhood. Finding the house he walked silently across the road and placed the bottle of pills in the window. He was shocked to feel a hand reaching for his. Ann had been waiting and was as surprised as he was to feel the enormous hand.

"You could be a pianist you have a wide palm and a long reach."

"Ann you scared me."

"Good thing it was me huh? How are you mon ami?"

"I'm well and I hope you are too and your family."

"We are doing as well as can be expected. In fact Stacia has started dancing again."

"Vraiment? She is dancing? How wonderful. I must go and watch her at the studio sometime."

"Oh she is not dancing at the studio. She is dancing in our basement. If you look through the little window on the backside of the house you will be able to see her right now."

All at once Frankie became highly motivated to wrap up his conversation with Ann.

"I would love to stay and chat but I am taking a little trip and I must be away. If you need anything call me won't you? Now where is my bread?"

Ann smiled and handed him the warm loaf. Then she patted his hand and said,

"A pianist, that's what you should be. You have large hands like Rachmaninoff; or you could be a basketball player like Magic Johnson."

He laughed, inhaled the lovely warm fragrance of yeast and dough, and returned the pat on her outstretched hand.

Then he asked,

"Do you miss France?"

"I do indeed and we have wanted to visit for years but with my illness and the medical bills we have not been able to afford it. Besides I was not strong enough. I am now, thanks to you, but there is still the problem of the money."

"Well then, I have something else for you." He put some papers in her hands.

"What is it mon cher?"

"Tickets, for you Jean Luc and Stacia. You can say you won a lottery of money and purchased them. Only you must go right away."

"But this is incroyable! How could you afford such a thing?"

"I have resources and I will not take no for an answer. I am going away too. I will be back in about a month."

"Merci, merci. How can I thank you? Merci et bon voyage Mon Ami."

Frankie had come close to losing his friends before and did not want to take chances. He had arranged all this for the De Lacy's and now was ready to call Elaina and tell her Dee Dee and she were to go to Boston Children's Hospital for some treatment that was long overdue for the child. Elaina was no longer in need of medicine and she had fully recovered from her addiction but as a single mom she still depended on Frank for assistance from time to time. Now that Dee Dee was her priority instead of heroin, she would welcome anything that helped her special daughter and they would enjoy some time away. While he was gone, those he loved had to be safe.

The Giant ran around the side of the house and towards the back with a mouse's silence and alacrity. He parked himself by the window being very careful not to let Stacia see him and watched as she played music and struggled with the steps. She seemed frustrated and progress was slow. He remembered how free she had been before the incident with the abduction. This trip to France might help her, he thought. He remembered how she flew through the air like a swan at the studio and how she had danced with that young male dancer out on the sidewalk that fateful evening.

He replayed the scene in his mind but of course he pictured her with a different partner. A vibrant tall Hispanic man; perhaps a man he once had been. They went through a complex and opulent choreography full of chemistry and passion. Its back drop was a place part in light and part in shadow. Lifting, twirling, chasing, and leaping they spoke to each other in movements fluid as liquid and warm as the rays of the setting sun on a tropical beach. Then it all gracefully resolved in strong but gentle embrace; two like creatures in species and mind. He awoke from his musings to shuffle into the night, knowing that for him such an encounter could never be.

Unknown to him and even as he had been playing the lonely voyeur, two pairs of eyes had been studying him; one from a Nisan sedan across the street and another belonging to a female Van Helsing on the roof of an adjoining building.

The Nisan with Andre in it drove after the giant shadow slowly and watched him disappear into an ally. The female closed in on the house he had just interacted with and wondered how this could further her cause. Andre found the connection to the De Lacy's from the call the department had when Jean Luc accidentally discovered Frankie. Andre put the pieces together when Elaina mentioned Dee Dee's progress with her teacher, Miss De Lacy. Babe had also found the De Lacy connection when she had been at the precinct and had access to the "Alien" records. She had considered it a dead end at the time but was now revisited it with great satisfaction. Both investigators were closing in on him and some of his people. Their intentions however, could not have been more different. One wanted him alive, the other preferred him dead.

10

Spawning the Dead

In the crosshairs of her devious purpose Babe felt that one minute all the ducks were in a row and then the next they had all left town.   They would be back however, and there was plenty to keep, the bounty hunter busy till then. Lupo would follow her activity with interest and even Alexi would be employed in that collaboration.   Andre would have to deal with some frustration for a month without Alien activity but he would have to live with it and Father Fergus also had some work to do.   He was determined to provide Frank with more information upon his return.

Gunta would be busier than he had ever been in his life. Because of this and despite his promise to Frankie, he reached out for help. He hoped beyond hope the giant would forgive him but he used his initiative and organized a few more trustworthy workers.   Gunta's street smarts had the benefit of global experience, dysfunctional origins and human cunning as a former addict coupled with the basic psychology of a med student.   He knew who he could depen

d on and who was a leech or a hazard.   He had "scanning methods" of his own.

Andre had to revisit the records of his brother's disappearance.   Babe had Ruskies to talk to, drones to purchase and a fortune to make in Krokodil. Lupo and Alexi had money to make, blood to shed, people to exploit for such is the life of vice, but for Frankie's retreat the world would stop and he would get off the treadmill. Father Fergus knew how much Frankie's activities kept peace in the city and he prayed that while the Big Guy was away things would not spiral out of control. For stasis the powers of good could depend on one thing. While evil does seem to make progress it also has within it the element of entropy. At this time, providentially, that element was manifesting.

The Russian who wanted to spread the new street peril Krokodil encouraged Babe not to limit herself.   She was advised to access as many vendors as possible. Why staunch the flow of wealth with only one customer? Take a lesson from the capitalist and extend your reach, they said.   Babe saw reason in this and it got her talking to the other big boss, Don Mecino.   She knew this was treading on dangerous ground but she also knew that she would be closing in on the big Shadow soon and she would be far away before Lupo was the wiser.   From a distance she would still have many tributaries of wealth flowing in. In fact with a little help from her friends she might cut Lupo out all together. Nothing was impossible. New York could be hers. She would not be owned by any man and who had a right to say that this male dominated culture of Crime should not be made female friendly.

What she did not realize was that Lupo's cunning extended to mob espionage. He knew right away of her treachery and much as he lusted after her body he began to think she would be prettier dead.   The fact that Babe could become a desirable competitor instead of a subservient ally both aroused and unnerved him. He wanted her more than ever but he wanted her compliant as well. Somehow he knew that the only way she would be, was if she was deceased. This was actually the first time the thought of killing someone ever troubled him. The witch had him under some sort of spell and had taken the piss right out of him? For this more than anything he had to have her. Besides, what had he floated all that money to Stein for? If he killed her and she could be brought back to his specifications he would have the best of both worlds. In addition the power of Krokodil would be in his hands.   He decided to pay the scientist a visit.

Lupo's #1 was Johnny and everyone knew it. But his son Angelo had to be by his side at all times and everyone had to treat him as if he were #1. Family was family. Fortunately he was not intelligent enough to notice this ruse for Angelo was as dumb as he was vicious. Unlike his other two brothers who had gone to law and architectural school he followed in his father's footsteps. He could eat pasta smothered in red sauce with gusto, right after a bloody hit.

When such brutish idiocy as Angelo's faced the intellectual sarcasm of someone like Stein it produced instant friction. Stein reminded Angelo he was stupid and Angelo reminded Stein of every bully he had ever encountered in school as a geeky kid. Stein wanted to dissect him and remove his hazelnut size brain and Angelo wanted to pull out Steins teeth one by one without anesthetic. It created a little tension when they were both in the same room.

Spending much of his time alone Stein had made friends with the guard dogs. They were a vicious pack but oddly enough they bonded with the man who fed them daily. They would also go down to the lake with him, from time to time, and scare off the ducks and swans. Stein, would play fetch with them and sooth them, after Frankie's infrequent visits. So it happened that when Lupo and his boys came to visit Stein had the dogs loose, which was not what he was supposed to do. They were only supposed to be released at night. The gangsters drove into the gated area with the dogs in pursuit of the car. Angelo got on the car phone.

"Hey booze breath, you left the dogs out. Call 'em in before I plug one of 'em."

"There were some prowlers around last night I didn't want to take chances." It was a lie but he wasn't expecting them.

"Whateva...do it?"

Stein went out. It was three o'clock in the afternoon and he was still in his bathrobe and pajamas. He called the dogs in and almost all of them were caged, when Sparky, an unusually stripped mastiff and Stein's personal favorite, broke free. Angelo got out of the car prematurely and the dog came at him hackles raised; not barking but roaring. Angelo put six shots into him before he hit the ground. Sparky was gone. In that moment the vitriol Stein had for the thug rose to stratospheric proportions, while the loss of the dog hit the depths of his shriveled heart. But Angelo gave him no time to mourn his pet. Pushing Stein he said,

"Get yer ass in the house we got business."

The Don walked into the house taking off his gloves and touched his nose. The place was not tidy and stank of stale vomit and scotch. He commented blithely.

"If your lab stinks like this I'll kill you myself." Stein dusted off a leather chair for Lupo.

"I wasn't expecting company. I would have tidied up but..."

"I'll get a woman in for ya. Ta clean up dis filth. You're gonna be having more company and I want your working area to be fit for a queen."

Stein trembled inside to think what this might mean. Lupo told the boys to wait at the door and only Angleo remained. Stein ventured an angry look at the gorilla but nearly got it wiped off his face with a back handed slap.

Lupo looked at the couch which was crumpled to the floor on one side.

"What happened to the couch? That cost me money you know."

"I got a little carried away with some of the girls I had up here for company." Angelo snickered and retorted.

"Yeah little pricks like 'em fat." Lupo didn't like "little" jokes.

"Angelo shut up."

The Don got to the point. He cautioned Stein to take care of the house he was "blessed" with and he dove into the purpose of his visit. There was a woman; a very special woman...

Stein was already living with the trauma of being accomplice to five murders. He had tried to think of them as inert materials but his conscience would not keep silent even under lakes of alcohol. Now he was being asked to use his skill to reanimate another person, who of course had to be murdered first. She (unlike the others) was a killer herself so he could excuse this as an execution but what Lupo wanted was not just reanimation. It would be a kind of resurrection of the damned that would be programmed to *serve him.* He wanted dominance over her and he wanted Stein to fix it for him.

Stein had been experimenting with DNA and cloning since his wife had died twelve years ago. He had some preliminary success. In fact Sparky was a product of that as he had been reanimated with some borrowed tiger DNA. This gave him his roar and his brindle striped coat, but that was not to the purpose here. The only way Stein knew of making someone do what they didn't want to do was either with diplomacy, deception or pain. A woman like the one described by Lupo could not be reasoned with or even bought, she certainly could not be deceived. Pain was the only solution. If NAI could be programmed to teach only minimally and to cause pain as well as end it then she would be in a hell of Steins making. She would be on a leash of torment held by the hands of a little devil named Romeo Lupo. Perhaps it was what she deserved. There was just one problem.

He had not been able to control for the content of melanin in Frankie, hence the giant's green appearance and yellow eyes. Lupo thought Frankie was dead but when Stein told him the "subject" had been green Lupo paused. He tried to imagine Babe with the eyes of a snake instead of her cat green eyes. He also thought that as long as her skin were smooth that pallid, green might not be so bad; like something out of the old Star Trek adventures. In fact it would be a rush, something new and exciting. He told Stein to go ahead. He would have the body in the next few days. Stein sighed and began preparations.

The delay also had to do with another problem. Alexi had hired Babe to do a job that would remain undone. Lupo did not fear Alexi but the broker helped him considerably in his semi-legitimate financial investments. Lupo could not afford to lose more money at present. Till the control of Krokodil was his he needed Alexi's good will. So he called Alexi and made a deal.

"You know she is planning to deal with Mecino and cut us out don't you?"

"I suspected as much. She's not one to limit her investments. I have helped her out a few times after she overreached."

"No one goes over Romeo Lupo."

"She almost has my job finished. Can't this wait a few more days?"

"We can't let her sell the Drone venture to Mecino that would mean far less for us. She's plotting something bigger I'm sure."

"Oh very well, I'll call her off but let me see if I can make a few friends first and at least get what she does know of the Shadow. I'll have a little party and invite her Ruskies. If I can make them a deal perhaps we can go around her."

"Yeah, you can count on my money for that one. See what she knows, play with the Ruskie's and then we'll plug her."

"What could be easier?"

Babe was not one to be caught off guard but she was juggling too many balls at once. When Alexi asked for a status report on the Shadow, in person, with a little down time in the bargain she readily capitulated. Alexi knew of late, that she had been in the constant company of Dema Karlovich her business associate and current bed partner. It seemed natural to invite him and his friends. They would be protection for her as well, she thought. But she agreed only if Lupo were not invited. Alexi bowed to her whims mentioning that he had notice her being encumbered by the Don's constant attention. However, he gave into her request too easily she thought. But no matter, she would be free to cuddle with Dema and that was enough. Even "hit women" and "drug devas" needed to relax now and then.

Meanwhile, after Frankie made sure Dee Dee, Ann and Stacia were safely away he focused his mind on his journey. As always he would carry only the clothes on his back and his large moccasins would leave ambiguous prints in places where even wild life was not likely to pass. He followed the Appalachian Trail for a short while then began to bushwhack as he was accustomed to do.

By this time so much of tree and animal life was known to him that he smiled at his earlier insatiable curiosity. The marvel of the creation however, was its incredible diversity and soon even NAI was stalling to bring to mind certain natural objects he would find. As an additional challenge he began to focus on the *parts* of things and become acquainted with natural objects on a more intimate basis. The shape of a dragon flies wings, the radar of a bat, the mycelium of mushrooms, or the bark of a beach tree all held hidden properties that he would use later for his medicinal and architectural inventions. All this was fascinating, but he did not forget his purpose for his time away. This needed to be his focus.

Frankie was mostly vegetarian due to his experience with the salmon. Years ago, in the presence of a Kodiak he ate fish raw but then realized he had killed it. He promised himself to never do that again. So bringing some gorp out of his hoodie pockets and finding some mushrooms under tree stumps he sat on some moss to partake. He had covered two hundred and fifty three miles that day and was now sitting atop a mountain in Maine overlooking a lake. It was evening and the moss was comforting around him. The aurora borealis greeted him and he smiled with familiarity. Finishing his simple meal he stood up and looked long at the green skies. Then he stretched out his arms and initiated the dialogue that would go on throughout the month he would wander.

"Oh Great One, forgive me for my existence and any part I might have in the death of good men. Hear me now and speak to me for only you can tell me the things I want to know. Fergus has called you 'All Mercy'. Have mercy on me in this regard and answer me."

Wanda had become nothing but a nuisance to Lupo by now. When compared to the urbane, intimidating and dazzling Ms. Lonagan, Wanda seemed like nothing but a cheap and childish, bimbo. He had basically shut her out of his boudoir and given Johnny his blessing to take her. This made Johnny very happy. For years, he had called her the "Viking Princess" and had idolized her every move. He couldn't believe the luck that brought the possibility of sending her his way, but Wanda had other ideas. Much as she liked Johnny she was not one to be easily set aside. She was also used to being a Don's woman and to the privilege and luxury that went with it.

She would take advantage of the situation of course, using Johnny to get even. She made it clear that if he wanted to have a Don's woman he needed to be a Don. "You're too smart to be lickin' Lupo's boots." "He's nothing without you." "You're his number one and all the boys know it. They respect you." "If anything was to happen to him, what about you? What about us? " "You're the real brains behind this outfit." And on it went.

Johnny wasn't just a mass of brainless muscle. He was a poor kid who Lupo took in, taught the ways of syndicated crime, and gave him a name to be feared. He wasn't great looking but he did know the books and the business front to back and no one could put him down with fists, guns or knives. If Lupo was still solvent and alive it had everything to do with Johnny. Like the good soldier that he was he had tirelessly and blindly served Lupo's purposes. Johnny kissed the Don's ring like he would the pope's because he was the only "father" he had even known, but every hooker he ever slept with had Wanda's face in his imagination. He was besotted with her and that trumped everything else.

Wanda made sure he knew, that she knew, why he was Romeo's top man. She also reminded him that if anything happened to Lupo, Angelo would get the business and Angelo was a moron. Further Angelo didn't like Johnny. He was jealous of him. Much as Johnny felt loyalty to Lupo he needed to look out for himself. If things were reversed Lupo wouldn't hesitate to send his "number one" to the big sleep. To make Johnny even crazier Wanda intermittently appealed to his lust and punctuated her remarks with the most persuasive satin lined reinforcement. Meanwhile Johnny knew that he had to take care of a woman like this, in the manner to which she was accustomed. He had to do this even if it meant that, figuratively speaking, like the Greek Oedipus, he had to kill his "father" to marry his "mother".

Thinking way ahead Johnny had already started making his own connections with the Russians, for drone shipments of the deadly opioid desomorphine, more commonly known as Krokodil. Even better he had gotten the street recipe and had two labs already manufacturing the crippling stuff from over the counter codeine and iodine. The product resulted in the same scaly skin, blotchy color and bloated aspect in the user. It was almost identical to the Russian variety. It also clotted the blood the same way even as it sedated, elated and cause overdose more easily than anything else on the market. The high was legendary and it was easy to use or to add to the dose of unsuspecting heroin addicts. Once you were a Krok, death was around the corner but few were able to go back. If you used Krokodil you were probably a user for the rest of your short life.

Johnny knew that customers in the states might be put off by the cosmetic results of the drug. With their culture of superficial beauty, even junkies who eventually might have to use their bodies as collateral for their dose would be concerned about looking like the scaly walking dead. Subsequently the strategy was to get them on the drug before they were aware. Johnny had that all figured out. He started Raves in every neighborhood possible. Ghetto hang outs, college towns, high school dances, arts bashes and fancy soirées. His people would be there to offer the hottest new high straight from the vogue party culture of Europe. It was all about marketing after all. The thrill seeking public would never know what hit them.

Lupo's fixation on Babe and her preoccupation with Dema and the big Shadow, made all this possible for Johnny in a small window of opportunity. Babe was taking a break to be just a woman and that was her big mistake. She had plans for labs and all the other things that Johnny had started but she had been dealing with the wrong man. Lupo had no idea Johnny was up to all this and Don Mecino was too old fashioned and wanted drugs to stay in the Ghetto where the "dirty spics" and "jungle bunnies" were. He didn't want this stuff near the high school of his grandkids. Johnny, as it happened, was the only forward thinker and he was not on anyone's radar but Wanda's. He also had the good sense to know he had to act fast.

At Alexi's party Babe gave her report about the De Lacy family and he was very pleased. He reveled in the thought of not only dealing with the "Big Shadow," but also, of finishing what he started with the charming sleeping girl in that room at the Ealú. Alexi promised the second installment of Babe's fee would be sent to her as soon as he could find his palm pilot and she would get the rest upon delivery. Of course he had no idea of paying because, as planned, Angelo and twenty other thugs had already disabled the surveillance in the parking garage and were waiting for the bounty hunter and her friends.

Johnny was there and would make sure Angelo was caught in the crossfire. Though the five Russians were skilled and could take twenty hoods in hand to hand combat, they were no match for hundreds of rounds of artillery. The "pthew" of silencers was heard in unrelenting succession and when it was over blood pooled at the drains of the dark and hollow open space, and many BMW's and Porches would be calling their insurance dealers about bullet holes and vandalism the next day.

The five Russians bodies would be left for the police to ponder but the Babe, with one bullet to the heart from Lupo's gun, was loaded up in a van alongside the wound riddled corpse of Angelo. Lupo stood between them holding the hands of both as they lay on their gurneys. He almost wept as they were loaded up but he had the presence of mind to brush a blood stain off of his cashmere coat with a leather glove and to remember to ask Stein for the slugs from Angelo's body. He wanted to make sure Russian bullets had killed him. It was odd that he was the only casualty on his side. He always knew Angelo's stupidity would get him in the end, but Lupo did not dream he himself would be so affected.   Still he had an "ace in the hole" with Stein and he made sure that even Johnny didn't know all about the details of this.

Stein had been working furiously since Lupo's last visit, to clean up the lab and get everything in working order. Lupo sent a couple of discrete cleaners who were good at hiding evidence. They were silent and came infrequently which Stein was very grateful for. Except for the usual Italian cuss word they mumbled they were efficient and thorough. The house was spick and span in short order. A new couch was also purchased.

During this time of preparation, and much to Stein's horror, Lupo also sent a present for himself to Stein's elegant place of confinement. Two large oval vats 8 feet long and 5 feet deep, made of high grade steel. These vats were soon after filled nearly full with industrial solvent. The Doctor knew well this could dissolve flesh and bone very quickly.

The scientist ventured a guess that these would be used to eliminate evidence. After all, "cement shoes" in the river, was so passé. The good news was he would have more body parts to experiment with and he could dispose of them before they might, like Frankie, escape to places unknown. The bad news was that more guilt provoking screams of ghosts would nightly haunt his imagination. Of course he guessed correctly, and all this was in his home which was becoming more of a house of horrors by the day.

Dalliance with the fantasy of a woman is not the same as having her; especially if she is dead. Lupo was sitting in his limo biting his nails for the first time in twenty years wondering if he had done the right thing to kill her. And then there was the death of his idiot son. Idiot or not a son is a son, and he wanted them both back.

When they arrived at Stein's the scientist was trembling with anxiety. He was concerned about reviving one and now he had to stay sober long enough to revive two. More than this Angelo's death was a dream come true for him.

What stinging irony that he would have to be the one to reanimate him. He wondered if Lupo would believe it if he told him he didn't have enough of some sort of chemical or voltage and that he could only do one. Then again he might choose Angelo anyway. What choice would Stein have then? He decided to get as detached and clinical as possible and just do the job. The rest would be up to fate. Perhaps Angelo, unstable from the procedure would stumble into one of the vats of solvent and dissolve. Stein could only hope.

Lupo was still strangely affected by the whole situation. He seemed a bit concerned and had a few questions about it all.

"Ya think you can give Angelo a little more, you know...smarts?"

Stein answered clinically as any inflection in his voice might give away that he was petrified. It was all he could do to keep his hands from shaking.

"If I did it would not be Angelo would it? Lupo, you need to let me work. I don't want to make any mistakes. And just so you know, I can't give him more brains but I can give him more strength. Would that please you?"

"Yeah, yeah that's Ok as long as he does what I tell 'em. That won't change will it? And that goes double for the woman. I need her cooperative see? You know what I mean."

"Beautiful as she is I can only guess." Stein remarked.

Lupo got dreamy eyed and loomed over Babe full of desire but still afraid to touch the cold form.

"Yeah...I had to kill her myself, you know, to make sure it was done right. I didn't want her spoiled."

Lupo then saw the shaky hands of the doctor and eyeballed him with his characteristic malice.

"You got this, right doc? Cause you don't give me my people back like I want 'em and there ain't no hell deep enough for you to hide in, you get me?"

Stein swallowed hard at the thought that this psychopathic lunatic was his boss and that his own life was in his hands. Still, as the intellect in the room, he might have some advantage. There might even be some means of a little payback for himself. He had promised Lupo more strength for Angelo and the quality of loyalty. What could be more loyal than a dog? Angelo had killed his Sparky and now in compensation he would be merged with him in the essence of the dog's DNA. A single hair from the brindle pelt of the dog would provide more than Stein needed for his revenge. Further he would *not* include nano-bots for body repairs or NAI for tutoring.

Lupo knew nothing of Stein's prototype. Therefore Stein could get away with giving Angelo none of Frankie's gifts. The girl was athletic and muscular. She needed only to be revived with a modicum of NAI and a few bots. The process would make her stronger but he would never again replicate the strength of his first reanimation. That was too risky. Still, Stein hoped she would retain the killer instinct and take it out on Lupo if he tried to get intimate. That would answer his deepest wishes. Lupo would die and he would be free. Therefore *her* loyalty Stein would not guarantee.

The doctor also did not want the repeat of equipment breakage. He had to replace quite a bit of equipment when Frankie was "born" which made Lupo quite cross. The fact that Lupo had stolen all this equipment made no difference. Lupo wanted his boys busy making money not pilfering lab crap. Half the things they got were superfluous anyway. Stein finally had to go in with them and point out what he wanted. Breaking, entering, knocking off security guards, he witnessed it all and it was traumatizing. Everything about all this was one trauma after the other. All he wanted to do was quietly reanimate dead people. What was he thinking when he got involved with this lunatic?

To prevent the breakage he prepared a strong sedative in case clumsy reanimates started thrashing about. And he also had a single morgue refrigeration unit ready for one of the bodies at least. He hoped that would be Angelo.

Hundreds of miles away, Frankie stood in the middle of a briskly moving river. His hoodie and moccasins were on the bank and his chest was bare. It was fall and no normal person who was not a member of the Polar Bear Club would be so engaged at this time of year, without hip boots and a flannel shirt. Temperature did not bother the giant. He merely enjoyed it. Just having bathed, his hair was wet. He pulled it back and tied it with a strip of leather then stood looking at the setting sun. He had forgotten how good it felt to be free of the need to hide his appearance.

When he thought to retrieve his clothes he noticed that a curious black bear was nosing around his hoodie pockets for the remains of the gorp. He was a big one as black bears go but scrawny compared to his previous acquaintances in Alaska. In Frankie's mind he could not help making the comparison.

He recalled many of the gigantic creatures foraging for food and wandering near the river. Most of them were agreeable to leaving him alone but there were occasions when game was scarce and hunting was bad. Then a big male might choose to challenge him. Prying himself from the jaws of a snarling bear was never pleasant even if Frankie's bots repaired him quickly. Then again, there were few creatures that could match him for size and strength. Except for the claws and teeth, the clash with these enormous creatures brought him a kind of satisfaction. When the bears discovered he was not an easy meal the tussles almost became play. He came to share berries and mushrooms with them and learned their language of grunts and moans. They considered him unthreatening and even respected him while he did them the favor of removing their parasitic ticks. He lived at peace with them for many risings and settings of the sun.

Back in the long ago he had taken a bite out of a fish and was sorry it died. Presently he was a confirmed vegetarian and he did not want to eat fish but from his vantage point he could easily catch them. He plunged his arm into the water and grabbed a fat bass then tossed it to the nosy intruder. He was entertained as he watched the bear fumble with the wiggly thing that tried to get away. In the end the fish was eaten and the bear's eyes brightened with a look that told Frankie he wanted more. This was punctuated when the bear sat on Frankie's hoodie obviously begging. Twelve fish later, Frankie hopped the bear might let him retrieve his things and he started for the bank. The bruin moaned with disappointment sensing his meal was over and he walked off into the woods.

Frankie washed the fur and bear smell off of the hoodie and hung it on a branch in the sun. Finding a large rock nearby he reclined looking up at the clouds. Why had he ever left the woods and bothered to go anywhere near people. The angst of hiding and rejection evaporated, like the water on his skin. He quieted himself and reminded God in his mind that he was listening. How God would speak he did not know. Time passed and he enjoyed the silence. Then he turned his head and sitting there, was that bear.

It was the same bear and he was not exhibiting any threatening behavior. Frankie tilted his head and looked at him then sat up and both their heads were level. There was something strangely familiar about this. Between them there were some river pebbles on the ground, smooth and round like marbles. Frankie looked at the bear and the bear looked at him. Frankie flicked a pebble with his finger and it rolled towards the bear. The bear kept staring and he changed into a boy. The boy rolled a pebble back at Frank. Frank shook his head and the boy was a bear again. Frank had not spoken for days. Not since he had said the prayer. He spoke now as he looked at the bear and what he said had to be another artifact. He said,

"Andy."

Three weeks to the day he had left, Frankie had his answer. The detective was someone who needed to know what had happened to his brother. Whether he accepted Frankie or not he needed to know, and Frankie was the only one who could tell him. He wasn't sure how he could do it but he must try. He would be directed to the right time and place. The Titan tossed another fish to the bear, turned around and began his decent from his wilderness paradise into the world of men.

As Lupo had requested Stein extracted the three bullets that were lodged in Angelo's neck and shoulder. The bullet that killed him had come from behind severed his esophagus with a downward trajectory and lodged in his chest. His windpipe Stein could replace with a flexible acrylic prosthetic created on a 3D printer. His heart and vital organs were intact and would not have to be repaired or replaced. As Lupo suspected two of the bullets were Russian but the one that killed him was not. This smelled of treachery and much as he hated to admit it he knew only one of his men to be capable enough to do this, and only one, inspired by a woman, would have the courage to dare.

Knowing his #1 was a traitor tempted him to leave Angelo and Babe in Stein's hands and go take care of business. Never-the-less, he decided instead to arrange things by phone and stay by the bedside of his loved ones. Marko was his second after Johnny and Marko was ugly enough and needy enough to make anything Lupo wanted happen. Johnny had been careful not to alert Marko to what he was up to. A full third of the gang was loyal to Johnny and the money was already rolling in from his krokadil delivery drones so they were already recruiting others.

While Lupo mooned about Babe, Johnny took off like a rocket in the direction of profit. He hired every kid that needed pin money, at high schools and colleges. They were given provisions to start kroc farms and were recruited as his dealers. Young New Yorkers seldom needed an excuse to party and Krokodil would soon hit the city faster than the plague hit ancient Europe. Johnny would use the profit to take over the organization and keep his pricey doll in furs and expensive bobbles but the Don was not totally unaware.

Lupo put his many spies to work and they soon gave him the intel he wanted. Johnny had set up quite a system and the Don of three boroughs would not be cut out of the action. The solution was simple; string Johnny up by his privates and pull Wanda apart, piece by lovely piece. Then he would act magnanimously towards the others who had been led astray and he would step in and take over. Once he was firmly in control he would pick off the other traitors one by one. His only reservation was the strength of his opponent. Marko was not a match for Johnny. As soon as this business with Stein was over Lupo would have to deal with this betrayal himself.

One other thing was concerning him. Stein was an obvious wreck and he didn't seem to be moving fast enough for him to deal with the reanimation problem. He had to make an administrative decision and this would force him do what he never like to do – postpone gratification. He needed men and so he chose to reanimate Angelo and leave Babe for later. Stein would be held to account for any mistakes he made with Angelo but Lupo figured the more he practiced on people the better he would get at it. Angelo first and then he would have more experience for Babe. Further he would force the scientist into detox and sobriety, before he did Babe. Lupo had a doc that was loyal to him. He'd bring him in to take care of Stein and in a week or so he would be sober enough to raise his "honey" from the dead. Babe was therefore "put on ice." And four days later Angleo was ready to be revived.

Lupo had procured for Stein much technical equipment, as well as a modest arsenal of weapons for himself, through connection he was developing on the black market via Alexi. Openly, as a loyal American, he disdained Middle Eastern sources but the Austrian had taught him not to turn his nose up at anything that could make him millions and he had learned the lesson well. Through these sources and his reciprocal trade in white sex slaves, much tech had been sent Lupo's way for this project and Stein could at least, depend on the best in equipment.

The procedure took a little longer than an embalming but had some similarities. Frankie had taken a full month to construct, with all the piecing together and reformation of damaged parts. That was hard but doable. Still, the power had always been the problem. In the end power for his reanimation was harnessed from a storm making the giant, forever after a force of nature. Power was made available for this new reanimation, from several high end generators that equaled the mega voltage of four Van de Graffs at 10 to the eighth power or 100 MV the potential difference between the ends of a lightning bolt. Half that power coupled with chemical and genetic preparations would make a robust reanimation and produce an individual with 5 times the vital energy of a normal Olympic athlete. Frankie had four times more than that and ugly as he was with all the scaring, would still be Stein's Opus, but these two would be formidable beings indeed.

Especially for Angelo, Stein wanted to be sure death would be possible. He hoped fervently that a stray bullet or something of the sort would take him down a second time.   He would then tell Lupo that reanimation could not be done again and that would be the end of it, but he had no idea what it would take to kill such a vital creature. This would have to be tested and he would certainly be taking notes.   He hoped the dog in Angelo would "remember" him in artifact at least, and that the creature produced by the union would be kinder to him that the man had been.

Four tireless days of work produced a live corps that even sedated was able to sit up on the edge of the gurney and look around. Lupo was there of course for the awakening and the new Angelo looked around disoriented and licked his dry lips continuously. Stein told Lupo to call him by name.

"Angelo, mio figlio." Whimpered the gangster and the creature answered in a hoarse tone,

"Angelo."

Lupo slapped Stein in the chest and commanded he give him some water. The licking and panting was making him nervous.   As Stein went to fetch the drink Lupo noticed there was a good deal more hair on the back of his son's neck than he remembered and though it had been years since he had observed his son wearing a "wife beater" undershirt or a bathing suit. He considered that his chest was very hairy indeed. Attributing this to his virility he passed it off as a positive.   The hair seemed strangely colorful but real men don't stare at other men's bodies in the gangster's opinion, so Lupo averted his eyes.

The gangster also could not help notice that Angelo seemed itchy. He scratched at his face with the back of his hand and when Stein brought him the water he smiled and pawed at the scientist and lapped the water right out of the cup. Stein was gratified but he told Lupo (who was disturbed by this) that his son would have to relearn many things. The process wiped away a good deal of memory so he would have to teach him. For the first time in years Lupo wondered if he might be able to locate the boy's mother in Sicily and convince her to come and work on this. Truth be told, she had a spiritual awakening after Lupo and was inches away from a convent in her piety. She wanted nothing to do with his business. Besides he needed a vicious contender not a priest. He and the boys would have to undertake his education.

Angelo looked at Lupo over the edge of his cup and Lupo took him around the neck and hugged him and kissed him on the cheek. The reanimate gave a toothy grin that revealed canine teeth Lupo never recalled as being that large. Angelo then scratched the wet cheek and sniffed his own hand. Marko, who was totally freaked by all this, was sworn to secrecy on pain of death and given the dubious job of dressing Angelo.

When he was done the man looked much more himself. In fact he looked elegant. Lupo made a mental note to have the barber shave the boy's neck as the hair there was looking a little less than sanitary to him. They put his favorite Fedora hat on his head and they walked him out of the mansion. Stein was glad to see him go but he was warmed by the slight whimper he heard as Angelo looked back at him before getting into the limo. Lupo was not pleased but again chalked it up to his reanimate immaturity. He would soon teach him to tow the line and be a man again. He left instruction with Stein to welcome his doctor and nurse in a couple of days. Stein was kept in the dark as to why they were coming. He would soon know and hate Lupo all the more for his forced sobriety.

Lupo squeezed Angelo's hand in the car and when the creature squeezed back he nearly crushed his fingers. Lupo pried his fingers loose and then slapped Angelo on the back. The Don was glad for the strength he had, that would serve Lupo well. Then he secretly nursed his fingers for the rest of the ride.

11

Chaos Unleashed

Before the signs were seen on the flesh of the first users, hundreds were ready to sell their souls for more. Bank rolls, even large ones, couldn't keep up with the demands the substance made on the human victim. The poor had to steal and kill for it and the rich had enough to die because of it. The crime rate went up exponentially over it and the overdose rate followed that escalation because of it. People, mostly young but not always, which became addicted grew terrifying in appearance and walked the streets at night to hide their desperate deeds, looks and shame.

Businesses and citizens had to double their fortifications against violent and thieving creatures that had only recently been, kids having a good time. Soon every household knew someone who was affected. And the war on drugs was being lost to the damned.

Frankie never saw it as a war. He saw it as an illness that he was determined to find a cure for it. These people were not enemies they were tragedies and the mercy he wished for himself he wished for them. When he came back to the city and Gunta apprised him of what was happening he immediately went to work on finding a way to help them. Gunta was already on the case.

The first thing the young man had done was start spreading the word through addicts cured by Frankie of other addictions. The word was the mob was sending this scourge through the city by promising the ultimate chemical experience. This campaign saved a few but they had little to say to the stream of kids who never entered the ghettoes where Gunta's little army worked. As a med student Gunta found some allies in other academic ex-addicts who were being helped by Frankie's medicine. They became part of his team and were soon spreading the word that the only ultimate about the Krokodil was the torment and death it caused. The experience would shortly turn the addict's short life into a brief money maker for the people who peddled it. Short lived elation would end in prolonged horror and certain terminal overdose. The Zombie apocalypse had arrived and its cause was Krokodil.

The next phase of Gunta's campaign was on social media. Zombie Apocalypse appeared in hundreds of memes on the internet and word went viral on behalf of stopping the drug, but thousands by then were affected, and the money kept rolling in for Johnny and his sources. Wanda was now the woman of the hour in the underworld of crime and she blessed the day she had "ditched" Lupo and snuggled up to the young buck with the forward vision. Babe could have "Lupo the loser" but Babe was probably dead anyway. At least that was the rumor.

It was now a fortnight since the reanimation of Angelo. Lupo was making sure everyone knew he would offer clemency to those who would return to the fold and sure death was promised to those who stayed with the betrayer. Some had come home to him and been handsomely rewarded. Lupo hated to temporarily lose the drug revenue but he had many irons in the fire thanks to Alexi's constant encouragement to diversify. Johnny would soon see Lupo was the master after all, and lament the day he ended his apprenticeship. Johnny was in fact, already beginning to worry, but Wanda would not let him concede defeat. She began to give him an inflated sense of what he was capable of, and under her persuasion Johnny began doing things he suspected might be over reaching. Her eye for luxury far exceeded any sense she might have had and she was glutting herself on it, at his expense.

There was also news of Angelo who was not as dead as Johnny had thought and who had been through some treatment that turned him into a vicious scourge. Of course Johnny was his primary target and everyone knew that. Johnny told his men that he could take Angelo with one hand tied but the rumors were scaring all of them. Rumors of not just killing but "eating" his opponents and bizarre things like that. Johnny was beginning to think he and Wanda should leave the country. He should have gone with his gut.

The showdown was inevitable. When enough men had come back to "Pappa," Lupo decided he would call Johnny out. Johnny begged Wanda to get her things and get on a plane to Greece with him. They would own an island and live in paradise for the rest of their lives but there was no more time to deliberate. Wanda spit the proposal back in his face. Her need for revenge was driving her and she said if Johnny didn't have the balls to confront Lupo she didn't want him. Johnny knew better but she owned him so entirely he would risk everything to make her happy. He knew in his heart, she didn't love him and that 'vengaza' was all she wanted but his desire was driving him. She filled his whole being with need. He would die for her, like the impassioned and tragic Sicilian he had always been.

On the day of the confrontation Johnny's men would gather by the river and Wanda, crazed by her need to see Lupo beg, would be there. She would dress in white leather with no end of gold chains. She would carry a gun and envisioned herself using it on Lupo when the smoke cleared. She wanted him alive after all his men lay dead, so she could pull the trigger on him. In his heart Johnny didn't think it would go that way. His only hope was to die in her arms.

The place for the fight would be under the highway on Bruckner Blvd. in the Bronx. The time would be-- midnight and they were just supposed to talk but Johnny knew that they would talk with bullets and the conversation would be more than hostile. They chose this place so collateral damage and bystander death would be the Black and Hispanic ethnic vermin they all loathed, rather than decent people like 'them'. Both parties agreed on that. The time would be two nights from then.

Meanwhile Lupo was getting impatient with his son. He was not making the progress he had hoped. His words were limited and he tended toward episodes of roaring and rage with some whimpering if Lupo yelled at him. He was compliant with his father and loyal to a fault but he was hard to leave with others who he had a tendency to hurt or even bite. Angelo also had trouble using cutlery and this made restaurants out of the question which cramped the Don's style. Lupo had to use simple commands; one or two words and Angelo even had trouble with that. What he didn't have trouble with (and this Lupo considered a plus) was the command to kill. He did this quickly and completely but he had a disturbing habit of using his hands and teeth instead of guns. Once or twice Lupo had to stop him in disgust from chewing up the target. There was a question among the boys as to whether he consumed the bits in his mouth or not, hence the "eating" rumor.

His struggle with his son made the Gangster long for Babe all the more as a relief from his parenthood. He held off on her awakening to ensure Stein's sobriety and efficacy. Having attributed the "defects" in Angelo to Steins addiction he would simply not bear unnecessary strange effects on Babe's appearance or character. To that end she lingered in her cold sleep while Stein was going through the inferno of detox. This was bad enough for those who wanted it but for someone like him who preferred the oblivion of intoxication and death rather than sobriety, it was a whole new level of hell.

When Frankie returned from his retreat he went to Stein's house first. He knew Dee-Dee had not yet returned from Boston and it was not the time of the month to see Ann. He felt quiet and rested as if something had settled deep inside of him since his time away, but now he knew he had to be on his guard.

He disabled the surveillance, quieted the dogs and examined the car that was outside the house. Stein had company so he would have to wait.

When every light was out, and all was silent, the giant crept into the vestibule and listened. He walked silently into the hallway and passed many closed doors. He stopped and listened again but heard no noise. Not even breathing from most of the chambers. Finally he heard snoring from one room and opened the door silently to see an older man sleeping, his arm around a young woman. He closed the door again and walked to the library where he was sure to find his reanimator.

Stein was there as expected and he was sitting, rocking and trembling. He seemed disoriented and was mumbling something about wanting to die. He repeated this many times over. The dark shadow of the titan loomed over him and his blood ran cold. He turned slowly and for the first time since he had reanimated Frankie he fell upon him desperately as if his salvation had come.

Strangely enough Lupo and Frankie were of one mind when it came to the question of Stein's addiction. They both wanted him to stop drinking but for different reasons. Frankie wanted to help him, Lupo wanted to help himself. But Stein saw Frankie as a possible oasis in the middle of the desert. He had relented and given him his scotch before when he started whining and complaining. Perhaps he would do it again, but Frankie had a better idea. He had made a preparation for the doctor from certain chemicals and a distillation of the kudzu plant. His expectation was that it would make Stein's drinking stop and his body have a sense of wellbeing. It wasn't what Stein wanted but he would take "any port in the storm".

The doctor felt some relief right away from the craving. He even felt well enough to thank Frank and to talk to him and tell him much more than he had ever told him before. The situation with his patron was approaching critical mass. He actually confessed it was Romeo Lupo and that there was another reanimate now in the world. He also told him what was happening with Johnny and that many people were dying because of this and many more would die. Last of all he told him there was a woman in the basement that was about to get reanimated. He wondered if that would interest Frank.

"If Lupo dies she will have no claims on her." The scientist remarked.

"No one should have a claim on her unless it is of her own choosing." Frankie returned.

"What I mean Frank, is that Lupo is a menace to humanity. Whoever kills him will be doing the world a favor."

"They will be doing you a favor that is certain."

"Yes well that's true but...look at her. She's gorgeous. You will be the same species, so to speak. She can't help but be drawn to you. You won't be lonely."

"You are so cunning and I'll admit I'm tempted but there is another."

"Oh yes your little albino friend. Be realistic, if you ever let her see you she would scream and run just like all the others."

"It is not her heart but mine that is not free. I love who I love."

"You're a fool."

"You should know. Here now, I can't stay while there is so much going on. I may not kill Lupo but I will stop him and his dog."

Suddenly the door latch was heard and Lupo's doctor walked in. Stein was terrified lest he be found out but smiled to think that now Frankie was obliged to eliminate this man or be discovered. He turned to ask Frank what he was going to do about this but all he saw was an open window and fluttering curtains. The doc was surprised to see the scientist so calm. His flippant nurse sauntered in and asked if they could have a snack and watch some Netflix. An owl hooted outside and no one saw the giant jump the fence as the surveillance came back on.

There was much to do, but if Frankie was to enter a challenging situation, there was always the chance he would be killed. He therefore wanted to be sure Gunta was well equipped to continue the work. Outside of the condemned tree house he called home, everything looked as usual. Walking inside, he saw a different story. There were at least ten people buzzing about, some on cell phones, others looking at maps or charts and others eating or laughing in the cooking area. Frankie's first thought was to kill Gunta for his betrayal but then he started to realize he knew these people. They were all among his dependents; former addicts whom he had helped. Among them was Elaina and when Dee-Dee saw him she ran right up to him throwing her arms around his leg. They must have come back early but why were they all here?

Gunta then called everyone to attention and said,

"Attention, attention everyone. Quiet please. I want to introduce you to the one who has changed everything for us. This is Frankie."

Everyone stopped what they were doing and turned to look at Frankie. No one was flinching or running. No one was acting like they were afraid. They all simply looked at him and then bowed to him in honor. He did not know what to do. He ran out of the house and sat on the broken front steps. After a few moments Dee-Dee came out and sat with him.

"Frankie you sad?"

Her little hand was on his scared face and she looked at him with sympathetic eyes. He sat in wonder at the fact that they could be together for just a moment without fear of discovery. Then he was swallowed in the ambivalence of shock and uncertainty.

"I don't know sweetheart."

"Come inside, I give you chips."

He took her hand and she escorted him in where everyone else began to laugh and applaud. Gunta had broken his promise and told. Now they were all in on the secret. Still, Frankie would soon realize this network was indispensible to the battle they had before them. He needed an army and these precious people were ready to fight at his side.

Gunta told him he had been busy while he was away and the amply stocked Credit card had purchased five vans that could be used to do the work he had asked Gunta to do. It became clear to the young man immediately that the tireless work Frankie had been doing could not be accomplished by one man. So he had recruited the ten most trustworthy among those Frankie had helped and he told them everything. He also had at least 50 more that did not know all but who were recruited to blitz social media with memes about the danger of krokodil and the distribution campaign of the mob. Gunta also made a plan for the ten to assist in the deliveries and in finding others in need. Things were going relatively smoothly but they had hit two snags. They were running out of raw materials for the medicine and the medicine was not working with Krokodil.

Frankie knew he must urgently work on these problems. But there was the matter of the bloodletting that was about to happen under the highway in two days. Gunta recommended they call the police but there was the matter of the other reanimate that might be a source of many casualties if he were not placed in check. Frankie felt he had to be there Police or no. Frankie also wanted to talk to Andre and he felt that this was the time to do it.

Angelo had taken to slipping out at night. He did not like the restraints his father put on him with his table manners and he liked the taste of a fresh kill and raw meat. He also enjoyed the company of stray dogs. And once or twice he ripped his shirt and shoes off and ran with a pack that was loose in the neighborhood. In fact he became the leader of the pack.

It was mentioned in the paper that a few winos and prostitutes were found in pieces by the river and that was disturbing to the Don but he figured they had it coming. In his heart he knew "the Ripper" as they called him, was Angelo but he learned to live with it. The first time he did this Lupo smacked him around and he whimpered. But after a while Lupo realized he was a grown man and how he had his fun was up to him. He just needed to be dressed properly and be available when his father wanted him and that, Angelo was happy to do. He was also told that he had to do his howling on the other side of town. Angelo loved to howl, and wherever he did it, he would get the other dogs started and no one got any sleep. Lupo would not have that.

Until he was needed in the Bronx, Frankie kept busy in the Caves. Gunta assisted him and marveled at the expertise with which Frankie handled everything pertaining to the medicine he was preparing. Time was running out and he had to work fast but he did everything with alacrity. Gunta asked him if NAI was his only source of information for what he was doing. Frankie stopped for a moment and thought. He said for now NAI was his source but it had provided him with many volumes of medical and scientific information and he had digested all of them easily. He was aware not all people could do what he did. It must be that he had been given a very remarkable brain. He also commented on how his hands always seemed to know what to do. At some point, when he had more time and if he survived, he must continue his search for the men who made up his "parts" and answer all these questions.

When Frankie saw how things were moving along with more helpers he commended Gunta. He also scolded him. He was angry because now all these people were taking risks with their lives. He saw Gunta had been very careful who he chose for the mission but there were logistic problems too. Some of these people had taken time off school or work to help. They couldn't do this forever. In addition, now more people knew of the whereabouts of the lab and that was dangerous. Also the formula was a gold mine for anyone with ill intentions. If anyone decided to betray them great harm would come. Most of all he was upset because Gunta had promised.

Gunta apologized profusely for that. He knew he had promised but he was overwhelmed with the task and he could not get hold of Frankie. It was a choice between getting help to do his work or keeping his promise. He decided that getting the doses to the people in need was more important. Frankie had to agree and made a mental note that he had to plan better if he was to leave again. Gunta agreed that they would keep the group of workers small for the sake of secrecy. He assured Frankie that these ten were as dedicated to him and this cause, as he was.

The ten were all profoundly indebted to Frankie. They knew how important his work was. They also knew they owed him more than they could ever repay. They wanted to do this to give back a little of what he had given them. They all swore they would never betray his trust. Ten promises were made to come and help whenever they could. Elaina and James were part of the ten. Then there was Radar whose expertise was electronics, Ben was a psych major now and Percy and Jamal were musicians and social media specialists. Angie was a political science grad student. Kurt worked at a garage and Hailey his wife was a waitress. In addition to the ten Rosa came along to cook and take care of Dee-Dee. Gunta made twelve.

Frankie's set up was a beautiful thing but needed a few tweaks. It looked quite like something out of a Tim Burton movie with gears and pullies, bowls and belts. But once the mixture was prepared for the pills, pressing them and packaging them was easy. In a day and a half they prepared all the medicine needed.

If time had permitted they might have celebrated but the urgency of the moment would not allow it. They all understood and like good soldiers they would leave the celebration for another time.

Frankie felt terrible that he had not been able to spend any time on the krokodil problem but he did his best thinking as he ran. This time he would not have to run all the way to the city because he could get a ride in one of the vans but he made them leave him on the outskirts of the Bronx because they had to be about their business with distribution. The messages for the meeting places had already been sent out. People would be coming for their doses. The distributers had to do their jobs. He also wanted them out of harm's way when the gangster war began.

Frankie had twelve miles to run in order to get to the highway at Bruckner on time. Fortunately he could run a three minute mile long distances and not break a sweat. He would be there in less than 20 minutes but there was something he needed to do first. NAI dialed the precinct for him and he asked for Detective Andre Poloche.

The two people in the van had been talking up to this point and Frankie hushed them. They all knew what he was about to do and they had assured him they would be supportive. In fact they cheered him on. He might be rejected, but then again, he might not be.

Angie and Jamal gave him an indisputable "thumbs up". No matter what happened they were there for him. This made it easier when the answer came,

"Detective Poloche here."

"Andy is it you?"

Andre had heard this unmistakable deep voice before. It was not his brother's voice but it had something to do with it. It was the Giant Shadow that he had been chasing for two years. But he wanted to be sure.

"Who is this?"

"I want to talk to you. I want to explain but I can't right now. I need your help."

"What is this all about? Do you know where my brother is?"

"I do and I will tell you but not now. Now I need you to send police to the place under the highway at Bruckner Blvd in the Bronx by midnight. Romeo Lupo will be having it out with Johnny Benotti who has been pedaling Krokodil behind the Don's back. It's going to be a blood bath. Come prepared."

"Why are you telling me this? You always work alone."

"You have to trust me. I need help this time. Lupo and Johnny don't care who gets hurt and there will be someone there that will be taking up all my attention."

"Who?"

"The Ripper."

Andre heard a click on the other end and the call was over. Adrenalin started pumping and a few phone calls were made. The detective couldn't take a chance on this being a hoax. It sounded like a feral fantasy and police nightmare double feature but if it was for real he needed a battalion dressed in Kevlar and armed to the max and he needed them ASAP. This was big and if it was Lupo he wanted him almost as much as he wanted the Alien. Plus the Ripper would be there. Perhaps Babe would show up too then Jasmine would be happy to bust her cakes as well. Meanwhile, there were "high fives" all around in the van and Frankie got out and started running.

As a social worker Jean Luc knew what a healthy relationship looked like. His parents had been through some ups and downs because both of them had problem with the law as college students and protesters with some drug use. They both wisely decided to sober up and did, but marriage and parenthood didn't come with a manual and as immigrants in a new country they had to figure things out. Fortunately they loved each other. There was a lot of passion and drama and then his father died. This was Jean Luc's example of happiness.

When Jean Luc started dating he found that he was inevitably drawn to bad girls or what Stacia called "girls with problems". Mother advised him to leave work at work and try to find a girl that had her head screwed on right. Unfortunately, girls like that seemed rather boring. Instead he got his heart broken a few times and finally settled on a little spitfire from the Bronx named Luna. She was Cuban and smart, taking nursing at Fordham University and she was beautiful. Unfortunately they had some differences.

While Jean Luc loved the theater and a variety of other cultural pastimes, she loved to party. He liked an occasional rave but for the most part he had grown out of the heated exchange of estrogen and testosterone on the dance floor and wanted to settle down. Luna didn't see it that way. To her, dance was a way to unwind after a hard shift at the hospital. It was also part of her culture and she argued it was an art form that allowed her to dress up and strut her stuff. She liked it and without reservation she wanted it--often.

A few weeks ago Jean Luc came home one evening and just wanted to decompress in front of the screen and forget everything with a good film. Luna had a hard day too but she wanted to de-stress on the dance floor. They talked about it and could not compromise. Finally, Jean Luc would stay home and Luna would go out with her girl friends.

At the club one of her friends introduced her to Weaver. He was a gay man and Luna figured that at least he was safe and wouldn't hit on her. As it turned out he was a riot. Just kept them laughing all night. He said he designed shoes and that if any of them wanted a pair no one else had he could fix them up. He gave all the girls his card; with just his first name and a number, no address. Then he offered to buy them a round of drinks. Luna said to make hers a Shirley Temple because she was the designated driver.

As she sipped she started to feel crazy good; better than she had ever dreamed of feeling. She asked her friend about it and was told, Weaver had just fixed her a little cocktail that would help her with any F'n stress she might have. She was told not to worry about it and at this point she didn't. Luna got on the dance floor and partied like she never partied before. Then she passed out. When she woke up, she was home and the girls were everywhere, on the bed, couch, floor and one was in the bathtub. None of them knew what had hit them but they all wanted to call Weaver and ask for more. Weeks later they were spending half their check on his "stress relief" and they noticed this strange eczema was encroaching all over their skin.

Jean Luc knew the signs of addiction and Luna had all of them. He was not just concerned he was devastated. This was the woman of his dreams and she was on the drug everyone was saying would not let you go--alive. Because of this, on that fateful night of the gang war he was in the Bronx. He had just been trying to talk Luna into going to a detox. She told him to lend her some money for the rent and he said he would if she went into treatment. She screamed obscenities at him and showed him the door. This totally broke him. Walking slowly he meandered towards his car which was parked near the highway. Then he heard the howl.

12

Conversations

Jean Luc had heard of the recent tragic deaths of homeless people at the hands of a howling maniac known as "the Ripper". His concern for Luna had momentarily eclipsed his caution and here he was, walking around alone, late at night. The moon was full and clear and he thought he could handle himself but not against a crazed fiend that might be carrying a weapon. Then again perhaps it was just a stray dog. But the Animal Control department had made strays in this area a thing of the past. Yet here was a chilling sound as savage as the jungle, echoing through the alleys and barrios of New York. Jean Luc's steps quickened.

Next he heard two things that seemed out of place in the city. It was a galloping or loping sound, like horses with padded feet, coming closer and closer. Then the more common sound of a jogger, but running like Hermes in frenzied approach. Bewildered he turned around and saw five dogs and something else coming straight at him. Shocked he began to back up. Knowing two legs cannot out run sets of four he frantically looked for something to climb on. He scrambled on top of a jeep parked under the dim yellow light of a lamp post. Reaching the top, he heard a mighty crash behind him. He turned to see a churning mass of arms and legs in snarling convulsion.

The frenzied dogs growled and barked as the thing leading the pack slammed into the massive jogger. Then savagely they tussled. From his vantage point it looked to Jean Luc like something out of a demonic dream with gothic overtones; dogs yelping and snapping as the two brutal wrestlers vied for the upper hand. And there was blood, oh yes, and Jean Luc thought he saw knives but then realized it was teeth that were producing the crimson flow.

He wanted to call for help on his cell phone but his fingers were simply not cooperating with his nerves. He stood there helplessly as one by one the dogs were mortally tossed by the giant against brick or cement and finally only the two biped creatures were continuing in the struggle. Then the giant gave the beast a mighty back handed slap that sent him reeling. It hesitated for a moment and Jean Luc heard a voice as deep and as low as the rumble of thunder shout a strange command,

"Sparky stay!"

The beast hesitated for a moment and it seemed to Jean Luc it was confused. It whimpered and held its head. Then, in the back ground, Jean Luc heard several rounds of gunfire. Like a starting gun in a race, it triggered the creature to move. "Sparky" turned and dashed straight in the direction of the gunfire and the Giant followed. Jean Luc crouched on the top of the jeep looking at the carnage. Five dogs were lying dead in pools of blood on the ground. He lay flat on the top of the jeep, peered over the side and threw up.

His stomach empty and his thoughts still spinning he dragged himself, terrified from the vehicle and stumbled away. Presently he realized that the safety of his own car was in the opposite direction—the direction of the increasing gunfire. By and by he noted one police cruiser after another converging on the area. Like the grand finally of a fireworks display, the snaps of gunfire increased till it became one thunderous cacophony ricocheting off the surrounding building. Emboldened by the police presence, Jean Luc moved cautiously towards the resounding tempest.

What he saw when he arrived, almost made him resume his retching. There were bodies everywhere, some not only full of bullet wounds but with their throats torn out. Bodies lying eyes opened in terror the blood oozing out of their silent mouths. The Notorious Johnny Benotti was among the ravaged. And he was grasping what looked like the leg of a woman whose body was a few feet away. She wore what was once white leather but was now smeared red and mangled unrecognizably.

In the stupor of shock Jean Luc recognized one man that was standing; the detective that had been involved in the case of his sister's abduction. He was there, disheveled but taking care of business and attempting to put his own adrenaline in check. As Jean Luc approached he heard the name of Romeo Lupo mentioned and he realized that the gangster was probably culpable for all of this. The detective was furious that the Don had been spotted and apparently escaped without a scratch. Jean Luc hesitated to approach, and Andre turning and noticing a civilian, asked him to move along. Jean Luc however, could not keep silent and spoke tremulously,

"I saw something…a huge man…"

The detective froze and wiping the sweat and blood from his hands on his jacket, he barked some instruction to some people and excused himself to talk to a terrified but available witness. The conversation that followed revealed that the creature involved in the more gruesome aspects of this mob scene had been checked by a large man who the detective very much wanted to interview.

Under the highway, the darkness had not allowed for the best view of all that transpired. When the police turned the lights on, much of the damage was done and Lupo was gone; so was the Ripper and the Alien, but here was an eye witness who had seen them both. Unlike the others who had been actually handled by the Alien, this witness was terrified but coherent; the first of his kind. As a Social Worker he was also trained to state the facts.

As police gave way to the cleanup crew and ambulances Andre accompanied Jean Luc to a quiet place for some wine to calm him and for a debriefing. At the end of it a shell shocked Jean Luc drove home and took a sick day the next morning. While Andre prayed the Big Guy would call again.

Lupo lost a lot of men in the fracas; but Johnny was dead and Wanda was history. The Don actually shed a tear for these two but mostly enjoyed the victory. The drug trade was now securely in his hands and most of the men he wanted eliminated were being bagged up by the police. A few were left to be dealt with but the information they were privy to regarding the management of Krokodil would be extracted before they were disposed of. All was right with the world except Angelo.

The doc who was tending to Stein, had treated Angelo since he was in diapers. He was trustworthy at least, if not approaching senility. Angelo had done his job exceedingly well and was responsible for many deaths but he had taken a lot of fire. Eighteen bullet wounds could not stop him tearing six people to pieces but ten more shots left him gasping for breath. By the time he got to Steins mansion, the limo was irreparably soaked in blood.

Lupo was terribly impressed that he had taken so much lead and was still alive. He made a mental note about that and wanted Stein to improve upon it, if and when Lupo himself needed reanimation. He didn't want the hair on the neck however, and that was not negotiable.

When Lupo's hoods carried the patient in, the doc was not hopeful. His voice took on a bedside tone and he prepared Lupo for his son's demise. Lupo was not pleased. He dismissed the Doc and called for Stein.

"Well, the doc says he's done for. What can you do with all this fancy shit I paid for?"

Stein cleared his throat and swallowed hard to prevent a giggle of pleasure.

"Don Romeo, respectfully, I have to say there is nothing I can do. Angelo's whole system has been over stimulated by his recent reanimation. To try it again would kill him even if he were intact. With all this physical trauma I'm afraid there is no hope of reanimation if he passes away. If I were you I would have the wounds treated and then leave the rest to his own extraordinary body's abilities to fight for life. I'm sorry. If there was something I could do I would."

The speech sounded convincing but as he turned he could not help an expression of elation. Behind him Lupo cussed a few times then sighed and called the doc in. By evening they were transporting the body to their piazano's at the family funeral home. What followed was a service, wake and funeral to remember with enough carnations to shame the botanical gardens. Then the Don turned his face towards the next reanimation.

Frankie was nursing his own wounds on top of a hill overlooking the city. He had pulled out his own bullets and was watching the wounds close with the help of the nano-bots active within him. He also felt the sting of the bites and scratches which were now added to his collection as mere scars. With every scar he thought he became less attractive but that was the price of being a protector and it was worth it. He had seen Angelo succumb to the gunfire and was too busy protecting the morbidly curious or the junkies and drunks that were too inebriated to move quickly away and save themselves. Once the shooting started it was hard to multi-task and deal with Angelo too. Johnny's boys took care of that job and Frankie thanked God, Stein had apparently not, given the Ripper his own great resilience. The creature had to be put down. He was a born killer and could only be stopped one way.

Frankie realized Jean Luc had seen him and that he would at least know that he meant him no harm. The Giant had protected Ann's boy and though Frankie would not trouble her with this information, at least he hoped it would not jeopardize his work. The thing was, Jean Luc would be considered a credible witness. What would happen if he reported?

After a few hours Frankie felt recovered and sitting on his hill overlooking the city he munched on some walnuts and dried mangos which Rosa had put in his hoodie for him. It felt so good to be mothered and when she made rice and beans and piled them as high as Bear Mountain on a serving dish and put them in front of him he was always too delighted for words. He could only pat her salt and pepper curls and smile his grimace of a smile. He bred roses and named one of his purple hybrid strands after her because purple was her favorite color. It was called "La Rosa Lila".

In that moment he very much wanted to go see Dee-Dee but he needed to make sure of what had become of Angelo. He saw Lupo leave and his cronies drag the expiring Dog-man out of the commotion. He also saw them drive away but Frankie could not follow as his work was not done. He only imagined where they would go and he was right. A few hours of running and he was disabling the surveillance and quieting the dogs again.

They curiously sniffed the scent of something of interest on him and he was sorry to have killed those other dogs in the Bronx. Seeing these friendly creatures cheered him. Perhaps it was the essence of "Sparky" they perceived. He wished he could ask them. Frankie made a mental note to learn the language of dogs if that were possible. He had so many questions for them. The bears taught him about so many things. He was sure the dogs would too. He would free these dogs someday; but not today.

The Limo was in the driveway and the lights were on in the lab. He entered the cellar via the side doors. His head was, so close to the ceiling in the lab, it made it easy for him to listen. Angelo was dead and Babe would be reanimated. The last thought sent shivers down his spine.

A companion; how he had longed for this since his early days of understanding when all the rejection of others painfully flooded his soul. He had seen lovers walking in private places and blushed at his voyeurism but how he hungered for a loving touch. He imagined himself holding Stacia in a passionate embrace but in fact he knew she could never be his. How could he even dare to wish it? But the lovely Babe was just inches away in her sleep of death waiting to be awakened.

He knew that wicked as she had been to endanger so many with the plague of Desomorphine, she too would suffer. She would become a slave to Romeo Lupo bound to do his dirty bidding on his bed and in the world. Lovely Babe; could Frankie reform her and make this remarkable creature a vehicle for good? Only if she wanted it so? And what were the chances of that? Then again, how shallow he was; how faithless. Dante had descended into hell to rescue his Beatrice in the Divine Comedy and Frankie thought to settle for another love so soon in place of his Stacia. No, he simply could not, even if she never loved him.

His solitude was now mitigated by his family of friends and his fruitful work. He also had the warm touch of Ann, the compassion and guidance of Fergus and the sweet adoration of little Dee-Dee. What more could he possibly want? God in heaven had provided for him richly. He would not compromise that or them for a possible liaison with a vamp. She would probably prove to be like the mythical Pandora, and open a cask of terrors into his precious world of good. If his strength and intelligence was great his heart was greater and it was already almost filled with all he would ever need.

He would return to see Babe's progress but not for himself, for the safety of the world. Lupo was alive and how he wished he had it in him to squash him like a bug and leave the woman to her fate as a corps. Spiritual warriors cannot however, use the weapons of their enemies. He would leave this in greater hands than his.

That night Jean Luc and Andre had quite a conversation in which pieces of puzzles were filled by both of them. The social worker had after all caught a glimpse of Frankie in his own kitchen long ago as he had been serving unmarked medications to his mother. He now realized this had to be the same strange guardian angel that had delivered him from the bloodthirsty cur who hunted people in the night. There was also the question of all the gifts, the tickets to France and everything else they had received anonymously and the matter of his sister when she was abducted then rescued in such a bizarre way.

Andre had up to now, thought the Alien a help rather than a hindrance. Because of this he had placed this case on the back burner of his professional agenda while putting it at the top of his personal one. This strange being had something to do with his brother and was working for good in an eccentric sort of way but-- this business with unmarked drugs-- this was definitely illegal and possibly dangerous. In the investigation the drugs were found to be absolutely benign. No harm was done to Ms. De Lacy and in fact she swore they did her a lot of good without addiction and that was confirmed by her doctors.

Could this have anything to do with the recent wave in recovery of so many addicts like Elaina and James? The Alien had something to do with Elaina he was certain. What was all this about? Who was this guy who could do all these remarkable things? Perhaps he was an alien--from an advanced civilization. Perhaps he was the devil himself.

Jean Luc requested the detective keep him in the loop if anything more was brought to light about this Giant. He felt sure it had something to do with his family and he had a right to know. In fact it was time to have a real conversation with his mother about it. Andre told Jean Luc he had been watching his house and had seen the Giant casting his shadow by his kitchen window at least once. He promised the young man he would be informed and he asked him to let him know if he uncovered anything else when he spoke to Ann.

Jean Luc walked into his house shaken to find Ann reading a magazine and sipping hot coco. By his bedraggled look and his rumpled clothing she assumed he had a rough night and that his business with Luna had not gone well. She offered him some coco and he looked at her like a disgruntled parent. She knew something was up, and it was.

Stacia had been worried about Jean Luc's trouble with Luna and his tardiness on a work night. She had the next day off for parent teacher day preparations and she had been up late reading. When she heard him come in she came down and poured some chocolate. Her feet up on the chair and her bathrobe around her legs she sat and listened then added what she knew. At the end of the conversation all was revealed. They all knew their family was at the hub of many remarkable events concerning a being that both unnerved and protected them. They determined upon a plan to discover more. The next time the Big Guy brought medicine he would be invited in and the whole family would be there to greet him.

Stein had been thinking a great deal about the reanimation of Babe. He knew it could go well or it could go badly. He did not want it to come back to bite him. Being the re-animator of a new kind of being would always bring them back to him and that was just more invasion than he was prepared to live with. Frankie was so innocent and benevolent. He had almost gotten used to having him around but Babe would be an incredible complication and would probably make demands that would equal or exceed Lupo's. With two such tyrants in his world he might just as well off himself.

To prevent this he would need one of them to control the other. Lupo wanted this too. He wanted to be in charge. How can you control a female titian? The only answer was pain. He had installed a limited form of NAI into the nervous system of the body. This version would give her tutorials to bring her understanding up to a graduate level in liberal arts and it would also control the pain and pleasure centers.   A far more sophisticated version of this had been placed in his first reanimate but Stein would do the female viper no such favors and the original version had been destroyed by Frankie anyway at his inception.

This NAI Safely installed he also designed an external remote control. Thinking back he wished he had installed something like this in Frankie but hindsight is 20/20. He hadn't thought of it and it was too late for that now. The remote would be placed in the hands of the happy Lupo and that would help him to keep his love interest in check, even against her hostile wishes. As for Babe she would be in torment but no more than she, in Steins opinion, deserved. The sedative was also prepared for her and this ensured that any outburst would happen in the privacy of Lupo's home. Stein still hoped she would burst her bonds someday and kill the Don. If Stein ever had an inclination to pray that would have been his fervent request.

The process was scheduled for the day after Angelo's funeral. Lupo lost no time in paying the priest handsomely for lying about his son at the grave side and left the reception early while the rest of the family still enjoyed the pasta and the open bar.

His arrival at the lake mansion was timely, as Babe had just been hit with 30,000 amperes of current and was quivering on the table.   Stein requested the Don wait in the living area till he removed hoses and electrodes. After this Lupo would not allow a man's hands on his woman and so he threatened the life of the ditzy nurse and forced her to dress Babe in an off white negligee and dressing gown from the exclusive "Bella Bella". This was after all to be her unveiling and Lupo wanted at least a virginal appearance. Bright white and the aloe green of her skin were not however, a good compliment, and Lupo may have been a devil but his taste was impeccable.

The eyes opened abruptly and the nurse had to be carried out in a faint. Stein was pretty sure she would be liquidated and he pitied her and the doctor who would miss her. But this was Lupo's way. Babe's eyes and her skin were a different shade of yellow and green when compared to Frankie's. He had residue of Spanish, Middle Eastern and Native American brown with red overtones which made his green closer to the color of fatigues or army green. Babe was almost translucent white in her life time with flaming red hair resembling the Tudor Queens of England. When she was reanimated she had the creamy color of palest mint with piercing yellow eyes that resembled a cougar's.

She needed no help sitting up and her posture was regal and deliberate. Lupo's temperature rose and his jaw dropped in awe at what he was beholding. He had leered at women and used or abused them frequently but here was one he could regard with a strange piety. He stood in front of her hovering his hand over her breast afraid to touch and with one dainty hand she gave him a shove that tossed him to the other side of the room. The scientist made a mental note for more sedation in the future.

Stein had already given Lupo a primer on the use of the remote but in his arrogance he thought he would not need it. His fantasies of Babe included her devotion and gratitude for her resurrection. He forgot that the last thing she might remember would be the fact that he killed her. As a man who understood "tit for tat" he was prepared to forgive this first reaction, but hereafter he would require obedience. She stood and looked at him with the eyes of a snake and the menace of a predator then he pressed the button that brought her to her knees in pain.

Andre had a lot to think about and one of his questions had to do with Jasmine. Her brother James had been one of the "wave of recovery" addicts and she was on board with turning a blind eye to some of the evidence coming forward on the Alien. She wanted him to keep doing what he was doing even if it was technically illegal. They had busted more real criminals since his appearance in one year than they had in the 5 years before. She had been sick of going after minor offenders when the real fiends were getting away. She was sleeping better at night now that many of these criminal superstars were busted and she loved her brother's new life and direction. He was doing well in school and now he had a new hobby and new sober friends. He wouldn't talk about it but as long as he was clean and sober she was ok with it.

Andre wondered how much he could trust her with all these new discoveries. Yeah the Alien was a vigilante but he was also practicing medicine without a license. Then again where was he getting his money? Or was he just continuing to pirate chemicals from the mob? Word was the mob was now using drones for chemical shipments. Was the Alien in on this? Krokodil was now the going thing eclipsing even Fentanyl. Was the "wave of recovery" a set up for this new scourge? If it was, this made the Alien a fiend; but that was not like his brother Frank. Back to the first question, SHOULD HE TALK TO JASMINE? The answer had to be yes. His judgment was compromised and he needed the accountability.

James and Elaina had been seeing each other for a few weeks now. Working for Frankie had brought them together and they became committed not just to the work but to each other. Dee Dee loved James and James thought she was teachable, cute and oh so sweet. Like Frankie, he believed she was one of heaven's angels that had just decided to live here. Frankie was mending from his wounds and work for distribution was done for now so James and Elaina decided to go home and take care of some personal business. James wanted to stop off and see his sister and they couldn't have picked a better time.

Andre was there and he had been talking to Jasmine about everything. James and Elaina just had a feeling about it all and they began to ask questions.

"So you caught the Alien yet? You been chasing that guy a long time huh?"

Andre caught the inflection and got suspicious.

"Yeah he's a slippery kind of guy. He must have a lot of friends covering for him."

Elaina had been there before with Andre and she didn't want to play.

"Why don't you guys go bust a crack den or chase Krok dealers instead of somebody who is busting up pedophiles and wife beaters and dirty senators then handing them to you in a basket?"

"Elaina we hear this guy is practicing medicine without a license. That could be dangerous. What do you think about that?"

"I still think he's doing more good than harm. It's the mob you need to tussle with not the Alien."

James had to step in. He put his arms around Jasmine and Andre and said.

"That's where my man and my big sister were last night. Doing just that; tussling with the mob in a hail of bullets. And look at them, Andre looks a little rough but sis is beautiful as ever and not a scratch. In fact I heard some creature showed up and the Alien too. Isn't that what happened?"

Andre's eyes opened like saucers and Elaina pinched James behind his back. Andre noticed and commented,

"As it happens that is exactly what came down. But it's not what we released to the papers. So how did you know?"

James mumbled something about his boys in the Bronx, and how they told him what they saw. Then he added that's all he knew, but both Jasmine and Andre were not convinced. The couple made a hasty exit and Jasmine determined she would keep her eyes open.

When James and Elaina were in the car they called the "tree house," as they had dubbed Frankie's place, immediately. Fully aware that phone calls and text messages could be used against them they measured their words. Rosa answered and she gave the phone to Gunta.

"Look, things are getting a little hot out here. People are saying the Alien is practicing medicine without a license. My cousin Andre the detective said so."

"Wow that's weird. Hey you guys coming over? We're having a get together and everyone is anxious to hear what is going on with you two. I mean you'll be moving into her place soon won't you?"

Elaina played along.

"Whaat? Who said that? We're just dating." James chimed in.

"Yeah, man this is the woman I have waited for." Elaina took the phone off of speaker."

"Don't believe everything you hear. We'll be there to straighten you all out tonight."

Gunta sighed with relief knowing they would come in to fill them in and added,

"Bring some chips and dip we're having chicken and roasted veggies."

"Might be late but we'll be there."

Babe sat like a manikin in a chair by the window as Lupo dragged a comb along her long red locks. She tried to move to prevent him but he pressed on the remote and she kept still. She was dressed in a Paris original dress a ruby color to match her hair with a lacy collar and an unusual angular cut. It was more fru fru than anything she would choose for herself and the heels were lower than she was used to wearing but she had no choice. The wardrobe was chosen for her just like the life. She felt she would rather be dead.

Lupo had determined he would take things slow. He wanted her but it would not do to make love to a robotic doll. He wanted to win her. He gave her leave to spend time alone and this she used to learn her lessons. Within a week she recalled enough with the help of NAI to know who she had been, who Lupo was and to know how much she detested him. She also remembered she had been set up by Alexi for this she would make him pay. Her strategy was to play dumb so Lupo would not suspect. She asked him for things and teased him but would always retract her affections at the last minute. This was getting to him but it was also working. The moment he let down his guard the remote would be hers and he would be dead. That was the plan but if need be she would fight through the pain at some point and get the remote away from him or die trying. This is what she lived for.

Andre lived in a condo with all the amenities his meager salary could buy. In particular he enjoyed the little balcony on which he had his garden. In Venezuela he had learned gardening with his grandfather on summer vacations and competed with Frankie to grow the best avocado plants. He started one the year Frankie disappeared and it now had bark and would bear fruit soon but only if he could get another avocado tree to cross pollinate with it. His brother Frankie had always furnished one in their youth but at this point Andre had not found one.

On this day he had shut the sliding door to the balcony as usual and locked it, as was his custom. He went to the gym that morning and he had a good work out completed by a five mile run. His sweats and hoodie had large patches of perspiration at his chest and pits. He earned that sweat and his reward was waiting for him in the form of lemonade made with the lemons from a little tree he had grown himself over the last few years.

As he walked into his apartment and bee lined it to the fridge he noticed his balcony door was opened and the curtains were waving gently in the breeze. He picked up the gun he had in the holster by the kitchen door and quietly looked around. He was used to keeping his cool in high anxiety situations but his eyes widened and his pulse began to race when he saw a Giant sitting on his living room floor with his ammo in the palm of his large hand. Then the Titan in the hoodie smiled and said,

"It took twenty five years but consider this pay back."

13

Woman on a string

This was a very emotional moment for both Frankie and Andre. Beginning conversation was a series of starts and stops. They kept sort of fumbling with their words. So they decided to eat something. But the first problem was Andre did not have enough lemonade for Frankie and himself. In fact like a typical bachelor who works more hours than he should, he had only a two week old half eaten salami sub in the fridge. Everything he ate or drank except his homemade lemonade was from a stand, bar or a restaurant. This situation was, to a Hispanic, with the cultural priority of hospitality, unacceptable. Further, for someone he cherished and had not seen in years it was totally scandalous. He was ashamed. Frankie came to the rescue,

"We could have some pizza. I hear they deliver."

They called the local pizza place and soon they had 5 large New York pizzas at the door. One was meat and veggie and four were simply veggie as Frankie was a vegetarian. They also brought some soda for Andre and a gallon of ice tea for Frank. Then conversation was possible.

Andre had not seen his brother for years, but he had not seen this big guy ever. Andre's instinct told him this was Frankie and he introduced himself as Frankie but he was obviously someone or something else. Andre was honest and told him so.

"Thank you for your honesty. I know you want very badly to see your brother and I want to be that brother very badly, you can trust me on that. But I have to tell you truly...only part of me is Frank the rest is 4 other men that I know nothing about."

Andre had no response to that. He could see this hulking creature could not be a normal human being. He also could see the scars and places on his hands and arms that might have been pieced together. But what other proof of what he was saying did he have?

"I'm a detective. I work with evidence. Do you have proof of what you are saying?"

Frankie sighed and lifted up his shirt. He showed a bullet wound there that had healed long ago.

"I was wounded in the recent battle under the highway in the Bronx. And you can see that those are still healing. But this one is an old wound inflicted by me when you angered me by taking the rest of Papi's ammo."

"No me hables con balas."

"Yeah."

"So you're saying you are a composite man, put together by a scientist you wish to protect for now, who put you together at the behest of Romeo Lupo. Is that right?"

"Pretty much."

"But Lupo doesn't know you exist."

"Well he knows I exist as "the Alien" but he doesn't know I am a product of his personal graveyard. My doctor told him I was destroyed. Lupo funded my doctor's reanimation research because he wanted to live forever. He heard my doctor could bring back the dead, theoretically, and he got everything that was needed by the doctor to do the job. He even provided the 'raw materials' or pieces of human bodies for him to work on. My doctor did not know who these people were. He just used them to make me. One of them was Frank."

"How did you find out that Frank was one of them?"

"When I was reanimated I could not speak. I was like a large infant mentally. But I had an artifact, a spontaneous throw back to one of my parts. I said the name Frank something and a string of numbers. My doctor only remembered the Frank and part of the numbers 571."

"127-69-9571. That was Frankie's dog tag number. When he was going into the army we had a party. He kept saying that if he was caught as a prisoner and tortured all they would get out of him was Private Frank Poloche 127-69-9571. He said it so many times, to so many people at his send off, that I remember it."

"I'll admit I was in a lot of pain when I was reanimated. Perhaps the Frankie part of me thought it was being tortured. Any way I didn't say anything after that till NAI taught me speech."

"NAI? You mean some kind of artificial intelligence?"

"Yes, do you know it?"

"A little bit, I heard this tech was in its infancy. Do you mean you have a computer brain?"

"No I have a human one but I am assisted in learning by NAI. This is something woven into my nervous system. My doctor did not want to be bothered with schooling a large child."

All of a sudden it hit Andre that his brother was really dead but not entirely. He got uncomfortably emotional.

"My mother was heartbroken when Frankie disappeared. I was too and wondered for so long what might have happened. I knew he would reach me somehow if he were still alive and...and you finally did, but this, isn't anything I could have expected. You are him but not. I don't know whether to go with the fact that he's dead or that he is still alive."

"I wish I could help you with that. I wish I could be your brother. I want to be because I desperately need family, but I also want to know who the others were. Will you help me find out?"

Andre phoned work and told them he needed to be away for a few days on family business. He hadn't taken a vacation or time off for almost four years and he was long overdue. No one argued about it. He told them he would call when the business was concluded. Then he pulled out his phone and started to look things up. Frankie told him NAI could give him a bigger picture and he asked him what to look up. Andre said, "The New York Citizen's Coalition for Human Rights and Safety."

As Frankie projected this into the air he asked why Andre had brought this up. Andre explained,

"The year 2004 brought a lot of race related violence to the city after a series of killings that were thought to be racially oriented. Jews, Blacks, Native Americans and Hispanics were the targets and white supremacist material was found at the site of the mass killing of eight students and one teacher at Columbia University. The students were all of the racial backgrounds I just mentioned and those of us who were investigating at the time naturally assumed the motive was racial. The publicity behind the whole affair ran with that and it caught the attention of the governor and the senate.

Because of this a coalition was formed by religious and governmental representatives to create awareness against anti-Semitism and racism. A large press conference took place with representatives of government, clergy and the faculty and student council of Columbia. One of the main speakers was the brother of one of the students who were killed. He was Native American; a 13 year old prodigy and already a chemistry sophomore at the university. This was a genius kid who had been in the shooting and lost two of his fingers trying unsuccessfully to shield his older sister.”

“This case more than any other, taught me never to assume. We later discovered that it was actually mob related and that Orlando Lupo (Romeo's father who died shortly after) had ordered the hit because he had discovered the Jewish teacher was secretly courting his daughter. Orlando wouldn't have that and had him killed. His students just happened to get in the way. This turned out to be Romeo's début as Don of the family because his dad's heart attack gave him the opportunity.

The coalition was almost disbanded but instead took up the cause against the Young Don. “Stop the Violence”, was their mantra. But Lupo as always had sharks for lawyers and they got him off even as witnesses and anti violence activists mysteriously disappeared, eight people in all. My brother and the Native boy were among them.”

Frankie saw where this was going even as Andre stared at this long black hair. The year Andre was talking about was the year he was reanimated. The boy sounded like the one Stein had mentioned. All this was very curious.

“Andre, I once questioned my doctor about the people who made up my body. He told me one was a dark boy with long hair and two fingers missing. What are the chances that two such young men would disappear at the same time?”

“I would say the chances are there was only one kid with that description.”

“What was the boy's name?”

“George Little Bear of the Oneida.”

“There was a eulogy I suppose.”

“Well, since there was no body his family didn't have a funeral. They kept thinking he would return.”

“But his sister had a eulogy.”

"Yes she did, her name was Sparrow; Sparrow Little Bear. She was a singer and was working on her thesis in Native Languages. George played the guitar for her and she played the drum. I went to the wake and paid my respects. They had a film showing at the funeral home of the two of them performing together. It was impressive; heart breaking really."

Frankie was very pensive. Both men were silent for a while. Then Andre spoke.

"I have a dilemma Frank. You are doing a few things that are not exactly within the law. I suspect there may be more things that are sketchy about your activities and as a detective I'm supposed to bring that to your attention and maybe even into the light. I would hate to do that because of all the good you do but it's my job. You aren't exactly my brother but then again you may be. Either way it's my duty to warn you. Do you understand me? "

"Completely, and I will consider what you say. You are a good officer. I'm trying to do the right thing but, in case you haven't noticed, justice is not being served for a lot of people in your world. I am thinking of ways I could do the things I do without breaking the rules but I haven't figured it out yet. When I do I will let you know. Till then I will continue doing what I do because a lot of special people are depending on me."

Andre admired his candor and it so sounded like Frank to say such things, but his hands were tied.

"Ok Frank, we understand each other. I'm not sure what I want to do about this either. I can't be an accessory to crime but justice is also what I am about and I'm sick of people getting legally away with murder just because they have the money to get them off. Best keep me in the dark about your activities because if I feel you are really crossing a line I will have to book you."

"You mean like when I hang 'em high?"

"I didn't hear that, but well, when you treat people medically without a license or when you give people medicine that is not approved by the FDA, or where you get your money Frank? You spend like a rich man, giving people tickets to France and getting people apartments and such. The scariest thing though is covering up for a mad scientist who is an accessory to mob murder. These are serious things."

Frankie began to doubt himself. He had never considered that what he did was stealing. He considered it more like redistribution of fund from those who had surplus to those who were needy. He had never mentioned the name of his re-animator but now he knew Stein was an accessory to murder. On the other hand Frankie wouldn't be here if he hadn't been and so many people would not have been helped. They both absolutely had some thinking to do. Frankie stood up and picked up the empty pizza boxes and crushed them into a tiny wad. He then took the compacted wad into the kitchen and tossed it in the trash. He spoke from the kitchen,

"Those are all good questions. I am beginning to see what you mean. I will have better answers for you when I have thought about all these things. As for right now, I have to go."

"Well now wait a minute Frank, I want some answers right now."

Andre listened for a response and none came. He called to Frank in the kitchen and still no response. He got up and walked into the kitchen then realized Frankie was gone. He had slipped silently out the window through the balcony twelve flights up. There was no sign of him. In fact Andre almost wondered if this were all some strange hallucination he had just had.

If it was real the giant must have climbed up the other balconies to the fifteenth floor and then up to the roof. The point was he was gone and what could the detective possibly report about such a visit? Besides, who would believe it? He wondered if he should even tell Jasmine? What proof did he have of any of this? Was he going mad? He stood there looking at the plants on the balcony as the tumult in his mind bandied him about. Then suddenly he realized that instead of one avocado plant about three feet tall, with bark forming on the trunk in an ornate pot, there were two and next to them was a huge wet moccasin print in some potting soil on the floor. Then he heard his phone ding with a notification and he looked at his texts. There was one from an anonymous caller who left him this message:

"I know things but don't know how I know them. These bits of thought are to me like a ghost limb, amputated but still in pain. The wonder is, I remember for all those who are a part of me. I am we and we are I. For instance I see two boys watching spaghetti westerns then playing cowboys and Indians. I am glad to have met one of them today."

Andre sank into a kitchen chair and wept.

Frank now had a great deal to think about. He thought he was helping people but now this person who had instantly become so important to him was telling him he had broken the law. He was a criminal. Lupo was a criminal? Could it be that he was like Lupo? When he had looked at the system of money all over the world he could not understand why so many people in the world had such a hard life because they didn't have any money and just a few people had life so easy because they had lots of money. Could it be that some people were supposed to be sick or hungry and die because they were poor? Was this alright? It did not seem so. He honestly did not understand. It was so easy to move money with NAI and help people get well and live a better life. Why couldn't that be the way things went instead of the way they were now?

At his palatial home in Chelsea everything should have been going perfectly for Lupo. Lupo's boy was still missed but frankly, he had been rather a challenge for the Don of late and it was better that he rest in peace than that he keep lapping water out of the toilet. Lupo attributed this flaw to Stein's drunkenness and was glad he had been sober for Babe. She was flawless except for the green tinge in her skin and the yellow eyes which were alluring indeed. He was crazy about her.

The greatest feature about this whole thing was of course the remote. The Don had always had complete control over his relationships by gift or by force, but Babe was not easy. He liked her resistance and strength. Every encounter was like another conquest. If she were easy he would have begun to disdain her the way he had Angelo's submissive mother or even the greedy Wanda who was easy to buy with a fur or diamond bauble. These women were boring and predictable. But not Babe; she was vicious and exciting, like impending death. She was his match in every way. But you can't take fire to bed without getting burned. So this "remote" Stein had given him was, to him, the best thing since the Uzi.

The remote was on a wrist device as he requested so that it could not be easily removed. When she wouldn't come to him he would bring her to him with pain. When she wouldn't dress or even speak the way he wanted her to the hurt would be applied. Sometimes he would let her go, with her words at least, just so he could punish her. She was like a beautiful but furious animal and he had no scruples about chastizing her to tame her, in every way.

As for Babe, she dreamed of ripping off his arm and taking the device then feeding him slowly feet first into a raging fire. The torment he put her through would have been horrible for any woman but for one who was used to control and dominance it was like suffering the tortures of the damned. Sometimes when she realized how futile resistance was she wanted to die. When Lupo discovered this he had her sedated and bound at night so he could sleep. Mostly she just obsessed about escape but at times she wondered if she was being punished by some great Warden in the sky for all the horrible things she had done.

The situation looked bleak for her till one day Lupo decided to go to Stein's lake house for some maintenance on the device. He took her with him of course.

While they were there Babe had seen the lake and the ducks and asked to be allowed to go feed them. She was forced to passionately kiss him before she went but since the remote had a mile radius Lupo thought what could be the harm. Marko was sent to watch her holding a long range dart gun with enough sedation to bring down a horse. Besides she was dressed in a tight skirt she could not run in and he wanted to talk to Stein privately about certain features of the remote and the rest of the equipment.

Lupo also encouraged Stein to keep working on the melanin issue. When the time came for his own reanimation he would rather not be green and if Babe could be brought back to her original color he would like the change. In fact, he thought, if she could turn different colors it would be even better. Stein secretly rolled his eyes and said he would work on it and Babe went down to the lake.

The creaturely act of tossing bread to birds was surprisingly delightful to Babe. Any change to the Don's constant attention was a plus, but this was even more so as she was relatively alone. Any moment away from him was a cause for celebration but the day was particularly lovely and the setting peaceful. She almost relaxed.

Her hyper-vigilance however, was never off. As a bounty hunter she was always aware of her surroundings and the recent re-animation had for better or worst heightened her senses. Ever on the alert for a chance to escape she noticed Marko leave his post for a moment to help bring in some body bags with contents for Stein's experiments. Quickly she surmised that having previously run a seven minute mile in her former life, now she might cover that distance in four. She ripped the side of her skirt, ditched the heels and took off like a gazelle.

The woods were not as easy to navigate in four minutes as was an asphalt stretch of road but she feared she would be discovered and intensified the pace. Bare feet were not easy to navigate over sticks and bramble. If she could make it to the highway she might flag down a car. With her skin color she might have a hard time with this but she had a silk scarf and her stockings covered her legs. She hoped against hope she would make it... and then she ran into HIM.

For a split second she saw what she thought was a large shadow in the woods. She was certain he had been in front of her and then without a sound like a ghost he vanished. She had seen this Shadow before. She had observed him speaking kindly at a window to an old blind woman and noted his expertise at covert movement. All records showed the Alien to be benevolent if unorthodox. This creature would not hurt her and might even help her. She took a chance.

"I know you are there." She whispered into the woods. "Help me, bad men are chasing me. Please, help."

Frankie had learned much about human beings and was hesitant. He weighed the possibility that she was lying and that this was a trap but he saw no weapons. He spoke back and the resonance of his voice warmed her.

"Who are you running from?"

"Romeo Lupo, he controls and tortures me with a device. I hate him. He is visiting the house up there and I need your help to get away. Please, my feet are bruised and bleeding. Help me."

Frankie hesitated but then thought he could not leave anyone to Lupo's mercy, no matter what they had done. They both stepped into the light of the clearing and he realized he was speaking to the re-animated woman he had seen at Stein's house. She confirmed that she was in the presence of the Shadow and now she knew he was a re-animated man. He lifted her up like a feather and started running.

A few moments later she began to squirm and groan like she was in pain. So much so that he almost dropped her. She explained in hoarse groans that Lupo was controlling her NAI and he accelerated his pace. She said that almost certainly he was in a car looking for her and that the range of the control device was a mile. Frankie quickly calculated the only way to beat it was to go up. So up and up they went into the hills. Till finally the pain subsided and she went limp in his arms.

He had never held a woman except for Stacia and she had been wrapped in a thick blanket. This woman was lovely and she had no scars that he could see except on her feet. Why were the bots not repairing her as they did him? He considered and finally concluded she had not been given many bots if any but he said nothing. She had been involved with Lupo and he still didn't trust her. He wondered if the device that tortured her might have a GPS. He asked and when she could finally talk she said she did not think so. She had attempted a few escapes and he never knew where to find her. He just kept applying the pain till she could not move and his boys could locate her. It had been brutal.

The place he took her was an old camp site of his. There they found the remains of an extinguished camp fire and a large pot for cooking. Neither of them felt the chill so he did not bother with a fire. He spoke little but he brought her berries, herbs and mushrooms and she wondered if he was an idiot or if he was just the strong silent type. When he finally began to give her a detailed run down on edible plants in the area she realized he was no mental slouch. Naming them all, including mushrooms and even saying their Latin names he proved his eloquence and intelligence. She reminded him she had NAI too but he soon asked her some questions and he understood her NAI was not the same as his. She realized this as well and assessing her rescuer she came to the conclusion her only advantage was in her cunning.

They chatted and she wanted to know all about him. He was not forthcoming but if she told him something about herself then she said he was obliged to share one thing about himself. This seemed fair to him so he played the game. She told him that Lupo had killed her and re-animated her because she did not love him and he wanted her. Frankie was angry at this and harrumphed like a bear. He told her he had been with bears in his early reanimated life. She thought this was funny but reasonable.

She was so beautiful. He thought of how Stacia had been taken for her beauty and that perhaps this woman had been taken by Alexi Brueghel and given to Lupo to Abuse. He finally had to ask about this and when she said, "yes" he soften considerably towards her. Of course she did not tell him she had been Alexi's friend and hired to hunt him. She kept it at the forefront of her thinking that Alexi would still pay for revenge. On the other hand, something inside of her was stirring concerning the Giant who had saved her, and she did something she did not expect to do. She told him her real name was Bronagh which meant "sorrowful". He said his name was Frank and a quick reference to NAI informed them both it meant "French man." But he did not think he was French.

When she told him the meaning of her name he could see this had special meaning for her. She, on the other hand, could see he was moved. If she wanted it this guy would be putty in her hands. After all if she was free of Lupo she would need money and if she could deliver him to Alexi she would be all set for a while. She also determined he would pay in more than one way. She suspected the Austrian had delivered her to Lupo and she was not pleased. She would get his money, kill him and burgle his place, which was full of fine art and other expensive items. She would then leave the country quickly, for parts unknown, where she could receive her Krokodil revenue remotely.

The only hitch was how to wrap Frank up in a package she could deliver. She had to assess all his capabilities. Knowing your target was crucial to one's success as a bounty hunter but this case, by all counts, would be a challenge. This was complicated by the next morning as he had disappeared leaving her some berries and a rudimentary map drawn on birch bark with charcoal from the campfire. It crudely depicted her whereabouts and how to get to the city by keeping to the higher ground of the conservation land. She understood it would be the only way to keep from Lupo's remote. Alongside the map was a pair of homemade sandals. She supposed he had crafted them from his own knee high moccasins. She was impressed by his consideration but she also felt abandoned. She had always been the "dumper" and now she was the "dumpee". She was indignant.

14

Seven Deadly Sins

Frankie realized that a visit to Stein was out of the question at the moment. "Besides", he thought, "Fergus was far more to the purpose just now." He needed to know the truth about himself and surely that was a spiritual as well as a physical question. Besides he needed to tell the priest about his visit with Andre. Fergus would surely want to know how that went.

Seated on the rectory floor, the priest and the Titan sipped tea. Fergus from a cup and Frankie from a pitcher; both refilled several times. Their conversations were always long and full of questions. Frank told him of the bitter sweet visit he had with Andre. He had so hoped to be helpful but instead seemed to disturb the detective. Fergus said it was all part of the grieving process. One had to come to terms with the loss through cycles of denial, sadness, anger and finally acceptance. There were people who got stuck along the way. Obviously this would help Andre come out of denial, but what of his accusations? Frankie would have to deal with those.

"I don't think you meant any harm in your dealings. You have been innocent and you just wanted to help. In fact you did help."

"But it's illegal. Andre could 'book' me. He wouldn't do that would he?"

"Well it's his job to book people who steal but you didn't know what you were doing. Still the law will not see it that way."

"Money is such an enigmatic thing. People put such importance on it but you can't eat it or love it."

"It brings people power. It is evil but it can also do good. I'm afraid I have had these thoughts myself and come to little resolution."

"Are people supposed to be poor?"

"I don't think it was part of God's original plan but it's a consequence of sin."

"And what is sin?"

"Sin is simply evil but for Jews and Christians it is the violation of the law or The Ten Commandments one of which is 'do not steal'.

"I understand that because it goes on to say one must not take things that belong to others. But all I did was move some ones and zeros with NAI and people were able to get what they needed and live."

"Well yes but..."

"And no one noticed the ones and zeros. I moved them from those who had so many ones and zeros they never missed them."

"Well yes but..." Fergus sighed then continued. "Alright, another way to describe sin is more classic way or -- a manifestation of the seven deadly sins."

"What are those?"

"Let me see, um, well there is pride, greed, sloth, envy, gluttony, wrath and of course lust."

"And these sins are deadly. Which means they kill correct?"

"Yes my son, sin kills and separates us from God. What others think is not as important as what separates us from God. "

This made sense to Frank because, he had never been so at peace and happy, as he was when he was with God in the wilderness, or when he was helping others. His life would be misery without these things.

"Jesus said there were two commandments more important than the rest didn't he?"

"Yes, Love God and love your neighbor as yourself. How did you know?"

"Just one of those artifacts. It just came to me."

"Some part of you must have read the Bible at one time. What a wonder you are my son. By the way, don't you think you should look at the list of people that disappeared during the disbanding of the group Andre talked about? You might find more of your people there. I did find one memorial service that happened at that time (2004). It was pretty high profile. It was the memorial of Senator Edmund Shea. He spearheaded that very Coalition Andre spoke of and he disappeared right around that time. A good Catholic and a champion of justice he was. His dear wife Kathleen was crushed and spent their last dollar searching for him without success. Their three children support her now but she went through a terrible spell. I got all this from my bishop who presided over the memorial service at St Patrick's Cathedral."

"Something calls to me about this Fergus. But first I have to ask my doctor some questions and then I am going to see some Oneida Indians about a Little Bear."

Stein had to drink gallons of fluid all the time even if it wasn't alcohol. He had taken to drinking tea and caffeinated drinks continuously and by the pitcher full. It was at least some tiny compensation for the booze but these could not bring him the blackout he needed and pot was his only ally there. He puffed and drank tea and hoped Lupo and his morose men wouldn't come back for a long time. Marko's body was on his table as Lupo had wasted no time in dispatching him for his failure to keep track of Babe. Stein had spent all afternoon and evening experimenting with his coloring without success and was weary of it all. He moved the table to the vats and pressed the hydraulics then watched Marko slide down and disappear under the flesh eating solution. At least this kept his lab clean. He would start again with the other bodies the next day; another day another corps. He didn't like his job and he wished many times he had gone into physics instead.

When he heard the zapping noise of static on the surveillance he welcomed the thought of a visit from Frankie. He still hoped someday, Frank would deal with Lupo for him. He wasn't happy about the news Frankie brought.

"You told a detective about me?"

"No name, no location."

"Well I've always known it was a matter of time till Lupo killed me or the police picked me up and somebody "took me out" in prison."

"I will protect you as much as I can."

"Why? You of all people."

"You are my father."

"How ever did you get so sentimental? And I'm not your father but thanks."

"You're all I've got."

"So Babe is on the loose. She'll want to kill me too and I don't blame her."

"She will stay away from here."

"No she will hunt me down and try to make me reprogram her NAI. That is unless you can charm her. If you kill Lupo she's yours."

"She doesn't see me that way."

"Give it time. She will have her own problems with people soon enough."

"She is beautiful and the size of normal women. She will be accepted; even desired."

"You like her don't you. Admit it. If you see her again explain to her I had no choice. I can help her to get free if she will help me."

"I won't be an accessory to murder. Even to the murder of a man like Lupo."

"Even the saintly Bonheoffer wanted Hitler dead and Lupo is a little Hitler. Do the world a favor."

"Someday I will turn him over to Andre as a present, but not yet, not till I know more. Now tell me about the boy with two fingers."

As always Stein became an emotional mess when asked about that subject. Frankie began to realize the trauma Stein had brought upon himself and how fragile his feelings were. That traumatic stress surely fueled his use of intoxicants but he needed to purge all this or he would never be free of it. So Frankie pressed him and he finally started talking.

Frankie's brain had been chosen from the boy as it proved to be the most robust of all the subjects. One other was also impressive (the old man's) but it had been damaged. He had taken the hands from him as they were large and strong and registered neurologically with great dexterity. The body was taken from the two taller men in the bunch. One he assumed was Frank Poloche who had a large chest and muscular upper arms along with a strong spine. The face was mostly Frank's with high cheek bones that were rugged but now badly scared. The lips were full but broken in a few places and very twisted. The forehead also bore a broad scare straight across it. But the eyes belonged to the boy. They were large and inquiring full of a thirst for knowledge. The rest of the body was from a tall man with muscular runner's legs and large feet.

The internal organs belonged to the fifth man who had a clean powerful heart along with great lungs and kidneys. All he could say about him was that he was a black man. The result was a seven foot jigsaw puzzle with green skin, vast intellect and a poetic soul.

This was more or less what Frankie needed to know. It would help him match people up with data from his queries. Somehow he also needed to know this for the sake of the people he might meet who were grieving family. Every little bit might help them in their process of loss. He was not certain now about his other activities with addicts and he was worried about the unchecked spread of Krokodil, but what he was certain about was that he needed to pursue this.

As for the seven deadly sins he would test himself for these and this might give him moral direction. He knew from Fergus the solution for a soul's corruption was repentance and forgiveness so he entered his introspection with hope that the results would be another step towards peace and perhaps even joy. In his conversations with God he asked for illumination.

It was time to make his delivery to Ann and he could almost taste the fresh bread with butter and honey that he would receive from her. He had the medicine with him and was about to climb down from the fire escape of a building across the way. When he spotted a black Mercedes sedan he had noticed before. Inside was a hooded figure that appeared to be watching the house. He waited and the figure just watched. His deliveries were usually at around 9:00 but he called Ann and told her the delivery would be late and kept watching. After about 11:00 the car drove away and Frank followed it. Its destination was a building in Soho, in a very high end neighborhood. The driver stopped and gave the keys to the valet. She then went into the building removing the hood at the very last minute to reveal a shock of red hair.

It was a warm night. Stacia and Lukas were watching a film and Ann decided to come out onto the porch for a breath of fresh air. The footsteps of the big man could not be heard by most, but her keen ears that compensated for her blindness knew he was approaching right away. He sat by her and she patted his head. Then she gave him a piece of bread slathered in butter and honey and she heard him make satisfied noises. She giggled then became suddenly serious,

"Frank, we have a big sadness in the house."

"Why what is wrong? Is Stacia alright?"

"She is fine. But Jean Luc is crushed as his love interest Luna, has become addicted to the Krokodil."

"This is tragic indeed."

"I know he has seen you. He told me everything about that terrible night."

"Does he still hate me?"

"No I do not." Frankie turned to see not only Jean Luc but Stacia in the doorway. His first thought was to run but Jean Luc stopped him.

"Please don't leave."

Frankie froze and turned away from the light. He feared above all things for Stacia to see him.

"Cheri, I told them you were coming and commanded them to welcome you." Jean Luc chaffed at this and said,

"No command necessary."

Jean Luc walked up to him and offered his hand. Frankie did not know what to do so he slapped it gently in a sideways high five. Then Stacia took one arm and Jean Luc the other and she spread a blanket on the grass and they had him sit down. Stacia went in and brought out some lemonade and chips. Then they all sat on more blankets and shared their hearts. By then Jean Luc had also told Stacia that Frankie had most probably saved her. She asked him and he modestly admitted it. She thanked him very much and for the garden boxes and the tickets and all the rest. Jean Luc also thanked him, even for his mother's medicine.

To Frankie this was the realization of the dream he dared not dream. He told them how he had seen them at first and become enamored with their family and the love that was apparent between them. Now Ann said they could share that love with him and though he did not presume, his heart leaped to think they accepted him. He would do anything for the De Lacy's. But in addition to all this good will, a warning had to be issued. He explained they might be in danger. There was someone watching them, most probably to get to him. He was aware and would not let anything happen to them. This was his vow.

Then Jean Luc turned to Frankie like a desperate man and said,

"Do you have a medicine that can help those addicted to Desomorphine?" Frankie said no but promised he would turn his mind to it that very night.

Andre was free but not used to down time. He therefore turned all his attention to the mystery of his brother's disappearance. The last glimpse he saw of Frank was in footage of the Coalition where he was coming out of a meeting with lots of media coverage. He was doing security on that day and was dressed in plain clothes. Tall and muscular he was almost as tall as Senator Shea whom he was protecting; a man known for his 6'8" height and his interest in the New York Nets. There were lots of people there and among them was George Little Bear.

He phoned Jasmine who was at the station.

"Hi Jazz."

"So you finally going to Disney I hear. You might have told me."

"Something came up quick. Family related."

"Alien related you mean."

He could never get one over on her.

"Well, maybe both."

"Damn son, you doing this without me? You're a sorry ass you know that?"

"Common, help me out. We can talk when you get off tonight. This is what I need. I need any peripheral footage that there might be at NBC, CBS, ABC and Fox news rooms for the final session of the Coalition on Human Rights and Safety in 2004. I also need a list of the people who went missing after that event and any information that might be found surrounding them and their disappearance."

"You ain't asking much are ya?"

"Common Jazz, it's all in the archives somewhere?"

"Well I'm taking me some time off to go to Disney too."

"I can't get it because Feldman banned me from this information. He said I was obsessing over it."

"And whatchu doin' now?"

"I got new evidence. You do this for me and I'll take you and little Pete to the real Disney myself. I promise."

"I'll hold you to that. You just lucky nobody else 'round here wants to work with me, else I'd be doing more than just twiddling my thumbs."

"That's the price you pay for being a Diva. Now get this stuff and I'll meet you at "Fish Cheeks" at 8."

"Ooh Thai, my favorite. You got a deal. Petie is with James, Elaina and Dee Dee tonight. They are going to Chuckie Cheese."

"Perfect, see you then."

Alexi had done some redecorating, particularly to one very private room with cushioned walls, soundproofing and covered over with white satin. It also had manacles as well as other sharp and questionable wall ornaments. Babe threatened to use them on him and he feared she might make good her promise. After he begged and pleaded they brokered a deal and the Austrian agreed to everything.   She said she knew all about the Big Shadow but would not tell all. If Alexi was good to her he would get his revenge but if he was naughty he would get pain.

About her unusual pigmentation she only told him she was back from the dead and stronger than ever. Confronting him with the knowledge that he had conspired with Lupo she squeezed certain body parts that ensure maximum disquietude and reminded him that nothing would bring *him* back if he did not cooperate with her wishes. As for her plans they were in process and she would inform him on a need to know basis. She told him she would be using his place as a headquarters and that if Lupo found out Alexi would die slowly and in wretched agony. Cooperative, sore and intrigued he escorted her to the private guest quarters. Her company was a pleasure as always.

"Stacia, Oh Stacia," the thought of her ate at Frankie's dreams incessantly but now so did Babe. When he finally sat with the De Lacy's he had kept his face in the shadows and watched her averting her eyes. Her demeanor was bashful and polite but he was sure she was revolted by him as she never looked at him directly. How could she? He was hideous. Babe on the other hand looked him straight in the eyes and engaged him like an equal. He could not deny his attraction for Babe but it was not like what he felt for the lovely swan he had danced with in his imagination. Babe grappled with a different part of him. He could only call it lust and now he knew it could kill him.

Following his talk with Fergus he was becoming more and more aware of the potential evil in his own soul. He was questioning and wrestling with all that he felt inside and it was so overwhelming. People were dying out there and he could be helping them, but here he was paralyzed by introspection. Fergus had warned him about messiah complexes. He was not the savior of the world and could never be. The priest gave him a prescription of rest and prayer and he needed to take him up on that, but then there was Luna. Jean Luc was counting on him and he must not fail. And there was George Little Bear. He so wanted and needed to follow up on that. Frankie was so physically strong but inside all these things were making him mush.

Gunta had done tolerably well on his finals and was now also taking a break. He made a bucket of tea for the big Guy and a cup for himself and sat down.

"Howse it going?"

"Don't know."

Ben walked in from the back yard where he had been sunning himself. He was done with finals too and looking forward to graduation but had taken some time to visit.

"When you can't think, you can do other things to check in with what you're processing. One of my friends does art therapy and she showed me a neat exercise. Wanna try?"

Frankie shrugged his shoulders and said, "Yeah."

Ben placed a large sheet of paper in front of him and asked him to write a word that was on his mind. There were so many but this question of Desomorphine was uppermost because of Luna. So he wrote:

Desomorphine.

Then Ben asked him to write three words that described this. And he wrote.

Ultimate, endorphin killer, scourge.

Ben looked at Gunta and Gunta nodded for him to go ahead. So Ben asked Frankie to write four words that expressed what he felt about this first word.

Frankie wrote,

Drug, missing stimulation, Itzak.

Both the students looked at Frankie and said, "Itzak?" Then Ben finished the exercise with,

"Now one last word that means the same as the first." And Frankie said,

"Dejavu."

Both Ben and Gunta felt they were tapping into something very important. Frankie was not just doing the exercise but he might be bringing up artifacts. The exercise was not over. Ben now asked Frankie to turn the paper over and to draw or scribble anything he wished with his un-favored hand. Frankie had never drawn anything before. He had watched Hailey who was very artistic draw pictures and admired her skill, but never tried it himself. He took the pencil in his right hand. (He did not even know which was his un-favored hand as he had never thought about it.) But he took a deep breath and with his right hand began to draw. When he was finished he had drawn the face of an older man with soft penetrating gaze, a hooked nose and a shock of grey curls on his head. The picture was almost photo perfect. Frankie looked in amazement at what he had done and said,

"This is Itzak and he is my hands."

Frankie thanked his friends and again felt supported and unconditionally loved. He renewed his need to help and support them and he wondered how people could ever think of addicts as horrible worthless people. With the right treatment they were amazing and compassionate, industrious and exceptional as far as human beings went. He preferred their company to that of most of the world.

This event had clarified things for him. He knew he needed to tell Andre and that delving into what Itzak was trying to "tell" him was the key to the problem with Krokodil. "Deja vu" meant "already seen" or the feeling that you had been somewhere or done something before. It was in the camp of precognition for a past event, if one could wrap their mind around that. It was strange enough for others but for Frankie who was prone to artifacts it was revelatory indeed. He was under the distinct impression that his hands always "knew what to do," when it came to chemicals and medication, because they had done all this before. NAI was summoned and a text was sent.

"Hello Andre, I think I know another person in my group. First name Itzak. Can you corroborate?"

Andre already had the answer from Jasmine's efficient research. The full name was Dr. Itzak Katz and he was known for his research on opioids and pain killers. Frankie wanted badly to find George Little Bear but the expedient at the moment was the solution for Krokodil and for that he had to find Itzak first.   NAI was put to work and soon they had information for a memorial service at Beth Qava Synagogue in Queens NY with a widow named, Dr. Esther Katz MD. They traced her practice and found out she had relocated to Schenectady NY. Gunta and Ben volunteered to go speak to her on the pretext of research for Opioids to write papers for school. They jumped in a van and headed for NY.

When they got to Schenectady they called on Dr. Katz at home and asked her if they could speak to her about her husband's research. She was not excited about it and acted a little frightened. She slammed the door in their faces when they arrived. Her husband had disappeared after all and she was there to get away from any further reprisals if any were to come. She suspected the mob and she wanted only to live in peace and practice her medicine. Ben spoke to her through the closed door with an excellent bed side manner he deescalated her and brought home the fact that they were safe people and only interested in the research so they could continue his good work. She opened the door a crack.

"We know you are afraid of exposure. We know your husband's disappearance might have some criminal involvement. We don't blame you for being cautious, but if Dr. Katz was killed, then it would be a shame to let all his work be wasted. The criminals would win. If we wrote the paper and gained any funding for the research we would of course give credit where credit is due. And of course, if his research, in conjunction with our own, went anywhere then you would be a major beneficiary of it all."

Ben's mom was an expert at Jewish guilt and his dad was a good poker player. This had served him well in his addiction but now it was a matter of life and death. Like Frankie he said a silent prayer that she would see reason. Dr. Katz opened the door wide and answered forthrightly.

"You think I care about the money? Is that what you think? No my poor Itzak was working for a cure to this addiction business because of our son. He died with a needle in his veins and we could do nothing about it. This brings it all back, don't you understand. I can't take anymore."

Ben told her he understood perfectly and sympathized with her pain. Then he and Gunta thanked her for her time and apologized for the intrusion. They backed away slowly and headed for the van. Before leaving Ben wrote his name down on a piece of paper along with a phone number and placed it in her hand. He said if she changed her mind they would be at the local Holiday Inn for the weekend. The young psychologist tried that one last thing and punctuated it with,

"We know a lot of people like your son who would benefit from something like this. Your husband could have helped so many."

They spent three days in the hotel, watching TV and reading. They ate pot roast and pan cakes at the local dinner and waited. Finally, on the third day, as they were packing to leave, the phone rang. It was her. When they got to the house again she was a different woman.

"My husband was an old fashion sort of guy. He didn't trust the cloud or the internet. That's why all his work was in, what they call "hard copy". Don't be frightened. When I moved I made sure to pick a house with a room that would accommodate all this. But the movers were careless and well what you will see is the result."

She opened the door to her back room and the boxes and stray papers filled the room from the floor to the young men's breast bones.

"My expertise did not extend to my husband's knowledge. I'm just an old fashioned general practitioner. But he was made for research and was very innovative. His creativity served him well for following the new and divergent solution."

"Was he artistic?"

"Was he? He was a regular Gotlieb or Chagall. I have his work all over the house. And the piano… it's silent most days now but when he was stumped on an issue he used to go to the piano to play and his inspiration would return. Come and listen."

She sat down at the piano and began to play a maudlin piece that was very beautiful but unknown to them. Assuming it was an original piece by Dr. Katz, Ben took his phone and texted NAI for Frankie to listen without speaking. Then he called NAI and allowed Frankie to listen to the music. Frankie was profoundly affected. He had never played the piano but Jamal's keyboard was there. Frank switched it on and sensing the music had a place inside him. He applied his hands and began to play along with what he heard. Note for note he reproduced it and where Esther missed a note he did not. It was his composition after all and the hands remembered that and much more. When Esther became overcome by emotion and stopped, Ben ended the call, but Frankie completed the music and lovingly caressed the final note.

Gunta and Ben returned to the hotel excited beyond words but they had a big problem. Where they hoped to bring home a few thumb drives of information, now, they had the dilemma of getting this mass of paper on e-files. They decided on purchasing a, top of the line, lap top with a terabyte of internal memory, a few external drives with 5 terabytes just in case and a high speed archiving scanner. They sat there for a week organizing and scanning files but in the end it was worth it.

When they were done they presented Esther with a one terabyte external hard drive full of her husband's research and they took a back up copy home for themselves in the laptop case. Esther commented on the marvel of modern ingenuity but she said she would never dispose of the papers. They were his and that was that. She did however thank the boys for organizing the documents and she sent them away with chicken soup and Reuben sandwiches, some knishes and some prune pastries. They were welcomed back any time and as they left she commented,

"I know Itzak is gone and this won't bring him back, but if it will show those mob Nazi's they can't win then find the answers and give 'em hell."

Provisioned for the journey, and petal to the metal, they made the trip back before midnight and Frankie was sitting at the piano waiting.

All Frankie's friend knew he was struggling with the morality of his activities. They were not the kind to tell him what to do but they were also there as a testimony to the fact that what he did made a wonderful difference. What was really right or wrong? They had many discussions about it. Rosa cooked her incomparable pasteles (boiled green banana pasties) and a sopon (various roots and mushrooms in a delicious broth), broiled fish from the lake for the meat eaters and they had fresh bread from the De Lacy's who came in response to an invitation from Gunta. The friends were all there with Frankie and they had a feast to remember.

Ann had not been to a party in years and the smells of food in the kitchen and evergreen and balsam in the rest of the house delighted her. Jean Luc was amazed by the stories the addicts told of how Frankie had helped them. The sound of music filled the Air as Percy and Jamal played tune after tune on drums, guitar and keyboard between mouthfuls of salad, chips and dips. There was no wine because of the alcoholics in their midst, but there was plenty of sweet tea and lemonade, fruit water and chocolate milk for Frankie and Dee Dee.

Stacia was content to wander in the fascinating house. The décor put her in mind of a fairy forest. Dee Dee saw Stacia come in and was happy beyond words to have her teacher all to herself. She took on the job of being a guide for Stacia showing her everything, from the room Frankie had set aside for children with a swing and forest play things, to the bathroom with round pebbles for a floor and a large smooth stone hollowed out for a bath. The toilets were in rooms of their own and there were several of those.

There were also at least 9 bedrooms and trees were everywhere. Fully branched trees were in the headers and footers of all beds and in the frames of windows and mirrors. Stairs were unusual but not functional. Instead there were ladders and a smooth wooden slide from the second floor to the first. This delighted Dee Dee and all the "big kids" as well. Ann climbed the ladder and slid down the slide at least three times.

There were lofts in the bedrooms held up by trees where things could be stored. On the outside it looked quite dilapidated but on the inside the house was a world of wonders. Dee Dee even took Stacia to Frankie's room where he had his huge nest of a bed and Stacia was quite surprised that a bachelor's lair would be so orderly and fantastical. When he came through the window Dee Dee ran to him for a hug but Stacia shyly excused herself and went to the kitchen.

Frankie tried not to give in to how he felt at her reaction. He moved his thoughts to the problem at hand. He had been working on the data that had come from Schenectady. He longed to see Esther and tell her all but he was afraid it might be too much for her. The boys promised to send her a copy of the paper, which Ben fully intended to write sighting Dr. Katz research, but the important thing was that the medicine was in process. They wanted to wait for a successful trial before contacting her again.

Frankie had taken to the data like he would take to an old friend. He recognized a lot of the formulas he had used on those addicted to heroin and Fentanyl and the one he used on alcohol dependent people. Frankie now knew exactly where Itzak had hit a road block. It was on chemically stimulating the brain's pleasure centers after the destruction caused by something like desomorphine in a human nervous system.

Itzak had come to the conclusion that the damage could not be repaired by medicine alone but he suspected it could be accomplished by a combination of medicine and external prompting similar to trans-cranial magnetic stimulation. This had been used effectively for depression and might work to restart the pleasure centers after addiction. He had been seeking funding to obtain a TMS machine that he could modify for his work. He had also done quite a bit of work towards locating the exact coordinates in the hypothalamus that would restart the pituitary glands for the needed sense of wellbeing. This was the intervention he had high hopes for. He was so close and then he was murdered. Now Frankie would have to continue where he had left off. But money, money was the great obstacle or was it something else?

The thing that made money such a problem was greed. Greed was one of the seven deadly sins. That was the thing. People in the drug industry with money would not get the kind of payoff they wanted from saving penniless addicts that they would get from other medications they could cash in on. He had noted pharmaceutical companies paying over 80 million for one medication to make over a hundred times as much on it. Was this to be the bottom line for everything? The seven sins killed. How could human being indulge them so? Frankie determined he would juggle his ones and zeros and NAI would procure for him a TMS machine. That was all there was to it. But these $90,000 dollar machines were only delivered to Medical facilities. They would need Esther's help and with all the progress Frankie had made he was sure they would get it.

When Frankie climbed into his bedroom window to get a clean hoodie he was surprised to see Dee Dee there but he was even more surprised to see Stacia. He almost climbed right back out of the window but the child was too quick and had him by the leg in a bear hug. For a moment yellow eyes met Stacia's pale blue and he thought he saw something more than disgust. Then she turned and left abruptly and he thought he had been mistaken. So, he asked Dee Dee to go make sure Miss Stacia went down the slide properly then he closed the door.

Combing his black hair back into a horse tail he washed his face with a cloth using the pitcher and basin by his dresser. He put his best hoodie on and wondered if he should go out there at all. The feeling of shame he struggled with threatened to consume him, but then, it came to him. No this was not shame it was really pride. He was too proud to accept rejection and really-- rejection was the fault of the other person not his. He thought he might be remembering something Ben said to him about all this but suddenly he realized it was true. Right then he decided not to give into this deadly sin of pride. He would walk out with the dignity of five good men. Well, at least the ones he knew so far were good, and he was all of them combined.

The rest of the evening was wonderful.   Frankie was a gracious host. At the end of the night Gunta asked Frankie to play Itzak's song and Frankie bent to the keys and performed. After hiding for so long he felt strangely warmed knowing all eyes were upon him in a good way. When the last note was played there was silence and he did not know what to do. Then Jean Luc began to clap his hands together and all the others joined in. Frankie tilted his head and took this all in like a child, and smiled but could not speak.

When people were ready to leave he was almost despondent. Greedy for their company, if given the choice, all of them, especially Stacia, would have staid. But he knew greed kills and he loved them all. He could therefore not hold them. They must go as they pleased and come again of their own free will. He went into the kitchen to wash the dishes. They had offered to help but he said he wanted to do it himself. As he did he thought of every detail of the evening and he was happy, moreover he was satisfied.

The next day was not so easy and he found himself a little down. He had to take a break from the research and wait on a few things. Gunta had spoken to Esther and she had agreed to let them deliver the machine to her office.

Gunta would be there to receive the training on the machine that was already paid for. Esther was thrilled to be a part of it all and she wanted eventually to meet Dr. Frank, the researcher who was in charge of the whole project. Ben and Gunta felt bad lying to her about Frank but if she ever met him it would be to tell her he was partly Itzak and that, they thought, would be traumatic enough.

Frankie was also waiting to hear if Jean Luc had persuaded Luna to be their guinea pig. She had lost her apartment and was living with a friend who was also an addict. Her savings were all exhausted and so were her credit cards. She had lost her job at the hospital and was about to lose the job she had gotten at a fast food place. Soon she would have to start doing illegal things to get money. If she were arrested she would lose her nursing license. Jean Luc hoped she would be desperate enough to try the cure. He would call Frankie as soon as he got her answer.

Meanwhile the Big Guy had to wait and he hated waiting. As he waited he found himself eating and the more he ate the more he wanted to eat. He devoured everything that had been left over from the party then he stared on the contents of the fridge. The food reminded him of the party and he wanted the party to continue. Then just as his belly was bursting he remembered that gluttony was a killer and he burped and decided to stop. But so much in his stomach made him sleepy and instead of picking up after his guests he sat lazily and closed his eyes. When Gunta arrived with the TMS machine the house was a wreck and Frankie felt guilty about his sloth. It seemed that one deadly sin lead to another.

Gunta told him he had lied to Esther and told her Dr. Frank was presiding over the project. Then he told Frank that she wanted to meet him. This disturbed the giant and in fact it made him angry. He was angry about having to hide and tell lies. He was angry he could not just get the things he needed to help the people he cared about without all these issues and problem. He was angry that men like Lupo got what they wanted and, and, and... he was just angry at everything. Gunta asked him if it was hard for him to have Stacia there the night before. Frankie remembered how she had so easily talked to and laughed with Ben and Gunta and all the others face to face but she always shied when it came to him. Yes he was angry that as Stein's prototype he was full of scars and hideous. He was wrathful, in point of fact, and envious of his friend's normal faces and he didn't like it. So he went out and split twelve cord of fire wood even though the weather was mild.

15

Lassoing the Moon

If Luna had been feisty as a regular nurse she was a wild cat as an addict. She threw herself at Jean Luc promising every sexual delight, then walked off with his wallet. He found her a few hours later and she was uncooperative, abrasive, and manipulative. She simply could not be reasoned with. Jean Luc almost forgot for a moment he loved her. Her skin was covered with dark spots that were potential blood clots and its once smooth surface was now rough, dry and scaly. When she was high she was zombie like and her speech was slovenly. She teased him, rejected him and disappeared once again. She was not the woman he remembered.

Jean Luc called the "tree house" and Gunta shared with him how he had been as an addict. Substances definitely altered personality and simulated mental illness they also bring about a desperation that manifests the worst of a person. He encouraged Jean Luc not to take it personally. Since drugs were illegal, a person enslaved by them would have to play dirty to get his or her fix.

This is why Frankie used drugs in safe dosage, to reel the addict in and then used those very drugs to help the addict change. Eventually if they really wanted they could wean off of those drugs safely with the used of his second stage preparations. Frankie learned about this from similar plans in other countries that were treating addicts medically and were helping them to normalize their lives. The only difference was that Frankie's medicine was far more effective for detox than anything else and it actually help to rebuild the addict neurologically. Jean Luc now agreed with his mother, that these drugs should become available to the world.

Unfortunately treatment for Krokodil did not work this way. Krokodil was much more addictive than other street drugs and caused increase in trauma for the body. It destroyed things other drugs only damaged. If one were suspicious one might even think Russia had sent us this "gift" to kill us all. It was spreading like lice and unchecked would soon be in every home in the country. Already the streets of many cities were full of its walking dead.

Luna was not in her right mind, this was clear. That being the case, her loved ones could section her. But all the friends knew nothing was more futile than treating an addict against her will. Still, for Jean Luc and for the sake of research they would try. It was determined that the Shadow would make a cocoon for an addict and instead of hang her out for show, he would bring her in.

The night was moonless and Luna had never done a trick before. She needed to look as good as possible so she dug up her tightest shiniest dancing dress and put on some tall pink heals. She made up her face with enough red lipstick to resemble a raspberry tart and sauntered out onto the street. The fact that her arms and legs had all those black and blues was a turn off and the only type of John she could attract would have to be the lowest of the low. When a fat drunk with a bank role approached her she thought to reach for the role and run. But her heels prevented quick getaway and he grabbed her. He also slapped her then went with the next pair of legs in the lineup. Luna was being schooled in lessons no woman should have to learn.

School for Luna that night wasn't over. The cops drove by and she ducked into an alley just in time to avoid an arrest. Thinking herself smart and tricky she turned to continue her solicitation but slammed into a huge hoodie that covered a chest as hard as concrete. She looked up and swore she saw two large yellow eyes staring at her from the darkness of the hood. Thoroughly freaked, she slowly stepped back from the chest to politely walk around it but the chest was not to be walked around.

What happened next she thought of as an impossible nightmare for many days to come. The hoodie's arms hoisted her on massive shoulders and began to climb the side of the building like a cockroach. If she started to slip he would secure her and so it went till the people below looked like mice wandering about in a cage. Reaching the edge of the roof the hoodie hoisted her over it and grabbed her, before she could escape. He rapped her tightly in soft bandages; duck taped her mouth and watched as she shook in terror then finally passed out.

The sedative she was given didn't wear off till she was strapped to a table in a sterile white room at Frankie's house. The room was Gunta's precautionary idea. He knew addict behavior and he knew this protocol was experimental. If it worked they were golden but if it didn't, Luna would be a loose end that might give everything away. She needed to think she was in the hospital till it was all over. If she was allowed to see the house all concerned would be in danger. So this large storage room next to one of the toilets was painted white the wall to the bathroom was turned into a regular door and the TMS machine was placed inside the room along with a bed. They would all wear surgical masks when dealing with her. Frankie could not be there when she was awake and would remained a terrifying hallucination until she got well, if indeed, she did.

Five days of intermittent sedation and treatment was performed. The chemical demon inside her worked violently to hold on to her body but towards the fifth day the old Luna seemed to be winning the battle for detox. Still they maintained their vigil, medication and treatment for two more days and on the tenth day Jean Luc was allowed to see her wearing a mask.

Her stomach was in tatters and all she could take was broth but he fed it to her and she looked at his eyes with recognition. He flipped the mask down momentarily, long enough for her to see who he was. Replacing the mask he explained that the process made her very susceptible to infection hence the masks. He told her why she was there. She told him about the horrible dream she had of being accosted by a giant hoodie.

It was still a few days till the sedation could be eased and she could sit up. Meds and treatment were continued three weeks in all and she was acting more like herself. She was given reading material and films to watch on a screen (no identifying TV). She started commenting on the medication because, as a nurse, she did not recognize it and she was saying she didn't know that TMS could be used for other things beside depression. She was asking to go to the toilet instead of the bed pan and being a regular pain by repeatedly buzzing the "nurse." She was the perfect stereotype of difficult patients who are medical personnel. She drove the crew crazy.

On the twenty fifth day she was asked how she felt by Dr. Jones (Gunta) and she said she felt no cravings. NO CRAVINGS! This was absolutely remarkable. She did however feel depressed and anxious and she wondered if her mother had been notified. Anxiety and depression were common to recovering addicts and those could be treated with Frankie's protocol #1 medications.

Jean Luc was brought in and he told her, mother had been notified. But they told her that mother and her sister were both sick with the flue and could absolutely not be in her presence till she was better. They sent their love because they had sore throats and could not be understood on the phone due to their condition. That was the best they could do. The crew was running out of lies and excuses. She would soon have to be told something or be removed. Frankie thought this might be the moment to start his original treatment method. True the ball would be in her court to continue recovery and she might not run with it but they had to take the chance. Jean Luc protested but true recovery does not happen without consent. They had to try.

Luna was given mild sedation, dressed and taken to a hotel where Jean Luc was waiting. When she awoke she looked at him and wondered what was going on. He soothed her and explained that she had been in an unusual experimental detox and that now she had a choice. She could continue her treatment or not. Continuing would require her getting honest with her family and moving forward. The alternative was go back to the streets and do what she had been doing before.

He gave her the stats on desomorphine and told her she could stay in the hotel for a few days till she decided. He would bring her meds daily and she could tell him what she wanted to do. He also told her the truth about her mother and sister. They didn't know. Finally he added that the program that helped her detox would also help her with a job and housing if she wanted to continue taking the meds and staying clean. It was her choice but there could be no compromise. If she got high it was all over.

Jean Luc placed her dose on the night stand and left her to think. He did not hope at this point that she would be grateful to him and return his love. He also knew that, if she wanted to prosecute him for forcing her into treatment she could. After all, nothing had been said about a section 12 and he was not a relative or an acting medical person. He was hoping she would see his desire for her wellbeing and not get legal but she had been so abrasive as an addict, he was not sure what she would do. He was not even sure how he felt about her anymore. He was concerned for her as a person but the romance had definitely faded. He was a little depressed himself after the ordeal. He wondered if there was a God and hoped if there was, that He or She would intervene.

On the following day Jean Luc brought Luna some clothes. She thanked him and told him she hadn't left the place. Frankie, who had been watching, could corroborate that. Jean Luc said he was glad and that he would send someone else to work out the housing and the work issues if she wanted. She sounded disappointed but she said thank you and he left.

On the second day he came in and asked how she was. She smiled and said she was feeling much better. The anxiety was almost gone and she was not too depressed. He sounded very professional and asked her if she wanted to continue with the program and get the benefits. She said yes and he brought out some forms for her to sign. He was honest with her. These forms relieved him and all concerned of reprisal for her forced treatment and they were a test. She signed them. He sighed in relief and told her the next day someone else would visit with further information. Then she took his hand and said, "I don't want anyone else."   Later that day she told him as they cuddled that she was not depressed anymore and neither was he.

The crew was informed of the results that evening and all rejoiced. They had pulled it off and at least one person was saved. Ben called Esther and she was told the protocol was a success. She was very happy and said she would love to have them over for a nice brisket and all the trimmings and she wondered if that doctor would be available to meet with her. She would like the medical details. Ben said Dr. Frank was extremely busy, especially now that this had succeeded and that he might be able to do a phone interview but he could not visit at this time. She understood and still said she would have Ben and Gunta up and that she knew a nice Jewish nurse who was looking. She would like to introduce her to Ben at the dinner. He thanked her and made the dinner date and Gunta ribbed him a little about the nurse.

"You lie like a bandit and get a date. You Yiddish dog you."

"I hope the dog isn't the nurse."

"Be nice now. Anyway beggars can't be choosers."

The process of the last few days had taken a lot out of everyone. The medicine and the TMS was not so grueling but the secrecy that kept information even from the patient--required "many hands on deck" and that was difficult. Also the chance that the patient might give the whole thing away was a big problem. Krokodil addicts were so physically invested in their drug it would be hard to pry it out of their control for treatment. Despite the gross physical manifestations of the addiction, most of them ended up dead not long after they began to use. The machines were also a problem. They could not be used for long without the inquiries of the company that manufactured the machines and the 'tree house' and caves were hardly medical facilities by normal standards.

All this clandestine activity kept the cures out of the hands of those who would legally exploit them but it also prevented thousands and soon millions from getting help. Frankie and his crew had some big decisions to make.

Then there was the problem of pain. It appeared that because of money, medicine that didn't help people ease pain was being sold and medicine that did help people was under terrible criticism and being withheld. Of course there was the problem of addiction and that was legitimate but people were still in pain and that was also legitimate. The motivation behind all these problems was not compassion but money.

Frankie found out that in some countries people didn't need money to buy medicine. They just got it. Medical people were paid by everyone through taxes. This seemed much more equitable to him. No one had to lose everything to go through the process of getting well. Why was medicine given, free of charge, in one place and was against the law in another? Why was it a crime to be an addict in one country, and in another it was not a crime at all, but an illness that was treated freely? Why would he be a criminal because he gave people good medicine here and not in other places? None of it made sense to him.

He discussed this with Gunta and the other members of the team and they all had opinions. Some said it might be good to go "legit". Others thought it would mean big problems. Some thought Frankie's medicine could be marketed as an Herbal remedy but others thought it had too many chemicals to be labeled that way. Some were in favor of selling it to "Big Pharma" to be mass produced and distributed. That would mean Frankie would not be able to make the medicine anymore and it would not belong to him. If his friends needed it they might not be able to get it if they were poor. The pharmaceutical industry would probably put a high price on it and that would mean not all the people that needed it would be able to afford it. Money would be a problem all the way around.

Some wondered if they could distribute it themselves. That would mean getting the FDA to approve it and it would mean lots of money to have it tested and approved then lots more money to make and distribute it. They would have to account for every penny and without NAI they had no pennies at all. They needed money and Frankie now knew that the way he had been obtaining money was not legal. It seemed fair but it was not legal. Obtaining money according to the law was extremely difficult and was made difficult by those who had lots of it and didn't like sharing. Besides, Frankie could not just apply for work. All hell would break loose if he were discovered. Stein would surely be imprisoned and die then the mob would kill all of them.

Frankie did not want any of his friends to get in trouble or to be in danger for helping him. They all said they didn't mind taking the chance and he said he didn't save them to see them get arrested or killed. Frankie told them all to go home. He said they could visit any time but he would be the only one taking chances from now on with distribution or TMS machines. The Machine was returned. The vans were dropped off by night at the dealership and except for Gunta, things were silent at the "tree house" for a few weeks.

Frankie would continue as he had before he had help. The problem was he had many more clients than before. The team had increased his distribution by almost ten times. So many people needed help. Frankie had to work round the clock and even for a reanimate that was an impossible schedule to continue.

Now, Frankie couldn't help them with school or apartments anymore because that would be redistributing money in an illegal way. Sadly what he discovered was that though they could get sober many of them gave up, because they were homeless or unemployable. Whether the reason was a prison record or no supports or disability, people remained in the street and lost hope so they went back to drugs.

Loss of hope led to crime in the short term and suicide by overdose eventually. Some could get jobs but because they were unskilled or unable to do anything but manual labor they had to work two or more jobs to make ends meet. Even then regular housing was so expensive they could not afford it and things would end in tragedy. Rehab and detox did not help their poverty and in the long run poverty would consume them. The state took their children and the drugs would take their souls and their lives in the end and all while the rich blamed them for the world's problems. It just didn't seem right.

So much tragedy was taking place just because the people who had so much money would not share it with those who had so little. Frankie could not abide it and went back to doing what he did before. He started to redistribute money to save them.   If prison was the price he would take the chance. But that left him with another heart ache.

He had just found his brother Andre and now he would lose him again because his activity would cause Andre distress. He simply could not face him and that made him feel very alone. He also could not talk to Esther because he knew she would be very cross about being used for the TMS machine.

Seeing his angst Gunta told him he would not finish school if it was a problem for him. Ben was done and it was not fair that Gunta would not finish. Frankie said he would not cut him off. Angie was finished with school but as a political science major she told him that what he was doing was righteous even if it wasn't legal. He was very torn. He did remember what Fergus said, the seven deadly sins killed but though he was subject to these sins, his reasons for helping others the way he did, was not because of greed or other sins. He could not help but feel God was alright with it.

Like Ben and Angie his old crew started to check in one by one and soon he had a full house again but they were not allowed to help with his work. He just would not risk them. Frankie figured what was done was done as far as they were concerned. They were now no longer dependent on him they were just his friends. They had a different perspective however. They were grateful and refused to leave him. They would continue to be supportive.

Frankie felt adrift as far as his healing activities were concerned but at least he did not feel alone. The twelve cooked for him, played music and cheered him and told him he was a regular Robin Hood. They even made him watch several movies about this historical legend and he found them very entertaining. He had no artifacts of seeing movies beyond spaghetti westerns. How could he turn his friends away?

But then again how could he stop helping? Ann, what about Ann? He would not, could not let her down. He also had about five more like her and they had to have their medicine. Could he save the whole world? No, only one could do that and He said poverty would be with us as long as greed was.

16

Real Criminals

As a genuine predator, Babe made a point of knowing small details about her targets. Now she knew Frankie, was a reanimate and that Stein lied to Lupo. She saw Stein as a possible means to get the Shadow. She also knew that as a reanimate, she was not as equipped as Frankie was. His NAI seemed unlimited or the deluxe model, while she was already exhausting her source for education via NAI and had to go back to her old sources for information. Fortunately she learned quickly. Soon she would be right up to speed.

She saw that the Titan was childlike and that intrigued her. A strong intelligent, capable man with the innocence (but not the irresponsibility) of a child; this was rare. She almost hated to kill him. In fact she might not. It all depended on him and what he was willing to do for her. Alexi could be duped or appeased in some way so she might not have to kill him yet either. Perhaps the albino girl would be sufficient to appease him and Babe could keep Frank. That would satisfy both herself and Alexi. The girl was albino but she would bleed red; blood on snow. Alexi would like that as this was also rare.

Then there was the little problem of Frankie's hasty departure. He was a busy boy but it wasn't nice to leave a damsel in distress half rescued. Why would he do that? Perhaps she was losing her touch. No, he was just shy. Those little sandals were so cute, how sweet of him. He must like her. The only way to find out was to spend some time with him, but how? He wasn't the kind you could just ask on a date. Or was he? And what was he doing with the old lady. Looked like he was supplying her with something and she would give him bread. Were they related? What was the attraction? The family had gone out two nights ago and come back very late. It was the time of month he usually showed up. Babe kicked herself for not following them. She wouldn't make that mistake again. Next thing was to talk to Stein. She would do that tonight.

Lupo had been to Alexi's house at least three times since Babe's disappearance. He also placed a man at the corner to watch for any indication she was there. She was aware of him and evading the mug was not difficult for her. If she had been wiser and richer she would have left the country. Further, she couldn't leave without money and she was used to living expensively as well as dangerously. A few times she felt twinges of the pain and knew Lupo was near. He kept the device with him and pressed it now and again nostalgically hoping it would cripple her so she could be found. This had happened before. But Babe was getting wiser about it. For her it now served as a bell did for a cat; a bell around a cat's neck that announced its presence to the mice. The pain did the same for Babe with Lupo. When she felt it she ran. In the Don's mind however, it was just a matter of time.

Concerning the investigation, Andre had a bead on eight people who had gone missing around the same time Frank did. Senator Edward Shea, George Little Bear, Itzak Katz and his wife Esther, Pastor Morris Gray, Melvin Diamante, Luis Batista and Gene Maroni.   Esther wisely moved to Schenectady, Melvin was later found full of led in the river, and this inspired Luis and Gene to ditched their spouses and run off to Costa Rica. That left Shea, Katz, Little Bear, Gray and Frank unaccounted for.

The investigative unit at that time of their disappearance included Andre. They watched the video of the end of the last CHRS meeting dozens of times. Many people were filing out of the hall where they met and security was in place. All the people who were missing were in the footage except Esther. Then the camera went to the Anchor man and the broadcast was over. But no one looked at the extra footage that was edited from the broadcast. Andre could have kicked himself for not thinking of it earlier but he was a bit emotionally compromised back then. After all, his brother was among the missing. Now he sat looking at the additional footage and he thought how stupid he had been. This was finally telling him years later, what he wanted to know. All five men went into the elevator together. They never came out. Understanding what he did of Frankie, it appeared that all but perhaps, Gray had been located.

Alexi did not like being the masochist in relationships but at the moment, he had a wild cat for a housemate that would draw blood on a whim, and this was a real problem. Often he wished he had never opened the door when she came knocking, looking very much like the unearthed dead in her strangely sandaled feet. Her story was macabre and made her both desirable as a sexual oddity and unobtainable as a female powerhouse. She had an ax to grind against rich perverts and men in general and he was all of the above. If she gave herself to anyone it would be a pliable saint and she didn't know anyone like that. Or did she?

In addition his life had become a game of Russian roulette. Lupo was a frequent visitor and finding Babe nestled in his apartments for refuge would result in Alexi being dissected in his own rumpus room by the mob. She assured him this would not happen and she also informed him that her aim was to put the little Sicilian sod to a gruesome end as soon as she could sever that infernal remote from his hand.

Of course Alexi was never too frightened to negotiate. He told her to be reasonable and throw him a bone. She knew he had been threatened into helping Lupo "win" her and he never dreamed he was going to kill, revive and enslave her in that order. How could he? Now she had him risking his life and art collections for her and there was nothing in it for him. He offered her a designer wardrobe and a trust fund in exchange for the secret of reanimation and the head of the Shadow. She said the secret was no problem but the Shadow might be. She would do her best. She also tried to persuade him that the albino girl, once she had served her purpose as bait, might be compensation for him if the Shadow proved elusive. It gave him pause.

The Austrian comforted himself with the possibilities his dilemma presented. Could he purchase a ticket to immortality with such a procedure? Would that mean death first? Not a pleasant thought. Alternately could he profit from any of this? Lupo was so busy making money from Krokodil it was amazing he had time for the Babe obsession. Besides, the Don had promised him a cut if he located Babe for him. This was substantial, but with Lupo out of the way the whole operation might be his if he played it right. Then also, by tailing the De Lacy's, Babe had learned that there was a cure for desomorphine addiction and Frankie or rather "the Shadow" had something to do with it. She wanted to know more about this treatment. So did Alexi. Perhaps there was a way to make money by afflicting people then curing them of this handy little drug. If this were the case the two criminal entrepreneurs might play both ends of the Krokodil and this was very exciting.

The giant ducked his head under the rectory door and the priest apologized for not having tea ready. He had been taking some night classes at a local college and a session had run late. Frankie brought some blue berries and they munched on these and some graham crackers as they talked.

"What I love about you Frank is that you are so earnest about what you believe. You are definitely not tentative about anything."

"It gives me problems Fergus. I can't let things rest till I have answers. I have been thinking about those deadly sins and found all of them in myself. I was not pleased."

"I am not surprised. They are in all of us. Part of the good fight is to win over these things in ourselves."

"I am losing the battle Fergus."

"On our own we all do, and this is where I secretly agree with my Lutheran brethren."

"Explain please."

"Well most religions profess good works and those as a ticket to paradise but this is their fatal flaw. We are so prone to mistakes and outright wrong doing that many of us despair of making the grade and give up. At our best we are scum Frank, that's all there is to it. We do good things for bad reasons and do bad things because we want to. So how can we be good? Just look at our planet. We've destroyed it and its people besides. We need help. That is where grace comes in."

"The grace and forgiveness of God."

"Yes! It is what cleans us up and sets us on a better path. I never meant for you to go around focusing on your sins. That's a sure formula for defeat. Just keep looking at God and he will put everything right. He will continue making you the good men you want to be."

Both of them smiled at Fergus' joke and Frankie felt better.

When Frankie got home he talked to Gunta, Ben and Angie about all this. They had been thinking about his struggle too and wanted to share some things with him. One by one they admitted that as addicts they had done some terrible things. No doubt, whatever makes us check in with our conscience before doing dirty deeds, is not working well when an addictive substance is introduced. They were not religious people but they liked the fact that Frankie believed in a God of love and forgiveness. It gave them someplace to put their guilt and leave it there. Still he needed to know they were not angels. He told them he knew and he loved them anyway just like God loved him.

Gunta also had another thought. When he graduated med school at the end of the following year he might be able to present Frankie's research as his own and see if he could secure grants for private distribution. NAI could fudge records with the FDA to make it look like they had applied for all the right things. They already had thousands of clinical trials with Frankie's meds and one at least with the treatment for Krokodil.

They would give Dr. Katz credit of course and nothing could make Esther happier. Gunta felt he could at least make a case for further testing and perhaps they might be able to legitimize their protocols and continue helping people. Once the meds started selling (at a reasonable price for even Medicaid) the proceeds could go directly into a fund for housing, jobs and education of these addicts. As soon as they were able to "wean" off of Frankie and take responsibility for their own upkeep they would graduate. Frankie liked the idea. So did everyone else. But till this could be put in place, Frank would continue as before.

Ann was coming in out of the raised garden. It was her job to water the plants while Stacia was teaching. She loved the smell of the dirt, the seedlings felt strong to her touch and all the plants were doing well so far. Soon they would have green salad and they didn't have to break their backs to do it.

She took off her garden gloves and was going to wash her hands when the phone rang.

"Hello, this is Ann." A woman's sultry voice was on the other end.

"Tell Frank to meet me on the roof of the Museum of Art. Midnight tonight."

The phone clicked and a shudder went through Ann as the dial tone hummed on.

Of course she dialed NAI immediately and warned her friend not to go. The voice seemed ominous and Ann's intuition was something Frankie had learned to trust. He knew within one guess who the voice might be and he did not like the fact that the De Lacy family had been used as a go between to get to him. He had half a mind to send them off for another excursion into some foreign land. Ann told him they could not keep running. Stacia and Jean Luc had responsibilities. She begged him to ignore the call but as usual he told her not to worry and said he would handle it. Then he called his big brother.

Andre had been hoping for that call. He knew he had been hard on Frankie and that life was full of answers that were not ideal. Truth was, in a few short months Frankie had been responsible for putting away over 53 elusive criminals and this was more than he and Frank had done in all the years of their career. Andre was curious about the odds and ends of Frankie's activity but he also wanted to salute him for his achievements. Family was never easy but Andre wanted it back almost as much as Frankie did.

"Frankie, oh I'm so glad you called. Look, I'm sorry I came down on you..."

"Don't be sorry big brother you are just doing your job. I have done a lot of thinking since then and maybe someday we can talk about it."

"For sure man, we can talk about it over a huge pile of rice and beans."

"It's a date, but not right now."

"I have information for you about your uh...parts."

"I have a lot to tell you as well but I need a favor. It's kind of urgent."

"Not another mob war."

"No I don't think so. I been asked on a date."

"Whaaat? Your razzin' me right?"

"Na, it's true but the woman is dangerous. She's like me—a reanimate."

"You're kidding me. How many of you are there?"

"Just her I think. The Ripper was one but he's dead again, permanently this time."

"Oh shit, I gotta sit down. Listen, you sure you don't wanna tell me who this Dr is cause it sounds like he's wakko and needs to be picked up."

"You gotta let me handle this in my time. A lot is at stake here. Trust me."

"Okay...so what did you call me for?"

"This Babe was someone you knew. She was killed by Lupo and reanimated. Now she wants to talk to me."

"You mean Lupo is involved with this? And that's not Babe Lonegan is it?"

"That's her."

"You're always stealing my women."

"She's bad news 'mano, I don't wanna date her I wanna stop her."

"So what does she want from you?"

"I don't know but she called me through some friends that I don't want in the middle of all this; the De Lacy family in Queens. I'll give you the address."

"I know the address. I staked it out quite a few times."

"You never told me."

"How could I? You were too busy eating my pizza and climbing out windows. And *you* never told me you had a phone number. Hook me up."

"Fine, look Bro I'll bring the pizza next time but you gotta help me by getting some suits over to the De Lacy's tonight at midnight so nothing happens to them while I deal with the Babe."

"Next time it ain't pizza its rice, beens and cuchifritos bro and I'll have the suits there as well as my handsome self."

"Keep it quiet, I don't want the family disturbed."

"Cayadito, shh…they won't know we're there. Man it's just like old time! Hang her high bro."

"She won't be easy."

"Too bad."

Frankie signed off and a text with an unlisted number was sent to Andre. The detective hoped he would never have to present it as evidence.

The roof of the Metropolitan Museum of Art in New York was not hard to access for someone who could turn off the surveillance and climb uneven surfaces but he didn't have to shut off the spy-cams. They were already off. Even with a full moon Frankie was able to achieve the summit of the classically columned edifice, unseen and undetected. He later figured out she had tampered with the surveillance cameras during the day programming for black out that night. Very clever for someone who did not have the same NAI access he did. But the real question was how she got in there; in a midnight blue evening gown and heals that made her as tall as he was. In addition she had set up a three course meal, champagne and candles. Those things might have been stored in a back pack but the Persian rug they were to picnic on had to be a real challenge.

She must have made two trips or she was stronger than she looked. Or maybe she set it all up during the day like the surveillance. That was probably what happened. That's how regular people with great intelligence did things. Still, he thought, she went through a lot of trouble, and Frankie was not sure why. Why was he even thinking of all this? He was meeting a beautiful woman; a naughty one. He had never been seduced before. He was scared and confused when he saw her and had to admit it. What could he do but come right to the point.

"Don't bother my friends anymore."

"But I wanted to thank you and I didn't know how to reach you."

"Don't reach me and if you are afraid of Lupo you should leave the country."

"That's rude. Where would I go with this color skin? I can't go sneaking around in a hoodie."

He had not thought about her plight as a reanimate. She would have some of the same troubles he had albeit she was beautiful enough to get by.

"Women wear makeup don't they? Perhaps you could..."

"Frank you and I are unique in the entire world. Shouldn't we get to know each other?"

"All right what do you want to know?"

This was not going as planned for Babe. Perhaps NAI was a bigger part of him than she thought. Perhaps he didn't have urges like other men. That would make him a big virile homunculus not a man. Then force would be the go to, but she liked a challenge. She would try again.

"You're making this hard Frank. But it doesn't have to be. Here, why don't you have something to eat? You fed me let me return the favor."

"What do you want? You have friends that do terrible things. I know you also have done things to hurt others. You have even killed. What do you want with me?"

"I like you, I see in you things I wish I saw in myself. Maybe I don't want to live badly anymore. Maybe I want to change. Won't you help me?"

Compassion--she had exploited it many times in other targets. In her opinion it was a defect of humanity that prevented survival of the fittest and she was a survivor. Never the less, Frankie, though full of compassion, and quite naïve, had one things in his favor; his love for God and Stacia.

"If you want to change perhaps you should pray."

"Oh no," she thought. "He's an altar boy." But she had also dealt with those before.

"Perhaps I should," She took his hands and brought them up to her chest. Then she wrapped her arms around his neck and kissed him. As she broke away she saw his stunned expression. Only Dee Dee had ever hugged him and it was never like that. He wasn't breathing and he was totally confused. She knew she had him. When he finally took a breath she said,

"Lupo forced me to do horrible things. I never wanted to be with him. I want to be with you. Please don't turn me away. I feel safe with you."

"I must consider, and you must stay away from my friends."

He started to back away and she tried to stop him without breaking the spell.

"But when will I see you again? How will I contact you?"

"I will find you."

"Meet me here, tomorrow night."

"Perhaps."

"Please."

"Alright."

He backed away from her and fell backwards off the roof sliding down one of the columns at the side of the building. On ground level he staggered a bit. He was dizzy and NAI informed him his temperature was elevated. He wondered if she had done something to him involving intoxicants. But NAI did not corroborate that. Apparently it was her and what she did to him. He did not know if he could face her again. It seemed that if he had stayed in her presence a moment longer, she could have asked anything of him and he would do it. It was frightening in a way he had never experienced. Bears claws and fangs were easier to deal with than this woman. But now he had promised. He had promised to come back the next night. What could he do? He had to check on Ann, Jean Luc and especially Stacia.

Many streets in NYC never sleep but side streets did and he was expert at running through them and then to highways and byways where a man in a black hoodie could run and not be noticed. The light from the moon was also bothering him. It had never done so before. Slipping quietly onto the top of a loan moving bus he crossed over the bridge and was at the De Lacy home within a half hour. A vehicle moving through traffic could not have done half as well. There he saw Andre's Nissan and a black and white. He stopped at a safe distance and called Andre.

"I'm here can we talk?"

"I'm with my partner; wanna meet her? Your friend James is her brother."

"Does she know about me?"

"'Fraid so."

"Oh boy, OK but I gotta talk to you."

"About the Babe? Damn."

"Shut up. Send the black and white home. Nothing's happening tonight."

"OK, OK good as done. Then come see me."

Frankie watched the police car leave and started walking towards the Nisan. When he got there they had to get out because he couldn't fit in the car. Andre and Jasmine were grinning knowingly. Andre spoke up first.

"We heard on the radio that there was a disturbance at the Met."

"Common Andy…" Jasmine chimed in.

"Somebody threw a picnic basket full of food and wine and a Persian rug right off the roof. Security had been having trouble with their surveillance equipment all night and it finally came on suddenly. They heard a crash and on the camera they saw what looked like a woman in a slinky dress climbing over the side of the roof and disappearing. When security got there nobody was around but there was a mess on the front steps. Was it something you said?"

Frankie was visibly embarrassed. Jasmine stuck her hand out and introduced herself. Frankie still not used to handshakes slapped her hand five.

"Hi I'm Jasmine and I just wanna thank you for all you have done with James. He didn't tell me but I'm a detective and between what James didn't say and what Andre said I knew you had something to do with Andy's brother Frank. The real story is fantastic no doubt but anyway I just had to meet you. Thanks again. I'll let you talk to your brother."

She looked at Andre, trying not to laugh but also looking like a scolding mother warning him to go easy on his "little brother". She backed up after that and got back in the car.

Andre took Frankie to the side and said,

"Common, tell me EVERYTHING."

Frankie did tell him everything and to his credit Andre restrained his laughter and told him what he thought was going on. The woman could not be trusted that was a fact but she was also a "one off" like Frankie and that might be making her genuinely attracted to him. Andre said that once you got over his size and the scars and the face he really was kind of buff and might even be attractive in a scary sort of way. Frankie was not encouraged and he did not like feeling so out of control. Andre just said,

"Well that's women for you. You can't live with them and you can't shoot 'em."

"I wouldn't dream of shooting anyone Andy, I know how that feels."

"No I mean it's hard to deal with how an attractive woman makes us feel. I'm just surprised you don't remember. You used to be quite a lady's man."

"There is one lady I wish would treat me that way but she doesn't think me attractive. She lives in there with her mother and brother."

"The albino girl. Yes she is beautiful, but that is also something that happens. You love the wrong people and the wrong people love you. It's the story of my life."

"You Andre? I would love to have your face."

"It takes more than a face bro. You gonna go back and see her? She seems to be kinda mad that you left."

"I have to. I promised. I keep my promises. Besides I have to find out what she wants."

"Uh huh, be careful then OK. I will make sure the patrols around here know to keep an eye for problems."

"Thank you very much."

"Sure Bro, we're family. Gotta get back to work. Now you check in OK? Rice and beans, right?"

"I'll let you know how it goes tomorrow."

"You better."

Stacia had been restless and looked out the window of her darkened room when she saw a police care and a Nisan drive up and stay. The blue light was omitted but she wondered if there was some sort of trouble. Descending to the kitchen she warmed milk and put a little honey in it; a remedy mother had long used to help her sleep on restless nights. As she sipped she sat in the dark and she looked out again at the police car. There was no movement and she began to think they might be there as a preventative. She was uneasy but not overly so, they were there to ensure safety after all and besides they were on the other side of the street. She finished her milk and went upstairs.

One last look outside before she got into bed and she noted the police car had gone. Not so the Nisan that now had two unknown persons standing outside of it and one more she recognized. It was him for certain, as there was not another like him. Not another, in so many ways. She stood there haunting her window like a delicate little specter wondering what other secrets and wonders her protector held inside. The teacher did not have the courage to tell the Titian she felt that way. Many others had approached her romantically and she dated now and then but she was having feelings now foreign to her experience. She sighed with the realization that having seen him out there she now felt truly safe. Retreating to her bed she slept well.

When Frankie got home the next day he told Gunta what happened and Gunta got an old film to show him. The film was Cecil B. De Mills, "Samson and Delilah." Frankie had responded well to movie therapy before and he sat there with a 13 gallon trash bag full of popcorn and watched the whole film. Gunta also wanted to show him "Fatal Attraction" but there wasn't time. After the film Gunta and he had a little talk about being careful and about how complicated women can be--especially bad ones. Frankie felt a little more educated and Gunta suggested he not let her kiss him unless he wanted her to. He also suggested he find out what she wanted before they did anything like kiss. Frankie agreed. When it was time for him to leave, Gunta felt like a worried parent sending his son out on his first date. He sincerely hoped it would not be his last.

Frankie instinctively did what every intelligent dater has done. He got many perspectives on dating before he ventured forth. Not that this was a "date" with Babe but it sort of seemed like one, according to what he had been told. If nothing else it was a very strange appointment with sexual overtones. So before he met with Babe he made one more stop. The light in the rectory was on and he was glad.

"I'm not sure I'm asking the right man Fergus but if anyone can give me a spiritual perspective you can."

"You think that because I am celibate I have no feelings?"

"I know you have feelings Fergus but you just don't have experience."

"You are right there. I was raised in a very strict way and then I went right into the priesthood but I have to make a confession to you Frank. I have been thinking our friends the Protestants have a better idea about clergy and marriage than we do. Marriage was declared good by God before man fell. It seems unfair to make a man—or a woman for that matter—have to choose between a godly spouse and a godly calling. I sometimes wonder if I should be a lay minister so I..."

"Your secretary is very nice." The priest turned a deep shade of crimson.

"Jesus, Mary and Joseph is it that obvious?"

"You should think about being honest yourself Fergus. Love is not a sin."

"You've turned my life upside down my son."

"I think I'm more your friend than your son, Fergus. I guess we are both having similar problems. But here is a question for you, whatever Babe might have done before she was reanimated, do you think she is still guilty of it now?"

"This is more new ground for me. I suppose it all depends on her present motives. Be careful ask questions."

When Frankie got to the museum he was disturbed to see several cars outside the building. One of them was a limo. He had intended to disarm surveillance and the alarm system but NAI informed him this had already been done. He wondered if Babe had seen Stein about an upgrade and he would be very angry at Stein if he gave it. Babe had been a thief. It would only encourage her to be one again. He started to climb the majestic front steps when two men went out the side entrance with what looked like a painting of a nude woman holding a parrot. This was in fact Courbet's "Woman holding Parrot" which was followed by two more men with Francois' "Toilet of Venus" and last of all, Gauguin's "Two Tahitian Women."   All these treasures were being hurried into a van by these thugs. They snickered as they went and they reentered the museum for more.

Frankie thought these men did not look like workmen. What would workmen be doing at the Museum this late at night? And why were they only taking paintings of women without any clothes. He stopped his ascent to the roof and waited behind the door. Peering through the door hinge he could see they were taking other pieces but obviously ignorant of good art they were only taking paintings that appealed to them, hence the nudes. Frankie recognized at least one of these as one of Lupo's men and he feared the Don had found Babe.

The museum was dark and the men were working with head lamps. This was unusual but whoever shut off the surveillance might have shut the lights off too. This would actually serve Frankie's purpose. His eyes were accustomed to darkness and one by one he silently approached the thieves removing and crushing their lights. Quickly he bound them in his usual way with whatever cord he could find. When he had six unconscious men in cocoons he carefully removed the paintings from the vehicle and flung all six thugs in the van. He returned the paintings to the inside and continued to move silently through the darkness. As he did he sent an NAI text to Andre telling him to bring help. The search continued.

Frankie guessed Babe had been waiting for him on the roof and Lupo might have found her there. Passing the security office he noticed three bodies lay bloody on the floor—the unfortunate security guards. This raised Frankie's hackles with anger and increased his heart rate with fear for Babe. Hurrying up the stairs he finally reached the entrance to the roof. It was open. Slowly increasing the gap in the doorway he saw Four more men with guns standing around Lupo and Babe was in their midst writhing in pain. She was wearing a beige gown that was covered in blood and her hands were tied behind her back. It was obvious she had suffered. At this point Lupo had her face in his hands and he was kissing her while she squirmed.

Frankie silently approached two of the men from behind and thumped them so hard they fell senseless eight feet away. The other two began to fire and clipped Frankie in the rib cage and right arm as he raised it to move Babe out of the line of fire. With his leg he kicked Lupo into the two others and leaped like a stag over the side of the roof with the bruised and bleeding woman. Again a column aided him to the ground and only speed helped them avoid the rain of gunfire. The bullets followed them as they ran together disappearing round the corner a city block away. A siren was heard and Lupo made it to his Limo just in time to avoid Andre with police back up; but that night the Don had to leave without his girl and eight good boys; on account of this gorilla of a creep. It was then that Lupo put his name on the list of those who swore revenge on the Big Shadow.

Strong as she was she had endured over an hour of torment at the hands of a crazed and verbose gangster. He used his remote to wipe the roof up with her and then had her bound and smacked her around himself. Her face was bruised beyond recognition, her gown was torn and she was at the end of her strength. She leaned on the giant but he feared holding her again especially when she was so frail. Finally she fainted and all he could think of was to take her to Fergus's church.

Up through the buttresses he climbed and down through the belfry they went. Morning was dawning on the city as he sat in the locked church asking God what to do. He laid her on the soft carpeted floor of a side altar, covering her as best he could with the flowing skirt of her gown then he went to fetch the priest.

Just then the large front door opened letting in the resplendent light of morning. There in silhouette could be seen the form of the tottering little Irish woman who had cleaned the church for over two decades. Her broom and faithful bucket at her side, in her broken brogue and flat intonation, she softly hummed a hymn from Ire which was recognizable only to God.

The lady began her labor of love at the front as she always had and moved from the side altar at the left past the golden Monstrance on display on the center platform to the altar of saints on the right. She worked as always but on this day a special gift had been granted her. On the floor of the right hand altar was the suffering form of what she could only think was Saint Brigit. She crossed herself as the consciousness departed from her head.

Just then Babe came to and sat up a little woozy, she saw Frankie on the other side of the church signaling to her with the priest and she walked over to them. The priest crossed himself as he looked at her and with alarm, noticed the elderly saint on the floor. Frankie bent down and listened to her chest nodded. She was alive. The Big Guy picked her up and placed her where Babe had been. It was the softest place he could find. The priest made the sign of the cross over her. Frankie put her broom over her chest and her bucket nearby, then they locked the doors and hurried out. When the cleaning woman awoke she swore to return to Ireland before her death and lay a wreath of flowers on the altar of St Brigit for she had received a sign and that is how she interpreted it.

Fergus had agreed to transport Frankie and Babe to the boarder of Connecticut then they would make the rest of their way on foot. They decided Babe needed medical help and the only doctor who could give it was of course Stein. This was risky because Lupo would be looking for her. But it was all Frankie could think to do and Fergus very kindly offered to help. Babe fully intended to kill Stein if he did not reprogram her NAI so that the remote would be rendered useless.

Fergus was however, a bit peeved and he told Frankie so.

"Frank I like you. You are my friend. I have no ill will for this lady but she is a criminal and I can't have criminals coming into the church and frightening the congregation. Mary Margaret could have had a heart attack."

"I understand Fergus but do ya think all your constituents are on the up and up. I happen to know that not a few mobsters come to your confessional."

"You know what I mean man. This is all too much."

"Am I not a criminal Fergus? I feel a calling to help the poor. I feel a need to end pain. My heart cries out for justice but I am a criminal?"

"Frank I just don't…"

"This lady may be a Magdalene someday. How do you know she won't be? Wasn't Jesus a criminal? He was certainly executed as such wasn't he? Even though it was done unjustly? Didn't He ruffle the feathers of those in charge? Didn't he walk with sinners?"

"I would say – yes, my son."

"Alright then brother, don't judge the girl."

"I'm not judging the girl only what she does. By their fruits you will know them."

"Yes their fruits; we will see what her fruits will be."

17

Complications

Alexi sat at a table on his balcony overlooking the city.   He was eating durian fruit and caviar while drinking a fine Chablis. This was a little snack he had a passion for that could also be served as an aperitif to the Middle Eastern prince he was conversing with.   They spoke of financial matters and settled on some investments that might further enrich this obscenely wealthy man. Then they got to the real business at hand; the skin trade.

This was of course Alexi's specialty and the reason all other business could come and go but his wealth would never wane.   This was also different than stocks and bonds, drugs and other things he dabbled in because it was his passion.   After all, his supply was ample in this highly populated metropolis and easily obtained.   In fact many believed there was a surplus.   The herd needed to be thinned and slavery with drugs in the mix was a useful way to do it.   "The rabble" or the "surplus population" as Dickens called it could be replaced by technology for labor, which was much cleaner and also a good investment.   Why should the super elite pretend they would ever want to spend money to educate and employ them? Put these useless people to work for those who were taking the so called, "financial risks" then dispose of them. Why else were those with less than 8 figures in their income bracket even alive?

Sex Slavery, like the devil himself, has always been easily hidden. No one wants to believe it exists.   Still, present data is revelatory. People disappeared, some even have a moment on the media, and viola, a client with money in hand has a lovely bed or wall ornament depending on their proclivity. Some need not even be shipped.   Given the right medication they could be employed here in the good old US of A.   They grace the tables of exotic dance halls, supply the entertainment for conferences and other high end venues, and of course become escorts for the wealthy in all colors, ages and genders.

Common sex slaves in US as in other modern countries exceed the numbers of temple prostitution of present day Asia or of ancient civilizations. These young women and men are encouraged to perform disgusting acts with feigned gratitude for their degradation. Like any other industries at present, they must provide good customer service. The consequences in their case may not be discharge but instead physical punishment or death.

The demand on them is incredible as they have to service a minimum of 5 customers a day meaning at least 15,000 people a year. The bodies of the slave, despite (in some cases) reasonable medical care, are ravaged by this constant demand. Prolapse, S & M injuries and venereal disease are rampant among them as condoms (when customers allowed them) do not always avoid aids, and other STDs. This does not include the psychological damage which is actually the hardest thing to live with and which is universal to them. These people are broken in a million ways but easy access and easy disposability encourages the increase of their numbers. Alexi took full advantage of all this and considered it, not only his business, but his pleasure.

The Austrian was not a religious man but he was spiritual. This was what had attracted him to the prince to begin with. For Sheikha Rashid bin Khalifa Al Maktoum, was involved in unifying the wealth of the Middle East by invoking the old Assyrian gods in place of factions of Islam that were tearing it apart.

Alexi knew religion was very useful in the acquisition of power and he might be able to offer something exquisitely unique. Would people after all not believe if one were raised from the dead? What if, say an ancient king, were raised and presented as the Day Star of the entire world? What if Tiglath Pileser III, whom Rashid's sect revered as a god, were to come back today and rule in the old bloodthirsty Assyrian way. Who would defy him?

The Prince leaned back in his chair and Aired his robes then holding his pudgy, bejeweled fingers together in a pensive clasp said,

"Those are very large "ifs" but *if* this could be done we would have the nine princes in the palm of our hand."

Alexi leaned in and was nearly salivating with excitement.

"This not only can be done but will be done."

Prince Rashid thought him mad but his own mind started racing with possibilities.

"Bring me some proof of this and I will make you wealthier than Midas."

"You shall have your proof in a few days."

Meanwhile the Prince's personal needs had to be seen to. Alexi was mad with ideas of power but he well knew these ideas might cause angst in his client and angst needed soothing. He therefore wanted to offer him something special. Something he might even have wanted to save for himself. He informed the prince he had his eye on a unique treasure and he was in the process of obtaining it. Within a few days perhaps less it would be in his hands. The prince was intrigued and shifted his corpulent form once or twice on his seat indicating his interest. He had never had an albino of any kind. If she pleased him he would pay well for this one. He emphasized he did not want to wait too long. He would be back—in a few days.

The way to Stein's was a difficult one. Babe's face was swollen her wrists were burned by the ropes, her feet were bare because heels were impractical for a long hike and her body was on fire from all the neurological pounding Lupo's remote had given her. She begged Frankie to have compassion and carry her. He could see she needed it and held her close as she sank into the warmth of his chest. They were more equal now than ever, due to the condition of her monstrous face. His sympathy was aroused at new levels for her. She could feel his tenderness and he was still not yet astute enough to feel her need to get even.

At Stein's the coast was clear. Lupo was also apparently recuperating from his losses the night before back in the city. Surveillance was disarmed and dogs befriended as always. There would be time to heal and Frankie would keep watch for a swift exit if need be. But Stein was ready to go back to the bottle because death was threatening his peace at every turn.

Babe's presence and demands were sure to bring the wrath of the little Mob Emperor. How could the doctor possibly reprogram NAI to ignore remote access? Lupo would surely dissect him and throw him to the dogs for food. Then again Lupo needed him. A bed was waiting for Lupo with all the trimmings so that he could be reanimated on demand as soon as the need arose. Only Stein could do that for him, but that did not preclude the possibility of torture in the interim.

Stein dreamed of joining Lupo's DNA to that of a rat's and seeing him scurry along the sewers of NY for all eternity. But Lupo's new number one (Anthony) would be watching. Tony had been carefully chosen for loyalty, muscle and stupidity. He had sworn on his mother's grave that he would never fail Lupo and that was a sacred trust. Tony could be trusted, and after Lupo's reanimation, Stein would be expendable. The scientist was 58 and did not expect to live to 60.

What Stein could do was throw a few more bots into action for Babe to speed recovery. She fortunately had no lesions as Lupo had been careful not to cut her skin but as the minute mechanical wonders began to do their work the pooled blood at her bruises began to disappear, the internal bleeding was repaired and the white blood cells that caused the swelling were reintegrated into their designated body parts. In one day she looked like herself and this was a gift, she was told, that would keep on giving. She would recovery speedily forever.

While she was recuperating Frankie got a call from Gunta and then from Andre. Both had good news and bad news. Gunta told him that Esther called and reported she had cancer. This was bad news but she was taking it well because she had lived a good life and she was sick of the state of things in the world. To complicate things however, she was very upset by the news that the TMS machine had been sent back. She confessed that her dearest wish before she died was to see this protocol implemented so she could give Itzak the good news on the other side. To that end she was staying at the local Comfort Inn and she demanded to see Dr. Frank to discuss a large endowment so the work could continue.

Andre's news also presented multiple conundrums. With all the Babe complications Andre had not told Frankie about the footage he had reviewed. Now they were certain of at least three of Frankie's constituents, Itzak, George and Frank but there was a good possibility that Senator Edmund Shea and Pastor Morris Gray were also involved. The common bond between them all was human rights and safety and a significant elevator on that fateful day. This would explain Frankie's rabid desire to help others and protect them. He couldn't help it, this was his essence multiplied 5 times.

Andre told him how all five of these good men had entered the elevator at the last meeting of the CHRS and they had disappeared. Frankie's head began to whirl and he crumpled to the floor like a child. His head was spinning and he was having artifact after artifact as if all five of the people in him were in a heated discussion screaming to be noticed. He saw families and homes, harassment and violence. He also saw the meeting and all the reporters. He saw Esther and posters with Sparrow's picture. He saw a tall man with great authority addressing the crowd and promising justice. He saw crowds of all sorts of people bow their heads as a Black Pastor prayed a heart stirring prayer begging Almighty God not to let justice die on that day.

Then he saw the elevator as all of them entered. He saw how in a couple of stops the elevator lights had gone out and the small cabled room began plumiting down, down into the darkness while 5 men screamed helplessly.   He then felt like a man who was being torn apart by five wild horses. Then, when all his parts were recognized they all reunited and he understood all at once, Stein knew.

Babe was asleep and Stein was sitting in the living area on the couch warming him-self in a beam of sunlight while illuminated dust particle slowly floated about him. He appeared more like a weather beaten part of the furniture than a man but there he sat puffing on some weed and hoping he would not be asked to do anything more today. This was not to be the case.

Frankie walked up to him radiating righteous fury and grabbed him by the hands extending them outward as far as they could reach and lifting him off the ground. His yellow eyes threatened to burn through the Doctor's own retinas as he stared into his dark soul. Then Frankie spoke,

"You knew who I was and you tore me apart. Now I will tear you apart if you do not give me closure. WHO AM I?"

He dropped Stein and the man collapsed limply on the ground. Then with trembling arms and aching shoulders the scientist reached into his pocket and retrieved a metal container the size of a man's hand. Within were Frank Poloche's dog tags, Senator Shea's cuff links, Pastor Gray's pocket watch, George Little Bear's guitar picks and the plastic encased patch of skin with numbers from Auschwitz that had been on Itzak Katz's arm.

Frankie held these relics gently in his large hands. He could see them in his mind--dressing for a meeting, looking at the time, playing the guitar, chatting up a pretty girl and sitting with Esther on a porch swing resting after a long day. He looked particularly at the Pastor with his laughing eyes and ready smile. And He said to himself,

"Justice did not die that day, God help me."

Frankie had decisions to make but in that moment his mind was too exhausted to conceive anything but one step in front of another. He walked out the front door and the dogs ran to him begging and playing. He took a stick and threw it then could vaguely hear the k-9s scrambling and fighting over it.

He walked in silence towards the lake and found there in the quiet water, his dark hooded image. Ducks started their noise approaching the shore for a handout. He had nothing to give them and so turned deaf ears to their squawking. The swans swam aloof and apart from the shore, to shy or too proud to beg from him. And that was always the way.

He had often watched them floating through the Air and heard their muscular wings thunder like those of dragons in approached. They had their own spot of sunlight that guided them to the far side where, unlike the beggar geese and ducks, they would tease him and avoid him. There in the morning sunlight they were enthroned the monarchs of all water fowl and he was but a minion to their beauty. He bowed to them, never the less, and thanked them for the pleasure they bestowed, which had always given his soul such ease. Then walking along the shore his moccasins ground the mass of duck feathers deeply into the sand and he thought them very dirty birds.

A large white feather among the brown and black ones told him that, despite their aristocratic demeanor, the swans also came to forage there. He picked it up and marveled at its delicacy and holding it to the light he thought of her. In the sun, auras of colors released from prisms of water droplets surrounded its fibers and he understood even colorless things bear more dimensions than we know.   With a sigh he tucked it into his hoodie pocket to accompany his other treasures and walked up to the house.

Babe had awakened and took advantage of Frankie's absence to speak to Stein. The man was a shell of a person by now and Babe made the astute deduction that if some pressure was not removed from him he would not be in this world for long. She was therefore offering a respite from the pressure, in the form of exorcising the demon that haunted him. When he asked her, "Which one, she of course said, "Romeo Lupo". He offered a lame smile and wanted to say something about the green man and woman that haunted his dreams but he didn't. She continued with this proposal. If he would consent to reprogram her NAI she would promise to kill Lupo. This was her plan.

When Lupo used the remote she would feign torment and would allow herself to be shackled to the table for his use. Stein could provide the table with the shackles but the key to the locks of those shackles would be hidden for her access along with a gun. She would free herself and kill him as soon as they were alone.

The plan sounded good and Stein could not be blamed for anything.   In fact to get things moving Stein called Lupo and told him Babe was there begging for medical help. He said he patched her up and would stall her till Lupo came. Lupo said he did good and told him he would be there shortly.   Babe got the things ready for her feigned bondage and Stein worked to reprogram the remote access to her NAI.

When Frankie walked in to take his leave he looked at both of them and suspected something was not right. He told them he had business elsewhere and he had to go. He wanted to know what Babe wanted to do? Staying there might be dangerous. She said she was still too sick to leave and would stay.

"What will you do when I turn on the surveillance again? You might be seen?"

"There are no cameras in the bedrooms I will stay in my room until dark then go out if I have to."

"And if Lupo comes?"

"I will stay in my room and lock the door."

"If he uses the remote?"

"I will suffer in silence."

"Seems kind of harsh. What are your plans when you are better?"

"I will wait to see you again then decide what I will do."

"I will return in a week and check on you."

"A week is so long? Oh, Alright, I'll be waiting."

She thought she pulled off the lovesick female quite well. Perhaps because she was a good actress but also because, to her surprise, some part of her was warming to him. Despite his looks he was more than she had guessed and more than most men she had known. He was a rare good guy. Babe could do worse than to end up with him. But she was an exceptionally bad girl. Would he ever have her?

Frank got to the "tree house" and Gunta met him with the same expression aficionados of soap operas have, anticipating the next episode.   Actually it was that expression he wore mixed with a good measure of concern.   They were both going to have to deal with the current problem. Gunta and Ben were after all, the interface in this relationship with Esther. And if there was any "splaining" to be done he and Ben would have to start off.   Monsters they could face but an emotionally formidable and physically frail old Jewish lady? Now that *was* frightening.

They decided to unveil the truth to her in stages starting with appealing to her medical experience with abnormality and deformity. They would tell her that Dr. Frank was a brilliant researcher but was afflicted with a rare disorder that gave him a frightening appearance. Only two people in the whole world had this problem that they were aware of. His distorted appearance disallowed personal interviews for the most part. He only consented because, understanding her to be a woman of medicine, she might be able to objectively view his physical appearance without prejudice.

She looked at them sideways with a wry smile and told them she had been in Africa with the 'Doctors without Borders' organization and she had seen things that would "curl your hair". In fact when she started to describe those things they informed her that they had enough information. She even made an offer to examine him, as Itzak had worked on many unusual disorders, and his records might have something to offer him. The boys smiled at each other understanding why a man like Itzak would fall hard for a girl like Esther. She was one of a kind.

For the meeting they needed a place and Frankie needed a wardrobe. The "Big and Tall" catalogue had quite a lot to offer by way of made to measure suits and formal knit shirts. Elaina said the guys had no fashion sense and she and Angie took on the job of selecting and picking out the outfit. Rosa (who was a seamstress) took his measurements. They specified it was a rush order, and in three days the suit was at the tree house.

Meanwhile they made plans for the meeting. They would show Esther the modifications they had worked on with all the meds and the data on the thousands of trial with heroine and fentanyl. They would also show her the one trial with desomorphine. She would want to see the coordinates that had been the most effective on the TMS machine which Itzak had 80% correct. They would apprise her of the details and problems associated with this population for treatment and follow up. Then, when she was fully in her analytic brain, reviewing the content and empirical data, they would tell her the truth about Frankie.

They rented a private room at a nearby restaurant, snuck Frankie in after the meal had been set up and they had Angie there to present data and take notes on the meeting. They figured a woman's presence might be a plus just in case there was any fainting.

To her credit, the little daughter of Israel was most definitely taken aback by Frankie's formidable appearance, but she was not daunted.

After blinking a few times she reached her hand out and took his (Ben had practiced handshaking with Frankie and he performed well). Her expression after that verged on emotional but she lifted her chin and swallowed hard, recovering nicely.

Frankie's outfit was a wonderful mitigating influence and the girls felt they scored big time on that one. Frankie looked as good as he could and that helped. After the initial shock, Esther snapped to attention quickly, and got down to business. She even lightened the tension by making a few jokes about being short (her head barely reached his solar plexus when they were standing next to each other). She sat in a chair with her feet off the ground and he sat on a sturdy bench the boys provided. They were all comfortable as they got technical.

The ample information left little room for eating. Esther was absolutely flabbergasted by the data and so very proud. She got emotional again when she thought what all this might have meant to their son who had succumb to addiction and died in squalor despite all their efforts to reach him. Thinking this couple to be exemplary parents Gunta wanted to ease her pain. He explained that addiction had many factors that also had to be dealt with. Esther conquered. Then she confessed that she always felt a childhood trauma incurred at the hands of an anti-Semitic neighbor when her Daniel was a boy, might have fueled his addiction. He needed a lot of help, and they were just learning about that when he overdosed.

All through the dinner Esther kept looking at Frankie's hands. Far from being appalled she looked at them with a kind of nostalgia. Finally she took one of his hands in both of hers and said,

"Forgive an old doctor's delusions but my husband had large hands just like yours. In fact it was kind of a family joke that his very skilled hands and forearms always seemed to belong to a larger body. In you they are proportionate."

She then noticed a rectangular scar that looked like a skin graft, where a number once had been, and she trailed off her words, almost to a whisper. Then there was silence and Frankie thought he needed to take the opening,

"Esther these look like Itzak's hands because they are."

She was livid at first that anyone would toy with her that way and then the worst occurred to her. This man might have murdered her husband and in a grizzly act taken his wonderful hands. She almost started screaming. Ben was able to soothe her and assure her they had proof for all they were about to tell her and that she would never know what happened to Itzak if she didn't calm down and listen. Flustered and angry but with great dignity she straightened her dress and sat back down. For the next hour she listened and at the end of it she was shaken but rational.

"I will need skin samples." She said.
"Of me? For what?"
"Come now 'doctor', a woman like me doesn't take anything at face value. I'm going to DNA test you AND examine you, then we will see what is what. If you don't submit to that you'll have to kill me because I will call the authorities."

"Wow" Angie whispered to Ben. "If she comes on board I'm gonna have her screen all my dates."

Frankie did submit and well that he did. The four skin samples and one biopsy she took, confirmed the identities of all the men who had items in that little metal box. Depending on what was decided this evidence could bury Lupo. The problem for Frankie was that it would bury Stein with him and much as the giant hated what the man had done he still had a soft feeling in regards to the doctor. He thought little of the fact that bringing this all to light might also bury the doctor's monster.

Esther held the little piece of plastic with her husband's skin in her hand then held Frankie's hand again and saw the scar where the skin had been removed. She then dropped it on the table. She understood all at once that what had been done was not his fault but it did complete her husband's work. How could she hold that against him? She said she wanted to talk to him further about many things but for now action must be taken. She took on an administrative tone and said,

"Well, this is the way I see it. This work was badly started but must go on. The control of drugs, in the hands of criminals, is causing a holocaust of sorts. It must be stopped and what is being done now is ineffective to stop it. Your methods have been unorthodox but they work. So we gotta legitimize all of this. We need legal help and we need political help. We need the Coalition back and we need to show them this data. We have to have a reunion."

All the people in the room were amazed at this little fire cracker of a woman. Feeling like she had no time to waste she took charge. She wanted to see some justice before she went into the cold earth. She also knew the others who were still wondering about their loved ones needed to be informed to find closure. What better way to get all this going than to have a joint memorial.

They set a date and rented the hall where the last meeting of the CHRS was held. They did not inform the media. This was a private affair for the families of the missing and the supporters of Frankie only. Dr. Katz would pay for most of it and would turn a blind eye to how they paid for the rest. Frankie's friends, including the De Lacys, volunteered to serve at the tables and bus them. Frankie would be the guest of honor and the data they had all collected would back up the story in the presence of all his families.

They decided not to accuse Lupo of the murders till the rest of those concerned were informed and on board with the project. They would have to understand that there was some danger involved. They also did not want to incur the animosity of the mob till they were sure they could win. Frankie listened to all this and knew the inevitable had come upon him. He had some decisions to make and these concerned Babe and Stein.

The next day Frankie made his way to Stein's informal prison. He determining the coast was clear. He petted the dogs and walked up to the house where he was seldom welcomed. Frankie had come to terms with Stein's ambivalence towards him and now it was not as painful as it was formerly. At present the Big Man knew what it was like to be respected and valued by others. He also knew Stein was a sick bastard who could not even love himself. How could Frankie hate him? It was a proposition not worth entertaining.

Babe was a villain but she was also a creature to be pitied. Her beauty had been a gift and a curse, and Frankie could only conjecture what might have made her the person she was before reanimation. None the less she had some soft aspects that were emotionally and physically moving to him, and he continued to wonder if her attentions had any veritas or if it was all a perverse trick.

Babe was in her bedroom "cell" as promised and she startled to see the Titian at her bedroom door. She was wearing an old white shirt of Steins and a pair of old jeans that he used when feeding the dogs or walking about the property. It appeared to him she was softened somehow by the look and it felt nice and earthy. He had left his hair loose and had his hood down. His shoulders were not stooped as they were when he walked in the city. At his full height he had a kind of otherworldly majesty that superseded his scars. She gazed up at him almost adoringly. Since he was present she knew the cameras were shut down. So she came out of the room to meet him.

"You have been away for a long time, more than a week."
"It could not be helped. There were many things I had to tend to."
"We had trouble here."
"What do you mean...trouble?"

Babe explained that Lupo had come looking for her. She did not tell him about the modifications to her NAI freeing her from Lupo's control. She also kept the assassination plan to herself. She just said she got away. The truth was she and Stein had colluded on all this but that would be their secret. She said she got away clean but came back-- for Frankie.

The facts were that there had been a tussle, and Babe killed two of Lupo's men. She then had Lupo pinned, and was about to kill him too, but more men came in, and she fled. In that moment she held the gun to Lupo's head, she told him she had modified the NAI herself using Stein's data. She said she would never be his punching bag again and hit him with the gun across the face several times. She also called him every name conceivable concluding with "mean, whiny, teensy Italian piglet." When the others came in she had to run, but his face and his pride would take a long time to recover. At least she had that and she promised herself that someday she would finish the job.

Frankie wondered about all this especially since Stein was in the lab and appeared to be covering up the vats of solvent. A crumpled Fedora was on the floor near the vats and Babe picked it up and said one of Lupo's men must have dropped it. He then noticed a spot on her hand that looked like a scar from an industrial burn. He took her hand and looked at it. It appeared to be repairing itself quickly, like his scars did. He looked at Stein. What had they been doing in the lab?

Frank really came to warn them but now he wondered if they should be warned. Deciding not to follow through, he just turned to leave. Babe clung to him and asked him not to go but he took her off his arm and walk on. Babe was livid. No man had ever snubbed her so. From now on it was war--and she didn't fight fair.

At the memorial Frankie was all dressed up again. He refused to wear a suit for the second time even without a tie and requested something more native looking. His fashion advisors (Elaina and Angie) finally settled on a loose fitting dashiki like top with the back longer than the front and cuffed sleeves. The pants were form fitting but comfortable and they were also black. His black moccasins were custom made as well by Kurt who worked with leather. He had made his daily mocs and was happy to make him a dress pair. Hailey did some fancy beading on his collar, cuffs and moccasins. He cut quite a figure. Esther made him bend down and wiped his nose with a hankie then pinched his cheek and said,

"A little orthodontics, a little plastic surgery and you wouldn't look so bad. We can talk about that after the meeting. You can also use a haircut." But he pouted and responded,

"Not the hair. You're not touching the hair." And she took his hands and put them close to her face then shifting gears she said,

"We'll talk about it."

All the people invited had RSVP'd and this gave Esther confirmation that they all wanted and needed to be there. Others get tired of people who continually talk about loved ones they are grieving. After a few years everyone is encouraging them to forget and move on. Still, when a person you love goes missing and you don't know what happened the wound is a never ending source of pain. So they filed in-- all the waiting wounded—they came hoping to talk, at least, to someone else that might understand.

Esther was there at the front with Gunta and Ben. They welcomed the wives Kathleen Shea and Vera Gray. Two of the Senator's sons came; Fred, a doctor and Simon, an attorney. Vera brought her son, Daniel, a marine in dress uniform, and her two daughter's Petula, a teacher and Francine, a business woman.

The Little Bear family came as well; Uncle Raven, Grandfather and Grandmother Little Bear. They came in native formal dress and brought gifts of sweet grass for the mother's. The grandfather and uncle had a head of hair much like Frankie's and they brought eagle feathers on leather ties for the mourning male relations.

Andre came and he brought Jasmine with him because he felt no self respecting Hispanic man would go anywhere stag. She thought he was a bit of a hypocrite because he hadn't had a steady girl in years but she would not have missed this for all the beer in the Bronx. She was also glad to get decked out for something. They both looked quite elegant and some said made a nice couple. Andre was also told he might have to say something. This induced mild panic but he swallowed hard and asked what he had to say. Frankie told him to bring the footage from the news cast and told him he would know when to speak.

Fergus was there dressed in regular clothes and he brought his admin assistant Mary Ellen a gentle spoken auburn haired lady looking lovely and fresh in an Irish green gown. She sat next to Ann to help her get around if need be. Kurt came over and whispered to the priest, that in the office attached to the hall, his professional expertise was required. He excused himself and left, thinking that even without his cassock he could simply not get away from his calling. Mary Ellen patted his hand and smiled with understanding.

The tables were arranged around a small circular platform. Frankie's friends all pitched in with serving and bussing as promised and no one dropped a plate. Ann dressed up and looked beautiful in a grey chiffon gown and was seated at Esther's table with room for Jean Luc who would also speak and Luna who by now was a friend of Frankie and would give her testimony. Gunta as a young intern was there to present the data. Ben would present an award.

Frankie was of course the reason Fergus was called. He was alone in the office and he wanted to prayer before he entered. Frankie was quite taken aback by what Fergus was wearing and was told not to ask about it till this was all over. Fergus was only too glad to pray.

Back in the hall Ben went to the podium and welcomed everyone. He confirmed that this was a solemn occasion but that he was also happy to hear laughter and good conversation among people who had suffered so long, after working so hard together, for such a noble cause.

He then introduced Esther as the one who had conceived of this evening and who had arranged it all. She rose to the platform and sipped some water then went right to the heart of the matter.

"My Friends it has been over fifteen years since we lost our loved ones and this place bring us back. This was the last place we saw them, felt them, encouraged them and the last place we were able to tell them our hearts swelled with pride at the work they were doing. It has been a hard fifteen years and I guess your pain is as fresh as my own. But I'm here to say that there is hope."

She paused...

"New evidence has been brought to us concerning their disappearance."

A gasp was heard around the room and several people started to cry. The pain in the room was palpable but so was the excitement. Esther paused again this time with difficulty speaking. Ben walked up and put his arm around her and she looked to him for strength. Then she said,

"The story that we are about to show you, sounds like a gothic novel, or something out of science fiction, but will be accompanied with definitive proof. It is a strange tale but as God is my witness I would not lie to so august an audience because I would not want you to lie to me about my Itzak."

There she began to cry and Andre knew he had to stand up.

"My name is Detective Sgt. Andre Poloche. My brother Frank was among the missing. He did security for Senator Shea on the day of their disappearance. Everything that I am about to tell you is pertinent to this case.

Early in the year 2012 we began investigating a series of strange events concerning a vigilante we called 'the Alien'…"

To Andre's credit he encapsulated the story very well and soon got to the visit he received from 'the Alien' himself.

"Bizarre as his appearance was his story was stranger. This benevolent but amazing creature claimed to be a reanimated composite of 5 men. He was almost certain of the identity of one; this being my brother Frank and he asked me to help him find the others…"

As Andre spoke, the audience it seemed had stopped breathing. When he got to the part of showing the footage a few of them stood up and some broke down.

At this point Esther had her nerve back and she asked if anyone was interested in taking a break. No one was. They had waited this long and they would hear all that had to be said. So Esther launched into her experience with the boys, the research and Frankie's hands. They presented their data and Lucas and Luna got up to tell their story.

At this point no one was nibbling and there was silence. Then Gunta stood up and said,

"We are not asking you to believe without evidence. Frank is here to answer your questions and confirm that he is what he says he is. The data we have collected concerning his DNA is also available as well as some items that may be familiar to you belonging to your love ones. We welcome your questions after you examine all this evidence. Ladies and Gentleman we are please to introduce Frank to you."

Till then the lights were off, so that the screen above the podium could present the data. At that point the lights came up and the timid Titian stood on a centrally located platform looking at all the people his parts had once loved and known. He fully expected all of them to start throwing food and jeering at him like so many others had done. But there was not a move or a sound.

Then from the kitchen a light shined as Elaina opened the door and sent Dee Dee out to stand with Frankie. The little cherub walked out and hugged his leg then one by one the others' stood and approached him in a state of wonder. The Little Bear family placed gifts at his feet and he knew to accept them in native fashion. Then they mounted the dais and hugged him. The Marine saluted him and the wives and daughters pulled him down and wept upon him. He was simply floored by the love. And he looked over the sea of people to where Andre was and Andy gave him a thumbs up. He could have died again in that moment and never been happier. But there was one face he missed.

Stacia had been standing by the kitchen where she had been talking to Frankie's friends. They all knew how he felt about her but were not telling because he had asked them not to. She on the other hand had been conflicted about him for a long time. She had gone from terror to admiration, to desperation over his work. Only recently had she admitted she loved his company, perhaps above all others.

The friends all walked up to join the general affection and Elaina took Stacia's hand and walked her through the crowd to where the giant was becoming reacquainted with his biological families. One artifact after the other was coming to him and he was convincing them all that he was who he said he was. He knew them and they knew him and were persuaded.

Then all of a sudden he was face to face with the delicate little spirit he had secretly studied for so long. She was looking at him and smiling. So he smiled back as if there was no one else in the room. At a loss for her next move she ran to the nearest table and poured a glass of water then brought it to him. He thanked her and downed the drink like a man would down the contents of a shot glass. He then returned the glass and in true native fashion signaled for her to wait as he produced his own gift. In her hands he placed a pure white swan feather he had held close to his heart for a very long time.

Then Esther nudged Ben and he took Dee Dee's hand and brought her up to the podium. Taking the mike the newly licensed psychologist hushed everyone and begged their attention. Then he said,

"I have been asked to give this book as an award to Frankie. He has no use for plaques or trophies but Esther thought he would like this book and he could read it to Dee Dee, so she will present it. For those of you who know the story it's titled, "the Gollum of Prague". It's about a man made giant who was called forth in a time of great need to help the Jews. We have been, and are, as desperate as they were at the time and Frankie may be our Big Guy of the hour. We love you Frank. Thanks for being you."

As the child brought the illustrated book to the giant and placed it in his huge hands the applause was deafening. He picked up the child and held up the book smiling, shaking his head in disbelief, but full of true happiness.

18

Plots and Plans

Everyone at the event agreed that they needed to meet again. Too much was revealed and needed processing. Plans needed to be made. The coalition would reemerge but in a different way. Precautions needed to be taken but after so long it was time to move forward. They only needed to strategize, as to how.

All the families wanted to spend special time with Frankie just like Andre and Esther had. He was only too glad to oblige them. The Little Bear family invited him to a sweat lodge and took him back into the tribe. They told him the legend of the Peace Keeper and said that perhaps Creator had sent him into the world in a similar spirit. As that great man had unified the five tribes for the Iroquois confederation, so Frankie would unify these five families, along with others, to bring urban peace. They also took a family portrait with the giant and all of them were in full warrior's regalia.

The Sheas taught him to play flag football and had him down to their home on Nantucket where Simon their legal advisor said he would begin looking into starting a legal entity to market the medication in conjunction with treatment that would aid the whole person. He also would obtain some grants for several TMS machines that could be purchased specifically for the modifications needed in their program. Kathy was thinking of running for office herself and she assured Edmund (through Frank) that she would make him proud.

Vera Gray fed him biscuits and gravy with strawberries and cream for breakfast then took him to church where he sat quietly in the balcony secretly enjoying the jubilation below and her family took pictures with him all wearing hoodies. They also started a campaign alerting students to tactics used to introduce them to desomorphine. Vera gave him a big kiss on the cheek and told him he was a gift from God to all of them. She said he was the answer to the last prayer Morris prayed,

"Lord, don't let justice die this day."

Frankie had never had so much socializing and fun. In this time period he would have been perfectly happy but for the storm brewing. On the streets and underground in the world of the mob, things were spinning with the momentum of a 6 point twister.   Frankie knew Lupo was an ever present danger and talked to Andre about shifting his gears from catching the "Alien" to helping him go after the Don.   Andre said it would be complicated but they could talk about it. Frankie was after all only a civilian at present without real identity or affiliation and not authorized to chase criminals.   But Andre wondered if that could change. He said he would love to see Lupo dangling from a billboard swaying in the wind and pleading to be arrested. If Frankie could arrange that before he was given papers—Andre wouldn't tell.

All this happened in the space of a month and everyone at the memorial agreed to meet at the "tree house" a few days after that month, to coordinate their plans.

During this time Frankie did not forget his dependents. He still made his house call to Ann then Ann and Stacia distributed the medication in the neighborhood to the other 4 people in great pain. He also continued to work with the dozens and dozens of people who were addicted to opioids and who wanted to change. The difference was he began directing these people to Lucas and other social agencies for as much help as they could get, then he assisted them with the rest. The idea however was always the same. If they did the right thing they would get their medicine. If not they were on their own. The end goal would be to slowly wean off as they became responsible citizens. The plan worked well 90% of the time. Krokodil continued to proliferate and things were on hold for that but without NAI's intervention for finance the wheels of justice moved very slowly.

Frankie was working hard but he felt so supported that he was floating around in a pink bubble of happiness. Then the bubble burst, because Stacia and Stein went missing on the same day.

Frankie came to see if Babe had moved on and found the dogs scratching for food and no one in the house. He dropped the dogs off at the Tree House and Kurt soon won them with some steak and leftovers.   Then Frank went hunting for Babe and Stein. The lab was in disarray and that frightened him even more. He had to find them. But just when he thought things could not get worst Ann called and said, Stacia had not come home and she was worried. He asked if she might have gone shopping but Ann told him she was supposed to go to a concert with Jean Luc and Luna and they were worried too. She was never late for such things. Frank said he was on his way. He also called Andre.

When Frank arrived Andre and Jasmine were already there asking questions. Stacia had called from school and said she was on her way, then, hours later, nothing. No show and no call. Jasmine made some calls and no one seems to have seen her after she left the building at school. She was walking towards the bus stop and that was all. No one saw her get on the bus. The Bus driver who had that route was questioned and he always noticed the unusual beauty when she got on at the same time every day. That day she hadn't. Somewhere between the school and the bus stop she had taken a detour.

The bus stop also attracted quite a few kids from the high school. Andre went there and asked around about anyone who might have seen her. The boys especially knew who she was as the fame of her looks preceded her. They said they saw her getting into a black Mercedes sport with another bangin' woman in costume. When Andre asked what they meant one kid said,

"Man she was wearing lots of leather with this short cape and hood, and boots, but dude, she had wicked long hair as red as blood. I mean like it's warm out and time to be showin' some skin but this woman wasn't havin' none of it. She even had leather gloves."

Andre knew the car and Frankie knew it was Babe. He also imagined where she had been taken and he almost ripped the door off the De Lacy kitchen heading straight for it. Where he went Andre could not follow, as the giant took to the roof tops, but Frankie sent him a text with the address and asked him to send help. The address in Soho made Jasmine a little nervous since it was a building with a lot of wealthy people who had a lot of legal protection. There would be no bustin' doors down without warrants or anything like that. Frankie would have to take the battle outside to them and that might be tricky. Still they would do what they could.

Frankie gained the roof of the building and understood stealth was of more use at this moment than strength. He had learned that NAI could be a great weapon in that regard and asked it to hack any telephone conversations in the building. At first there was a cacophony of sounds beeps and talking but finally he heard the words, "Albino girl" and he honed in on that. He noted the Nisan had caught up with him and had parked in a dark corner of a side street. He shimmied down the side of the building to let them hear.

"I will be at the Museum in an hour your Excellency and the girl will be waiting for you here when you return to my apartments. We have sent the scientist with a most delightful creature named Ms. Lonegan she will give you access. The Assyrian exhibit is on the first floor. The rest is up to your men."

Andre said the Assyrian exhibit was at the Museum of Natural history but apparently Stacia was here. Which apartment was she in? That was the question. Frankie suspected but he did not know for sure. He was uneasy about waiting so he stared circling the building peering into windows. He saw a lot of strange things but did not see what he was looking for. He left the channel open in NAI to hear any other conversation that might transpire. Down he came again to ground level and with the detectives he heard this,

"I don't care what time of day it is. I pay you an obscene amount to keep my home tidy and it's an absolute Middle Eastern bazaar at the moment. Whatever it costs I want someone up there right now and I want it immaculate by the time I get back in two hours. I have a very important guest with me and he doesn't like hummus on his tush when he sits. Am I clear? It's the Penthouse, I will tell Bradley the private elevator man to let her in."

Frankie started to move but Jasmine held him back.

"No dude, going in like gang busters might get Stacia killed. You will have to leave this one to me."

She took off her scarf. Put it around her head. And went to the trunk of the car where she got a box full of rags, Windex and other cleaning supplies Andre had, to clean his Nisan, which was his "baby". Then she twiddled her fingers at them in "goodbye" and went into the building. Frankie was concerned but Andre said,

"Relax, she knows what she's doing, AND now she won't tease me about the cleaning supplies for my fine car."

Frankie sighed deeply and impatiently and waited.

Five minutes later a limo drove out of the building's parking garage and away in the direction of the city. The windows were darkened but they assumed that at this time of day there would be few people leaving for business. It was Andre's guess that this was the voice at the end of the call

NAI had intercepted. NAI also had a bead on Jasmine's phone and she spoke to them as if they were her employer,

"OK I'm at the client's apartment and the fine elevator operator just let me in. So tell the other girl she doesn't need to come. Oh what? She's on her way? Well I'll just have fine Bradley here tell her she can get her fat but home to sleep. I was here first and I ain't sharing the money."

"See I told you, she's good. If Stacia is in there she will find her."

Jasmine got to the door and blew a kiss to Bradley. Habitually, she felt for her gun tucked in her jeans and under her t-shirt. When the door opened she was escorted in by the Butler who was overwhelmed with the company inside. Jasmine looked around to see three swarthy men in robes guzzling assorted drinks and ogling Cable porn. The Butler threw his hands up in dismay and said he would be working in the kitchen. He wanted her to start in the living room. Fortunately the trail of empty bottle led into two bathrooms and she indicated she would start there.

She took a trash bag and began throwing bottles into it. She also looked in various rooms. One had sleeping mats all over it and she took this to be the temporary dorm for the hoods in the living room. She counted ten in all. That meant there might be seven at the Museum with his "Excellency", who ever that might be. She was not about to clean that and the Butler came over to check on her and shook his head closing the door. He told her to concentrate on the bath rooms and hallway.

She then noted he walked into a room with a look of concern. She slipped over there and barely got a glimpse before he shut off the lights and closed the door. He locked it.   This room had disturbing white satin walls and some sharp things that looked rather dangerous. She acted as if she had not seen anything and continued to pick up bottles. The Butler left and she continued till she had looked in all the other rooms. These were relatively normal looking and she was certain she had the information she was looking for.

Moving back through the living room one of the men spotted her and grabbed at her making lewd remarks in a foreign language. She slapped his hand and waved her finger "no, no" then hurried into the kitchen where she informed the Butler she was not going to put up with these men and their nasty ways. She picked up her box of cleaning supplies and marched out of the place. The Butler dropped his head in desperation and kept cleaning.

When Jasmine got to the Nisan Frankie was ready to explode. She gave him the information and he shot up to the penthouse in less time than it would take a bird to fly. Over the balcony rail he went and he crashed into the glass windows like a hurricane. The men stood up and began to draw their weapons but it was too late for them. Frankie was tossing them like rag dolls and had all three unconscious in short order. The Butler was hiding under the table and could not believe what he was seeing. The yellow eyes of the giant glanced at him briefly and that was enough. The elderly gentleman grabbed his hat and a framed coin collection on the wall of the hallway then made his way to the elevator wearing his apron with a plan never to return.

Frankie went towards the hallway shattering doors as he went. Finally he arrived at the white room and stood there aghast at what he saw. Manacles were on the wall, and sharp bejeweled weapons and tools of extraction lined a nearby table. Blood covered another table and was smeared onto one wall. His heart sank to think of what might have transpired there. Stacia, however, was not there. He called for her several times but no one answered. Crushed he took a sample of a bloody cloth and walked out desperately confused, but unknown to him behind the satin wall of white were three closets like chambers. The first held a once beautiful dead young woman and the other two had drugged women who were still alive. One of these was Stacia.

The Big Guy came down to ground level and showed the cloth to Jasmine and Andre. They both looked at him with pity and told him it might be hers but it might not be. He should not lose hope. They put it in a plastic bag as evidence. They then called for backup and forensics. Both detectives knew Frankie wanted to follow the Limo to the Museum. It may be that whoever was in it decided to take Stacia with him. It could be the blood was hers and she was dead. Either way Frankie had to know. Besides, Stein was also apparently with them and that meant big trouble. Frankie thought it was time to tell. He no longer felt the need to keep Stein a secret from his brother. Perhaps prison was where the man belonged. The world would certainly be safer if he was out of commission.

Jasmine volunteered to wait for the back up and Andre told Frankie to lie flat on the roof of the car and hold on. When they arrived at the Museum the police were already there. Frankie slipped off the car and behind it to avoid exposure then snuck into the Museum to look around. Andre walked over to the suits and asked what was going on.   The commissioner was there as this was the second time a museum had been broken into in the last month. This job had apparently been planned better than the last one. The surveillance had been disabled and the robbery perpetrated before any police got there. Andre asked what had been stolen. The commissioner said, so far, the only things missing were three Mummies.

Alexi felt a sense of accomplishment every time he had a satisfied customer. The fact that most of the leg work for this deal was accomplished by Babe was incidental. He had conceived of the master plan and he would get the credit. Riding high on what had been accomplished, and the daring plan they were about to undertake, Alexi congratulated himself, then his cell beeped and he received a disturbing text.

Dear Sir,

I am leaving the country and will not be available to continue in my position as your serving man. Forgive me but, I have taken the liberty of removing the rare coins you had on display in the hallway as my severance. Thanks to the internet they are already processed on E-bay and I have my money. Thank you very much. I endeavor to maintain discretion as long as I am allowed to live in peace far away from you. My "insurance policy" is very good and should anything unpleasant befall me, would reveal to the authorities the foresight and intellect you neglected to recognize in me during my time in your employ.

 Regards, and best of Luck,

or as they say in America,

"Good luck with that."

Wendell

This of course released a stream of invectives from Alexi but showing Babe the text she assured him of reprisal as soon as their plot was executed. They had the doc and they had the goods. What could possibly stop them? Alexi's thoughts turned to what might have happened to cause Wendell to leave. He hoped the cleaning lady showed up and did her job. The "three little pigs" the prince left at the house to guard Stacia, might have been rude to

Wendell. If they damaged anything the Prince's bill would be astronomical. Besides he had other plans for himself and discussed this aside with Stein. He might soon be in a class of his own as far as his abilities and power.

Stein, who had hoped that his last two years with Lupo would be quiet ones, was suffering sensory overload. He sat in the Limo staring at the mobile bar and nearly cried when it was retracted into the consol because they wanted him sober. He was considering suicide but hoped that perhaps Frankie might save him for old time's sake. After all he was like a "father" to him; a bad one, but a father never-the-less. True narcissist that he was he continued to hold the hope that Frank would pity him and pack up all his enemies for delivery to the police. Then again that would mean he would be in trouble himself. He waited for them to cross a bridge and tried to get out. If he had been successful he would have jumped but Babe prevented him. She would watch him more closely thereafter.

The prince was also suffused with adrenalin. His nerves needed soothing and all he was thinking of was the sweet white haired prize that awaited him. His dreams of power would enable him to continue indefinitely with acts of cruelty. He believed such acts had given the Assyrians their triumphs in the conquest of their world. In the present he contended that the hegemony of the entire planet could be accomplished with this kind of totalitarian resolve and ruthlessness.   A resolve without pity or compassion would be invincible and his place would be by the side of the master of inhuman barbarism as soon as he could be reanimated.

As for Babe she was riding high and confident that all would be well. If they succeeded in this plan their power would be unassailable. It was intended that Stein would use parts from the mummies of two conquering kings (Egyptian pharaohs) and the DNA of the third Assyrian conqueror Tiglath Pileser III who's genetic material could be found in the last Sarcophagus. Stein would then reanimate the composite lord. His education would be assigned to NAI and a professor who was the companion of the prince. This done and with NAI at the limits of its power in Steins system, they would be on their way to harnessing the wealth of the Middle East and the world. The next step of course would be global conquest.

Babe planned that as a re-animate and the woman responsible for his awakening, the Great Lord, would favor her. He would be world Emperor and with little effort she would become his Empress. Yes they all had plans but none of them had counted on the seismic disruption they found when they got to Soho.

Babe intuited and warned that the Prince's "fun" should be postponed till later and that the girl be brought to Steins house instead. The Prince, however, was so impressed with the white satin room and the practice session with the other unfortunate woman that he wanted to repeat the process with the delicate white flower. After all, the Assyrians murdered children, which he had not yet reached the fortitude to do. This girl's innocence would be a preparation for greater things that would relieve him of all pity, which was his goal. Babe's instinct, however, proved correct.

Approaching the apartment complex they found it swarming with police. Alexi told his driver to drive on but he could see that there was a great deal of debris on the ground and his balcony was in shambles. The three men in robes, that had been found unconscious in the apartment, where being hauled off in handcuffs and were acting very skittish; at once babbling and crying. Alexi knew this meant the end of his "day job" as a credible financial consultant. The world of crime would also be leery of his involvement since he had been discovered. Lupo would become aware and go after him for Babe, as the three men had also been blabbing about a green woman and Lupo's spies would quickly digest and regurgitate this information. His cover was blown in every way. Now all his "eggs" were in one proverbial basket, but if they succeeded in "hatching," it would be the only basket he would need. They changed course for Stein's house where the van with the sarcophagi had already been sent.

When the satin room was found by the police, one rookie officer vomited at the site of all the blood. Forensics began their work of bagging up evidence and three hours into the process they heard a thumping sound. Further investigation revealed the hidden compartments with the corps and two other women.

Stacia had been traumatized by the event at the Ealú and she was shaken by this one but now she was also angry. The therapy she had been through and the work she was doing with the coalition had grown her up and given her new courage. When they were taken, the plight of the other girls who were no older than fourteen or fifteen had awakened her own protective strength and the news of the third girl's death was enough to infuriate her.

In her new focus, this was something the Titian and the coalition should somehow address. Drugs was a scourge but sexual trafficking was flagrant daring and unmitigated evil. She felt sure the Big Man would agree. As she looked at the apartment they were extracting her from, she saw signs that Frankie had been there; so did the police. She understood it was not his fault that she was not found, but she was comforted to know he had come for her. Stacia was then able to tell the police that "the Alien" was not responsible for their abduction but had come to the apartment, to save them. Once free, she called Jean Luc and Ann immediately and when he picked her up they headed directly for the "tree house".

19

Reanimation 101

When Stein realized he had the answer to reanimation he thought he would be very rich. After all how many people would readily pay a handsome price to be revived once dead. He never suspected there would be factions and squabbles about who was to be revived and who would stay dead. Then when he went to work for a man like Romeo Lupo he really didn't think it through. Not only was the Doctor not rich but he was a prisoner, and further; now he was a prisoner in the midst of a battle field.

Here he was in Lupo's house with Lupo's equipment; being forced to reanimate Lupo's enemies. Even speaking to Lupo's enemies guaranteed a bullet in the brain. What would the Don do to him now? Besides, Alexi and the Prince were both demanding services for themselves and for an ancient personage of some importance, and there was no talk of protection from anyone or financial remuneration for him. In fact it appeared they wanted the services simply for the fee of keeping him alive.

Babe was also demanding and threatening. She wanted upgrades. She had the repairing nano-bots now, but she also wanted full NAI like Frankie. Stein had no illusions about what she would do with that. She might bring the whole world's economy to its knees. He explained to her the upgrade was not possible after reanimation, but she wasn't buying it, and she promised to get ugly about it. Though, Babe was incredulous and ever suspicious of the doctor; regarding this, he was not lying. In actual fact the formula for that upgrade had been destroyed by Frankie at his genesis. In the end it would be a godsend that he inadvertently wrecked the laptop the formula was in, but Stein didn't want to tell Babe anymore than he had to.

Babe was keeping secrets too. The features providing virtual invulnerability and global knowledge were not made known to the others. Alexi and the prince were suspicious but still in the dark about much of it. Stein had not told anyone about how Frankie worked out moving money either. This would, no doubt, increase their desire for the feature even to the extent of execution and torture. They were always on the verge of applying that anyway. What a web of intrigue the doctor found himself in? Where was Frankie when he needed him?

Frankie did a search of the museum and found no clue to tell him where Stacia was. He then spoke to Andre who told him to think with his head and not with his heart. The criminals had Stein and three coffins full of remains. Perhaps he needed to find out what they were up to. Frankie said he knew the man that held Stacia as the owner of the restaurant that was burned down.

"You have no idea how perverse this man is. She is in grave danger."

Andre called the team that was working on the apartment in Soho just in case they found something. They told him the details and he told Frankie there was good news and bad news. The good news was Stacia had been found and picked up by her brother and mother. They said something about going to the 'Tree House'. The police thought it was some sort of restaurant. The bad news was another woman had been found with her, tortured and dead.

Frankie's eyes burned orange with rage when he heard about the murdered girl. He turned and started to run but Andre whistled and yelled for him to wait.

"Let's pick up Jasmine and I will give you a lift. You may need further help on this one."

Frankie considered and got on the hood of the Nisan. It was near daybreak but still dark, and Andre drove like a mad man.

Near the 'Tree House' Frankie leaped off and ran the rest of the way. When he got there lots of people were milling about. Frankie had forgotten they were gathering for their meeting and he needed to be with them. Not all were yet assembled but Stacia was in the kitchen with a bunch of people preparing breakfast. Frankie stumbled and fell at Stacia's feet and everyone else quickly disappeared leaving them "sort of" alone. Of course they were listening in the hallway.

"I'm so sorry. When I think of what could have happened...I should have been there."

"But you were there mon ami, I know you were, you have nothing of which to repent."

"But I couldn't find you and if anything had happened to you I..."

"Nothing happened except that I am so angry for that poor girl."

She looked at him emotionally crumple in her presence and put her hand on his head smoothing his hair. He was afraid to look at her but with two hands she lifted his face to hers and in silence spoke her concern and her affection. Then she became all business.

"Please, stand up I do not like this groveling. We as a group must discuss what can be done to prevent such terrible things from happening but now we are making breakfast and the others are listening in the hallway and we can talk later. N'est pas?"

"Vraiment," Returned Frankie. He had never seen this commanding side of her. He liked it, and he obeyed. Walking out of the room backwards he stepped out of the door to see the guilty listeners chagrined at being discovered. He turned with a great deal of embarrassment but just a tiny bit of swagger and went to wash up in the rock bath.

From Stein's piecemeal telling of the story Frankie had learned that his body had taken a good month to assemble so Frankie felt like they had some time. Besides, there had been some damage in the lab since Babe's reanimation and that would have to be remedied. Certainly, whatever was going to happen with these ancient mummies was not going to happen in a day, but there were other problems. A more immediate concern might be a clash between the Don's men and the foreign contingent who were working with Babe and Alexi. If this man was truly a prince then there might be political ramifications. Frank had to think all this through.

Frank consulted with the friends and they agreed safety and the preservation of life was the main concern, even if Frankie had to come into the light of public scrutiny. Andre wanted to call in the feds. This case after all had crossed state lines as well as national borders and it was their jurisdiction. That would, however, mean a battle. Therefore, Frankie thought, perhaps he should see what he could discover by paying Lupo's mansion a secret visit. Everyone concerned deserved to be legally punished, but if possible, Frankie wanted Stein alive. If there was a chance the man could change he wanted the scientist to have it. Like a son with a wayward father he never stopped hoping for some sort of miraculous transformation. It was probably a pipe dream but he had to try.

Andre and Jasmine unsuccessfully tried napping. Then, that evening, Andre made some calls. He started with the local Marshal's office and they met him near Stein's for a run down. They would call the FBI in, if the situation really warranted their involvement. When dealing with the average population no one seemed to mind an occasional oops in judgment by the authorities, but people with money and connections could cause trouble if mistakes were made. They had to be careful. Andre said he had a man on the inside and wanted to wait to hear from him. The Marshalls took issue with this but he begged them to give him time, as night came on.

In silent approach to the house, NAI informed Frankie, surveillance had been permanently disabled. The dogs were now residents at the "Tree House" but men with riffles had replaced the dogs and were standing watch at the gate. The Giant silently jumped the wall this time carefully avoiding the lake's nervous and noisy water fowl.

There were lights in the house and guards at the front but there was also activity in the back field. Stein was there tinkering at the generators surrounded by portable flood lights. Babe was by his side. Frankie wondered what they were up to, but perhaps Stein's equipment needed work since he last used it on Babe and Angelo the dog man. Frank noted the doctor seemed to have aged. He was bent and worn and looked like a corps himself. But Babe drove him, asking dozens of questions for her notes and she was relentless. Stein was speaking,

"These generators are very specialized and I'm afraid I haven't been doing the maintenance as I should have. The last time I used power for Frankie quite a few transformers were blown and the whole town went dark. So Lupo "acquired" these things for me to reanimate you and Angleo without detection. Your boys may recognize them, they are Russian made but we got them through Middle Eastern connections."

"Alright spare me the history lesson. What will we need to get them ready?"

"I've made a list. Let's go in and see what Alexi and the prince can do for our budget."

Hearing this Frankie quickly reached the front of the house ahead of them. Arriving at the Veranda he could hear another conversation between the Prince and Alexi. They were enjoying some Sheri in the fresh air which Stein seldom visited in his solitude. Large French doors opened to too much light during the day for his taste, and at night there was too much exposure to the darkness beyond. But for the sadist and the fanatic nothing was expansive enough. The night was warm and sipping from their glasses they thought the veranda a good place to dream their dreams of power and form their plans. They sat occupying a cushioned couches in the cool of the evening and Frankie slipped into an obscured niche to listen.

"This Shadow or Alien...Ms. Lonagen says he is a Reanimate. Does the process of reanimation make one so powerful?"

"You have seen what it has done for her. She hardly sleeps and five of your men could not best her. If she is wounded she repairs herself. If she is sick she heals quickly."

"A luscious and formidable woman; but the color of the skin is quite unusual."

"Small price to pay for the other perks wouldn't you say?"

"Yes, as the bard said, 'tis a consummation devoutly to be wished.' One might even feel it was a process worth dying for."

"I have considered this myself.   After all won't the Lord of the Millenniums require strong advisors? People of his own kind, who could stand by his side, to help him manage the millions of this unruly planet?"

"In truth I had not thought of this till now. There are other princes who might wish to build upon my work and who, in their laziness or cowardliness have proven they are unworthy. I would need every advantage to put them in their place, but can such a thing be arranged?"

"At the right price anything is possible."

"Name your price my friend."

"I require no money, only that you give me a position by your side. You the Lord's Prime Minster and my humble self his chief administrator."

"What you are asking is a great deal."

"I am not lazy or cowardly and without me all this might not have come to pass. I have served you faithfully. Are those not worthy qualifications for such a position?"

"The Woman might have other ideas about this. She has spoken of the Lord needing a Lady. I think she wants the job."

"Then you will need assistance in managing *her*."

"I think we have an agreement, only do all you can to expedite this process. First, our reanimation; then the revival of the Great Lord and his cult of death and blood. We have much work ahead of us."

When Babe and the doctor came in for their status report, the prince said he was far too tired to look at figures. They would have to discuss this over breakfast. Babe was impatient but she relented. The Prince and Alexi smiled at each other tacitly enjoying putting Babe in her place. This did not go unnoticed by the lady. Stein just wanted to go to bed and for once he got his wish.

Meanwhile, Frankie now realized there was so much more going on than he had expected. Reanimation was turning out to be life for a few that would mean death for many. Babe was plotting and being plotted against. She was also standing between him and rescuing Stein. He felt compelled however, to speak to her. There was an uncomfortable responsibility he felt for some of her corruption, after all, hadn't he rejected her? Because of this he sat by her window on ground level and waited.

Babe had learned a thing or two about securing prisoners especially during her experience with Lupo. She employed one manacle in securing Stein for the night before she took her own rest. This being done she got into something comfortable and slipped into bed but though she slept on command like a soldier, she also slept lightly. Something shifted by the window and in a flash she was up and next to the sill holding her Rosewood Crimson Trace revolver with sound suppressor. But her intruder was already in the room. From a dark corner she heard his hoarse whisper,

"Bronagh."

She lowered the gun and turned.

"You shouldn't be here."

"That sounds like concern."

"Why should I be concerned about you? I just don't want to have to kill you myself. You did save my life a few times after all."

"I appreciate that but you shouldn't be here either."

"Get out! This is no place for boy scouts."

"You still have time to get away. The people you work with can't be trusted."

"Of course they can't. That doesn't matter, the stakes are high and so are the risks but I'm willing to take them."

"If you leave now with Stein, I can take you to a safe place."

"You want to save me again? It's too late for that."

"Very well, I will take the doctor then."

"No you will not." She pointed her gun at his head. "He has work to do for us."

"When Stein reanimated me I was not what he expected. This all may not be what you expect. Bronagh--you trusted me once with that name and with a little of who you really are. Trust me now this is not going to end well."

She shot him twice in the shoulder and said,

"NEVER call me that again!"

He looked at her more with obvious emotional hurt. "What must she be going through inside to carry such rage?" He thought. Frankie touched the blood on his shoulder and said,

"The hate and anger inside you is festering. It will find and destroy you. Get out of this while you can."

Then he was out the window and gone. Babe did not bother to follow him. Lupo had put her through less pain than she was feeling now. Too late she realized she loved him. If she had been more genuine could the gentle Giant have returned that love? But it was too late, too late.

STEIN! Was he there? She ran to the room next door where the scientist was drugged and manacled and he was snoring. She flipped him so he would be quiet and walked out locking the door. Frank had made a big mistake coming to her first, she thought. Moving slowly to the library she downed a half glass of vodka to help her sleep. When she came back she checked on the doctor again and the doctor was gone. The window sill was stained with Frankie's blood.

Waking the house she drove all hands to make a thorough search with night vision eyewear but it was futile. Frankie was not as naive as she thought and she never again would underestimate him. Far from being stupid he used her to find out where Stein was being kept. As soon as she left the room he was in there pulling the chain out of the wall and flinging the scientist over his shoulder. Despite the bleeding, he ran like wild horses and was away before she upended her glass.

At least five miles away in the woods, Frankie put the doctor down just long enough to pull out the bullets with his fingernails and allow the bots to work. They sealed the wound in minutes and he was again on his way. Pocketing the bullets he ran on. Stein who had been drugged to prevent escape was oblivious. They zig zagged across the countryside and over stones and water whenever these were available. He heard nothing behind him and thought that either Babe had given up or she decided to pursue in the morning. She might also have taken his advice and left, but most probably not. He called Andre and told him where he was. When his brother arrived Frankie asked him to head for a local hotel, get a room and open the window. That being done the giant entered in his unorthodox way with the semi-conscious scientist draped over his shoulder like a feather boa.

Needless to say, Andre did not approve this scenario. The only thing that made this plausible to him was that he would have time to interrogate the "mad scientist" responsible for taking his brother apart and joining him to the bodies of four others. In fact, if Frankie had not intervened, he might have taken Stein apart himself.

"Give me one good reason why we don't turn this piece of human excrement in to the Feds to process in Guantanamo?"

"I don't have a good reason."

"Frank, we're about to have our first fight."

"You think you got a chance?" at this Frankie smiled. "Look at him. He's just a shell of an old man."

"Look at you! You are pieces of 5 people put together with crazy glue by this son of a motherless goat."

"A what?"

"Never mind."

"I might still be dead if not for him. He just did what he was told and he became their prisoner. He might have gone to the police but he couldn't."

Andre grabbed Stein by the lapels and growled at him.

"Would you have?" Stein knew an opening where he saw one.

"Well I certainly wish I had. It's better than living like a crime boss's ping pong ball. And now this new crowd that wants to use me is driving me mental. I've tried to end my own life but they prevented me. I can't take it anymore."

Andre looked at him wrathfully but his breathing slowed and he sat down in a chair. Frankie sat on the floor and the conversation became, at least, civil. In the end Andre was glad for all the intel he acquired from the scientist.

What they heard from the doctor curdled their blood. During the time she was with Stein Babe had not been idle. She took many notes about the process of reanimation and had most of Stein's data. She now sort of understood the principles by which it worked and she had notes on the parameters for wattage and chemical solutions, regimen for infusion and notes for NAI, Nano-Bots and DNA combinations. She had been working hard to make the doctor expendable and to make herself indispensable. She was now only keeping him around for trouble shooting. The mummies stolen from the museum were basically too ancient for functional body parts but the DNA was of course still useful. All they needed was a healthy freshly killed body to be the host.

Joining that, to the information about the two super creeps who wanted to "get green" the scenario looked quite bleak. It got a little bleaker when Stein told them they had taken the sarcophagi away and disposed of them. If the Feds came in they would have nothing to arrest anyone on. They could say the equipment was just part of experiments for genetic engineering of crops and who could blame them if they wanted to be off the grid with those generators from Helsinki. Even if the generators were Russian; buying army surplus from Russia was not against the law. In addition the prince's international status would give him immunity and harassment might cause an incident. They had nothin'. Alexi, on the other hand was wanted for murder, this was their ace in the hole.

Back at the mansion the lab was hooked up to the power generators and the lights came on as all the monitors and instruments hummed to life. Babe felt like the captain of a space ship about to take off. There might be a few things she would still like to ask the mastermind but it was too late now. She was going to take her maiden flight. All she needed was a test case. That was easy to find since she wanted to kill Alexi, but the prince had prior claim. They were still going back and forth about it and finally decided that the Prince would need to be first. He thought his death of course would be painless and under anesthetic but Babe wasn't that patient or nice. She shot him and said,

"If a gunshot was good enough for Mamma its good enough for you."

She was nearly dispatched herself but managed to calm his body guards with "It's all part of the process." As soon as he was cold she stripped him with Alexi's help laid him on the gurney and wheeled him into the lab. Then she discovered something. Alexi had a thing for blood. He wasn't afraid of it; in fact, quite the contrary. He liked to play in it. She caught him smearing it around and he finally started licking his fingers. This rather disgusted her and she told him to leave the room. He refused under the pretext that this was their arrangement. He would supervise the prince's reanimation and vice versa. In other words they didn't trust her, and well they should not.

They knew a fraction of what she had studied with Stein. They also understood she had more vital force than they did for everything, even her thought process, was greater than theirs, thanks to reanimation. If she did something shady they wouldn't really know and she was way ahead of them. Though she planned a straight forward simple reanimation with the Prince, she had in mind to give both of them less NAI potential than herself and less nano-bots. In other words they would heal and think faster than regular humans but much slower than her. Babe intended to remained Queen Bee at all times.

Practice with the DNA binding also had to happen before the ultimate reanimation. Though she wouldn't try anything fancy with the Prince Alexi would have a surprise in store. For this purpose she had collected samples of DNA befitting his creeping and conniving character but she could not settle on which to choose, a fruit bat or a spider. Still, that was not the expedient at the moment. She prepped the prince and whatever would be, would be.

Fluids and electrodes in place the process commenced. Everything was humming along and the numbers were right. In two hours they would see vital signs beginning and in four hours the prince would be conscious. They had time for a drink and would check his status in an hour or two. Alexi took this time to "bond" however he could with the woman of the hour. He told Babe that he had always admired her ability as a mercenary but that now he was in awe of her ability as a scientist. She told him she was hardly a scientist and apart from what Stein had taught her she knew very little. As a technician she was not bad however, and those accolades she would accept. He told her the prince's men would kill her if she failed. She affirmed that -- she would not.

Four hours later she was good for her word. Her first reanimated infant sat up and four of his men were there to dress him. He did not have Frankie's curiosity but he was immediately hungry and started putting things in his mouth. He was brought bread, cheese and wine and taught how to eat it. He had in fact arranged for the professor from his country to be there for his immediate instruction. Between this person and NAI he would move along quite nicely. The bots were put in immediately and bullet hole in his chest took four hours to repaired itself via nano tech so it was done by the time he woke. Never the less Alexi realized that it would take days maybe weeks for the Prince to be adult enough to supervise the process for him. The alternative was to trust Babe. He decided to wait.

Lupo had undergone a strange transformation after his last encounter with Babe, proof that even a sociopath had feelings. The only way the men could describe it was that he was broken. Listless and quiet he could not be tempted, with anything he used to find pleasure in. Expensive booze, drugs, the torment of his enemies; nothing seemed to help. They got him one high class hooker after another and he was no good with any of them. They told him Babe was some kinda monster now with her green skin. She wasn't even human. Why bother? All their arguments fell flat. His bravado history, his moxie flattened, his appetite even for pasta evaporated and he acted clinically depressed.

Tony and his men were catching the depression like the flu. They had no direction without his orders, but he wasn't giving any orders, so they just sat around and ate and got drunk and picked up his drug money. They knew if something didn't happen soon everything would fall apart. Tony as number one was elected to say something.

"Boss, you left sometin' in that bitches house that you ain't never been widout. Your nerve."

Lupo looked up at him with a look that never failed to inspire fear. Tony got nervous for a moment and the boys thought the reaction was promising, but then the Don shrugged, turned away and continued to mope. Tony tried again.

"Boss de boys and me wanna go to the doc's place and drill dat Babe full a lead. She's there in your house, drinkin' your booze and payin' no rent. She gotta pay for what she done Boss. Where's your self respect? It would make you feel better to take care of it. You could get...whatta ya call it? Closure. Common where's that Don we all know and love? Wha de ya say? "

Lupo thought for a minute. He wasn't certain of anything anymore. But the boys were like dogs, they had to be taken out or the crap would be everywhere. Further he would lose everything he had ever built. Without her it didn't mean much but he owed his men something. He didn't sound too convincing but he said it anyway,

"OK, load up the guns and fire up the limo, let's go make the Babe pay."

What Lupo lacked in enthusiasm the boys made up for in excited commotion. They loaded up their best Glocks, Berettas and a few sawed off shotguns. Breaking a few crates open they took out some new "peace keepers" they had been dying to try out. It felt like ages since they had stepped out, fully armed. It was like old times.

The job was supposed to be an easy one. They thought they were going out to scare an old man and shoot up a dumb broad. What they found when they got to Stein's was a small army and a war they were not prepared for. The exchange started like popcorn and ended up like Pearl Harbor. Lupo's boys got the worst of it but the Don managed to get into the house with his Berretta thanks to Tony and two others behind him with riffles. Alexi who had not fired a shot finally took out one of Lupo's escort with a bottle of scotch to the head, but he was now exposed and that was unfortunate.

When Lupo saw Alexi something switched on. He could see everything clearly. Alexi had been playing double cross with him and Babe all along. He was here to ensure his own immortality at Lupo's expense. Without his interference Babe might still be his. He knew gunfire was following them but he just wanted to see the old blood sucker suffer. He signaled for the boys to take hold of him and they dragged him down to the lab. There they shut the door and took the cover off of the vat of solvent. Then they hoisted the

Austrian up kicking and screaming and were about to dip him in slowly when the legs of Bobby, Lupo's second, were shot out from under him.

They looked and it was Babe with her own Crimson Trace revolver in hand. Tony would have completed Alexi's execution on his own but he had to take cover so his "load" went sprawling to the floor and crept into a corner. Babe had control now and was ready to shoot whatever moved. Tony tried his luck and got it in the gun hand. His Glock fell into the vat. Lupo knew this was the end so he stood up like a man and faced her. He said,

"I loved you Babe, from the beginning you always did it for me, you were amazing but you were also like death." She shot him three times and said,

"You got that right."

Tony looked at her and knew he was next but Babe paused.

"You wanna be the next Don?"

"What are my chances?"

"Zero." And she shot him between the eyes.

That evening the vats were both well fed. Lupo and his boys along with a couple of the Prince's men were disposed of in this clean and efficient way. The enterprise of the Great Lord acquired a second Limo and inherited the Krokodil business in three boroughs. Babe thought life was good and getting better by the moment. The police did hear the gunfire and made an appearance but they were told by the professor that it was just target practice. There were no bodies and all the guns had permits. The household was just told not to hunt and to stick to targets. They politely agreed to do so and that was the end of it. No other questions asked. So this was the way the Don of three boroughs met his end. Like so many he had sent to early and anonymous graves, he went without memorial, prayers or hope and was gone.

20

Creepy on Steroids

Everything Babe did these days scorched her soul, but she had learned from many experiences that sentimentality was the enemy of survival. She wanted to be Queen of the world and that would require some sacrifices. But the last words Frankie said to her kept echoing in her head and she could feel the warmth of his chest on that day when he carried her like a baby. It was a sweeter memory than any she could recall and she hated it.

The debate in her head went from tender to tenuous. Her guilt told her he could never love her, his recent visit told her he might. Then there was the Albino--whatever did a Titian like him see in that fragile stick of a girl? Only a goddess could match him and Bronagh was that, but she wasn't Bronagh anymore. She was "Queen Babe the Serpent Charmer" or something like that, and her consort would be the Great Lord of the Assyrians. He would make Frankie tremble and regret choosing the Toe head over her. That would be her solace, as her internal conflict with love drowned, in her growing desire for power.

Frankie was having his own troubles with romantic love. Stacia had changed since her last terrible experience and now she was hyper-focusing on woman's issues and rescuing victims of sexual slavery. Frankie was all for that but he was also interested in pursuing her feelings for him. It seemed like whenever he would say something personal or gentle to her she would begin to spout statistics about sex traffic and intimate partner violence. As interested as he was in protecting victims, this reaction kind of quenched his mood. Frankie had done his bit apprehending predators and protecting abuse victims but Stacia seemed to be working something out of her own and unfortunately he was not invited to join in the process.

At the moment she was going on about a certain case in the news of a wealthy entrepreneur who had been caught with a prostitute. He had been observed by witnesses and the case seemed open and shut. If he did the usual thing and took a guilty plea he would probably get a slap on the wrist. Instead he was fighting the accusation and protesting his "innocence." Then it was discovered that he was protecting a political figure of his personal acquaintance who had also been imprecated in the scandal. It looked like they might get away with it too-- not because they weren't guilty-- but because they had the money to say they weren't. This flew in the face of all the thousands of sex traffic slaves and victims that were enduring the abuses for the pleasure of those who could make their managers rich. Stacia was livid that such travesties were going on everyday and she especially took issue with the fact that these men claimed to be Christians.

Frankie did not like what she had to say about that. He was quite a fan of Jesus Christ by now and knew that the Lord would never endorse such horrible behavior. He told Stacia that these men were obviously lying about who they believed in. A real Christian was someone who followed Christ and tried to be as loving and kind as his Lord. Stacia got very angry at this point and said he was being foolish and naive. This was absolutely shocking to him. He did not know what to say for a while. He went away to consider and finally came back and told her she was being unreasonable. This brought on a great silence between them for the rest of the day. She went home that evening and did not even say goodnight.

Frankie remembered an artifact he had of what must have been Itzak and Esther. It was more of an impression or feeling of being close to someone and of being single minded and profoundly loved. Having such a disappointment with Stacia he felt drawn to that body memory. His deliveries done, he had some time on his hands and thought to go and visit with Esther. Her condition was getting in the way of her being able to travel and they were all missing her, but Frankie missed her (because of Itzak) most of all. The walk/run took him part of the night but he was there by morning in time for breakfast.

"Good morning zeeskeit, how are you feeling?"

"Zeeskeit, that is just what Itzak used to call me. You devil, you know how to play on my heart strings."

"But you are a sweetheart, why shouldn't I call you that?"

"If I took a scissors to your hair you wouldn't call me that."

"You wouldn't. Not my hair. It's my best part."

"Don't sell yourself short. Stacia thinks there's more to you than that."

"Stacia doesn't like me very much right now."

"She loves you."

"Does she? She has never said so, but I'm not here about her, I wanted to see you."

"Me, I'm dying—and please don't let anyone reanimate me. I've had enough of this world."

"Esther, don't talk that way. It's not like you to quit. We need you."

"I'm tired Frank, I just want to rest. Is that so bad?"

"No I guess not."

"It's all part of the cycle of life."

"One that I seem to have interrupted."

"Did you read that book I gave you?"

"I read it to Dee Dee as you told me to do. She didn't quite understand it but I was very touched. Do you think I'll disappear when I'm no longer needed like the Gollum did?"

"No one lives forever Frank. Not even you, but you are a kind of goel for us."

"A goel, you mean a family redeemer. How am I that?"

"In Torah God had people administer justice differently than they do today. A goel took care of family justice. He helped poor members of the family get on their feet. Sometimes if a relative died and left a widow the goel would take her into his home. If a family member was killed wrongfully it was the goel's job to avenge them. That's how families made it through."

"The man responsible for the murder of your husband is dead. I didn't do that."

"No God did. It's always best when He does it and it lets the goel off the hook. But you have taken care of poor humanity and helped, single moms and done so much that amounts to justice. You are a good goel to the human family. I am personally proud to know you."

"From what I hear you have administered quite a bit of justice yourself. I am your humble student."

"You're a menche. Any woman will be lucky to have you."

"Don't know if a woman is in the cards for me Esther."

She looked at him with love and patted his cheek.

"Itzak and I had a good run. I'll tell him to wait for you at the pearly gates when you are done with his hands and research. And don't be so impatient with Stacia. Ann told me what happened. We old yentas talk on the phone ya know. Stacia is doing a little overcompensating for now. She got scared a few times and she doesn't want to be scared anymore. Sometimes you gotta get mad before you're courage kicks in. She'll be alright and she'll be back."

"Do they teach you mind reading and prognosticating in medical school?"

"Na, but they do in the school of hard knocks. You should listen and learn. Now how about a nice whole grain bagel with cream cheese and a few locs? Help me up and we can fix it."

Frankie wanted to get it for her but she wouldn't hear of it. So he brought the table with the toaster and all the food and put it in front of her and she made breakfast while still in bed.

They chatted and while she ate half a bagel he had 6 whole ones with no locs and after a few more hours he finally went home. Before he left Esther grabbed his hoodie sleeve and said,

"Ya know I been thinking about your "Robin Hood" antics. I know they give your tender conscience trouble, but there are cases in Torah when people took back what was taken from them and God had no problem with it. Israel spoiled the Egyptians after their long slavery and Jacob took back his wages from the flocks of Laban because Laban had cheated him for 20 years. God didn't have a problem with taking back what was stolen in the first place."

"Dear Lady, that does give me ease as I see wealth has taken much from the poor and this has never seemed right to me. Thank you."

Esther leaned her head back and smiled a tired smile then waved him away. Frankie let a tear roll down his face as he walked out of the house. A few days later Ann called to say Esther was gone.

The passing of Dr. Esther Katz left the coalition with a huge heart ache but also quite a bit of money which she had bestowed for the purchase of a TMS machine. She also bequeathed her home which they sold to buy a property near the Tree House that they intended to use as an office. Ben and

Gunta would both eventually establish a practice there but they were able to get two more doctors Fred Shea son of the deceased Senator and Dr.Levine, a friend of Kate Shea who had quite a few helpful connections. They would all work to oversee the research. The ministration would go on but Esther would be sorely missed.

Andre went to the station and met with the local Marshalls in person. He told them that most probably a known pervert wanted for murder was hold up at the mansion that belonged to Piazano Enterprises. He told them presently foreign elements were there as well, that might be planning terrorist activities. The Marshals confirmed that at a recent visit quite a few visitors of the Middle Eastern persuasion had been seen coming and going from the home. They knew nothing of any perverts or murderers and they went on to say,

"The doctor that lived there for the past nine years said they were attendants of a foreign dignitary that was staying with him for the season, at the behest of the company. After neighbors reported what sounded like a major gunfight there was further investigation which revealed gunfire damage to the house. The spokesman for the group said the Doc had gone away on business and that they had been doing some target practice. Police did look over the premises and found nothing untoward outside of the ammo damage on the outer walls.

We also met the spokesman for the Prince that was visiting there. He said he would pay for the damage. Seemed like a gracious sort of guy. He said that having heard of the violence in America he wanted his men to be practiced in protecting the person of the prince. This was understandable since he was a big wig. Police told the spokesman they didn't blame him for being careful and went on their way. We read the report. The long and the short of it is we've been watching the place. So far nothing more than a violation in hunting regulations issued for shooting a few ducks. But heck," the Marshall said, "people get bored. We warned them though."

Andre turned away in silence rolling his eyes and sighing in frustration. If they were only aware of the lies they were swallowing and the seismic terrors that were about to spill over into the world from that place. But there was nothing he could do at the moment short of exposing Frankie and the time was not right for that. He wondered if it would ever be.

Meanwhile inside the mansion Alexi waited for his turn at potential immortality and the emotionally maturing prince was busy with his first adult project since his reanimation. After consulting with Babe it was decided he would pull some strings to acquire the appropriate body for their project. This hulk of flesh would be privileged to bear the DNA of the three Ancient kings for the composite man that would become the Great Lord. The Prince also had in mind some element of the animal that had always been their totem; the sacred cobra.

A great fan of wrestling, the prince had chosen an Olympic Wrestler of their country who was known for his height, strength and dashing looks. Babe ogled him through NAI and heartily approved. She also liked snakes and wondered how that combination would pan out. Sedatives would be in place should things go awry. She would take no chances.

The Prince was doing well at recollecting his connections with the help of the professor and his admin assistant. It would take a few weeks but Kirjath Arvio Yazid the undefeated wrestler, would come to "compete with American champions" at the summons of his Prince and—unaware of the plan, would meet his destiny.

In his conversations with his friends, Frankie had been compared to many heroes of old. Being a rare and humble man he wondered at these comparisons and could not see all the fuss. He was who he was, and channeled all the noble qualities of 5 freedom fighters. Justice therefore rushed to the depth of his heart through his ample veins. Even if he couldn't see this his friends could and they wanted to make up for his earlier loneliness and rejection by building up his self esteem. So they made comparisons to Job the suffering penitent, Robin of Locksley, Samson, the Beast from the legend of the Beauty and the Beast, and the Golem of Prague. He could see glimpses of each one of these and accepted them but one he just couldn't see was Martin. When Vera Gray compared him to Martin Luther King Junior he could not accept the honor.

Martin was recent, historical and uncommonly authentic. There was too much detail about him in history books for Frankie to flatter himself with a likeness. He admired the man no less for his brilliance but for his triumph under the duress of an era of titanic hatred and oppression against his people. Like the blacks, Frankie felt it was hard to hide or assimilate. While others could pretend to be part of the crowd they were always black and obvious even as he was big and ugly. That was his only concession to Vera's argument. Then she told him that she and Morris had marched with Martin to Washington when they were just kids. She said she knew what she was talking about and this gave her argument more credence. He still disagreed but Frankie wanted to know more.

Vera explained that her husband and she had grown up in the shadow of that great man and it was always his humility and prayers that gave his words power. She recalled Morris, who had grown up in the church had fallen into drunkenness and dissipation. He then got involved with some low down people frequenting honky tonks and he finally ended up on heroin. That resulted in her relationship with him temporarily ending.

A light dawned on Frankie.

"You mean Morris was addicted? Wow, it makes sense that is another reason I am so interested in addicted people."

"That's the way it is love, sometimes we don't know a problem exists till we have it." Vera went on to tell him more.

"When word of this boy's dissipation got to Pastor Martin, like a good shepherd he went and found his lost sheep. He found him and prayed such a prayer that without process or recovery Morris was delivered of his addiction. Now this was not the way the good Lord worked every time and Lord knows Morris still had a lot of healing to undergo but that powerful prayer worked for Morris. He got up out of his "dope fiend hell" and became a freedom fighter like his mentor."

Frankie thanked Vera for this disclosure but was markedly disturbed by it as well. He had always loved the peace of God but trusting him to such depths was foreign to him. He thought it the ultimate kind of courage and was certain he had none of it. He walked away confused and upset and he came back to Vera days later angry.

"If Martin was so perfect why was he killed?"

"First of all," Vera retorted, "Martin was not perfect. He and Coretta had lots to work out in their marriage. He made mistakes and blunders just like the rest of us but his trust in the Lord was unassailable. If he fell he got up again with the help of the Mighty Hand. That is one place I see you are alike. You are both like weebles that wobble but don't fall down."

"He's dead Vera."

"That don't mean he's down. Martin's done more good dead than he did when he was alive. All us lazy britches, who depended on him for our courage, had to take hold of God and find courage of our own. We continued the fight and so it should be because all this should not be on the shoulders of just one man."

"Part of my work has to do with breaking the law to help people. This was not Martin's way."

"Yes and we need to talk about that Frankie dear, but Martin did break lots of unjust laws in order to bring their injustice into the light. It was against the Law for black and white people to do just about anything together back then. That was wrong and if breaking the Law was what it took to get it fixed then he did it."

"Alright then it's wrong that people can't live decently, have no homes, can't feed their families good food and get the right medicine when they are sick. It's wrong that some should have so much and others so little."

"You got that right, but if the sustenance of people depends on you and something happens to you then they are back where they started. Ain't that so?"

"Yes."

"Then things have to change so that, with you or without you, people will have what they need."

"I try to help people change so they will become independent of me. But some people need more help than others."

"Yes Frankie you do that and that is wonderful but as long as the system stays the same we will always have drug addicts, alcoholics and poor people. You get me?"

Things were beginning to dawn on Frank in pellucid forms.

"All right then, alright...I will do justice, I will equalize the world. I can move ones and zeros and give everyone the same amount of money that all may have an equal share in the wealth of the world." Vera raised an eyebrow and shook her head.

"If it were only that easy. But Frank, do you think you will solve humanities problem by doing that? People would only find another way to best each other without money. You cannot eliminate greed and the desire for power, it resided in the human heart, and the solution must include that fact.

The unassailable Lord above has a solution to all this and He is working it all out perfectly, even as we speak. Meantime, like Job we must bear pain and know that there is no real reason for it, except that chaos temporarily rules here on this planet. This is the reason we can help but we cannot eliminate injustice all together because evil still reigns on earth, but not forever. Soon and very soon all will be well. The change is coming and it is happening-- one heart at a time.

If all money were removed from the planet people would use force to gain supremacy or some other means. Things could get worst. Money is just a tool at the moment for good or ill. It may also be a small deterrent to worse things."

Frankie bowed his head and shuffled his feet.

"Vera, you have made me feel very young. I know so much but I don't know anything."

"No dear you are just a good man and good men like to fix things. But some things have to be allowed to develop. You can't fix it all immediately. Sometimes slow development, continuous work and some waiting is the best fix. Otherwise we start fighting spiritual wars with carnal weapons. Malcolm X's solution was violence. Now that precipitated things but it sure caused a lot of animosity."

"He was killed as well wasn't he?"

"Yes he was. And so may we be but some things are still worth fighting for."

"Then I will fight my way and if I go down, so be it."

"Working to change things is always a dangerous proposition any way you do it. If we put our head together there may be things we can do to permanently help the poor and oppressed while we wait on God's plan to unfold."

"Like the Coalition. We got killed too."

"But we're back stronger than before, Praise the Lord. Now we gotta work to make some changes for freedom that will not depend on us but live beyond us."

"You mean with the church?"

"Heavens no, not the church alone. Unlike some, I'm not one for church uniting with the state. No, no politics is a dirty business and as the church we need to be free of that dirt to do God's work in love. But good people everywhere voicing their concerns and voting and marching and working through legal means. Well you know all that. This is giving Cesar what is Cesar's and God what is God's."

Frankie saw how wise she was and wished he could be like her. It did not however, help his anger. He saw how people, years after Martin's work, were still so evil and hateful towards those who were different than they were. What really had changed?

Vera said "Oh people still profile us and still even hate us but we can ride the same buses in the same seats as white folks now and we fight on for more. As for you my dear, we got to find some way of making what you do with addicts, work legally. You are just one person and too many people need this."

The Giant was in awe of her. It did seem to him that glorious things come out of pain and poverty, not because God wanted poverty but, because God had a habit of working all things around for the good. Perhaps that was His job. As for the human heart, good and evil did not depend on how much money you had, it depended on who and what you loved.

Alexi once had a mother and that mother had two sons. One grew up to be a sadistic, lubricious fiend with a lust for money and a knack for making it. The other brother Jerrod was successful business man who ran a company dealing in factual data. He was a trusted provider of credit reporting, risk mitigation, flood and verification services to the mortgage lending industry. He hacked into people's deepest darkest financial secrets and moved money and data around on the net much like Frankie did. Only he did it legally, even though he was a controlling sociopath who did it for no one's good but his own. What did these two boys learn at their mother's knee? What might a psychiatric analyst make of it?

Alexi had spent as much time as he could tolerate with the Middle Easterners. He did not favor their cuisine and he did not enjoy conversations with the mental equivalent of a spoiled teen age Prince. Babe was busy as well, moving drug money, and studying the data for the ultimate reanimation. Bottom line was, Alexi was bored and he longed for some sauerbraten and potatoes in a cream sauce instead of the heavily spiced meats and grains these people liked to eat. His brother lived in Connecticut and he decided that while they were waiting for the wrestler to come he would take one of the limos and go see him. After all, he would soon be among the gods and dear old Jerrod would just be an ordinary worshiper. Now was the time to go and say his goodbyes without giving anything away.

Nora walked down the dusty road pushing her cart. She looked bleary eyed and bedraggled but she kept on. Why she appeared once or twice a month on this route near the Tree House, no one knew. She was a street woman who now lived part time in the back of Frankie's Tree House and the rest of the time, who knows where. Whenever she came Frankie always offered her more safe and comfortable accommodations than the dilapidated car port, but she would always decline in terror. Still she returned but when she did, it was as though she had forgotten all about Frankie and was visiting for the first time. It appeared she had lost her mind. Frankie and Gunta built a little insulated shed with a bed in the back of the house for her. That was the most they could do.

One cold day in November Angie was finally able to talk Nora into using the shed. After that the friends would give her food and she would continue her cryptic circuit and inscrutable behavior. It was plain she had once been beautiful but mental illness had altered everything, till she was not even able to say more than a few garbled words.

Nora's shopping cart was full of plastic bags that held her treasures. These consisted of who knows what. Assuming them to be full of moldy clothes or aluminum cans, no one was interested in investigating their contents, until one day Nora fell and sprained her ankle.

Gunta was quick to do some first aid and they discussed whether they should take her to the hospital or not. She had no medical insurance and she would probably not be seen at the ER with the new rules that had basically eliminated free care. So they decided to make her as comfortable as possible and take care of her themselves. The ladies took charge of helping her get washed up, found her a night gown and put clean linen on her bed in the little shed. She panicked whenever the cart was not at hand. So the cart was rolled into the shed with her.

As Ben and Kurt helped to bring the cart in Kurt noticed there were a bunch of neatly kept files in one of the bags. This seemed remarkable. Everything else looked bedraggled and dirty but the 12"x12" box with the documents was spotless and orderly. Nora's intrigue doubled as the files were seen to be arranged with great care. She was restless and Gunta knew she needed to sleep so he gave her some of Frankie's pain meds and some melatonin, valerian and chamomile tea. When she started to snore they took her box and thought they would have a look. Stacia thought this was invasive but the boys said she might be in trouble and in need of help. Or perhaps these files were someone else's and they might be missing them. Whatever the case was they thought it prudent to investigate.

What they found were a bunch of legal documents that had to do with a man named Jarrod Breughel. It so happened, that Simon Shea, the Senator's attorney son, was at the tree house discussing Esther's estate with the Friends. They asked him to have a look at Nora's documents and then things got really interesting. The papers were arranged in groups of one document labeled "falsified" attached to one or two documents stating they were proof that the first document was fabricated. Document after document were similarly arranged. These papers were mostly regarding a divorce and alimony case. Simon quickly determined this ragged woman (Nora Breughel) was the one these documents were referring to and that if all was true, she was owed a great deal of money by her Ex-husband. Therefore, why was she destitute? Her Ex must have certainly paid off some high profile people to get these falsified. These documents must have surely robbed her of her upper middle class home, her children and her sanity.

When Frankie heard of this he was livid. He wanted immediately to go to this appalling man's home, tie him up and hang him high for all to see. It was Simon who counseled him not to. He would look further into the case and get back to them on it. In the meantime whatever they could do to keep Nora with them and to restore her back to coherence might be best. He also asked Frankie to use Gunta's high speed scanner and scan all the documents to Simon's computer. With both Angie and Stacia's help this took a good part of the afternoon.

Ben, whose specialty was mental illness, thought Nora might be a lost cause. She was so non-verbal so incredibly depressed and anxious. Gunta confirmed that she was a bit malnourished and certainly infested with bugs but she was not in bad health. Frankie took care of the bugs in short order, with his laser works, which the friends affectionately called, "the

blue aura." The girls fed her. All this helped, but it did not take care of the babbling and the obsession with the papers. It was Simon in the end that was able to calm her. He put all her papers back in the box and gave them to her. She snatched at them indignantly and shook her head tremulously. Then he pointing to himself and said,

"Lawyer," then he pointed to the papers and said,

"I think you have a strong case." She caught her breath as if she would choke and responded in clear language,

"Oh God, thank you, thank you."

After that, little by little, and with the help of TMS treatments she started getting more and more rational and understandable. Ben said she had PTSD probably from all that had happened to her so he also did EMDR treatment with her and that made a big change. The best therapy was for her to talk about it all and resolve it.

She was happy to unburden her soul with the story that had haunted her for years. Her husband had always kept her dependent and ignorant about his work and pay. He had never treated her well and kept her on a short leash financially but the children were everything to her so she quieted herself in their care. Life went on. Then one day he tired of her and began to accuse her of little things. Soon those became big things and she found herself in a dirty divorce without resources to fight. She was thrown out of the house and this left the children in shock over being left with their vicious father. But with all the false documents and friends that were paid off Nora was powerless to do anything about it.

Jarrod then launched a final dirty plan. For a large sum, he got a friend of Nora's acquaintance to "share her pills" with Nora. This was done in the guise of easing the emotional pain of the divorce. Nora fell for it and was soon addicted. His plan was working perfectly. He portrayed her as a dirty addict and unfit mother. He even paid off a judge to back him up.

Without credibility in the world and without resources or self esteem Nora became destitute. She was stigmatized by her wealthy peer group and she would never see her children again. She tried and tried to get someone to listen but no one would go up against the powerful people who might be accused in order to defend her.

Jarrod was never really liked by anyone because he only used people, he never befriended them. He also liked to lie about himself, saying he had studied at places he hadn't and knew people he really didn't know. If one got too close to him they would eventually find out about him; another reason why he might have wanted his wife to disappear. She had been asking about his supposed acquaintance with a certain sports celebrity and he simply told her to buzz off like a good little bee. This was a catalyst for the divorce. It was time to displace her.

From the documents he felt that Jarrod was probably in league with a powerful woman (Rachel Margarite) who had access to all records in that area and who was married to a district judge. It was rumored she "helped" some people who "helped" her in return. There was a whole list of victims on the internet who had been ruined and destroyed by her activities and Nora was obviously another one. Simon came to believed that Jarrod had purchased "friends" in the lower courts and that was the reason all the copies of documents Nora had given to lawyers kept disappearing and never getting to judges.

Well, Jarrod had friends locally but Simon had friends in the Senate. It was easy enough to get the scanned documents to these powerful friends and not only was Jarrod arrested but Rachel was as well. Many people under Rachel were exposed and a few people like Nora filed a class action suit against her and got justice. Simon got media coverage with the headline "Son of Senator helps Homeless Woman and uncovers Judicial Corruption." When it hit the front pages Shea's name was again a household word.

When the police showed up Alexi, who had comfortably installed himself in his brother's house, bolted of course. As he drove away he thought, he had only been there a week and there was family trouble already. Would the inconvenience to his person never end? He turned his limo back towards the mansion even as Jarrod got cuffed and carted away. Jarrod's teen age children were only too glad to corroborate their mother's terrible treatment as they hated their dad. They also told the police that their creepy uncle had been staying with them and that he was a pervert and they were afraid of him.

When Alexi's name was mentioned and checked, police confirmed that this man was wanted and on the run. The young people were commended for their courage and Nora was reunited with them. By now she was counted among the friends of Frankie and the coalition. After Jarrod was investigated and his fraudulently attained assets were sorted, what was left was just enough to cover the alimony that was due Nora and the support that was due her children plus their home and health benefits. When he eventually emerged from prison in about ten years or so from then he would be destitute. Nora pitied him but she was restored and grateful.

Back at Stein's mansion, Alexi saw the newspapers. The police net was tightening around him and he did not think he could wait till the Prince was mature enough to protect him. He decided to promise Babe some of his Swiss accounts for her care in reanimating him. She would receive part payment now and the rest when he was restored to himself after reanimation. She agreed. He punched the numbers into his phone to transfer the cash to her account as they had always done. She then turned and shot him through the heart. Why dilly dally? That was her motto.

Babe had him stripped and the limp body was plopped onto a cold slab where she circled it like a sculptor contemplating her next stroke of the chisel. There was no love lost between her and Alexi, it had always been business, but of late she had accumulated some animosity towards him due to his collusion with Lupo. Now Lupo was gone but Alexi's turn to pay had come. She had long contemplated his odious character and wondered what she would make of him. Certainly a man like this should be given no more cunning than he already had. Therefore the minimum of NAI, just enough to get him through adolescence then he could figure the rest out himself. No enhancements with bots. Oh, but well, he had paid for some so a minimum of those. Then what about some additional DNA? Hmm? A rat, a worm, a cat?

She recalled his blood fetish and thought it would be a hoot to make him a vegetarian. She had gathered samples of the genetic material of fruit bats that were plentiful in the chimneys of the old house due to the orchard in the area. He might be angry about that but--oh well. Still, she needed his money. She could have his phone hacked and the source of his accounts linked to hers but that would take finding an expert hacker and lots of time. On the other hand Alexi would be pliable for a little while as he was regaining his mental capacity. She could be like a mother to him and if mommy played her cards right he might even become her pet forever which would be useful. Regardless

of the outcome it was worth the experiment and, never mind, he would have to
live with his new self, as she had learned to live with hers.

18

CIA and Show Biz

Pam Johnson was going from Hershey Pennsylvania to Manhattan to try her luck at journalism. She had her MA from Penn State and was hoping to stay with an old friend who was in textile design and had a studio apartment in Queens. She had been warned about the traffic and the crime but she was so sick of being down on the farm that she was ready to risk anything. With a "Can do" attitude and a good moral compass she knew those city slickers wouldn't get the best of her. She would work hard and show them all.

Her city wise friend had warned her of the rash of street people and junkies who had been barraging cars at stop lights. They would pretend to wash people's windshields with dirty rags then demand payment for their "services". Pam had already decided she would not fall for that scam and would drive on triumphantly if they even tried such a thing with her, but she was not ready for the scenario to follow.

It was early in the morning when she drove into Flatbush and there were some (what she called) "low life's" gathered on the corner. Distracted by the gathering on the left of the road she did not see others who emerged on the right. Both groups converged upon her car with buckets of dirty suds and soon her windows looked like she was driving through a murky car wash. Disoriented by the lack of visibility she honked the horn. That is when the thumping began. They were thumping on her windows. She applied the windshield wipers to get enough visibility to move forward but she was horrified to see grimy hands and a scabby lizard like faces with oily hair grimacing and yelling at her.

Another thump and her windshield cracked into a smash pattern, web like, oozing suds and mud. Then she felt the car rocking. Terrified she realized they were trying to tip her over. In desperation she applied the gas and heard an awful thump like she had once heard when she hit a large raccoon on a back road in Pennsylvania. She floored it and heard screaming and wheels screeching. Then she heard an impact and Pam never heard anything again.

Stein sat in his hotel room, ginger ale in hand surfing the internet for scientific journals he had not read in years. He was so ahead of his time on reanimation but so behind on other things since Lupo had never allowed him access to the growing cyber universe. The advances in genetic research especially fascinated him and he could not get enough. When Frankie would stop by and ask if he needed anything he always declined saying room service was available if he did. After being alone for so long at the mansion he was a bit agoraphobic and being a person who liked solitude anyway he was happy to stay put. He was also scared to death.

Lupo was the source of his night terrors but Andre brought him word through Frankie that no one seemed to know where Lupo and his men had gone. The restaurants they frequented, the Italian tailors they patronized and the dealers who inquired about them were all quite curious about their disappearance. Informers for the police said they suspected someone had "offed" them all in a big secret hit or maybe they went to Italy but they had never been gone for so long. A sister of one of Lupo's men finally walked into the station and said she and her mother hadn't seen their Dominic in a week and none of his friends either. She was worried. He always called every week and the boys came round for Mamma's pasta at least twice a week.

Though it seemed like Lupo was gone it did not mean the coast was clear for Stein. Babe still had devious plans for him and Alexi was also at large. If not for the political status of the Prince the FBI might have made a serious raid on the mansion but certainly local tales of monsters and mad scientists would not move them to action. Furthermore, in discussions about what to do with Stein it was finally disclosed to Frank that Babe had enough information and power in the generators to conduct reanimations of her own. This was really bad news. The world was not ready to have beings loosed upon it, of Frankie's kind, with Babe's character. Still if anything was to be done Frankie would have to do it. He had to consider.

The one silver lining was this; Babe did not have the data for maximum NAI. The reason for that was this research was the brain child of a former colleague of Stein's--Dr. Samuel Benavent leading the field in neuroscience and artificial intelligence interface. While attempting to blend the 10 billion transistors of high tech computers with the 100 billion neurons and 100 trillion synapses of the human brain, Benavent had an episode of conscience. He told Stein about it over a few drinks and said he was going to destroy his work, return to Spain and retire. Just prior to that, Stein, who had no conscience, managed to steal his data. Babe didn't have it because Frankie was the only repository of this tech and "broke the mold" so to speak, when he was reanimated, by accidentally destroying the lap top upon which it was filed. This was in fact the thing that had enraged Stein the most at the time. The thing he later discovered would have made him an unspeakably wealthy man.

Still the good news was Babe had no information on this subject. With Stein's minimal notes on artificial intelligence and neuro interface and his prescriptions for basic levels she could only go so far. Had she been more adept at neurology or savvy in cyber science she might have been dangerous with just that, but she wasn't. She was just a reasonably "good cook following a complex recipe" without real knowledge of the principles. Even now she was planning quite a "queer dish" and the results would be chilling.

Alexi's body lay in the mini morgue in the lower levels of the Mansion while Babe searched the chimney for a fresh furry subject. It was warm weather and without a fire to deter them there were at least a dozen or two sleeping in the stack. Night vision goggles helped her locate one without a light to disturb them. She reached in and grabbed it with a gloved hand and it hardly squeaked at all. It was an ugly little thing with its snubbed nose and pointy cat-like ears. In fact it was perfect. Its genetic essence was all she needed and she would keep it safe for the appropriate time.

Tolya Karlovich owed Babe a blood debt for killing the murderer of his brother Dema and it was not difficult for him to join hands with her on the import and distribution of Krokadil. He was well in with the Russian Mafia as well as the KGB and whatever put the USA in its place and money in his pocket was A'Okay with him and all his associates. Never the less, both Babe and Tolya were surprised when another drug started invading the market from China called simply "X". When an overdose of Krokadil was in progress the subject might respond to large doses of Narcan to save life but "X" did not respond to Narcan at all. It was a tool not of commerce but of carnage.

It was a killing drug and heroin, Fentanyl and now even Krokodil were being cut with it. Doubtless someone thought it a grand idea to make drug addicts then exterminate them. That was the bad news. The good news was that it was frightening people into rehabs but there weren't enough beds and some of the wait lists were six months long. Not only was this bad for the regular drug business but it suspiciously looked like something that had happened before.

From his perch high atop buildings Frankie could see the streets were becoming war zones where decent people were afraid to walk even during the day. Businesses were closing left and right as people decided to sell and move away for fear of the drug zombies that constantly wandered in search of sustenance for their habit. Police were stretched to the breaking point. Every family of high or low income had an addict and every addict would rob his family blind to get what they needed. They were dropping by the pod but more were taking their place daily. It was a true plague in every sense of the word. Frankie tried to do his part but he too could not keep up with the need for help.

The war on drugs was obviously failing. There was too much money in the traffic of it and criminals were winning. The coalition's efforts to make the treatment medical, which had been a success in other countries, was moving far too slowly. Frankie was feeling kind of helpless and very low.

When he discovered Babe's involvement in all this he was not surprised but he was again disappointed. There was this need in him to save her, perhaps because she was the first woman who had ever looked at him with more than horror in her face or perhaps because she was his own kind. He didn't know which and perhaps it was both, still it was hard for him to move against her. Besides, legally there was no proof. What would she be charged with besides impersonating an officer? Making a cocoon of her and offering her up to the police would in the end, do no good. He would then, also be discovered.

The Russians were a different story and their cronies were frequently found hanging by their feet in precarious places. But even they were not involved in the peddling of this new drug. Neither was Don Mecina. Who...who was to blame?

Frankie was not one to listen to the useless chatter on the internet but when he was looking for information about the current drug crisis memes kept popping up that were quite disturbing. Things like:

"No Narcan at all"

"Let 'em die"

"Druggies deserve death."

Who was promoting such horrible ideas? He knew people on drugs could behave badly and act out of selfishness and desperation but he also knew that once they were clean many of them were among the most compassionate and wonderful of people he knew. He also understood many of them started taking drugs because they were hopeless or abused or in terrible emotional or physical pain. How could people think of them the way they did? Between that and the injustice that urged Stacia into action on behalf of sex traffic victims, his heart and his head felt like they might someday burst. In one episode of this kind of turmoil he sat on the top of his hill overlooking the city and cried out:

"Is this the way it is God? You see everything, you can do anything will you not act on behalf of justice? If this is the way of it...If there is not a remedy for the selfishness of human being and their hate, then destroy us all. We are nothing but a blight on the universe."

The wind sped past him in warm gusts blowing his long hair about his face and tangling stray leaves in it. The earth beneath his feet was mixed with bottle tops and glass. He kicked at a can and hurrumphed like a bear. Tucking his hair in his hoodie he turned to go thinking the Almighty might be too busy to care about this cesspool of a world. Listening to the cricket's symphony he thought it ironic that when humanity was done killing itself the last opus would belong to the insect. He did not know when he had been so low. His sigh moaned like the wind. Then pivoting to shuffle into the woods he paused.

There was something in his head or close to his ear...tones forming and flowing in and out of him, sounds of many kinds...then one sound forming a voice; soft, low and melodic like the lowest woodwind. He thought perhaps Fergus had followed him and was praying, or had been listening to his ranting but there was no one there. The a message hummed in tones as deep as the beat of his heart,

"Love endures."

That was all. That was enough. His questions though unanswered were satiated. Walking into the wood he felt strong confident. Guidance would come, and it did come in the form of a man named Branford Wilkes.

Branford lived about a mile away from the tree house. He made his money landscaping in the warm seasons and plowing in the snowy ones. His house was as dilapidated inside and out as the tree house was externally. He was a drunk and had arthritic pain in every bone in his body from breaks he had sustained in battle. They reminded him of his history and his age every time he pulled the cord of a lawn mower or fastened his plow to his old truck. He was a hoarder with a penchant for antiques and historic scenarios of warfare. He collected much but never sold anything and cataloged it all carefully on a computer that was also ancient by tech standards. He was not a military man but he was ex-CIA.

Branford had served his country well, doing whatever righteous or unrighteous thing the moment required. Swallowing his pride and his conscience he had finally retired without family or friends and drank his pension away like many other decorated heroes and residuals of espionage or war. He was used to chaos and crisis and now he was too old for both so he wallowed in his self made never land.

On several occasions, returning from his hill top retreat, Frankie had taken a short cut through Branford's property and the old spy had heard his quick agile foot falls as they disappeared into the gloamin. He had never been able to get a glimpse of the thing that so swiftly sped away but he had seen a print or two that made him wonder what was stalking his woods. Like a true "boy scout" the old man was prepared with ample sets of this tool and that, rope, bungee cords and such things as fishing nets and twine.

An assortment of these would aid him one night, as he set up an elaborate trap. He might not catch the thing to keep as a trophy but he would get a good look at it and, if he was lucky, scare it away permanently. He also had flood lights and cameras, a shot gun or two and an antique elephant gun fully loaded and in mint condition. It had bullets the length of a man's hand. In addition his collection boasted an animal stun gun which his CIA cadre used for practical jokes when things got dull on office picnics. In this case the plan was to trap his trespasser and take a few pictures of it for his collection of oddities *and* only if necessary, kill it. He was not one to kill what he could not eat.

The night Frankie heard the Voice, Branford had everything set up including a folding chair on the other side of the trap with a little table full of salsa, tortilla chips and lots of booze. He was hunkering down for his "stake out" to see if the thing would show up. He had a hunch and his hunches were usually good. The old spy was also confident he could get the thing. He had snared pesky bears this way and gotten them to stop digging in his trash. The net would trip some wires and elevate the prey at least a few feet off the ground on a sturdy branch he would then sedate it and do his photo op. Unbinding it after, he would allow it to awaken in a few hours. Then hopefully it would leave for good, duly warned. The old sod hadn't had this much fun since he caught a fisher cat in his hen house last winter.

Jogging lightly Frankie turned the corner to head up through Branford's as he had a habit of doing. His mind was on the wonderful experience he had just had. Then suddenly he found himself entangled and hanging inside a pouch of ropes and wires the soft gentle darkness pierced by blinding white light. He struggled momentarily and then stopped to consider. The pouch of nets that held him turned slowly and finally revealed a disheveled man seated on a lawn chair holding a bottle of Sam Adams with his jaw wide opened and half chewed chips dribbling out of his mouth.

Frankie said,

"You are an alcoholic, I can help you."

At this point Branford thought he was hallucinating and seriously considered taking the AA cure, he tossed the bottle into the bushes and wondered if IT would speak again.

The Coalition was to meet at the Tree house that Sunday afternoon and everyone was concerned that Frankie had not come in at all the night before. It was not like him to miss preparations for a meeting. He was always there at the crack of dawn cleaning house and preparing food. Rosa, Elaina, Dee Dee Kurt, Hailey and Angie were all there at 8 AM ready to help but though Gunta had bought ample provisions no one had even heard from the "Lord of the manner." Dee Dee was the only one who was not worried. She said, "Frankie commin' and sat in his nest playing with her legos (Frankie often found one or two of these angular, poky little things in his bed) then she took a nap.

When he finally did walk in everyone was there and they were laughing and joking as always. Voicing their relief they asked about his new friend. By way of introduction he said,

"Hi everyone, sorry I'm late. This is Branford. He's a new friend for us and NAI tells me he is a retired agent for the CIA."

A few chips fell to the ground and no one was breathing.

Frankie began treating Branford immediately and in short order the old curmudgeon was a believer. He didn't want the booze any more but he began to want the company. In fact he began to feel that all this energy and righteous excitement was far preferable to his solitude. To tell the truth, justice and excitement had first lured him into the CIA. He had been sorely disappointed in practice as a spy but down deep the desire for justice was still there. Here the fire inside was kindled again.

The ladies took care to give him a lot of TLC and he began to remember his manners. Ben sat with him from time to time and was just sympathetic and the old spy soon began admitting he had been living in seclusion because of the millions of shocks received in his work experiences. Ben urged him to talk about any subject he wanted to. He didn't reveal any government secrets but just talking about his questions and fears helped him feel better.

The food, the fellowship and the stimulating banter were all a little overwhelmingly at first but soon he found them indispensable and wonderful. He and Kurt shared a love for planes and old weapons but he still felt accepted by all the other pacifists. A Patriot all the way he admitted his faith in his country had waned after President Carter whom he had served under. He had not voted in a single presidential election after that. He just knew too much.

As an addict he saw a great need for helping people like him and wanted to help the cause of the coalition. After pretty Stacia caught his ear he told her he knew only too well how the sex trade was exploding and he thought it demeaning to humanity. To make money off of such slavery was positively neanderthal in his opinion. He finally admitted he had never had any children because he was afraid to bring innocents into the kind of world he knew existed. But these young people were the type he was proud to know.

The friends soon discovered just how intelligent and resourceful Branford was. They were all ashamed they had not trusted him at first. They apologized for profiling him as CIA the same way most people profiled them as addicts. So, Branford began to get involved just as a matter of course. It felt good to help and he thought it might be a way of paying for his sins. Vera assured him he could not pay and that grace would cover those sins for him if he wanted. But he still felt he had to atone, to make some amends.

He would not reveal secrets that were unknown to them but he could confirm certain things were fact not internet conspiracy theory. Then again he was also a strategist and he was really happy to be assisting with good strategies in this peculiar sort of "war". One day the subject came up about who was promoting drug "X" and having studied historic clandestine governmental initiatives in his training Branford recalled something that sounded similar. He said this:

"In 1926 the US was smack in the middle of prohibition. It was Christmas Eve in New York and drinking was still illegal, but Belleview Hospital was filling up with people who had some weird version of alcohol poisoning. They were hallucinating and paranoid and their alcohol levels were sky high. Over sixty people celebrating the season were treated in this condition and 31 died of it. That was just the beginning.

Doctors were used to dealing with alcohol poisoning during those days what with secret stills and bathtub gin and all, but this was different. It was an enormous increase. What they later found out was that the government was behind the rash of deaths that was overwhelming hospitals. They were sick of chasing down drunks who were killing themselves with alcohol and decided to just help them along. They wanted them to die. Now I'm not saying this is what is happening with drug "X" but the signs are similar, perhaps too similar. It might be the Chinese but I would not be surprised if the in higher ups in corporate or government did have something to do with this."

When the friends got this information they were all pensive. A couple of them (Angie and Gunta) said they had suspected something to that effect but what could they do about it if it were true? Stacia and Lucas said that the media might be their best bet but of late so many controls had been placed on the internet and the media by the government that they would have little success. They could not, of course, attack the government or even wealthy parties, corporations or criminal factions that were controlling lobbies or who had politicians in their pocket. What they had to do was get the message to the people somehow.

Jamal and Percy were of course the ones who came out with the artistic solution. If they could put together a super show with Music and Art and offer it free at a huge venue, with "must see" publicity they might be able to create a sensation that would move the masses to action. They had connections who had connections and there were music forums and performance forums on line that could be tapped for top notch performers and artists. They could call it

"Bringing down X". Of course NAI would have to fund it but even Frankie could participate in the show as if he were wearing a stupendous kind of costume. The coalition could be named as participants but if questioned would not have any knowledge of the organizing agency. They would say they were approached as collaterals and of course wanted "in" for this worthy cause.

As they planned it the show would have more audience interaction than "The Wall" and more special effects than "Star Wars". Simon of course had to turn a blind eye to this project since NAI funding would be involved but performers would be asked to donate their services for the cause and they were told it could be a tax right off, they were also told that everyone who was anyone would be there.

Known drug users among the entertainment community were offered free treatment with new and exciting protocols provided from a third party by the organizing agency and they were sent samples. Also, thanks to NAI's access to private numbers contacting these people was easy. Simon did suggest, hypothetically, that they should have a false entity to be the organizing agent and they called it "Clean and Painless Inc." This company would produce the show and worked in conjunction with Katz Labs.

Both agencies were given a full profile on the Net courtesy of NAI and Percy who had been in the background with music up to now, was in his glory designing websites and keeping them updated. Since no money would be generated for profit but only by donation there would be no contracts for finance. Insurance for liability, loss or injury would be needed but NAI could get that. Branford was used to keeping his mouth shut and committed himself whole heartedly but of course would have to stay low profile.

So in this way the Coalition armed for war against this onslaught of the Drug X. Wherever it was coming from it was going down as far as they were concerned. Stacia was going to be a part of this and she got out her dancing shoes and started going back to the studio. If this worked, sex trafficking would be next on their battle agenda and she wanted to be ready.

As for Frankie he was terrified. There were many things he had learned and begun to understand with his friends. He always had a fascination for Art both graphic and performance; but, to perform himself? Well, he would have to dig up more courage than he had ever done before. He was not sure about it, at all. The artists seemed confident however, and burst into action. It was amazing how quickly things were coming together for this. Without the hindrance of finances they took off like a rocket, networking, writing, composing, and setting everything up.

Frankie also soon had more friends who needed help, but who also had skills. Jake the agent was a client of Clean and Painless and Tammy and Iris – Dancer's from the studio that Frankie had saved at the restaurant Ealú had also benefited from the medicine. The girls especially were all over Frankie with special gratitude and affection. Stacia was almost sorry she got them on board.

Babe had dawdled concerning what was happening in the city long enough. Something was going on with the arts community that was getting major media coverage and she suspected it would bode ill for her business. She also had some recent expenses and needed money. The quickest way to get it was to reanimate the old Popsicle in the morgue that was once Alexi. Dealing with him initially would be difficult. But she wanted to use basic NAI to tutor him herself. This would hopefully ensure his cooperation so he would eventually give her what she wanted; his wealth. Molding his mind would always risk his ire when he started having artifacts of his former self but she would have to take that chance.

She didn't start having them (even with more advanced NAI) till she was well into being Lupo's slave. She recalled she did not appreciate the deception much at any time but she went along with it because she did not know any better. When she came to herself however, she was livid. She hoped Alexi would be as compliant for a while as she had been. She would teach him math first and hope he would at least remember his passwords. She would also have to do this away from the prince, as the prince's servants had vowed they would guard against the Babe's devices. They, however, might be bought. She would see.

The prince was anxious to have another reanimate with him. He was told by Babe that the generators needed some time to recuperate after the last surge used to reanimate him. This was a lie but there was no one there to tell him any different. She just didn't want to have to deal with the two of them. Now she had no choice. She hoped the advantages she had in her awakening would be enough to give her an edge. If it came to a battle between them and Frankie they would also come in handy and she knew they would band together on that. When the great Lord arrived they could all be easily disposed of as she knew he would love only her.

Babe went down her check list and everything was in readiness for Alexi's process.   But another event was about to take place that took precedence-- even over this. Alexi's money was in fact, needed for the arrival of Kirjath Arvio Yazid and she had purchased a few things already. A lovely red Porsche convertible and some outfits sure to entice, but she needed more. She needed to be sure of him. When he arrived she would need to wine him and dine him, take him to some sporting events and, most of all, take him somewhere they might have some privacy. She had also acquired some Air brush techniques for social events that gave her a decent color. She was prepared and wanted to plant some memories in him that she could call back as artifacts. Nothing could be left to chance. He was to arrive in a week because he was completing a wrestling tour in Turkey. That would hopefully be enough time.

The day of Alexi's reanimation nothing went right. The generators were acting up and she had to contact her Russian friends to make repairs. Fortunately one of them had been a repairman in the Soviet Army and he did it for Tolya but Tolya was curious and Babe had to promise to fill him in on her project at some point. He said he would hold her to that. She didn't like his tone. Perhaps it was time to start thinking of cutting ties.

After Kirjath was reanimated things would change subject to the game of world dominance. She would soon be done with the Russian Thug's drug peddling and connections. Still she lied and said she would cut Tolya into the deal if things went as planned but in her mind she saw his body sinking into the solvent in the basement along with his men. Meanwhile, she had to wait the whole tedious, gray day for him to leave.

The evening was dark and the night was stormy but they were ready and she felt it was now or never. The prince was an unruly adult/child and as many boys are, he was fascinated by dead things. He insisted on poking and prodding the body and touching the tubes that would infuse it with the proper solutions. She slapped his hand away several times while his body guards glowered in disapproval. Finally she said that it was unsafe for the prince to be present as the current of energy would be considerable and they removed him from the room. It was then she applied the fruit bat DNA and finally threw the switch. The snap, snap of surging power came sharp and fast with blinding white potential. When she powered down and detached the tubes his fingers were already twitching.

Four hours later she sat him up. His shoulders were slumped and his head was still unsteady. She wanted to dress him before the others returned as she didn't like looking at him. He was never beautiful naked though now the reanimation had filled him out a bit. The fluids had done their work. She noted a slight lift in his nose that had not been there before in his Germanic profile. And looking for any other signs of the visiting DNA she noted downy hair all along his back and neck and a small growth between his shoulders that looked like small flaps or skin tags. His eyebrows were also darker it seemed. She thought that if he were his usual vain self he would have them shaped immediately. His nails had grown also as most corpses' nails do and his hair was still silvery but a little longer than fashionable. She brushed it back to reveal his widow's peak hairline and waited for him to react.

Unlike the prince he did not seem to have a need to get up and start stumbling around. Instead he sat, or more like perched and raised his hands to his eyes shading them from the light. Perhaps he had inherited light sensitivity from the bat DNA.

Babe turned her back on him to dim the lights then noted that in removing the tubes she had cut her finger. A trickle of blood ran down the injured digit and she ignored it. The bots would soon have it repaired. Then behind her she felt Alexi's presence breathing faster than before. She saw his pale green/gray hand reaching for hers then turned to see eyes that gleamed with peculiar fascination. He would have taken her finger off if he could have, but she was faster than he.

Outside the thunder rolled and the lightning flashed. She slapped him to show him who was mistress and though he did not flinch in pain he did cower as if in shame and turned away showing his back. The growth between his shoulders seemed to be engorged. It had grown just a bit bigger.

21

Prince of the Air and the Prince of the East

Vera and Nora were talking in the tree house family room. Daniel, Francine and Petula were there by the piano and guitar practicing a song for church. They were waiting for Fergus, Mary Ellen and Ann, Frankie, Raven, Grandma and Grandpa Little Bear. Brandon wandered in with some vegetables from his garden that he wanted to share. Rosa with a coquettish smile, told him to put them on the table and she would wash them. He asked if the meeting was special and they said no but it would be spiritual. If he wanted he could stay. He did and so did Rosa. Kathleen Shea and Simon wandered in and finally Kurt and Hailey.

The friends had never made any spiritual profession but of late some of them had been gathering to pray. They felt that there were spiritual forces they were also fighting against and they wanted to be covered. Frankie agreed whole heartedly. All five of his "parts" where men of faith and he felt the need to consult with the Big Guy upstairs daily. It was a wonderful experience for him to consult God in a group of people he cared so much about. The group started with three but as time passed more and more of the friends joined in. With this big initiative coming on more and more of them felt the need. Vera was a pastor and could have taken control but she said she wanted the Spirit to do that. Everyone was in agreement and music and prayer happened as the Spirit led. It was always good and they did it more and more as time passed.

They were going into the public arena like never before and it seemed like certain powers didn't want them there. As they prayed they found that doors opened for them and soon even Jamal and Percy, Lucas and Luna and Ben and Gunta with Tammy and Iris were bowing their heads reverently and asking for the forces of good to win. The only one that didn't want anything to do with it was Stacia. She would always wait outside till it was over then she would come in. This pained Frankie and put distance between them.

Today they were praying for the program itself. How would it be arranged? They had received quite a few RSVPs from big names who were intrigued enough by the free samples of Frankie's meds to donate their time for just plane fare. Because of this, the program would be a "shoe in" for Madison Square Garden (paid in advance courtesy of NAI so entrance to the public would be free) and several networks had already approached them about TV coverage. "Clean and Painless" were going to film it and they had lots of T-Shirts they would be distributing, as well as hats and other paraphernalia. Actors and performers who had battled with drugs or alcohol and were now clean said they would be available for testimonial. Andre was tearing his hair out to get security for all this and Brandon who still had a few connections called them in for ex-CIA and FBI who were now high end security or body guards.

Gunta and Ben would speak about their new treatment for opioids, alcohol and krokodil but the big push would be "Taking down X". Safety measures to avoid the drug were peddled on T-shirts and hats as memes, like "X Stranger Danger" or "Party with the Trusted," or "Poison X", "Get Clean and Mean, X bites." Stories of how people were tricked into taking it and died would be told, but they wanted more.   They wanted a grand finally. This would be a short but powerful musical to bring this message home at the end of the day. The play needed to show X was poison and it was a way of killing off a lot of people deliberately. This was the big issue they were praying for because the big day was two months away and they still had only half a script.

Stacia had been sitting outside in Lucas' car and she was getting bored. In actual fact she had been working on some ideas for the script and some choreography.   One of those possible scenarios included a giant named "Justice" lifting up a man and a woman who were addicted and nearly dead out of the darkness of addiction into the light of freedom, only to see them bury a friend who died of X. The giant would weep over this and the whole cast had to come together to support him so that X could be taken down. Together with justice they would succeeded.

The story was simple but powerful and she knew just the Giant who could play the part of "Justice." She looked in the window of the tree house and saw that people where walking around indicating that the prayer meeting was over. So she entered and declared she had a possible script. Everyone was excited and liked it very much. Vera said,

"Praised God that's an answer to prayer,"   And Stacia got upset and walked out.

Babe's experiment with Alex's vegetarianism had obviously failed. His preference for fruit had increased but so had his blood fetish. Soon raw meat began to disappear from the kitchen and the cook had to ask Babe to remove the Austrian incubus many times when meat dishes were being prepared. Alexi was like a puppy begging at the pantry door. Finally the cook found that doing prep for supper in the bright afternoon, with the windows open to let in the sun, was a deterrent. Alexi's light sensitivity was quite pronounced. Still, they had to lock up the fridges and even then a few times the lock was broken.

On the upside Alexi's verbal and math skills were moving on apace. He was a good student and Babe gave him lots of reinforcement by way of bits of raw bloody meat. At the end of a week he was an expert at his cell phone and to the Prince's disgust he found him face deep in bucket of bloody ground beef after he gave Babe access to three of his Swiss account. She had rewarded him with it and then left the room to make her transactions. The cook came in screaming Persian epitaphs and Alexi snarled at the irate chef. The cook then raved to the Prince. Body guards got involved attempting to restrain the crazed and red faced stock broker which ended in a tussle that the guards lost. By the time Babe came in to sooth everyone Alexi was panting hard and the thing on his back, which seemed to grow with hostile emotions, was taking on a very strange configuration.

Three more similar situations happened before it was apparent that the growth, increasing in size with every outburst, was a pair of bat-like wings. Two days before the arrival of Kirjath, on a particularly sultry night, Alexi spread those very wings and took off into the blackness to find his own bloody meat.

Andre and Frankie had engaged in this discussion before. Stein was a criminal and needed to be arrested. Frankie begged him not to do it because it would expose him as "evidence". That might mean lots of bad things. He might even be confined for the study of science. This would bring reanimation into the public eye. All the friends agreed reanimation should be shut down not opened to discussion. Andre didn't want Frankie to become "Exhibit A" in a trial but Andre also wanted very badly to get even with everyone who had destroyed his brother. Frankie begged him to wait till after the show at least.

As a compromise, Andre insisted they not keep Stein in a hotel with room service on NAI's tab, but that they place him in Nora's old shed where they could watch him. Frankie agreed to that, though it might present other problems. Branford would help keep a watchful eye and so would Kurt. Stein had no gumption to run, given a lap top with Wi-Fi he was actually no problem.

As more and more tasks had to be completed for the show Jamal and Percy, Angie and Stacia began to think they needed an office and rehearsal space. The studio where Stacia danced was still struggling after being shut for so long. They had lost a couple of teachers and needed some financial assistance to stay afloat. "Clean and Painless Inc." made an offer and they told them they would need dancers for the big show. They were only too glad to collaborate. The office was opened, phones and computers installed and rehearsals started. It was a win, win for everyone. It was also summer and Stacia could apply herself to this whole heartedly since she was not teaching. She came alive with it all.

Meanwhile, the CT police had promised Andre they would keep an eye on the foreign element at Stein's place. They did have reports of those generators humming and sparks flying a few weeks prior but everything seemed copasetic with that now. The police were also concerned that the doctor had not returned. The middle easterners said he was now in Geneva presenting a paper on GMO as a solution to world hunger.

The officer nodded his head with understanding then announced another disturbing problem in the neighborhood. It seemed that a number of missing pets had recently been reported in the area. The Police had actually come to speak to the guests at the mansion and warn them that there might be some kind of large animal in the area making off with dogs and cats. They had at least six reports and people were very alarmed by it all.

The professor, who was the Prince's right hand, assured the police they would keep an eye out. They had gotten rid of their dogs a months ago and did not want any pets around as the Prince was allergic and the barking annoyed him.

On a different note and by way of friendly exchange, they introduced the police to Kirjath and he impressed them with a few feats of strength and told them it was his goal to compete against the American Campion and beat him. The police wished him luck to his face but "flipped him the bird" behind his back. Then the officers left without knowing the large vicious animal they were looking for, was staying in one of their guest rooms and flying around the neighborhood on nightly hunting expeditions.

It was in fact, on one of these forays into the neighborhood, that Alexi spied a large shadow running at great speed (for a biped) then disappearing into the wood. This excited him and he followed the movement of the trees for as long as he could then was distracted by a young deer which he victimized in short order. Never the less the shadow intrigued him and in nights to follow he would seek it out and finally follow it to a ramshackle house that appeared more overgrown that lived in. His eyes well adapted to the night could see as clearly as in the day that there were stirrings of others in that place and cars, though hidden by trees, were parked here and there around back. Landing quietly in the wood he folded his wings and made his way to a window where he was able to spy quite a lot of folk milling about and enjoying each other's company.

An artifact of parties in a stately apartment with a grand view of the city came to him. His blood lust had given him so little time to reflect and recollect. Only short artifacts had filtered through, enabling his business acumen to emerge briefly for the benefit of his domineering tutor, the beautiful Babe. Then as he watched through the window, that lust sparked his thirst, when he noticed something that might serve as easy prey.

It was a small child. He had up to now never tasted man flesh and his desire was aroused especially since the "Shadow" was for the first time identified as a grotesque giant reanimate, and the child seemed to be his darling. Artifacts came fast and furious of the things this large simpering buffoon had taken from him and the desire for vengeance, grew almost to rival the desire for blood. Now, as more than human, Alexi would even that score. He had already dined that night but there would be other nights and soon his revenge might be more than complete.

Inside the tree house Frankie sat with Dee Dee next to him. He was cross legged and she was still small enough to fit under his arm watching all that was going on. The elemental storm, flying above them in the form of a reanimated incubus, was not on her radar and she felt only peace next to her big protector. He patted her little head as he listened to Raven Little Bear who was explaining the smoke process as he lit up some smudge herbs.

"Smudge does not usually burn but smokes and gives off a good scent. This smoke represents our prayers to Creator. Grandfather and Grandmother have been worried about you. They both feel you are about to enter a great battle and you have to learn to dance like a warrior."

Here Grandmother and Grandfather Little Bear began to play the heart beat rhythm on the drum as they sang a warrior's song. Raven demonstrated the hunter's dance and showed Frankie (and everyone else who was watching) by stomping and moving his head and upper body in ways that indicated alertness and awareness of all his surroundings. He crouched and looked up and around as he stomped, as if expecting possible enemies even from the skies. His hand was on his knife by his side and his fan made of hawk feathers wafted the sweet grass smoke upwards.   Then he continued to explain.

"We have gathered eagle feathers for you, some were George's for his accomplishments at school and this one was for his attempt to save Sparrow on that terrible day. The physical strength he lacked you have in spades my brother but his brain helps you to think and this gives you great power in planning. Grandmother has made this regalia for you. She put a lot of work into it because you are so big. You don't have to wear it except when you meet with the people of first nations but this choker is something you can wear any time. It bears the cross of Tesa since we are believers and it blesses in the four directions."

Frankie accepted it and everyone clapped.   Then Frankie gave Grandmother a big kiss and a silver bracelet with turquoise heart. To Raven he gave a silver arrow with red flight feathers and to Grandfather a large bear claw on a leather strap. Then he said,

"I have been collecting silver spoons and making things with them. I hope you like this Grandmother. I found the stone in New Mexico as I passed through from Alaska. And for you, Grandfather. I pulled this claw out of my arm years ago. Keep fighting for your health with the strength of the bear. Raven be careful what you shoot with this. You may not want to lose it. It flies true. If great Spirit sees fit, I will come to you all soon." They were all well satisfied and smiles were everywhere.

"I will not shoot with this at all my brother, unless it is a great enemy I seek to bring down. Hey we gotta go. Work tomorrow. Got a big art show to get ready for. Come see it."

"Would love to. We'll talk."

The grandparents got into the car and Raven stood outside of it with Frankie. The moon was full and had a hallo of diffused red and gold giving the night a solemn mystery. Raven was going to get into his green mustang then looked at Frankie and said,

"I got an old convertible Chevy you might fit in I'll bring it next time and we'll go for a ride." Frankie smiled but just then a shadow passed across the moon. Both heads looked up and he remarked,

"Bats?" But Raven said,

"Big ones…take care."

"Sure, you too." And the big Indian that looked like a child next to the giant drove off.

Babe thought the handsome wrestler quite a dish till she realized he was an inch shorter than she was. But that was incidental to the fact that he was a good Muslim who thought women in slinky clothes were to be used and not admired. Despite her Air brush, he discovered her pale green skin and was put off by it. She wondered if he might change his mind when he became a god instead of a worshipper, but if he didn't, she was quite miserable thinking that she, as a reanimate, might end up the handmaid of this egomaniac instead of his queen.

Of course part of his destiny was in her hands, even if he did not know it. Never the less, she had to rethink all this and make some plans of her own. Babe would short him on all the things she had shorted the other two but the political power she could not short him on if the prince accomplished what he and Alexi were planning. Babe therefore began to think, this muscular upstart should not get back to the Middle East. For this she might need Frankie but since Stein's disappearance he had not been around. How could she find him?

Playing all this out in her cunning mind she sipped wine late into the night when Alexi flew in. She envied him his ability to fly and wished there was some way of giving herself such a gift but Stein was not around to question about such possibilities. He was another she wanted to locate. She looked at the Austrian covered in the crimson evidence of his ghastly table manners and wished him swimming in solvent. He was beginning to get a clue that she did not have his best interest at heart but he intended to get some rest before the sun started to peak into the window. She stopped him.

"You really have lost quite a bit of your fashion sense since I reanimated you."

"Other considerations are of greater importance to me now. Besides you cleaned me out. Now that I know this I'm a little peaked at you."

"You agreed to my price when you were desperate. It was the cost of your divinity. When things are rearranged in the world you will have all the pocket change you like."

"I'm counting on it. But I have noticed things are not going as well with you and the wrestler."

"No, he is not as charming as I had hoped."

"He had two dark lovely ladies brought in for his amusement today. One could say they were children, no more than 14 or 15 is my guess. Apparently he prefers adoring brunettes to a red head that wants to be adored."

Babe held her tongue for a moment then changed the subject.

"Notice anything of interest on your nightly rounds?"

"As a matter of fact I did. I found the large Shadow."

"Oh?"

She tried hard to sound disinterested but her heart was racing. Alexi told her she didn't have to finish her job. He could now take care of the Shadow himself. She said it didn't matter to her now as she had other plans. She asked if Stein was with him and she said that perhaps they should both go to finish the job, at no extra cost to him, of course.

"You'll have to tell me where he is though. *I* can't fly you know."

"Yes, pity that."

He told her the location and that day when he fell asleep in his darkened room in the basement, she went to pay Frankie a visit.

Parking the car in the woods Babe walked to the house and tried some observation before she knocked on the door. Everything seemed quiet except for a shed that had some Bach softly wafting in from its humble recesses. The only window appeared to be on the roof. She thought to climb a tree to peer into it when she heard a noise normal ears might not hear. Frankie appeared from between a small grove of birch trees.

"You found me Br...Lady."

"The bullet wounds have healed I see."

"Yes they have. What brings you here?"

"You are in danger."

"And you are warning me? How kind."

"I owe you, but I won't after this. Get your friends away from here. Alexi has been reanimated and he is hunting you."

"How did he find me?"

"Let's just say he did. Look to the skies tonight."

She stroked his face and Frankie did not recoil. But he did think of the large bat he had seen the night before with Raven. She stepped into the woods and disappeared.

In the back doorway of the house, stood Branford, silent as a stone, holding his elephant gun. Frankie asked him to put it away.

Meanwhile, silent and ghostlike in the upstairs window, stood Stacia. She did not look pleased in her navy blue night dress, but displeasure was her default of late and Frank could do nothing about it. He had told her about Babe and she knew Frankie did not want to reciprocate, but the sultry attention Stacia witnessed smarted a little. Ann, unaware of the exchange, beckoned her to help with breakfast. They had been sharing the room overnight after the meeting but guests were all getting ready for their day and needed to be fed. Frankie went inside and with a sense of urgency told everyone they needed to get ready to leave.

Ben and Gunta were dressed and eating granola. They needed to get to the Katz Center by 10:00 as they had a full load of treatments to do. Jamal and Percy were going to give Angie a lift to Grand Central as she was going to visit her mother in upstate NY. Stacia would also go with them to open the Studio and work on some PR for the show. Elaina and James had planned to go to the conserve and do some hiking with Dee Dee. Frankie was not happy about them doing this but James promised they would be back for their things before dark, and then they would leave for the city.

Rosa was getting a ride with Ann, Jean Luke and Luna that morning as the two professionals had to work and the retirees were to do some gardening at the De Lacy's. Kurt, Hailey and Branford remained to clean up and get the house ready to be vacated for a while. It was agreed Stein would go wherever Branford went. All the rest of the friends were home or at their business. All were called and told their meeting was cancelled and that they should stay away from the house until further notice.

It was a gray day again and the hike was not as cut and dry as the little family had expected. Dee Dee was a trouper and kept right on going all the way to lunch. After they ate they wanted to walk off their meal but by 4 o'clock Elaina and the child were quite tired and James was not reading the map correctly. They did reach the lake where they dipped their tired feet and splashed around. But they wanted to keep moving, and being city folk after all, they got a bit disoriented. One tree started looking like another. Finally they completed the hike at around six. Hungry and in need of refreshment they drove to a burger place for dinner and then to the tree house by eight to get their things. The sky was darkening by then.

In the house Kurt, Hailey and Branford were all getting tired of hearing Stein say "We have to get out of here," especially since he was doing precious little to help. It was just getting repetitive. Certainly he knew what might be coming their way but enough was enough. They had done a great job of cleaning up but the last few boxes of flyers and equipment for the show had to be loaded in the van and they didn't have time for the aging neurotic. Frankie was just closing up on the second level. He had considered staying but he wanted to pick his battles. So he would flip his hoodie up and go patrolling in the city that night. If there was an attack they would be disappointed. There would be no one to fight.

When she came down the ladder Dee Dee was looking for something. She was upset. Elaina said she was just tired but she kept saying, "Mama, my egos." Frankie of course knew that meant her legos and he told her they were in his nest. He was going up to get them when Kurt asked him to please help with the last box that was really heavy. Frankie just told Dee Dee she could get them herself and she kicked her foot in frustration and went up to do just that.

Frankie lifted the box with one arm and opened the door of the van with the other. Then they heard it; a screech of demonic glee and the scream of a horrified child. Frankie dropped the box in the van. Without hesitation he climbed along the outside of the darkened house, like an orangutan on amphetamines. He was in sight of the window of his room before James and Elaina reached the ladder.

There Frankie could see a massive bat's wing spread out and ready to take flight. This was attached to the body of what looked like Alexi who was dragging something else. In moments Frankie could see it was Dee Dee screaming and crying and held by one arm. The incubus Alexi was trying to make off with the little girl. Frankie was having none of it. With a great lunge the giant grabbed for the extended wing and caught the demon's leg instead. The wings flapped madly and the bat started skyward laboring to rise with his prey and his passenger. Alexi had one choice for escape and that was to drop the child. Of course the hero would choose the child over the bat and he did. Surrounding Dee Dee with his arms and chest they both fell into the tops of the trees.

The fall was hard but broken by many layers of branches and leaves. They were safe. Dee Dee clung to Frankie terrified but she was unhurt and he quickly handed her to Elaina. He would follow the high flyer as far as he could, swing from one tree to another. Finally he came to a cliff and in a rage found he had run out of terrain and mobility. He saw the bat in the distance and swore this was not the end of this. Turning he ran in the direction of the Stein mansion.

Frankie had his head down and was running at full tilt like a sprinter in a race. He had never felt such anger. A killing rage surged through him, but even as he hastened towards his destination, his adversary caught a lift on a moonlit breeze and sped away beyond his reach.

Alexi, furious at being deprived of his prey once again, by the infernal Shadow, saw his opportunity for reprisal. From his great height in the glowering skies the demon spied a flickering light. Someone was enjoying an outdoor evening with friends and had a good fire going. A can of kerosene was at hand to stoke the flame. The craven swooped near the gathering and unseen, snatched the can. Swinging round in a deadly arc the predator swept the sky on a return visit to the tree house.

Meanwhile, another car drove up to the house below. Fergus and Mary Ellen had not checked their messages before they left and did not know about the cancelation of the regularly scheduled meeting. Both of them were just getting out of the car when they heard Dee Dee crying inconsolably at the back of the property and ran to see everyone getting into vehicles. The other friends informed them of the incredible details and he and Mary Ellen added their soothing words to the child's angst. Suddenly the very creature in question was behind them hovering over them like demonic bird of prey. Fergus turned to face him spreading his arms over the family behind him in a protective stance. He was terrified but with reflex well honed in his holy practice he screamed:

"Back Satan, no one here belongs to you."

Breughal stopped flapping his wings. Suspended in mid Air he paused in unexpected disorientation. The Icon of Fergus' faith was on a chain around his neck and the bat spied it with horrible fascination. He reached for the little group of friends as if to snatch some stray limb or bite some extended digit but he could not. He screeched in anger but to no avail, though his mind did not believe in or fear God, *something* possessing him did. He beat his wings in retreat and instead landed on the grass covered roof of the tree house and poured the kerosene he brought with him in a wide circle. Standing there in his soiled Armani suit, as if outside a theater, he pulled his silver cigarette case out of his jacket pocket and lit one up. Airborne once again he tossed it on the roof and cackled with laughter as it went up in flames. Surveying his handiwork with satisfaction, his thirsty obsession turned again towards the child. He began his killing decent but in a moment quick as lightning an explosion aborted his trajectory. Brandon's elephant gun blasted a hole through Alexi's belly and the blood sucker went down in the blaze he had just kindled.

The pause in the terror gave everyone time to frantically get into their respective vehicles and leave. They did not want to see if the thing would reemerge. The roof had just caved in and the fire was now licking up the sides of the house, faster than any of them had thought possible. Fergus called the fire department and reported the blaze as it had already started to spread quickly. Brandon grabbed Stein and drove towards home hoping the fire would not spread through the woods to his house nearby. He turned his short wave radio on and planned to remain informed as always. Everyone else drove away in shock and prayed Frankie would be alright.

While all this was happening there was much activity in the Mansion. Tired of Babes excuses for not reanimating the Great Lord, the Prince impulsively commanded everyone pack up and make ready to leave. He called the local Airport and had the pilot of his private jet fuel up and stand by. Then he unapologetically shot Kirjath and demanded that Babe reanimate him immediately. She was of a mind to resist but thought instead that 30 guns aimed at her might be hard for her bots to handle. She reluctantly complied with the procedure which included the royal DNA cocktail and ample portions of cobra genetic material all infused into the chauvinistic wrestler as requested.

When the fireworks were over and the generators were powering down what emerged (with much sedation) was a thick necked creature with a majestic pattern of black and gold scales down his back. These were complimented by penetrating vertical pupils, a forked tongue and a short tail protruding from his caudal area. If this behaved like Alexi's wings he would soon have a dragons train following him. She hoped he would not live long enough to see it.

As Kirjath's body was adjusting, the Prince informed her that she was not coming with them and neither was Alexi. The betrayal burned within her but fearing for her life she acquiesced and pretended allegiance to the Prince. She spoke submissively and told him she would be there to serve him when the Great Lord emerged victorious. After all they might have need of more reanimations and all would be in readiness when the request came. The Prince was dubious about her sudden cooperation but he saw some sense in what she said. He chained her to a pillar of concrete in the garage and left. When Frankie arrived Babe was just extricating herself.

"WHERE's the BAT?" Frankie thundered.

"I'm not his keeper Frank but I warned you didn't I?"

"I am waiting here till he returns."

"Suit yourself. I'm going after the others."

"Where did they go?"

"Frank, brace yourself. I've reanimated a greater nightmare than Alexi. He's a genetic composite of the pharaohs and the Assyrian king. The prince forced me to do it. This thing also has Cobra DNA and the body of a champion wrestler and what the Prince intends for it is terrifying even to me."

"Sounds like you've been dumped Bronagh. But I need to deal with Alexi."

"Well you ought to know about being dumped. How is your pasty little lamb these days? No matter, while we're wasting time on personal quarrels the world's safety lies in the balance. If these guys make it to Egypt they will pool the wealth of Middle Eastern oil and power, to begin the next world war. Millions will die."

"You didn't care about *that* when you were included in the conspiracy, did you Babe?"

"I now realize what I've done. I'm sorry alright. Common, are you going to help me stop them? I can't do it alone. Or are you going to sit here and wait for Alexi? He doesn't come till morning sometimes. I'll show you where he sleeps. But this won't wait."

Frankie huffed in frustration and shook his black mane of hair. She loved it when he did that. He didn't trust her but he knew Dee Dee was safe and his duty was to the many.

"Very well, where did they go?"

"Danbury Municiple Airport where the Prince has his jet."

"We'll never make it. They're far ahead of us. But wait..."

His NAI began to beep as it dialed Andre.

"Hello Poloche here."

"Andre, we got trouble, big trouble."

"What's goin' on?"

Frankie filled Andre in and asked him if it were possible to get some police presence to stop the flight or at least stall it till he got there. There was a very dangerous reanimate on that jet and it would cost a lot of people to have him reach his destination. Andre said the fastest way might be to say there was a terrorist threat which was kinda true. He was on it. Then Frankie called Branford. The old spy filled Frankie in on what happened with the bat and then said he could get some CIA guys out there with the same threat of terrorism. These kinds of buzz words got results.

Frankie was not conflicted anymore. Alexi was taken care of and he could focus on helping Babe. Regardless of her intent these people had to be stopped. It was always a gamble to trust her, but she was so alluring when she played the "good girl" even though she was never really good. She smiled at him and for a moment she felt a thrill thinking she was on his team. Oh, what was she thinking? She would be lucky if he and Kirjath killed each other. Then she wouldn't have to worry about interference from either of them. She knew neither of them would ever be hers. Never the less the moment was sweet but all this momentary musing stopped when they heard a huge thump on the dark veranda.

Their eyes met with apprehension and she pulled out her gun. He whispered,

"If it's an animal please don't kill it. I will deal with it."

"It's not an animal."

"How do you know?"

"I can feel it."

One thing she had on him was an uncanny intuition. She stepped closer to the window to take a look and they heard another thump. She took cover and listened then moved again. Frankie just stood there trying to see past the glare and his own reflection on the window. He took a book and threw it at the light breaking the bulb and dropping the room into darkness. A third thump came. Then she whispered again.

"It's not an animal...it's a monster."

Seconds later through the window burst a rage filled creature splintering wood and glass. They could not have anticipated its appearance but they knew who it was. That once human thing was twisted and charred. It endured a misshapen face that resembled melting wax but was really pealing flesh. It's clothes were shreds of once fine fabric burnt and hanging from sagging flaps of seared tissue. He resembled something out of Dante's infernal pit. A hole was featured in its abdomen that was a wound almost healed--donut like in its malformation. The wings were mangled and twisted. How it flew in its condition was a greater mystery than that of the bumble bee. Obviously his bots had attempted some recovery but moving more slowly than was useful they warped his appearance beyond recognition. Roaring in rage it then sagged in exhaustion and spoke,

"Help me Babe," his gravelly voice more a moan than human language. Then he collapsed. Babe stood over him aiming at him with her revolver. Feeling pity for him in that moment she thought. "Not worth killing." Babe lowered her gun. And right before their eyes, Alexi writhed, gasped and perished in greater pain than he had ever caused.

Babe picked up the corps and carried it to the basement where she yanked off the cover of the first vat. She then eased him into it watching the acidic substance swallow and digest him. A solemnity took her for a moment but a moment was all she gave him. Then she turned ready for business. Running for the back of the house she uncovered the last vehicle that was left under a tarp; a dusty Porsche. It wasn't functional.

Frankie looked up and thanked the Lord for friends. Then he dialed Branford. In ten minutes the man who had become indispensable to the friends was there with one of the Vans. Kurt and Stacia were with him. The two women faced off but remained civil. Stacia thought, "She's very beautiful," and Babe thought, "Maybe she'll die," but no words were spoken. Babe got in and there was just enough room for Frankie to squeeze in lying down with his feet hanging out the back. He thought, "All of this is awkward," but he told them where to go. Andre called Frank just then and said help was in process and he was halfway there.

The Prince, his August Charge and six of the Prince's men were on the jet. Beside these were two terrified stewardesses, the pilot and co-pilot.

The Serpentine man was half reclining, half draped on one of the jet's luxurious chairs and still quite woozy. One of the men was of course the professor who had brought enough sedative to dull the senses of six oxen for twenty four hours or more. He sat next to the would be "Great Lord" with the medication at the ready in several gold tipped syringes as befitting the rank and divine status of the recipient. All they needed to take off was the permission of traffic control from the tower.

They were being delayed and the holdup was wearing thin on the impulsive Prince. This delay was coming courtesy of the CIA agents in the tower, who were there at Branford's behest. They had instructed the controller to blame the delay on fog therefore giving their people time to act. Meanwhile heavily armed men and women in Kevlar were taking their places and preparing to board through the luggage compartment. They had been commanded to carry heavy artillery as what they might find would be shocking and armored.

Police and bomb squad stood at the ready in the terminal. Andre had to mediate when Frankie and Babe arrived, as every gun pointed in their direction. Andre questioned the wisdom of such exposure but Frankie was done with secrecy. He knew there was a chance this battle might cost his life but he did not think he could be a good man and do anything different. That meant the whole world would be watching. Stacia knew this was emotionally huge for Frankie. She walked up to him and said,

"We're all with you." And he answered seriously making the comment personal,

"Are *you*?" Stacia was cut to the heart and turned away pursing her lips. Frankie looked and saw Babe pouting. He turned and grabbed her arm walking as he spoke.

"Bronagh focus please. Is the Serpent still sedated?"

Andre just smiled at the whole interaction and seeing Frankie grimace at him he got serious and spoke to one of the officers. Babe answered Frank,

"We'll know in a minute."

It was too late to call back the troops from the plane so Babe and Frankie watched as one by one CIA agents were flung from the open hatch of the air craft or shot down.   Frank and Babe exhaled deeply and jumped into the fray just as one of the stewardesses ran down the ramp screaming in terror while the other was thrown out dead. Then, to their horror and amazement, the hatch was closed and plane began to move away from the ramp.

The luggage compartment was still dragging and that had to be in place in order to fly; to do that a few more agents had to be tossed out like rag dolls. Inside the Serpentine man was fully awake. The sedative had worn thin and the next dose was preempted by the attack. Unaware of who was friend or foe it had perceived danger and begun hissing to defend itself. When it heard the shots its tale began to swell with adrenalin and its neck also expanded in a collar of scales which amplified the hisses emitted by the split tongue. The vertical pupils narrowed to better focus on whatever came. Like birds before a serpent the agents were paralyzed by the sight of him. They were soon overcome.

Of course the attackers were first to go but soon anyone with a gun became a target of its defensive posture. When every armed person was gone the survivors included the prince. Hoping it would ensure his survival he prostrated himself before the abomination and that seemed to appease it. Something came into its mind as an artifact, thousands bowing before it. He then understood on an instinctual level that he was back in the world of men and this was how they should be treating him. The Creature calmed and the hooded neck retracted into more human form. He draped himself over one of the posh chairs and seemed to enjoy the soft leather. The Prince who, had been watching him sideways from a prostrate position, spoke softly to him in the Persian tongue.

"You have been victorious in battle my Father, this is your chariot that travels the skies like those of the gods. We must away to your palace for it is a long journey and we must prepare for war."

The Serpent was not absolutely certain of all that was said but he liked the sound of it. Pileizer nodded to the Prince and he in turn gave the terror stricken pilot the order to move even as the two remaining men and the professor pulled the luggage hatch shut. Wine was offered the Serpent in a golden chalice and he licked then sipped it. Outside there was much commotion but the Prince just told the Serpent there was nothing to be concerned about.

As the plane started accelerating the Serpent got excited. Having heard his native language he began to remember. He exclaimed to the professor that this was faster than any horse he had ever traveled upon. The professor chuckled a little thinking they were probably only going around 40 miles per hour. Then he mentioned that they would need to go much faster to fly. Pileizer accepted this with anticipation and asked why they were not riding on the outside of the sky chariot called a plane? Would it not be easier to steer it. The professor then asked permission to show the Great Lord how the plane was "steered". Two men were reluctantly commanded to carry his tail like the train of a robe and the Snake followed the prince. At the cockpit the door was opened to reveal the petrified pilot that looked over his shoulder and almost fainted.

Understanding now that the fog was a ruse the professor smiled with satisfaction as he looked out the cockpit window and thought they were finally free and clear to take off. But just when he was breathing easy an army green monster with wild raven hair jump onto that same window and punched a hole through it. The Serpent Hissed and roared in ancient Persian,

"HOW DARE YOU ATTEMPT TO STEER MY SHIP! UNDERWORLD VERMIN! A SWORD, SOMEONE BRING ME MY SWORD!"

Finally the pilot could take no more. Almost by reflex he slowed the plane down and passed out. The Serpent grabbed the pilot by the collar and threw him straight through the plane where he hit the rear lavatory. Then like the wrestler he was the Serpent lunged towards the Titanic Aggressor knocking him off the nose of the plane. Simultaneously he got his first taste of broken plexi-glass. The shards that stuck in his arms and caused them to bleed were fascinating to him and he crouched on the nose of the jet that was still slowly moving and lifted them off his skin. Then he watched the skin heal as the bots did their work. He stood taller than Frankie now in his Cobra's cowl. The adrenalin continued to puff him up as he raised his arms and shouted in triumph, and his tail lashed away the remaining glass. His victory, however, was not yet won.

Frankie was once again on the nose of the moving Aircraft and he landed a punch on the snout of the snake that knocked him off the plane and onto the tarmac. What followed was as epic as the battle of Heracles and the Hydra. Limbs entwined with serpentine constriction, teeth and claws all tussling in chaotic fury. Not to be left behind Babe was on the tarmac too waiting for an opening, her gun ready to assist whoever happened to be winning. Stacia by contrast, stood at the Airport window frustrated and afraid for Frank.

The battle was fully illuminated by the lights on the runway. Stacia could see everything and thought the Big Guy was handling himself masterfully but the Thing had razor sharp fangs. If they were poisonous the outcome might shift in its favor. Then she noticed there were wounded agents on the tarmac who might get in the way of the landing gear of the aimlessly wandering plane. The EMT's on site were obviously overwhelmed and Fergus with Mary Ellen (as clergy) followed others to help. Stacia snuck in as an informal assistant showing her CPR card. But the deal breaker was Branford. He had his Elephant gun locked and loaded and all he needed was a clear shot.

Frank had all he could handle to keep the fangs away. A few times he found that going for the Serpent's throat was the only way to get him to retract them. One hand on the neck and the other to fight with was a handicap but despite this he still had the advantage of strength. The wrestler had a few moves as well that came to him as a matter of kinesthetic artifact. He also had that lethal tail that tripped Frank up more than once.

Frankie snatched the tail and finally pinned the Serpent to the ground only to have the tail wriggle free and grab his own throat from behind. He gasped and again squeezed the neck. The tail released Frank, and he had cause to thank Raven's choker for its protection. Thankful but indignant Frank again took hold of the wriggling tail and used it to lift his opponent off the ground like a lariat. He swung him around and around his head then let go into some dumpsters. Dizzy and covered in trash it was now the "Great Lord's" turn to be indignant. He did not wear indignation well.

Pileizer was now more serpent than man. It lifted itself up on its inflated tail and Frankie could not manage its escalated size. The serpents vertical pupils were now very thin, a ploy these kinds of reptiles used to deepen the field of their focus. This also had an added psychological benefit of hypnotically charming its prey. Frank thought he was just impressed by the size but presently he looked into the eyes and felt himself fascinated by their gleam and the slow, serpentine movement of the head. Seeing Frankie's dilemma Fergus wasted no time. He left a wounded agent in Mary Ellen's care then swallowing hard he started to move towards his friend. He waved to Branford who nodded and move into place across from the Serpent that with fangs bared, was poised to strike. Stacia also saw the configuration of friends and stood up ready to help in any way possible.

Fergus intended to yell at Frank and warn him not to look into the serpent's eyes. Branford knew he would get only one shot. The tail swished back and forth rhythmically and Frankie began to reel a bit on his feet. Suddenly Fergus moved forward yelling, "Frank look away," but the hum of the maverick jet engine muffled his voice. So Stacia started to jump and wave in Frank's peripheral vision.

The Snake's tail answered her movement smacking both Fergus and Stacia cold with one stroke. It then opened its massive jaws to swallow them but Frank snapped to and lunged to take hold of the spear sharp fangs protecting them. The toothy lances pierced his hand but he held on as powerful venom began to course through his body. Then there was a thunderclap as Branford took his shot. The old agent landed on his backside with the kickback but the shot was effective. The serpent's head sported a hole the size of a softball and it was enough to bring it down.

Delirium was beginning to take hold of the Titan buy still he carried both his friends to the medics and asked them to help them please. Regardless, his job was not done. The Serpent was mortally wounded and limp on the tarmac, but the plane without a master had turned itself around, and was heading towards the building where hundreds of police, passengers, medics and others would not be able to get out of harm's way in time.

In the cockpit the professor had revived the unconscious pilot and was attempting to get him to steer the plane away from the building. Disoriented, the pilot only succeeded in pressing the wrong buttons and the plane began to accelerate. Frankie had only one choice that he could see. He latched onto the landing gear and dug his heals into the tarmac. The thrust of the plane and his strength parted the landing gear from the body of the Aircraft. It dove into the hanger with minimal human injury but Frankie was not visible under the wreckage.

22

Evangeline

Frankie's eyes were closed but the light still streamed through his lids. He wondered for a moment if he was out in the sun on a bright Alaskan day. His eyes opened slowly and what met them was not what he expected. Blinking continuously he saw no clouds or trees only pure light; so much so no shapes could be distinguished.

"He can't see. The goggles Tralain bring them here."

"I have them Temon. Oh no, I don't."

"No I have them. You dropped them in the entrance to the vestibule."

"Oh thank you Talius, put them on."

"Tobias brought the berries."

"Not the berries he can't eat our food till he is here to stay."

"What do you know Temon? Is he going back?"

"Yes he is Tuku. His work is not done. He can't sleep yet."

"So why is he going to see us? They don't see us till they are done and resurrected."

"He's special, you know that. That is why he has five of us instead of one. He needs more help. Father says he needs to see. He will need us right now."

Frankie tried to sit up but he couldn't. So he just lay there and waited. Some strange sort of eyewear was placed on his face and what he saw was five luminous beings of different shapes and sizes with smiling faces.

"Who are you? Where am I? Is this..."

"Heaven? No. This is the vestibule," one of them said. Frankie thought for a moment and said,

"Vestibule to what?"

"To eternity, what else?" Temon answered.

Disoriented Frankie thought he was supposed to be doing something but he could not think what. Still he asked,

"What time is it? I mean what day is it?"

"There is no time here. But don't worry we are sending you back and we will be with you as usual." That was Tobias that answered.

"As usual? I've never seen you, or anything like you, before in my life."

"No but we've been with you since you were reanimated as we are with other people from the time of their birth. Think of us as protectors." Tralain seemed proud of that fact.

"Where is this vestibule?"

"Not where…um I mean between. Between everything." Tobias explained. "Most people sleep here after they die till the end of all things then they are resurrected but you sort of did that early."

"Why am I here? Did we die again?"

"Not exactly. You see they, that is, the five, did die and they are here asleep and waiting. For them no time at all is passing till He calls them forth. You are different and have not died yet, you were close but there are people struggling to keep you alive, AND they will succeed!" Temon was very excited about this.

"You mean I have a consciousness apart from the five men that make up my body?"

"Yes you do. You were given one at reanimation." Quipped Tuku.

"Why?"

"Because everything that has life is given one. It is His will." Tralain spoke this fact solemnly.

"Then why do I remember things they knew?"

"Oh Shaqad you are so full of questions." Tobius giggle at that one.

"Did you just call me Shaqad? That is Hebrew for 'Awake'?" Frankie's languages were kicking in.

"Yes of course that is what we always call you. Because you are so "awake inside" we like that in a human."

"And to answer your other question you have named your body memories artifacts. That is a good word for them. Yes they are things that remained of the men who made up your body but your consciousness or "spirit" as they used to say, is your own." Talius paused for effect and Frankie was even more awe struck than before. Then Frankie asked,

"Can I see HIM?"

At the St Francis Hospital and Medical center in Harford, Frankie was of course, the strangest patient they had ever had. Not only did he look dead but he appeared to be repairing himself. It was all the doctors could do to keep the media away long enough to take a good look at him. Dr. Gunta Doree the controversial head of the Katz Institute for Chronic Pain and Addiction Research (KICPAR) got in with the remarkable statement that he knew the Giant and needed to be there to treat him. The team at St Francis welcomed anyone who had a clue about this case. Meanwhile Gunta got several other friends in as "family". Fergus got in as clergy and so did Vera.

CIA and FBI were both all over the hospital asking lots of questions. Branford told them a little but kept quiet about the man in his car. He mentioned in passing that he was a fellow drunk who he knew from some AA meetings and was unfortunately along for the ride when all hell broke loose. Branford had the presence of mind to also tell the science crew examining the Snake man that he needed to have his head removed because he had similar body repair properties to those of the Green Man and they didn't want this thing recomposing itself. The head that was indeed reforming in distorted ways was removed and disappeared into the secret recesses of one of the agencies. All the other people found in the Aircraft were dead but police reported two individuals (a man and a woman) with unusually colored skin who escaped them near the perimeter of the scene and disappeared into the woods near the Airport.

The friends knew Frankie did not want Stein delivered to the authorities. So they all said they were not certain how Frankie got the way he did. This was true after all since none of them knew anything about the reanimation process. They just knew he was a remarkable person and they admired him. Imaging revealed some electronics in his cerebral cortex that Dr. Doree said he had been told were for pain management. That was true of course but the rest of NAI's functions were kept secret.

Footage of the incident at the Airport was played over and over on every news network. It was recorded and viewed by people everywhere like some cult classic. People of course assumed many things. They wondered if he was some sort of experiment gone awry, or a super hero or an Alien. There were several reports of former victims of the famous NY vigilante called the Alien, who phoned the networks claiming hysterically that it was him. After examining him, all the hospital added to the original footage was that, for a man who had tangled with a thirty foot snake and was then smashed under the fuselage of a small moving Jet, he was doing remarkably well.

Sadly however, in the same hospital another person's life was taking a different turn and ebbing away. Though she was unique and a hero in her own right she was being ignored by media. That is till reporters noted that the friends of the Alien were also concerned about her. Stacia had received a blow from the serpent's tail full in the face that sent her and Fergus sprawling. Fergus had caught the worst of the blow to his body but Stacia landed on some equipment and she received a sharp wound that injured her spleen. She was not doing well. Ann and Jean Luc took turns sitting by her bedside and getting an hour or so of sleep but they both new the prognosis was not promising.

When Frankie opened his eyes in this world, he was surprised to find himself in two hospital beds that had been put together to accommodate his great size. His leg which had been broken was now perfectly healed. He removed it from the wench above his bed and ripped off the cast with one maneuver. Then he sat on the end of the bed holding his head. The poison had been removed by the bots and what anti-venom the hospital had given him was helping. All that was left was a whopping headache that he commanded NAI to work on right away. He also looked at his hands. The marks of the serpent's teeth were still there where the bots had repaired the wounds but he could see an oval shaped hole perfectly healed right through each hand. Later Fergus would tell him it was "stigmata" but though he had fought stigma all his life he would always answer, "I am not worthy of such things."

Gunta, Ben and Angie were Frankie's mouth pieces to the public. They had been watching him through windows in ICU for days. They laughed at what he did to his leg cast and rushed to the door as soon as he was awake. Gunta was allowed in but the other two were not. A few minutes later Gunta got them in too by sending the guard off to fetch a fictitious doctor.

They were all so glad to see him. When they asked him how he felt he only smiled and finally said,

"Is the Serpent dead?" and Gunta answered,

"He is but," knowing Frankie would feel guilty about killing he added,

"There was no other way. Would you mind if I examine you? "

Frankie was not in a mood to resist. He let Gunta have a look at him and all he found was a lot more scars. Frankie was unusually quiet as he was still in the afterglow of what he had experienced in the realms of light. This was what he later described as the inter-dimensional vestibule. In addition he was not of a mind to bring glory to himself so he would save the telling of that experience for another time.

The Agent who was on guard was sent by Gunta to fetch a certain Dr. Whoosh. There was no such doctor but not to be daunted he found a Dr. Whume who was a plastic surgeon. The agent thought surly as ugly as the big guy was he would need the services of such a doctor so he assumed this was the doctor in question. He fetched her. Glad for the opportunity to appease her curiosity, about the "monster" in ICU, Dr. Whume hurried over.

She walked in smiling and the agent who noticed the other friends in the room shut the door scowling. But Gunta was impressed by the pretty young plastic surgeon and he let her have a look at Frankie as he had a look at her. The result of all this was a promise to have lunch with Dr. Doree and confidence that she would be able to help with the scars and deformities on Frankie's face at least.

Frankie could not help but notice the chemistry between them and of course thought of his own pure desire. Gunta pronounced him well but Frank was thinking about the true concern of his heart. Why wasn't she there? Did she hate him that much? He looked at them and finally asked the question they did not want to answer.

"Where's Stacia?"

The concern in the room was palpable. All three of the friends froze and looked at him with great pity. Rather than say, Angie took his great big hand and like a child led him through the pastel hospital hallways that had bivouacked dozens of reporters for three days. These disheveled men and women came alive with questions and cameras as they walked through the halls. Frankie remembered being shunned by people for so long and now those that wanted to talk to him came at him in droves. The feeling of popularity was not what he had hoped. He felt like an organ specimen in a jar. Walking close to his friends he did not raised his yellow eyes to the crowd. His heart was full of dread.

When he got to Stacia's room he let out a great sob and fell on his knees next to her bed. She was so bruised and deathly white he could not endure it. The hallway came alive with phone calls and questions. The Alien had a love interest and she was dying. Who was she? They even tried to crowd into the room. Frankie roared at them like a Kodiak and in a menacing stance let them know they needed to go far, far away. Without hesitation--they did.

Stacia opened her eyes at the roar and raised her hand. Ann and Jean Luc stood up since they had not seen her stir for two days. She even parted her lips and opened her eyes slightly.

"Cheri." She whispered. Ann and Jean Luc grasped each other's hands and stepped away from the bed. Frankie could not believe his ears. She was calling him "dearest" but she was also dying.

"Stacia, my dearest friend. I will help you, I will find a way."

"I'm dying Frank. Everyone dies. Please keep going, don't forget the abused."

"Stacia you must stay and help me. I can't do this without you. I have seen God Stacia. He is real."

She smiled weakly and felt around the covers then grasped a white swan feather she held near. She lifted it slowly to show him then quietly breathed her last. Frankie crumbled in a heap on her corps. Now that she was gone he had to feel the final ebbing of her warmth. He prayed to the God, his own eyes had seen in the form of glorified man, among the sons of light, and heard him say to his spirit,

"Stein will give you good news." And he knew this was permission to do what he deeply desired to do.

A quick consultation with the friends and NAI was initiated for the purchase of a hearse along with documents to take the body from the morgue of the hospital. NAI also caused quite a disturbance and not a few errors in the automated calling systems of the hospital for prescription pick up. This has nothing to do with the story but did annoy quite a few people.

Ann and Jean Luc were alerted to the plan and Gunta and Ben were on site to sign the death certificate and for the removal documents needed. Kurt picked up the vehicle and the body was loaded by hospital staff. Branford brought Stein to the Mansion and the Generators were fired up. Frankie was the only problem at this point. He was, after all, being watched carefully by CIA, FBI and the press, but the hospital window, a climb to the roof and a slide down a drain pipe that night solved that issue. Automated telephone communications at the hospital were restored to normal and the Alien was at large again.

About a mile away from the hospital Angie waited in the van. When Frankie came through the woods she opened the back doors and he slipped in tucking his feet as far in as he could. She closed the doors from the outside holding them together with a bungee cord. She reminded him that there were longer vans they could trade this one in for. He said he would keep it in mind.

An hour later they were converging with the hearse onto the property of the mansion. They passed the ducks and geese that squawked their welcome and Frankie noticed the pair of swans that majestically glided by in silent approach. He recalled how a swan had welcomed him into the world the day of his reanimation and how he had found the feather that Stacia had held up to him in the hospital. But he could not enter the house. He felt it best to let the scientist work while he waited outside wondering if she would even have anything to do with him after her reanimation. She would be one of his kind but that would give him no guarantees of her affection. Angie parked the van and went inside leaving him to his thoughts. She did not want to miss the action.

In the building the scientist was humming "Fanfare for the Common Man" under his breath while he was setting things up. He seemed glad to be doing something besides reading or twiddling his thumbs over computer keys. There was a different feel about this reanimation. He was actually helping someone, doing something worthwhile with his invention.

He had never admitted this to himself before but he felt terrible guilt over all the pain he had caused Frankie. Despite his bulk and strength, the giant was such a gentle soul. Stein had treated him so callously. He thought so little of his creature in his drunkenness and ignored his needs. All along he knew Frankie was his responsibility. If he could help Stacia this might be some amends. He also remembered his own pain over losing Elizabeth, the only human being he had ever loved. He knew Frankie was feeling like that now. Stein had never made anyone happy before. This might be the first time and it felt, well…satisfactory.

He had taken some skin sample from the subject and was evaluating the genetic material for deficits or brittle conditions that might be eliminated or in need of support. He noticed the corps was clutching something and when he opened the hand that was stiff with rigor mortis he saw it was a white feather. Swan perhaps, he had seen enough of them on the shore of the lake. He wondered if some genetic elements of the sturdy bird might not improve the makeup of the fragile girl. Some fibers from the feather were all that was needed; the finishing touch before the power was applied.

Ann and Luna were waiting outside the lab with Jean Luc. As soon as the Doctor emerged, the ladies crowded passed him, as prearranged, to dress her. They had been warned that she would be very new mentally and emotionally. Since she was also a gentle soul, Stein gave her as many reconstructive nano-bots as possible and the maximum access to NAI that could be had without Dr. Benavent's specifications. She would be able to achieve several doctorates and this would make her a near match for Frankie. The doctor only wished he had taken greater care with Frankie's looks. After all, she was very beautiful.

Jean Luc went out to talk to the big guy. He knew the women would take some time with her and he was also anxious about his sister. What if something had gone wrong? They were both relieved when Angie approached and said the procedure was successful inviting them in. Jean Luc went in to see her readily but Frankie pulled up his hoodie and said he would come presently. He couldn't just now. Instead he climbed up to the Veranda like a thief, to steal a glance at the one he had no right to look upon.

She was brought in, wearing a pale blue gown and he thought the process had not changed her much. If Babe had been aloe colored due to pale skin, Stacia was the color of milk as she had no pigment at all. Her eyes were the bright yellow of butter cups and her hair was platinum colored giving her the appearance of a Celtic fairy. Like Frankie at first she was curious about everything, picking up pens and dust and art objects and feeling fabric and hair and faces. Wonder surrounded and infused her. So they let her walk about and get her bearings as NAI explained things.

Much to Ann's delight, Stacia's NAI was speaking French, perhaps because it was her native language. In her exploration, the lady in blue finally got to the French doors of the veranda and Angie made sure she did not put her hands through the glass. She had her feel the transparent medium and she beamed with fascination. NAI commented saying, "Vere transparent" (transparent glass). Curiosity, twice amplified by the large stranger on the other side of the glass, made her smile. Her bright eyes met his golden ones and he knew he had been discovered. He shuffled a bit but noticed she was not afraid. Like Dee Dee, she did not yet know fear.

He came into the light and as she had examined everything else she examined him and marveled at his great size. She pulled back his hood and wondered at his glossy black hair comparing it to her own. She examined his scars and she compared her small hand to his large one. She appeared so impressed and far from rejecting him she asked NAI and it said "Frankie" and she smiled repeating the name. A tear rolled down Frank's face and she picked it up with her finger. Then she held it near the window and said, "vere transparent". Everyone smiled at this especially Frank. It filled his heart with such joy he could hardly contain it.

In days to come the only "blemish" on her, noticeable to anyone, was a small growth between her shoulder blades. It was also observed that she had white and downy material on her back. This far from being unnerving to Frankie was becoming. In his eyes she was perfect and everything she was beguiled him.

After the fire the coalition needed a headquarters and they finally decided to purchase the Mansion which had been given to the state when the owners disappeared and stopped paying taxes. The Coalition extended their reach to the state of Connecticut and Ann and Stacia moved there to avoid nosey paparazzi. Jean Luc and Luna married and made the apartment in Queens their home.

Of course Stacia stopped teaching. Her poor little students had been told she had passed away and the school had grieved for her. She could not return like a ghost to haunt them. Dee Dee was tickled that she had her teacher and that nobody else in the class knew about it. It was hard to keep the secret but she did. Eventually however, things changed for that family too. New York was too far from Elaina and James' new friends. For a long time they felt the city was too congested and dangerous for Elaina and Rosa. Schools were better for Dee Dee in Connecticut. Elaina could work with Gunta and Ben at the Katz Institute, and James found lots to do with "Clean and Painless" so Frankie had an eight apartment building constructed on the property as part of the Katz Foundation and they all move in.

The generators were just sitting there for the most part so they finally decided to use them to get off the grid. Frankie gave a lot of the mansion furniture to the others for their apartments and he started to bring in the trees and drift wood for his own home. Soon the inside of the big house looked very much like the Tree House only a bit more spacious. Stacia liked it very much and spent a lot of time there learning and coming up to speed with her artifacts.

Another development happened that changed things for the little group. Stein decided to help. He did not have all the specs on Benavent's NAI but he learned enough to reconstruct the neuronal pain blocking stimulation (NPBS) aspect of it. This was something he had been working on since his sobriety and it was now at a point that testing was needed. Of course he could not bring it to light without going to jail. So he figured he would broker a deal. Let him go to a private place where he could live out the rest of his days in peace, and he would give them the tech to help those in pain. Gunta and Ben thought it would make a wonderful addition to the Katz Institute. Frankie agreed and the tech was acquired for testing. Ann was the prototype for that. Stein was sent to a Scottish island where he would live peacefully in solitude for a few years.

There had been so many interruptions to the production, but "Clean and Painless" was determined that the "show would go on". Stacia was not yet able to perform but other dancers were and even as she watched them her abilities started to come back to her. The hitch was that whenever she was excited whether for good or bad reasons the growth on her back engorged and enlarged. Soon it was apparent she was growing a pair of wings.

At first she did not know what to make of them. She was of course concerned that she was growing this deformity. Many people stared at her because of her coloring. Now where would she go with this peculiarity, to be away from the morbidly curious? Frankie of course went straight to Stein and demanded an answer. Stein told him what was in his mind when he did the

DNA blend. He had no intention of deforming her only strengthening her. He had no idea it would turn out this way. He callously recommended surgical removal of the wings but by then Stacia had started to wonder if someday she might be able to fly and she decided to keep them till she found out for sure. In fact, if she could, they could incorporate it into the show.

The script for the final skit was a logistic nightmare but the story was a simple one. Poor people, people who struggled with addiction and people in chronic pain or with mental illness were all stigmatized. Stigma was portrayed as a villain. Because of this they were not getting the help they needed. In fact they were being left, more or less to die. Justice was also portrayed as a character (by Frankie) and justice was frustrated because of the success of Stigma in the general population.

As powerful as justice was he was defeated by Stigma. But people started becoming aware as their own loved ones suffered and soon they were prepared to fight on the side of Justice. In the end the people got rid of Stigma and they supported justice. This was shown in a great way with this enormous see-saw that all the people jumped on with "Justice" on the other side. In true Cirque du Soleil fashion they balanced and danced on the see-saw. Then, when they all decided to stand with "Justice" they jumped on the huge teeter-totter together and gave "Justice" the momentum to fly into the Air doing a fantastic flip and landing on his feet on a platform center stage. Then "Freedom" which was played by Stacia would fly up onto the shoulders of "Justice" and there would be fireworks and the musical grand finally.

On the night of the performance the whole day was nothing short of spectacular. Celebrities in recovery from drugs or who suffered with chronic pain held court with common addicts and victims of pain and they had wonderful experiences that were filmed all day. Finally night came and it was time for the skit but they were having some trouble with the rigging. Frankie was supposed to be rigged for safety and so was Stacia to accomplish the grand finale. Try as they might things were not going well. Frankie finally said he would do his leap without external help or safety net.

He had done many such moves evading the eyes of people. And he was sure he could accomplish it. Stacia was another story. They thought that Frankie might certainly be able to lift her up onto his shoulders easily enough, but would she be stable on his shoulders. A strange look was in her eyes when the moment came. Flushed with excitement, she looked at Frankie, and smiled. Then, instead of taking his hand to climb, she spread full wings and shot up into the Air like a flare. Suspended in space for a moment she reversed direction and gently descended downward, landing on his shoulders with perfect balance. A dove could not have been so precise or so ethereal. He was so overcome with wonder he almost fell backwards and she was the one that held *him* steady, with her feet. The crowd went wild, the word got out, and the donations rolled in.

In the afterglow of the show the congratulations and sober good will spread in great swaths around Madison Square Garden and the whole city. Frankie and Stacia were paraded out of the garden on a truck bed along with a lot of the other dancers and performers. Everyone was talking about the costumes and the special effects and they all wondered if the giant was really the Alien and how they did the winged "freedom" stunt with such ease. They all thought it was the best makeup and special effects ever. No one could figure out how they put on those realistic wings.

Everyone else got off the truck and went home but not Frankie and Stacia. That truck became their special limo. Neither one felt the cold and the ride seemed magical out in the open. Like many performers when the lights are out and the show is over they experienced a certain melancholy. Still, this was not a time to be sad. This moment was theirs and it was full of triumph and joy. When the truck dropped them off they were laughing. Kurt and Hailey had been driving and they went into their apartment ready for bed with a backward glance and a smile on their faces.

Neither one of the passengers were tired. She folded her wings and they walked in the moonlight.

"You looked like an angel up there you know."

"And what does an angel look like?"

Frankie was silent as he didn't want to get into a debate with her. She realized what she was doing and apologized.

"I'm sorry Frank. It's just that I can't believe what I can't see."

"I'm surprised you believe in love then, or do you?" Now *she* was silent. But he continued.

"I've seen them you know. They told me I was going to live."

"How do you know it wasn't a hallucination?"

"It was as real as you are. I felt them. I heard them. But you don't have to believe me. Only it's hard for me to understand why you can't believe. I see so much evidence."

"I don't see God or angels Frank but I see you. You're a good man."

With that she blushed pale pink, stroked his arm, spread her wings and took off. He watched her climb into the sky and prayed she would be safe. Then he also asked that she would be able to see what he saw. When an hour later she landed on her building and went inside, he was still there keeping his lonely watch.

Babe sat in a jet that would stop in Spain first and eventually end its journey in Egypt. She sat across from the Prince who was pulling on a water pipe and trying to calm his nerves. He was nursing the wounds he had gotten in his encounter with the Titian. He was healing, but much slower than Babe. This was disconcerting to him and he made mental notes about her shorting him on benefits due to a reanimate.

She was intent on a screen where a broadcast of the free extravaganza of "Clean and Painless" was being replayed with interviews proclaiming its success. Of course they replayed the finale and when it came on she could not believe her eyes. Her vision narrowed and she promised herself that far from all this acclaim, she would drive the "Justice" and "Freedom" characters back into the wilderness of obscurity, where every creature that affronted her belonged, before she killed it.